Praise for *In Bed with the Earl*

"Exceptional . . . This series launch is an intoxicating romp sure to delight fans of historical romance."

—*Publishers Weekly* (starred review)

"Sizzling, witty, passionate . . . perfect!"

—Eloisa James, *New York Times* bestselling author

Praise for Christi Caldwell

"Christi Caldwell writes a gorgeous book!"

—Sarah MacLean, *New York Times* and *USA Today* bestselling author

"In addition to a strong plot, this story boasts actualized characters whose personal demons are clear and credible. The chemistry between the protagonists is seductive and palpable, with their family history of hatred played against their personal similarities and growing attraction to create an atmospheric and captivating romance."

—*Publishers Weekly* on *The Hellion*

"Christi Caldwell is a master of words, and *The Hellion* is so descriptive and vibrant that she redefines high definition. Readers will be left panting, craving, and rooting for their favorite characters as unexpected lovers find their happy ending."

—RT Book Reviews on *The Hellion*

"Christi Caldwell's *The Vixen* shows readers a darker, grittier version of Regency London than most romance novels . . . Caldwell's more realistic version of London is a particularly gripping backdrop for this enemies-to-lovers romance, and it's heartening to read a story where love triumphs even in the darkest places."

—NPR on *The Vixen*

Someone Wanton His Way Comes

OTHER TITLES BY CHRISTI CALDWELL

Lost Lords of London

In Bed with the Earl

In the Dark with the Duke

Undressed with the Marquess

Sinful Brides

The Rogue's Wager

The Scoundrel's Honor

The Lady's Guard

The Heiress's Deception

Wicked Wallflowers

The Hellion

The Vixen

The Governess

The Bluestocking

The Spitfire

Scandalous Affairs

A Groom of Her Own

Heart of a Duke

In Need of a Duke (A Prequel Novella)

For Love of the Duke

More Than a Duke

The Love of a Rogue

Scandalous Seasons

Forever Betrothed, Never the Bride

Never Courted, Suddenly Wed

Always Proper, Suddenly Scandalous

Always a Rogue, Forever Her Love

A Marquess for Christmas

Once a Wallflower, At Last His Love

The Theodosia Sword

Only For His Lady

Only For Her Honor

Only For Their Love

Danby

Winning a Lady's Heart

A Season of Hope

The Brethren

The Spy Who Seduced Her

The Lady Who Loved Him

The Rogue Who Rescued Her

The Minx Who Met Her Match

The Spinster Who Saved a Scoundrel

Brethren of the Lords

My Lady of Deception

Her Duke of Secrets

Nonfiction Works

Uninterrupted Joy: A Memoir

Someone Wanton His Way Comes

CHRISTI CALDWELL

Montlake

Published by Montlake, Seattle

www.apub.com

Amazon, the Amazon logo, and Montlake are trademarks of Amazon.com, Inc., or its affiliates.

ISBN-13: 9781542021395
ISBN-10: 1542021391

Front cover design by Juliana Kolesova

Back cover design by Ray Lundgren

Printed in the United States of America

To Marietta:
Thank you for every note you've ever written
and every story you've ever shared in.

Sylvia and Clayton's story is for you!

Prologue

1826
Gentleman Jackson's
13 Bond Street
West End of London

It took a moment for Clayton Kearsley, Viscount St. John, to register his friend's words.

In part because of the din in Gentleman Jackson's, where too many noblemen had packed into the club to play at being gentlemen gladiators.

In part because of the casualness with which the words had been delivered.

And in part because what he'd heard made no sense.

"Beg pardon?" he blurted.

And for a moment he thought perhaps he might very well have imagined that question—a request, really, after all. For the Earl of Norfolk, his closest friend since their Eton days, attended to the wraps on his hands with a good deal more focus than he did to Clayton.

He lifted his right hand up close to his face and angled it back and forth, inspecting his knuckles. "Someone is going to have to look after her," he finally said, confirming that Clayton's ears, in fact, hadn't deceived him. That he'd heard what he thought he had.

And yet hearing it changed nothing, as Clayton still struggled to process the implications of precisely what his friend was saying. Because there could be no doubt: it was more a statement than a request.

"*You* will look after her," Clayton said slowly, at last finding something meaningful to say. That was, after all, the other man's responsibility . . . and had been for three years, twelve weeks, and a handful of days. "She is your wife."

Norfolk flexed his fingers several times, as if testing the feel of the wraps before setting to work adjusting them once more. When he bothered to look up at Clayton, he wore a frown. "Have you been listening to anything I've been saying?" There was an impatient quality to his question.

"Have you been listening to anything *you* are saying?" Clayton countered, loud enough to garner looks from several sets of gentlemen.

Norfolk's frown deepened. "Have a care, St. John. Show a little calm, would you?"

Clayton had long been the equanimous one of seven siblings—the rest being sisters for whom he was responsible. The Kearsleys were a volatile lot, tempests, really, and he the voice of calm and the family member of reason. As such, he drew on the thirty years of inner calm that had prevailed amongst the chaos that was his big, unruly family.

And yet, all that went out the proverbial window as he finally saw that Norfolk spoke with an absolute seriousness of intent. "Be calm? You're telling me to be calm?"

More stares were directed their way. Long, curious looks that could come only at finding one of society's most even-keeled, scandal-free lords raising his voice—to his best friend, no less.

"My God, man, you are talking about . . . about . . ." He couldn't even get out the rest of what his friend intended.

Grabbing him by the arm, Norfolk forcefully guided Clayton back to the corner of the studio. "Quiet."

The moment they had that flimsy privacy, Norfolk resumed speaking, this time in more measured tones. "I am talking about going away with the woman I love."

Clayton had known Norman Prescott, the Earl of Norfolk, since they were boys of eight. There'd been times he'd been in awe of Prescott's ease around people. In awe of his boxing. There'd been times he'd envied him.

He could count just one time he'd resented him.

But this? This was the first time he'd ever actually hated the man he'd called a friend.

"You have a wife, Norfolk."

"I don't love her," the other man said simply on a little shrug that served only to overemphasize the callousness of his admission.

A haze of red fell across Clayton's vision, briefly blinding, but not before he caught the casual way Norfolk went back to tending his hand wraps. That was . . . it? That was all the man would say? He'd just speak of leaving his wife and gallivanting off with his . . . lover?

"It is a little late on that score," Clayton gritted out between his clenched teeth, and this time when he looked up, there was something akin to surprise in the other man's eyes. Yes, but then why should he be anything but shocked at being challenged by the ever affable viscount? "You asked her to marry you." *Just three weeks after meeting her.* "You courted her."

A sound of impatience escaped Norfolk. "I do not need you to remind me of my courtship with Sylvia. I assure you, I am well aware of it. I did that which was expected of me."

Clayton didn't relent. "The moment you said 'I do' and promised to love her, comfort her, honor and keep her, in sickness and in health? And forsaking all others, keep only to her as long as you both shall live . . ."

Grief contorted the other man's face in the first hint that Clayton had managed to break through whatever madness had compelled this reckless, and heartless, thought.

Sensing that weakening, Clayton put further pressure on him. "You'd just leave her to her own devices?"

"She is well loved by her family. There's Waterson." As in her brother, the Parliamentarian earl, who was known for his devotion to his kin. "He'll care for her."

Clayton tried once more. "But she is *your* wife." And when that made no difference in the other man's implacable features, he appealed to Norfolk's commitment to his family's title. "There's not even an heir." Even as those words left Clayton's mouth, he cringed in shame at having spoken them. But if he could get Norfolk to reverse course, god help him, he would.

The earl spoke in quieter tones. "Sylvia's maid informed me that my wife missed her menses. As such, I've done my duty by the Prendergast line."

Hatred tightened Clayton's gut and seared his veins, threatening to burn him from the inside out in a fiery ball of fury. "I don't even know you," he spat. And fearing he'd do something like put his hands around the other man's neck and choke the life from his blackhearted body, he started from the room. Ignoring the friendly greetings called in his wake, his gaze forward, his intent just one: escape. Flee this thing his friend intended to do. And what Clayton now knew would come.

He reached the front doors of the posh club, grabbing the handles before the servants stationed there could, and let himself out.

The London heat, higher than usual, slapped at his face, cloying and clawing, the thickness of it only adding to the nausea that churned in his stomach.

I am going to be sick.

With quick steps, Clayton headed for his horse.

"St. John!"

That frantic call rose above the hubbub of Bond Street's bustling thoroughfare, and he whipped around to find the other man rushing over.

Norfolk stopped before him and tossed his arms up. "What would you have me do, Saint?"

"I'd have you honor your commitments," he said, as matter-of-factly as he could manage. "I'd have you be a husband to your wife, and a father to your child."

"I can't do that." Another would have at least had the grace to show some compunction at that charge. With the rapidity of his response, however, Norfolk didn't even bother to feign false hesitancy.

"There is . . . nothing I might say, nothing I can do to convince you to not do this thing you intend to do?" Something. There had to be something. The man Clayton knew . . . would never do this.

"I tried to play at this life, St. John. I tried to be the dutiful, devoted husband, to the dull and proper lady—"

"Have a care," Clayton snapped. "You may regret having wed her, but she is *still* your wife and as such deserving of, at the very least, your respect."

Norfolk's brows drew together. "I don't regret marrying Sylvia."

That gave Clayton pause. He continued trying to reach his friend. "If you don't regret it, then you wouldn't be doing what you"—he glanced about the bustling streets, confirming they were unobserved—"say you intend to do," he substituted, unwilling to risk uttering the words aloud.

"You misunderstand me. I don't regret it, as our marriage served its purpose." Rage tightened each of Clayton's muscles, every sinew coiled tense to the point of snapping. "There is a child, a future marquess, and as such, I've fulfilled my obligations."

And yet . . . what if that was what might delay Norfolk's flight? Perhaps if Clayton could stall his plans, the other man might see reason. "You don't know that. Because you have already stated your intention to leave before your own babe is born . . . What if . . . what if it is a girl babe?"

"Then I'll return when I must and give her another child until there's the damned Prendergast hei—"

Clayton buried the remainder of that vile deliverance with a fist to his lifelong friend's mouth.

Norfolk crumpled, landing hard on his arse. He gave his head a dazed shake. "Never felt you deliver a blow like that," he said, the hand he had pressed to his bruised mouth muffling his words.

Nay, because there'd never been a reason to, before. Clayton's knuckles stung, and his heart pounded hard as he stood over his *friend*. "I don't even know you."

"You know I love her," Norfolk whispered.

"I thought she was . . . just your lover." And even when he thought as much, nearly all his respect for the other man had died, and his resentment had burnt strong.

"Never. She is my everything, St. John. My everything," he repeated. "And you don't know what she's been through. Hell," he whispered. "She's been through hell." His features were a twisted mask of grief and regret, and it was the first time since the other man had revealed his wishes that Clayton felt a wavering . . . because . . . he *did* know about loss.

The moment proved fleeting.

For honor meant more.

"And instead, you'd rather put your wife through hell?" he asked bitterly.

Norfolk came slowly to his feet. "I never intended for Sylvia to be hurt."

But he had no intention of altering course. That truth was clear. "There is nothing I can say?" Clayton asked tiredly. "No way to make you see reason?"

Color splotched Norfolk's cheeks, and once more, Clayton thought he might have helped the other man see the wrongness and the madness of what he'd proposed here, with the public just out of earshot from the scandal they now whispered of. That hope proved fleeting.

Norfolk shook his head, and this time when, with a sound of disgust, Clayton turned to go, the other man rested a hand on his arm. "Can I rely upon you?"

He shrugged off that touch. "What does that entail? Caring for your wife? Raising the unborn child you are leaving?"

"Of . . . course not. Just see that they are well. Occasionally check in on them. I know you have your own obligations and responsibilities and— St. John," Norfolk called after him. "St. John."

"Go to hell," Clayton shouted, ignoring that faint plea. He didn't look back, just headed to his horse.

Later that afternoon, he learned it was the last time he'd ever see his friend alive.

Chapter 1

London, England
1829

The March family wasn't one that had been left unscathed by tragedy or scandal.

Quite the opposite, in fact.

Lady Sylvia Caufield, the Countess of Norfolk, had been made a widow after her husband died from an errant blow on the fighting floor of Gentleman Jackson's.

Her sister, Lila, nearly dead on the fields of Peterloo, had lived the life of a recluse after that tragic day, having only recently rejoined the world.

Then there had been Sylvia's brother, Henry, the notoriously prim, proper Parliamentarian, the Earl of Waterson, who had been beaten and left for dead in the streets of East London, only to be saved and nursed by a former courtesan whom he'd gone on to marry.

One would think as such that their mother, the dowager Countess of Waterson, was capable of bravely facing anything where her children were concerned.

One would be wrong.

"Wh-wh-wh . . ." The dowager countess wept into her crumpled kerchief.

"Is that a 'wa-wa-wa,' as in she's crying, or is she trying to ask a question?" Lila whispered behind her hand.

Sylvia peered at their blubbering mama. "I . . . cannot be altogether certain which," she replied, keeping her lips absolutely motionless as she spoke. And if the countess was distraught over this small revelation, what was she going to say to the second item Sylvia had called her here to . . . *discuss?*

The door opened, and the sisters looked over.

A maid entered, bearing a tray in hand. The longtime member of the family's staff hovered at the doorway, briefly considering the path over her shoulder.

"Lovely. Thank you, Patricia." Sylvia smiled widely and, holding a hand up, gestured the girl over. "Refreshme—"

The rest of that announcement was lost to the dowager countess's enormous gasping sobs.

And the usually attentive servant set the tray down, then fled without so much as a curtsy or waiting to see whether anything else was required of her.

Smart girl. Sylvia eyed the doorway covetously, knowing all too well how the young woman felt and envying her that escape.

Alas, this exchange had been . . . inevitable. There had been no way around informing her mother about her intentions. She was never going to take well to Sylvia leaving the respectable household she'd shared with Norman and moving not back in with her family but to another, less stylish street. Sylvia, however, was more than ready—and eager—to put this exchange behind her.

Donning another forced smile, Sylvia lifted the porcelain pot. "Tea?"

"I think tea is a splendid idea," Lila exclaimed, albeit a bit too forcefully to be sincere, and yet her efforts were only appreciated. As was her support this day.

Sylvia proceeded to pour, and then she looked to her still-wailing mother. "Would you care for tea, Mother?" she asked loudly enough to penetrate the dowager countess's noisy blubbering.

Her mother lowered the kerchief to her lap, revealing her swollen eyes and red cheeks. "Tea? *Teaaaaa?*"

Her mother managed to squeeze a whole four extra syllables into that single word.

Lila promptly looked down at her delicate floral cup and put a good deal of attention into stirring its contents.

Sylvia offered her most serene smile to their mother, the same one she'd practiced with her governesses to perfection as a girl. "You always *did* say tea is the great equalizer of sentiment and emotions." Which she'd secretly thought to be vexingly redundant. Alas, using the countess's oft-delivered lessons could only help in calming her.

Their mother's lips fell agape, and she floundered about several moments for words. "*This* is the lesson you should choose to remember?"

"This one is as good as any," Sylvia countered, taking it upon herself to pour a cup anyway. She tried to hand it to her mother.

The countess made no attempt to take the offering. "No. No, it is not. There are any number of lessons I've imparted that are a great deal more important."

"Such as not moving out by oneself?" Lila volunteered.

Their mother looked to Lila. "Precisely."

"Thank you," Sylvia mouthed.

Her sister winced. "I'm sorry." Clearing her throat, she lowered her teacup to her lap. "I . . . What I intended to say is though it might seem sad and disappointing to see Sylvia leave"—Lila's recovery emerged halting and disjointed—"many women move outside of their family's households."

"She is a widow," her mother cried.

When no other response was forthcoming, Sylvia asked, "And?"

"And you belong at home with us. Widows are prey for"—their mother dropped her voice to a loud whisper—"all manner of scandalous, wicked men."

"Why are we whispering now? Are there scandalous, wicked men about whom we fear offending?"

The door opened, and they looked to the front of the room as Henry strolled in. "Lila!" he exclaimed. "I heard you—"

Both sisters spoke as one. "Get out." The last thing Sylvia required was two overprotective family members attempting to dissuade her from her course.

"Do not order your brother gone," the dowager countess commanded. She thumped a palm on the curved arm of her chair. "I would have him join us."

The three March women stared back at Henry.

He looked amongst them and must have seen something more menacing in facing a pair of March sisters than a single angry mama, because he hastily backed out of the room.

The moment he'd closed the door behind him, Sylvia refocused on the countess. "There are no worries about scandalous gentlemen. I've no interest in letting myself dally with the wicked." Or dally with any man, for that matter. Not ever again. No good came from such dealings. Life and love had taught her that much.

Her mother pounced. "They'll do it anyway. The world will take it as an indication of how you intend to live, and . . . and . . . there is your son."

Sylvia's heart pulled. Her son, Vallen, was her world. The only gift left to her by a husband who'd never truly loved her. Not in the way she'd loved him. Not in any way, really.

Pushing aside that useless self-pitying born of an understanding she'd come to terms with, Sylvia took the opening left by her mother. "My son will be with me. I'm not leaving him here."

"And do you expect he's going to serve as a protector?" her mother asked incredulously.

"Of course n—"

The countess's challenges kept coming. "He should not be exposed to all the widow-hunting gentlemen who have their sights on *you*, Sylvia."

"He's not going to be exposed to widow-hunting gentlemen," she said, exasperation sweeping in. "Quite the opposite." What she intended in moving out would see her home insulated from all men.

"Furthermore, are they *realllly* gentlemen?" Lila pointed out.

No, her sister was correct on that score. Sylvia joined in. "And are they *really* hunting?" After all, women weren't fowl or deer.

"Yes!" their mother cried. "They are, and that there is the very reason you should not do this thing you are suggesting."

"I'm not suggesting it, Mother," she said gently. "I'm doing it."

That pronouncement was met with a sudden onset of thundering silence so heavy the distant rattle of carriages rumbling past filled the parlor.

The countess's lower lip trembled wildly, and she raised her wrinkled kerchief to her mouth.

"Here." Lila collected the forgotten cup of tea from Sylvia and handed it over.

This time, their mother took the offering. The tip of her index finger sticking out, she raised the cup to her lips and sipped daintily at the contents. With her other hand, she dusted a tear back from the corner of her eye. And when she lowered the kerchief to her lap, Sylvia's stomach turned over.

For she recognized that glimmer in her mother's eyes. She recognized it all too well.

Setting her teacup down, the countess moved to the edge of her seat . . . And for one fleeting moment born of hope, Sylvia thought her mother would storm off.

But then the countess wouldn't do anything so uncouth as walking briskly, which was why the leading pillar of society was responding as she was to Sylvia's announcement.

And only one of her announcements at that . . . What would she say when she discovered the other reason Sylvia had called this meeting together? Her mother rested a hand on Sylvia's knee, as she'd done whenever she'd doled out some maternal request she expected met.

Not allowing her that opportunity, Sylvia spoke quickly. "I'm not intending to live alone. I'm planning to have company."

Her mother froze, from her silvery eyelashes on down to the gloved palm that still rested on Sylvia's skirts; not so much as a part or sliver of her moved. And then her shoulders sagged slightly.

"Companions! Yes, that is a splendid idea," she said, clapping excitedly. The dowager countess sagged slightly in her seat. "You should have said as much. We shall find you the most respectable ones!"

Both sisters exchanged a look.

"No. No," Sylvia said. "That won't be necessary. I already have them."

That brought the countess up short. She swiftly found her footing. "Very well . . . You found your own companions." And since the door closed and their meeting began thirty minutes earlier, their mother smiled her first smile. "That is *very* reliable of you." The countess trilled a laugh and gathered her teacup. "And here I was worrying, and all for naught. I should have known better, as you were ever the most dutiful of the daughters."

"I'm sitting right here," Lila muttered.

The most dutiful of the daughters. But then, that was how everyone and anyone in Polite Society and her family had come to view Sylvia. Always proper, always doing that which the *ton* expected of good young ladies. And mayhap that was also why no one had ever truly been able to love her . . . because she had been sculpted by the most illustrious governesses and shaped into a clump of colorless clay.

Sylvia tensed her mouth.

No longer. The days of being the vapid, soporific lady were at an end. "They are not companions, Mother."

Her mother's smile wavered ever so slightly. "Beg pardon? You just said—"

"They are not *paid* companions, that is."

"Un . . . paid companions?" That teacup found its place once more on the countess's lap. "Are you in dire financial straits?" Not awaiting an answer, she looked to the doorway. "I knew we should have had your brother remain. He would—"

"My finances are in order." Sylvia's husband had offered little in terms of happiness, but he'd left her comfortable enough with resources to see herself cared for.

"Then why aren't you . . . paying them?" Puzzlement underlined her mother's question.

"Because they are not employees, Mother." She spoke gently with her elucidation. "They are friends."

Lila, silent through all that exchange, raised her cup to her lips and looked up at the ceiling.

Their mother whipped her head over to her younger daughter. "What is it?"

A blush bloomed on Lila's cheeks. Lila, the only person who was even worse at dissembling than Sylvia. "I didn't say anything," her younger sister said.

The countess didn't waste any more time pressing Lila. She narrowed her gaze on Sylvia. "What is it?"

Smoothing her hands over her peach skirts, Sylvia met her mother's stare with a brave smile. "I take it you mean . . . who?"

"Sylvia." Her name emerged as a warning.

"They are very dear ladies, who not unlike me have found themselves the unfair recipients of—"

"Who?"

"Lady Annalee," Sylvia blurted, starting with what would be outrageous, but still the lesser so, to her mother.

Silence met that pronouncement. There was another moment of stillness as the countess turned motionless. "Lady Annalee?" A young woman who'd been at the Peterloo tragedy with Lila. Unlike Lila, who had dealt with the aftermath by isolating herself, Annalee had used alcohol and society as a distraction from her pain. As such, it was to be expected Sylvia's announcement would be met with some degree of shock. "As in . . . *Lila's* friend?"

"Yes." Annalee may have not at first been Sylvia's friend, but since Lila's reentry to the living, Sylvia had become close with Annalee as well. "The very same."

There came another wave of silence that Sylvia filled. "She was visiting with Lila when I also happened to be visiting, and we were both remarking on how unfair it was that grown, unwed women should be expected to live with their relatives, and then I said . . . 'Why do we have to? Why can we not have a place of our own, as gentlemen do?' And"—Sylvia lifted her hands—"here we are."

Her mother stared blankly back. "Here we . . . ?" And then she erupted. In . . . laughter. Unrestrained mirth, which was the first ever shown by the older, proper matron.

She'd driven the countess to madness. Splendid. Sylvia looked over to her sister.

Lila lifted her shoulders in a confused little shrug.

This had decidedly not been the response they'd expected. Hesitantly, Sylvia allowed herself to join in that amusement.

"And here you, the least humorous of all my children, are telling jests."

Indignation killed Sylvia's laughter. "I beg your pardon?"

Her mother dashed the tears of hilarity from her cheeks. "You aren't even friends with Annalee."

No, she hadn't been. As Annalee had been her previously reclusive sister's closest friend, their mother was certainly entitled to some . . . confusion.

Lila took heart and came to the rescue once more. "They were not friends; however, I took the liberty of introducing them, and they've since become so. Isn't that right, Sylvia?"

Steadied by her sister's support, Sylvia nodded. "Indeed. We get on quite well, and—"

"You . . . get . . . on . . . quite . . . well?" Their mother's disjointed question emerged garbled. "But her reputation. She is unmarried. She is . . . a scandal." The countess hissed out that last word on a whisper. Though it was unclear which she found to be a more egregious offense.

"Mother," Sylvia said gently but firmly. "I would not judge a woman unfairly. She conducts herself no differently than most gentlemen living their lives."

"Yes," her mother cried, nodding frantically. "That is precisely it. She is not a gentleman, and you are not one to invite scandal. I forbid it."

Another time those three words would have effectively quashed any hint of rebellion from Sylvia. Not anymore.

Sylvia took a deep breath. "There is more."

"Of course there is," her mother muttered. She set her cup down hard. "What is it *nowww?*"

It was a dire day indeed when the dowager countess was a-muttering and sloshing tea over the rim of her glass.

Just get out all of it. "And we will also be joined by Valerie Bragger."

There was a time when that name had brought only the greatest hurt and resentment and outrage. No more. Sylvia had come to find a compatriot in the unlikeliest of women.

"Your . . . *husband's* . . . former . . . *lover?*" The countess strangled on each syllable of each whispered word.

Sylvia's body stiffened. The truth of her late husband's betrayal still landed a blow square to her chest. Not from any love that she carried or felt for the man who'd deceived her. That had died. Rather, it came from her own naivete. At having loved where she'd been wrong. At the lie she'd lived for so very long.

"Mother," Lila said chidingly. "That isn't fair."

"Well, she was," the countess hissed. "That is precisely what she was, and she isn't deserving of Sylvia's kindness"—the countess jabbed a finger down at the Aubusson carpet as she spoke—"or financial support or . . . or . . . anything. And furthermore"—her voice crept up—"you'll simply dismiss the fact that she was following you and Vallen at one point. Now, this matter is officially at an end." With that pronouncement, their mother grabbed a small plate, added a chocolate biscuit to it, and proceeded to nibble at the corners.

Yes, of course. Because ladies nibbled like mice. Just like ladies didn't do anything that would earn any manner of attention from Polite Society. Living with one's husband's former lover would certainly fall into that category.

"It is not," Sylvia said quietly.

And for a moment, as her mother continued to take those small bites and dab at her immaculate face with a napkin, Sylvia thought the countess might not have heard her. Or perhaps the dowager countess was simply ignoring her show of defiance? Or mayhap it was just that she was so unaccustomed to Sylvia being anything but an obedient wife, daughter, and mother that she couldn't hear when Sylvia went against what was expected of her. "Valerie explained her reasons for seeking me out."

"Following you," the dowager countess snapped. "She was *following* you."

Because she'd been filled with the same curiosity Sylvia had for her. That was something the dowager countess, however, would never and could never understand. "She is my friend."

"You simply have not thought it through. You are a young mother. It will be expected that you carry yourself above reproach, and if you do not, then you risk losing your child."

Vallen. The son whom she'd been carrying while her husband had been betraying her and their vows to one another. And whom she alone had cared for, after Norfolk's death. Yet, even as his mother, she was held to entirely different standards than men . . . where if she did not conduct herself in a way society deemed appropriate, she might have her child ripped from her. Following Norman's death, the court had approved multiple guardians for *Sylvia's* son, and as such, there existed the possibility that Vallen could go to someone else's care if she were found to be *unfit*.

Resentment lent her heart an extra beat, that organ pounding harder from the unfairness of her lot. Of the lot of all women.

"I have always lived my life above reproach," she said when she trusted herself to speak through her bitterness. "I am not suggesting I live in a townhouse with two unmarried men. I am going to reside with a lady and—"

"And a woman born of the streets, who also was your husband's former lover."

"There is *no* scandal in our living together," she murmured, this time not allowing those words to sting. Refusing to be sidetracked by her mother's matter-of-factness. "No one is even aware of . . . what happened."

"What happened? As in your mother-in-law having been responsible for organizing a horrific fight society in which children battled to the death for entertainment?"

Sylvia's entire body tensed, and her stomach revolted, just as it had when she and Lila together had made the discovery and tracked down the head of that heinous group . . . only to discover it had been Lady Prendergast.

"And now, one of the women you are choosing to live with also happens to be a former fighter whom your late husband was in love with?" Her mother spoke in barely audible tones, because of course she'd be aware that only danger would come from anyone overhearing such words. "Have I missed anything?"

Sylvia winced. "I rather think you've summed it up quite sufficiently." Yes, when her mother put it that way, she could certainly see her point. "I have reached an agreement with Lord and Lady Prendergast. No one is going to say anything about . . . about . . . what happened." All the evil perpetrated by a woman whose mind wasn't sound would remain secret. Wealth and power could buy anything— and that included sweeping away, into silence, Lady Prendergast's deeds. "It is in their best interest to say nothing. And few others"—aside from her family and her late husband's—"are aware of any of this." Even knowing that hiding the family sins would protect Vallen's title and future reputation, guilt still reared its head. In her opting for silence to protect her son, Sylvia's brother-in-law, Hugh, and the other fighters would go without the justice they deserved.

Her mother threw her hands up. "Secrets such as this, they do not stay secrets forever," she insisted. "And certainly not with you helping it along as you are."

Nor could there be any disputing the world would devour such a scandal.

As if she sensed a weakening, her mother shifted closer. "Having *that woman* in your life will raise questions about how you know her, and about her identity." The dowager countess looked to Lila. "Tell her what I'm saying is true."

Sylvia glanced over at her youngest sibling.

"Mother is correct, in that you will be closely scrutinized and questions will be asked." Her younger sister held her eyes. "The question is, do you care?"

Their mother sputtered. "*Of course* she cares. She has to. If not for herself, then for Vallen."

As her younger sister and mother launched into a quiet debate, Sylvia sat silently, asking herself Lila's question: Did she care? Yes, there was merit to their mother's warnings. Both logic and reason said moving in with these two women was the last thing she should do. And yet, perhaps that was the fuel to her determination. From when she'd been a girl to when she was a young lady out for her first Season, and then through her marriage, she'd always done what was expected of her. This, this was her stand. And despite her mother's horror over Sylvia's decision, it remained hers. In a world where men were free to exist in any way and have complete control over their choices and decisions, she should have, at the very least, the right to decide where she would live.

With her resolve firmed, she spoke quietly, interrupting the debating pair. "I've told you what I intend to do."

The dowager countess went absolutely still, and Lila edged closer to Sylvia.

She braced for the fireworks, which was why she was thrown off balance when her mother's face fell and her words came out not with a shout, but with a whisper. "She hurt you, Sylvia."

"It was not her fault," Sylvia said simply. In the immediacy of learning all she had about her husband's betrayal, that realization had come surprisingly easily to her. "She wasn't aware he was married." He'd lied to Valerie Bragger just as much as he'd lied to Sylvia. As such, she'd felt more of a kindred connection to the woman for how she'd been wronged than she ever had resentment at the relationship she'd had with Sylvia's late husband.

"I knew it was a horrid idea when you insisted on finding this woman," her mother spat. "No good could come of it, I said. But no. You had to search her out and meet her"—Sylvia bit the inside of her cheek; it was better not to point out that it had, in fact, been Valerie who'd come to her—"and now . . ." The dowager countess gave her head a hard shake. "Suggesting that she live with you? I cannot allow this." Only, those four words emerged as an entreaty from a woman whose tone indicated she knew she would not and could not win.

"It is already decided, Mother," Lila said gently.

Sniffling once more, their mother set aside her favorite dessert in favor of the steadying tea.

"That doesn't change the fact that there will be a scandal," the countess persisted, her voice restored to its earlier strength. "Is that what you want for Vallen?"

She'd gone there. To Sylvia's one and only weakness. The child whom she'd sell and barter her soul for.

"That is also unfair, Mother," Lila chastised.

"Unfair because the truth hurts?" their mother countered. "Because it is true. Do you think society will be kind to a child who lives with a drunkard socialite and a street-born woman who was his father's lover?"

Sylvia winced. Yes, well, when presented that way, she could see the damning possibilities, and yet, her husband had opened her eyes to one truth.

"He will be fine." Sylvia's assurance came from a place of knowing.

"Oh?" Her mother shot a brow up. "And what makes you so very certain?"

"Because he is a male," she said, "and a future marquess."

And as such, he would never know the lack of freedom and control of his life that Sylvia and all women did.

Ever.

❧

A fortnight later
Waverton Street

Sylvia had done it.

She had moved out and into a *new* residence, free of her life as a married woman.

The newspapers had been intrigued, but unlike her mother had feared, there'd been no great uproar caused. There'd been, at worst, mild curiosity.

And there was something so splendorous in having a household that a husband or a mother or an older brother truly wasn't in charge of. For here she had something she'd never known: people who accepted her and allowed her—nay, encouraged her—to speak and think freely. And however worried her mother might be, Sylvia had found herself thriving in this new environment.

"This is all yours," Valerie murmured. Wrapping her arms about Sylvia's waist, Valerie hugged her, resting her chin atop Sylvia's shoulder.

Sylvia glanced back at this woman who'd become her friend, and then at Annalee, who looked over the room with a like happiness. "This is *ours*," Annalee said. And after living without ever really having anything of her own, there came a thrill of triumph in this.

The moment proved short-lived.

Someone shoved the door open hard, and as one, Sylvia and her new living companions whipped their gazes in that direction.

Their butler, Mr. Flyaway, a former fighter Lila's husband had arranged to work in the new role of head servant, frowned at them. "There be someone at the door," he said without preamble or bow. Unconventional in his delivery, the burly man had nearly brought Sylvia's mother to a faint upon her first visit. "Not a relative." Sylvia, however, found his direct style refreshing. "It be a young lady." He handed over a card.

Accepting it, Sylvia looked at the name emblazoned there. "Miss Emma Gately," she murmured, and looked questioningly to her friends.

Valerie shrugged. "You know I don't know . . . any of those sort. Not *ladies*."

Yes, having been born outside the peerage and living on the streets of East London, she hadn't had many dealings with members of Polite Society.

"And she's not someone I keep company with," Annalee offered, and then she flashed a wicked half smile. "Which likely means she's polite people."

Polite people. As in members of the *ton*.

"Shall I send her away?" Mr. Flyaway asked impatiently.

"Yes," Annalee said. Uncorking her flask, she took a sip. "See that you do."

And yet . . .

"Wait!" Sylvia called. Three sets of eyes went to her. "Show her in. I'll see her."

"She's got company with her. Two other ladies, one a sister. One a friend, she said."

Sylvia's intrigue redoubled, along with her worry. What reason would not one but three ladies have to seek her out? Unless they were somehow connected with the Fight Society?

The moment the thought slid in, she shook her head, refusing to let herself think of it.

"Sylvia?" Valerie spoke in a gentle voice. "Are you certain you want to receive them? Annalee and I can go see what they are here about."

They would shield her. It was thoughtful and kind, and yet, Sylvia was tired to her soul of being someone whom people felt they needed to protect.

"Please send them in, Mr. Flyaway," Sylvia repeated, and the butler hurried off.

A short while later, he showed in a trio of ladies. The three, all dressed in meticulous white, high-necked, heavily ruffled gowns, filed into the room. That was, however, where all similarities ended: one possessed crimson curls, another dark ringlets, and the third, the somewhat gangly, tall leader of that group, honey-blonde hair that had been drawn back severely at her nape.

Though Sylvia assessed the tall one to be a mere eighteen or nineteen, the young lady had a serious look to her. She also possessed a determined set to her mouth as she glanced amongst Sylvia, Annalee, and Valerie . . . before ultimately settling all her attention on Sylvia.

Mr. Flyaway drew the door shut behind them.

"May I help you?" Sylvia asked gently.

"Are you the Countess of Norfolk?" the blonde asked in surprisingly firm and decisive tones for one so young. Sylvia hadn't been anywhere nearly as self-assured when she'd been this girl's age.

Annalee reached for her silver case and removed a cheroot. Touching that tip to a nearby candle she always kept lit for such a necessity, she took a draw and exhaled out the side of her mouth. "Who is asking?" she answered for Sylvia.

"I told you," the dark-haired woman whispered none too discreetly to the lady at the center of her group. "This was a silly idea—"

"Hush," the blonde lady said dismissively . . . and commandingly. She proceeded on with introductions. "My name is Miss Emma Gately, and this is my younger sister, Miss Isla Gately." Her sister dipped a curtsy. "And my dear friend, Lady Olivia Watley." Lady Olivia offered a curtsy of her own.

There came a brief pause. "And how may I help you?" Sylvia asked, looking at them.

There came the first spark of indecision in Miss Emma Gately's eyes. "You are independent. Establishing this . . . society. And I would ask to be part of it. To learn from you, how to assert myself and to be interesting, and . . . also, to determine what I might do to win the heart of a gentleman."

A . . . society? Sylvia rubbed at her temple, wholly befuddled. "I'm sorry?" she ventured, as even Annalee, who was always ready with a retort, found herself gape-mouthed and silent.

"Her betrothed doesn't like her," Isla Gately blurted, earning a sharp look from Emma. "What?" The younger girl shifted back and forth. "He doesn't."

Miss Emma Gately bristled. "That is neither here nor there; the part that matters is . . . learning how to assert one's independence. How to be in control of one's life and future marriage and—"

"Why don't we slow down a bit," Valerie interrupted.

Sylvia motioned to the sofas. "Please, won't you sit?"

Moving in unison, the girls ventured deeper into the room and claimed the indicated seating.

"Now," Sylvia began when she and Annalee and Valerie had also found their chairs. "Perhaps you might explain a bit more about who you are and how you think I might help you, Miss Gately?"

"Emma," the young woman offered. "My name is Emma, and"—she drew in a breath—"I've been betrothed since I was a babe of only six."

Silence met that pronouncement.

"That is . . . horrific," Annalee said, and took another pull from her cheroot.

"Indeed," Emma agreed. "To the Earl of Scarsdale. Our families are close and thought the best way to cement that connection was through two of their children."

Sylvia stiffened. The earl, one of her late husband's closest friends, was a rogue of the first order.

Emma's gaze homed in on Sylvia. "You know him." It wasn't a question but an astute observation for one so young.

"I do." And perhaps it was only that she'd just moved in and was tired from the work they'd done in their new residence, all while caring for a child, but Sylvia spoke without restraint. "And neither do I think you should go about transforming yourself for him, or for any man. But especially not him."

"I told you!" Lady Olivia exclaimed, and then shifted her attention from Emma over to Sylvia. "I've told her time and time again that she doesn't want to win such a man." Unfamiliar to Sylvia until now, the young woman grew in her estimation.

With her cheroot clamped between her lips, Annalee clapped her hands. "Clever girl."

"I'm twenty-one years old. Not so much a girl," Lady Olivia replied.

"You came here, asking me to help you marry a man?" Sylvia said to Emma. "Well, I'd be more inclined to tell you how and why to avoid marriage to such a man." She paused. "Any man," she amended. "Not a single one of them is worth tying oneself to, particularly a scapegrace like Scarsdale, who wouldn't have the sense to see you."

Color leached from the young woman's cheeks. *Oh, dear.* She'd said too much. "Forgive me," Sylvia said quickly. "I don't know what came over me." Actually, she did. She knew scoundrels everywhere who were still attempting to swindle young women out of their hearts and then carry on as her own late husband had.

"No," Emma whispered. "Please, do not apologize." The young woman came to her feet, and Sylvia winced, bracing for the lady to storm off.

Instead, the girl began to pace. "I have attempted to snare his attention. I've wondered as to my failings. And for what?" Her strides grew increasingly frantic. "Why? And"—Emma abruptly stopped midpace—"I love everything you've said here," she whispered. "I'd not thought of it, but that . . . You are right. For seventeen years, I have been lamenting his lack of interest."

For . . . seventeen years? Sylvia studied the young woman before her, reassessing her youthful looks. Her self-possession made a bit more sense now.

The lady's sister interrupted Sylvia's musings with an admirable display of loyalty. "You've done nothing wrong," she said. "He is the one."

"Yes!" Emma exclaimed, her spine growing more erect with every word of truth she spoke. "Why should I change and seek his approval? Or be different? Or proper or . . . any of it?" Her jaw hardened. "When all along I should have been asking, 'How might I live an independent life, free of some cad?' It is just that it is—"

"Ingrained in us?" Sylvia supplied.

"Exactly," Emma said with a firm nod. "And I appreciate the society you've formed for opening my eyes to this grievous fault that exists amongst society."

Sylvia was nodding in agreement until that last statement registered. She stopped mid–head bob. "Come again?"

Valerie leaned in. "I believe she called us a *society*," she whispered.

Confusion creased Emma's brow as she returned to the sofa she'd vacated. "Do you prefer a different name?"

Hopelessly, Sylvia looked to Annalee. "What are we?" she mouthed.

Her friend gave a little shrug.

Sylvia turned back to her suddenly enthusiastic guest. "Forgive me, I believe you're mistaken. We are *not* a society."

"You're not?" Emma asked, bewildered. "A club, then?" She continued before Sylvia could disabuse her of the notion. "And here I thought a society a more officious and elevated group than a club." Her nose wrinkled. "Those clubs that all those men spend their time at."

Sylvia shook her head. "We're not either."

Emma's face fell for a moment, and then she brightened. "Well, you should be." The young woman folded her arms across her chest. "We should be. All of us. After all, I gather we're of a like opinion on . . . men. It would be worthy of us to help not only one another in seeing the light, as I have done with your guidance, but also other women, as well."

Silence met Emma Gately's declaration.

A society. It was . . . a peculiar thought. And yet, an interesting one. One that, the more Sylvia turned the idea around in her head, grew upon her.

"What are you thinking?" Valerie asked.

"That perhaps we might be an accidental society, after all," Sylvia murmured. "A mismatch society."

Miss Emma Gately started, laughing brightly. "I like that very much! The *Mismatch Society*. After all, there are so very many women who are in need of similar saving."

It was certainly a truth that resonated with Sylvia.

Annalee looked questioningly over at her. "What say you, Sylvia?"

This was . . . preposterous. The height of absurdity. Assembling here with her friends, and now strangers, to debate. But mayhap . . . mayhap it could be more than that. Mayhap it could be a way of helping young women find their voices and assert themselves in a world so very determined to keep them silent.

"Welcome to the Mismatch Society, ladies." Sylvia smiled. "It is an honor to have you amongst our ranks."

Chapter 2

One Month Later

Every girl from age four up to twenty-four had gathered.

Given the sheer size of the Kearsley family, it was a rarity to have all six ladies assembled. Seven, when including the mother of their impossibly large brood.

It was even rarer to have the utmost silence from any of them, let alone *all* of them, at the same time.

Something was decidedly amiss.

With a wariness born of knowing just how much trouble each lady present was capable of, Clayton eyed the collection of his kin, crammed three sisters per Louis XV Marquise settee, with their mother at the head chair.

Each woman and child stared back innocently, saying absolutely nothing.

There wasn't a tangle of words all rolled together as they vied to have their story, request, or question put to Clayton first.

There wasn't screeching and squealing over having another sister's story, request, or question addressed first.

And they may as well have replaced the ringing of St. Lawrence's bell with the one now clamoring away loudly in his head, for the sheer enormity of its power.

His littlest sister, Eris, at very nearly five, and also the most tempestuous of the lot, would be the first to break the silence. She shot a hand up. "I'm getting—"

Sixteen-year-old, Shakespeare-loving Delia, an identical twin, slapped a hand over the mouth of the youngest of the Kearsleys. More babe than girl, his littlest sister waved her hands about excitedly in a bid to speak whatever words had now been silenced.

Delia whispered something into the little girl's ear . . . that managed to penetrate her eagerness.

Eris promptly lowered her hands to her lap, and in a foreign display of primness, she folded her chocolate-stained fingers upon her once immaculate white, and now chocolate-stained, skirt.

Clayton's suspicions . . . and fears . . . deepened.

Had he been simply an observer and not the one summoned, he would have been endlessly fascinated by just what Delia had said to manage to silence the chatterbox.

As it was, as the summonee . . . all he knew was a healthy dread.

His mother came to her feet and motioned to the lavender-upholstered gilt-wood armchair beside hers. "We have summoned you today, Clayton."

He made his way through his gaggle of sisters, none of whom rose, and all of whom looked up at his approach. "I see that," he drawled after he'd settled into the chair.

Except again, that dread-inducing silence met his response.

He looked from sister to sister to sister.

But for the lone leather book resting on one of his sisters' laps, everything from their expressions to their blinking was a perfect match.

Clayton squirmed. When he'd been a young man at university, he'd been set upon by footpads and had his purse and fob snatched before suffering a cuff to the head for resisting giving over his timepiece. Even with all that, he always said he'd take a turn with even the most ruthless pickpocket over the whole of the Kearsley sisters together.

His mother smoothed her wrinkled grey skirts. "Shall we begin?"

"The suspense is killing me," he said, and that response was met with a bevy of identical frowns from his less-than-pleased siblings. He shifted. "I was not being sarcastic." And he wasn't. He was terrified.

Out of his damned mind.

Anwen, the eldest and most practical of his sisters, pushed her too-large spectacles back on her nose. "Good. I would advise against that. This matter is of import." The round wire rims promptly slid back into the improper place.

Alas, all his efforts at having them replaced were met with outrage and indignation by his sister, who was as loyal to her spectacles as she was to their sisters.

"Very serious stuff," Daria, the most notoriously morbid of his sisters, murmured.

At her side, her younger twin, Delia, picked up her book and proceeded to read.

"Ahem."

When the other girl made no attempt to lower her reading material, Daria tried for her attention once more. "I said, *ahhem*." Finally, Daria slapped Delia's fingers and favored her sister with one of those haunting, dark looks Clayton had once caught her practicing in a mirror.

Sighing, Delia lowered the volume to her lap.

Daria returned her attention to the group. "As I was saying . . . *very* serious stuff."

Once again, six of the ladies present nodded.

Eris looked confusedly between their mother and her elder sisters. "But we already did that part," she said on a loud whisper.

"*Shh.*" Daria and Delia promptly covered the younger girl's mouth.

Clayton leaned across the elder of the twins and whispered for Eris's ears only: "It's all right, poppet. I've already determined there's a play been scripted— *Oww.*" He winced as Eris brought an impressively strong foot down on top of his own.

She glared back at him with enough fire in her eyes to make him fear the future down the road. "*We* are talking, Clayton."

So much for being the loyal, avenging brother. "Very well." He straightened. "Then why don't we dispense with all the dr—" All eyes narrowed on him. This time, he was wise enough to edge his foot away from his youngest sister. "Er, that is . . . Why don't we dispense with all the"—Clayton fiddled with the fabric of his cravat—*"dithering?"*

"You were going to say 'dramatics,'" Brenna charged.

The bluestocking of the group, Brenna could recite any of the Enlightened thinkers, and debate a person into forgetting their name. As such, Clayton took several moments to fashion a response. "I—"

"Furthermore," Delia interrupted, "if *I* may point out, 'dithering' is not much better. It suggests one does not know one's mind, and we each know our own mind."

This time, their nods were perfectly synchronized.

Yes, there could be no doubting the Kearsley sisters knew what they wanted and when they wanted it, and Lord help the one who served as a possible impediment to those wishes.

Unfortunately, in this particular instance, it appeared that he was the unlucky one pegged as the "impediment." "Forgive me," Clayton said with his best attempt at a suitable-enough-for-them level of solemnity. "If you would be so good as to continue?"

"I will be the one to say it." Cora, his science-minded sister, pulled back her shoulders. "I am—"

"I am getting *marrrried*," Eris cut off.

Silence met the little girl's announcement.

She smiled, revealing the wide gap between her two front teeth.

Clayton didn't so much as blink. Of anything the noisy, oft-demanding, but always loving lot of Kearsleys might have said, that was certainly . . . not it. *"I . . . ?"* He scratched at what he trusted was a thoroughly confused brow. *"Whaat?"*

Cora frowned. "*I* was going to say that."

"Well, in fairness, if we want to be accurate? It was decided that I should be first," Anwen corrected with a little sniff. "I am just twenty-four."

A series of protests and challenges went up with sister fighting over sister for that dubious pleasure of—

Clayton sat back in his seat and just took in the scene.

Long, long ago, sometime between Anwen coming to blows with a doctor who'd refused to fashion spectacles for ladies, and Delia crashing upon the stage of a Royal Theatre performance to confront the player delivering his lines from *Hamlet*—or incorrectly delivering his lines, as she'd pointed out—Clayton had ceased to be nonplussed by anything they said or did.

That was . . . until now.

Because from the bits and pieces he was able to make out of a scene that seemed dangerously close to descending into an all-out brawl, his sisters, each of whom had expressed a distaste at even the mention of the marital state, should now be quarreling over who would have the honor and privilege first.

Their mother clapped her hands once. "Girls!" Her voice, however, was muted by the din of her quarreling daughters. "I said, girls! That is *enough*."

Alas, she may as well have been any one of the unsuccessful governesses they'd brought in over the years to tame the wild beasts.

Putting two middle fingers into her mouth, the viscountess whistled loudly.

That "emergency gesture," as she'd come to refer to it, had the necessary silencing effect. Each of her daughters fell quiet, though they each still took time to periodically glare at their last debate partner.

"Now," the viscountess went on, "it hardly makes sense for Eris or Delia or Daria to marry first."

"Yes, as I see it, they still each have at least another year or so before they venture into the bonds of matrimony," Clayton said dryly.

Eris and the sixteen-year-olds glared his way once more.

"Forgive me," he murmured, having committed the folly of shifting their ire away from their previous opponent and back toward him.

Their mother cleared her throat. "As I was saying, our youngest girls, despite their offer of sacrifice and their willingness to do so, should *not* at this time, or at any time within the nearest of futures, be wed." She drew in a breath and, bringing her shoulders back, looked straight ahead. "It shall be . . . *me.*"

Oh, good God.

Clayton slumped in his chair and dropped his brow into his palm.

"No other. It should be me . . . I shall do it . . ."

"I am the *eldest* sister . . ."

"But I am the one who . . ."

There was never a dull day in the Kearsley household. That held true from Clayton's earliest remembrances of his wild and free family. One that he'd sought very much, as heir to the earldom, to raise himself above. And yet, it hadn't been until his father died four years earlier, on Eris's first birthday, and Clayton had stepped in to fill the role of viscount and de facto father to his sisters, that he'd come to appreciate that he'd not had any idea of just how wild his family, in fact, was.

From the overdramatic debates and discussions that frequently ensued, to each sister's eccentric interest, to all the sisters' devotions to their respective interests, the Kearsley girls were the pieces upon a chessboard that he still hadn't been able to make heads or tails of.

"Are you quite through?" he called loudly over the racket.

"What manner of son are you?" Cora cried out. "Have you not heard what Mother said? She said *she* will be the one to marry. When she loved Papa so desperately, she should be the one to wed another." The girl sniffled and dabbed at nonexistent tears in the corners of her eyes. "Why . . . why . . . at her advanced age, she is very near the end and should hardly be thinking of marriage."

The viscountess's lips formed a displeased moue. "I beg your *pardon*? I am not so very old."

"Yes, you are," Eris piped in. "You have white hairs."

"I have three white hairs." Their mother lifted her three middle fingers. *"Three."*

"Either way," Brenna murmured in sad, somber tones, "no woman with white hair should be the one to enter into marriage."

As Anwen touched the streak of white hair tucked behind her ear, her frown deepened. "*I* have white hair." As she'd had since she was a girl of sixteen. Society had been less than kind to her for it.

"Precisely." Brenna stuck her tongue out. "That is why it should be me."

Leaning over, Anwen grabbed the younger girl's loose ringlets and gave them a sharp tug.

"Owwww!"

Before the display could dissolve once more into a debate as to who would have the right to wed first, Clayton raised a hand. "If I may . . . ?" His mother and sisters quieted once more, and each looked expectantly his way. "Now . . . this . . . sudden desire to marry—"

Cora cut him off. "I don't have one."

Clayton gave the ever-sharpening ache in his head another rub. "Weren't you just fighting for that privilege?"

"*Privilege?* I hate men."

He furrowed his brow. Now had it been Brenna, reciter of Condorcet, advocate of women's rights, well, then, *that* he would have expected. "Since . . . when?" As soon as the question left him, he frowned as a more pressing query slipped forward, an important one. "Why?"

"Why, but there's many a man hath more hair than wit," Delia said in dramatic tones, and with that, she picked up her book and proceeded to read.

"Shakespeare," her twin explained to Clayton.

"I know that." When she wasn't reading the Great Bard, one could count on Delia to be reciting his wisdoms. "I want to know—"

Delia made a flourishing motion of turning the page in her copy of *Macbeth*.

"Oh, never mind. Can someone please explain the sudden about-face amongst so many of you where marriage is concerned?"

His mother looked at him as if he'd sprung a second head. "Because *one* of us must do it, Clayton. I'm not sure if you are aware, but in a family of six daughters and a mother, there are many who will require looking after."

When he wasn't there.

That thought hung unfinished without a need to be spoken aloud, as the Kearsley curse, which saw the men struck down too quickly and the women ravaged by tragedies of other sorts, was common knowledge to each sibling present.

"I assure you I am quite aware."

And for the first time since he'd stepped onto the makeshift stage of whatever farce this was, a somberness descended upon the gathering.

An understanding of what the future held—or rather, did not hold—had been with him from early on, and as such, he'd accepted the same fate met by the other men who had come before him. Be it his father, who'd choked on a plum pit and died too soon, or his grandfather, who'd taken an errant bullet from poachers on his Scottish estate, the list of peculiar, untimely deaths went on and on.

Anwen cleared her throat lightly. "Then you must also be aware, Clayton"—her words came haltingly, with an almost pained quality to them—"that we cannot rely upon the charity of distant relations."

No. He well knew that.

"Mr. Meadows." Their mother spat the name like the epithet it had long been in the Kearsley household. Clayton was now all that stood between the distant cousin several times removed and inheriting the title.

"It is hardly Mr. Meadows's fault that he is the heir behind me."

Gasps went up, and Cora flew out of her seat. "You would dare defend Mr. Meadows?"

Their mother, however, held up a hand, and that brought the young lady back into her seat—albeit stiffly.

"Mr. Meadows has done nothing *wrong*," Clayton insisted. "That is, with the exception of being next in the line of succession. Which is no fault of his own, I should point out."

"You *would* defend him," Delia muttered.

"He is frequently writing to Mother, and he always asks after you, Clayton," Brenna shot back. "Why would he do something like that? Hmm?" The gangly girl folded her arms across her chest, and all her sisters immediately followed suit, daring him with their expressions and poses to defend the man.

"I don't know," he drawled. "Perhaps to be friendly?"

"Friendly," Anwen muttered, giving her head a disgusted shake that sent her spectacles tumbling to her lap. Nearly half-blind without them, she felt around, searching, finding, and then jamming them upon her face once more.

"Yes," he went on when she could see him again. "Forgive me for not thinking his motives are anything but pure. He is not a villain in a Shakespearean play—"

Charging to her feet, Delia brandished her book. "Though those that are betray'd Do feel the treason sharply, yet the traitor stands in worse case of woe!"

He winced. "Et tu, Brute?"

Delia's eyes flew wide. "You should use my Shakespeare against me?"

And wonder of wonders, his mother took pity . . . on him. Sailing to her feet, she placed herself between Delia and Clayton. "Come, Delia. It is hardly your brother's fault."

He gave his head a wry shake. *That* was the defense? Clayton peeked out from behind his mother and caught the fury flashing in his sister's eyes. She made a slashing motion with that book across her throat, and thinking better of it, he ducked back and took what protection the viscountess had offered.

"Now, can we please resume this ever-pressing matter?" she asked the room at large.

The moment she seated herself, Cora spoke. "This is a waste of time, Mother. We have already decided that we have to be the ones to look after us." *As Clayton would not.* That meaning came as clearly as if it had been spoken.

"I agree," the viscountess said sadly. "Your father, God rest his soul, did not leave us well off."

All the girls made the sign of the cross.

The late earl had known precisely what fate awaited him. And yet, instead of attempting to live a life where he had things in order before his passing, he'd believed in living for the now and indulging the whims and wishes of his daughters. They weren't destitute, but neither were they comfortable.

And there was the matter of Clayton's sisters requiring security and stability . . . none of which they'd have when he was gone. The fact of the matter was, building a fortune wasn't something that happened overnight. Most of the lands yielding profits would go to the heir to replace him—a distant cousin who was a nice enough fellow. But to expect the man to care for six female relations and Clayton's mother?

As such, where would his sisters be if Clayton failed to produce an heir? If he did, however, marry and provide a future Viscount St. John, all the land and fortune would stay with his immediate family. As would the poor wife left to look after his sisters . . .

It was something Clayton had not allowed himself to think of since his father's passing.

Not as much as he should have.

Because there could be only one solution that would ensure the properties and monies they still had did not pass to Mr. Meadows. Another person.

An heir.

An heir only he could provide. He and . . . a wife.

Oh, bloody hell.

He slumped in his chair once more.

"Why is he looking like that?" Eris whispered up at Delia, and when the twin didn't answer, Eris turned her questioning gaze up to Daria. "Is he . . . going to be sick?"

He certainly felt like he was going to cast his contents up. "I'll do it." His voice emerged strangled.

Eris screeched and, flying out of her seat, rushed to the opposite end of the gathering. "I don't want to get his sick."

"I'm not . . . going to be ill," he assured. "I'm . . . I'm . . ."

All his kin looked back expectantly.

"I'm going to be the one who marries." He managed to get the words out.

He braced for the onslaught of shock and disbelief.

Oddly, there was an almost bored expectation from the group. It lasted no longer than a moment that might have been imagined.

"Are you certain?" His sisters spoke over one another, their words of praise rolling together.

"That is so very wonderful of you . . . You are the very most devoted brother, you are."

And with that, the group came to their feet and, following behind their mother, filed from the room, leaving Clayton thankfully and blessedly alone.

Chapter 3

One week later
White's
London, England

Clayton had inherited his friends through his connection to Norman, Lord Norfolk, at Oxford. He'd always been the odd man out of the group.

With their penchant for womanizing, drinking, and wagering, that much remained true.

Their friendship, however, remained strong.

And given the state of his best friend, the Earl of Scarsdale, his head buried in his arms on the table, the man was in dire need of friendship.

Waving off a servant who came forward to pull out his chair, Clayton availed himself of the seat closer to his other best friend, the Marquess of Landon.

Landon cupped a hand around his mouth and whispered, "He's in bad shape."

"I . . . see that."

As did all the other patrons and servants stealing curious looks the way of their table.

Scarsdale groaned. "Broff-off, shedid."

"Another drink will do." Leaning over, Landon patted Scarsdale hard between the shoulders. "It always does."

Clayton was in possession of an entirely different and unpopular opinion to the one Landon now spouted. At this particular moment, however, that seemed neither here nor there. *Broff-off, shedid. Broff-off, shedid.* Alas, no matter how many times Clayton tested those mismatched syllables in his mind, he came up empty with the deciphering. "What was that, Scarsdale?"

The Earl of Scarsdale downed a drink, and hadn't even finished the swallow before he had his arm up, gesturing to a White's servant for another.

The notorious rogue, who'd recently decided to settle down and see to his responsibilities as earl, set his glass down hard. "She . . . broff it off." With that, the man slumped forward, letting his head fall hard on the table with a *thunk* that earned winces from Clayton and Landon.

Clayton slid a questioning glance over to Landon.

"Broke it off. His betrothed, Miss Gately." The other man silently mouthed the latter part.

Ahh. So this was the reason for Scarsdale's misery. "But you didn't want to marry her anyway."

"Notthepoint, St. John." Either grief or too much drink added a slur to Scarsdale's response.

"Uh . . . isn't it?"

Landon lifted his half-empty brandy Clayton's way. "It is because you are the optimist of the group."

"It is trueyouare." That response, buried into the smooth mahogany, came muffled.

Clayton frowned. "I'd hardly call myself an *optimist*." His sisters and his mother, yes. Clayton himself? Decidedly not. After all, a man who'd accepted his fate was to die young and likely to leave a family of hoydens and hellions to their own defenses would hardly ever be confused as someone with a rosy-by-nature look at life. "But as I said before, you didn't even *want* to marry the girl." In fact, Scarsdale had done nothing but complain about his fate since the day he'd offered for the young lady.

"That's not the point." The other man surged forward, but Landon put a calming hand on his arm.

"*Tsk-tsk*, St. John," Landon chided. "Bad form, piling on a man when he is down."

"I'm not attempting to pile on; I'm just pointing out that detail for solace's sake."

"Solace's sake," Scarsdale muttered. "As I said . . . *optimist*." Grabbing Landon's glass, the earl saluted Clayton, then drank down the remainder of their friend's fine French brandy.

A servant arrived with another bottle.

No sooner had the young man left than Scarsdale let his head fall to the tabletop once more.

Landon continued. "Either way, it isn't just you, Scarsdale," he pointed out commiseratively. Grabbing up the bottle of brandy, he refilled Scarsdale's glass and put it within reach of the other man's fingertips. "Lots of men are in the very way you are." That managed to bring the earl's head up, revealing tired, bloodshot eyes. "Why, look at Bowick over there." Landon gave a discreet nudge of the chin, and they followed that gesture over to a gentleman with his head in his hands and a drink framed between his arms. "And Cobham."

Cobham, who was currently cradling a whiskey in each hand and alternating sips between the two.

"All of Polite Society has gone insane; you are just one of the many, many victims," Landon said, helping himself to another drink.

"Whatever are you talking about?" Clayton asked, looking about the room at the men Landon had listed.

The marquess paused midpour. "You gentlemen don't know?" There was an almost gleeful relish from that member of their group, who'd always taken delight in being the first in possession of any information.

Scarsdale turned his head so he rested his chin upon his palm. "Know *what?*"

Dragging his chair closer to the table, Landon spoke in hushed tones. "Ladies everywhere are refusing to wed. They are breaking their betrothals, turning away suitors, and calling for greater freedoms. All of society is in an uproar over it."

What? When there was a whole time of the English calendar dedicated to that very institution? Clayton snorted. "That is preposterous. I've heard nothing of this."

Landon shrugged. "You aren't often abreast of what is happening in society."

No, that much was true. "Gossip," Clayton corrected. He'd at least have his friend call it what it was. "I don't bother with it."

"Which is why you don't know," the other man pointed out. "Either way, call it what you will, it also happens to be how I know, and you"—drink in hand, he stretched his littlest finger out and wagged it in Clayton's direction—"do not." He shot his left arm up, and held two fingers aloft.

A liveried servant immediately came forward with a silver tray in hand.

Landon plucked free a copy of *The Times* and tossed it across the table.

Clayton caught it in the chest.

"Front page," the other man instructed when the servant had gone.

Unfolding the paper, Clayton scanned the page.

The London Season Is in Upheaval

"Not a very clever title, is it?" he drawled.

"All fun and games to you until it affects you," Landon charged.

He resumed reading.

All the while, Scarsdale's pathetic, forlorn sighs punctuated each detail Clayton skimmed in the gossip column.

> Ladies are calling into question not only the institution of marriage but also every institution this kingdom holds dear . . . crumbling marriages and shattered betrothals . . .

And his earlier confidence that his friend had, in fact, been exaggerating, as he was wont to do, flagged with every damning inked word upon the page.

> London's most notorious rogue, reformed, has been the latest to suffer the effects of a broken heart. Lord Scarsdale's betrothal was officially severed and the nuptials . . .

"Canceled," Scarsdale finished on a shaky whisper.

Oh, bloody hell.

In short, the Marriage Mart was officially closed.

He dropped the newspaper to find Landon smiling back, wearing a smug "I told you so" look.

"Surely not . . . *all* ladies are part of this . . . this . . . movement?" Clayton asked dubiously. After all, gossip columns were given to exaggeration. That was why they were gossip columns.

Landon shrugged. "Look around you, friend."

And Clayton did.

From Scarsdale vacillating between pitiable sighs and agonized groans to the various other lords scattered throughout White's being comforted by their own friends and acquaintances.

Clayton let loose a string of silent curses.

It should so work out that he had chosen to settle on the responsibility of finding a wife when all London's ladies were in revolt—specifically against the state of marriage.

This time he did reach for the bottle and glass that had been set out for him and forgotten until now. "What in thunderation has happened?" Because revolts weren't born of nothing. They rose from the ashes of firebrands.

Landon leaned back in his seat, stretching out the moment, relishing the attention paid him as he often did. "The Wantons."

That managed to penetrate even Scarsdale's haze of misery. The other man picked his head up.

Clayton scoffed. "There have been wantons and all manners of wicked sorts since the beginning of time. And yet there was not a revolt before now." *When I vowed to my family that I'd be the one to wed and secure their fates and futures.*

"No, not as in a specific person or another," Landon said in the frustrated tones that should be solely reserved for annoyed tutors. "As in a title. The Wantons. *Of Waverton Street.* They call themselves the Mismatch Club, or some such, but all the *ton* refers to them as the Wantons. It all started with three ladies living together. Now their membership is growing, and the number of ladies in the market for a *husband* is dwindling."

Clayton tried to make sense of that. "It is a club, then?" A club comprised of women determined to break down societal order.

Landon nodded. "Indeed. They meet weekly and discuss ways in which to make our lives a living hell."

Clayton scoffed. "I'm sure that is not the purpose of their group."

"Have you *seen* the men around you?" his friend retorted.

He glanced around once more. Yes, his friend had a point there. "What, exactly, occurs at these meetings?"

"The ladies provide instruction to other women on how to avoid the state of marriage," Landon said, rolling his snifter between his palms.

"They school their members on how to instead push that task off onto brothers, guardians, and fathers, who will then see to the responsibility of raising a family's wealth and status through marriage."

Clayton couldn't help it . . . nor did he even try—he laughed. He laughed until both friends were glaring his way, and every sullen peer was glowering, no doubt disapproving of the one person finding mirth that day.

"So glad you have a reason to laugh," Scarsdale groused, tossing back his drink.

Clayton regained control of his amusement. "Forgive me. It's just that it's utterly preposterous to feel sympathy or pity for those men who allowed themselves to be so duped."

"It's all very amusing until it is you with the broken heart or you have become a victim of the Wantons."

"I assure you," he said in response to Landon, "I've no intention of finding myself anyone's victim."

"I remember when I was that arrogant." Scarsdale's shaky voice dissolved to a whisper.

Landon leaned over and gave the other man a commiserative pat on the back.

"Confident" was how Clayton preferred to think of it. Not "arrogant." Alas, neither was he a person who'd belabor the point with a friend who'd already been knocked down.

As Landon's earlier levity faded and an uncharacteristic somberness fell over the usually lighthearted lord, they sat in silence, each sipping their drink. While they did, each to his own thoughts, Clayton studied the room at large; the somberness that had fallen over it was an even more pronounced indication of the situation Landon had spoken of and about.

This place, usually so filled with conversations about Parliament and business and other casual discourses, had been reduced to a silent, solemn club.

But then, given what Landon had shared and the newspapers had written of, why shouldn't there be that gravity?

The fate of futures and families fell to the men here, and those futures and families were reliant upon gentlemen making matches. It was, simply put, the way of their world.

And now that world was threatened.

And not only that but apparently their hearts, too.

Clayton glanced over at Scarsdale, sprawled out across more than half of the table, his head buried in his arms.

Granted, he'd not known the viscount's heart was engaged either way, and yet it had been. Clayton picked up *The Times* and found the mention of Scarsdale there. Surely the women responsible for these unfortunate changes to society hadn't intended for . . . *this*? Any of it? Or, at least, not the parts that had led to the complete breakdown in social order?

"What are you thinking?" Landon asked.

Clayton lowered his newspaper. "Someone needs to just . . . explain the chaos resulting from these meetings of theirs."

"There's a leader of the trio," Landon shared. "They call her Madam Leader."

"Of course they do," Clayton muttered. That probably fed the lady's ego and only further fueled whatever madness this was.

Landon waggled his eyebrows. "And is that what you intend to do, St. John? Patiently explain to her what she is doing wrong?"

"Why . . . yes."

It was harder to say who was more shocked by Clayton's pronouncement: the wide-eyed Landon; Scarsdale, who'd at last picked his head up from the table; or Clayton himself.

What in hell had he agreed to do? And yet . . . how difficult could it be to reason with the woman? "As I said, I'm sure if the lady has pointed out to her the effects that her meetings are having on society, she'd be more inclined to make some adjustments." That pronouncement was met with silence, even managing to put a stop to Scarsdale's infernal sighing and groaning.

"Adjustments?" Landon echoed.

Why was he repeating back everything so? "Yes, adjustments. I'm not suggesting that they don't meet."

Scarsdale straightened, looking more like his usual composed, sober self. "What are you going to suggest to her, then?"

"That some changes be made to whatever discussions are taking place. I'm sure they can't mean for *all* women not to marry. Just as I'm sure rebellion is not what she set out to create." And yet, here they were.

Both men looked at him, and he bristled. "What?"

"You're going to be the one to speak to this lady?" Landon didn't give him a chance to answer, clearly feeling further clarification was required. *"You."*

Clayton bristled. "Yes, me." Was that really so hard for them to contemplate? Yes, his volunteering to show up at the residence of a scandalous lady's household was uncharacteristic enough to merit those looks. It was the manner of boldness that would have always been better suited to the colorful, sociable men he'd called friends over the years. But still . . . they needn't look *quite* so surprised.

For the first time since Clayton had arrived to find Scarsdale bereft, the man burst out laughing. Nay, it was more a hysterical fit that left the earl sputtering and wiping tears from his eyes.

Landon joined in. "You . . . ? You . . . ?" He opened his mouth to speak but couldn't get anything else out before dissolving all the more into paroxysms of hilarity.

And Clayton couldn't sort out whether Landon was trying to determine if that single word he'd sputtered in between his merriment was what exactly Clayton intended to say when he paid the Waverton house a visit. Or whether it was a rhetorical utterance, at the overall preposterous idea of him doing what he'd stated he'd do.

"Oh, bugger off," he muttered, swiping his glass from the table and drinking down the contents.

When both men's laughter had dissolved to the periodic chuckle, he gave them a look. "You may laugh, but if the both of you and the gentlemen of London on the whole had it their way, they'd be sitting here licking their wounds and their sorrows while this scandalous society carries happily on."

"Whereas you intend to go and be the voice of reason." Landon apparently wasn't anywhere near close to done with his amusement, his words sufficiently cracking him up once more.

"Laugh as you may," Clayton said on a frown. "But anyone can be reasoned with. Anyone," he added for good measure.

"I've it on authority that the angry papas and guardians who've attempted to speak with the lady of the household have all been turned away."

He scoffed. "That is . . . rubbish. They can't simply turn everyone away."

"They have. And *they* do . . . After all, remember, there are three of them."

His stomach fell. Yes, he'd forgotten that detail.

"Three," Landon reiterated with more of that obnoxious amusement in the emphasized word.

Oh, hell. It was daunting enough to have taken on the job of speaking with the lady responsible for Scarsdale and the rest of the broken hearts at White's. But . . . three women? Three, when he'd never been known for being . . . well, anything of a charmer.

Clayton pushed back his chair and stood.

His friends looked up questioningly.

"Where are you off to?" Scarsdale asked.

"I have a meeting with the Wantons."

"Wait . . . You were serious?" Shock laced Scarsdale's query.

"Deadly so." Clayton didn't have time for this Marriage Mart revolt. No doubt this was fate's way of manipulating his life, a means of ensuring that he broke the promise he'd made to his sisters, one that had been relatively easy to make because their futures depended upon it. Clayton hardened his jaw. He'd be damned if he allowed some free-spirited women to turn every lady against that state. Not when he was in need of a damned wife himself. He grabbed up Landon's copy of *The Times*.

Landon jumped up quickly enough that his chair went tumbling back and skidding over to a nearby table of equally aggrieved patrons. "Wait. You're really doing this?"

"I am." It was somewhat unlike him, but also what needed to be done. As such, there wasn't time for the nice gent he usually was . . . but rather a gent in action.

"There is something else you really need to know before you make that visit." Landon spoke quickly. "The lady—"

"I already know everything I need to." The last thing he had time for was finding himself at the source of Landon's baiting and jesting.

Ready for a battle, Clayton quickened his stride and headed out of White's and off to Waverton Street.

Chapter 4

Sylvia hadn't *intended* to create a stir amongst the *ton*.

Just as she hadn't planned to forge and form a society.

Alas, after a little more than a month of living on Waverton Street, that was precisely what she and her new living partners had, in fact, created.

They had set all the peerage abuzz.

And Sylvia had never found herself happier with her changed circumstances.

Thunk-Thunk-Thunk.

The silver lorgnette, the makeshift gavel that began and adjourned all meetings, landed three times upon the turquoise-painted pine desk. "This meeting is called to order," the most vocal of their group, Lady Annalee, announced to the crowded room of women. She paused to take a draw from her cheroot, and exhaled a perfectly formed circle. "First order: new business."

Sylvia looked to her sister, Lila.

Lila, who, following her attack at Peterloo, had withdrawn from the world, and had recently returned to the living, thanks to the support of her now husband, Hugh. And yet, Sylvia still detected a tension and palpable unease in her sister at her changed circumstances. Perhaps it would always be there. "Lila has something to share with the group," she volunteered in a bid to help her sister along. "Lila?"

All eyes went to the dark-haired woman, now proprietress of her own establishment, where men and women learned the art of self-defense. Lila cleared her throat. "As you are aware, my husband is a carver. He fashioned this for our group and our meetings." Reaching into her bag, she withdrew a small, circular disc, carved and painted yellow. Next, she took out an intricately detailed gavel; with a ribbed handle and a daisy carved upon the top and bottom of the head, every part had been lovingly attended to. Holding both aloft, she came forward, extending the set to Annalee.

Annalee stubbed out her cheroot in the little porcelain tray of ashes and discarded the scrap, then reached for the offering. "This is . . . splendid," she said in reverent tones as she took the gifts and held them up for the gathering to admire.

A number of sighs went up.

Nor did Sylvia believe for a moment those exhalations of air were anything but romantic expressions.

After all, it would be impossible to not be in awe of a husband as devoted as Lila's.

Sylvia stared on, her gaze fixed on that lovingly crafted set Annalee showed to the room at large. A devoted husband, one who supported her dreams and efforts. In short, it was what Sylvia had wanted . . . and for a while, what she'd believed she had.

More fool she . . .

But then, what dreams had she really had? What had she really done in her life other than be the perfect lady and hostess?

Returning to her desk, Annalee set the small yellow disc down and banged it with the gavel. She turned a smile on Lila. "This was long overdue, it was. Many thanks to His Grace."

"To His Grace." The other ladies all lifted their fists and pumped them twice in the air in a collective show of appreciation.

Lila inclined her head. "I shall be sure and let my husband know his efforts were appreciated." A little blush rose in her pale cheeks. "I have been thinking," she hesitantly ventured as the room attended to her, "about our meetings, and I have some concerns."

Murmurs rolled around the room.

"Concerns?" Annalee echoed. "What concerns, exactly?"

"About the views expressed regarding men as partners and husbands," Lila said quietly. "I fear that we are speaking in a blanket way about all marriages and all gentlemen when not everything is so very black and white."

"Marriage and men are equally terrible." Sylvia's response sprang from an automaticity of truth and earned a laugh from Annalee.

Lila shot a look at her childhood friend, and then shifted her focus once more to Sylvia. "Surely you don't feel that way about all men?" She continued before Sylvia could speak. "What of Hugh? And our brother, Henry?"

"The exceptions," she said bluntly, and the other members nodded in concurrence. "They are the exceptions." It was far easier for Lila, who'd not suffered a broken heart, to believe there was good in that union. But she was the exception, not the rule.

"I do *not* disagree with that assessment," their sister-in-law, Clara, put in with a husky laugh, rousing like laughter from the other women around the room. A former courtesan who'd saved Sylvia's brother and ended up falling in love with and marrying him, the music hall owner had every reason to be cynical where men were concerned.

"And knowing a handful of good men is hardly reason for me or any of us to advocate for the prison that is marriage," Sylvia added when the laughter subsided.

"Not all marriages are the way you are describing them." Lila spoke with a quiet insistence.

"How many others here have parents who entered into a love match and had it remain so during their union?"

The Kearsley sisters raised their hands.

However, aside from the siblings, not a single arm shot up. Certainly not Lila's or Sylvia's, whose parents had had a businesslike arrangement. Yes, there'd been affection, but there'd not been more than that.

Lila, however, clung to that lone family who lent the only support to her argument. "See?" She pointed to the Kearsleys. "Between them and me—"

"You married a gentleman who spent the bulk of his existence outside the *ton*," Annalee gently reminded the other woman. "Men who've spent their entire lives in this world? They care only about title, rank, and privilege."

There came more murmurs of assent.

"She isn't wrong," Sylvia said for Lila's benefit. "Peers marry ladies with only one intention . . . to continue their line and maintain their wealth." And all the while they sought their pleasures elsewhere. They found love with women who weren't their wives. Once, just thinking that would have cut off her ability to breathe without pain. Now, the realization of who her husband had been and the lie her marriage had been caused only a dull ache in her breast. Pushing back thoughts of her late husband's betrayal, she refocused on the debate at hand. "As such, given the motives of greed that drive men, I could never, and would never, encourage a woman to entertain the prospect of marriage. Now, is there anything else?"

"I suppose there is not." There was a sad glimmer in her younger sister's pretty brown eyes. And there was something more there: pity. At the changes life and love had wrought upon Sylvia? At the cynicism that should exist within a room, when Lila had proven that in the rarest of times, real love could not only exist but also thrive, as it had for her and Hugh?

And if there was even the rarest of times when a woman might want to trust herself to that state, and even . . . find what Lila had, who were they to stifle it?

"Continuing on." Annalee banged the new gavel, calling the group back to the real focus of the day's agenda. She looked over to Valerie, who'd become the official secretary of their society. "New business."

The young woman scanned her notes. "The second order of business pertains to the topic of marriage." She stole a sideways peek at Lila, and then Sylvia, and cleared her throat. "That is, more *specifically*"—she turned the page with a flourish—"avoiding the marital state when others within society and one's family have the opposite expectation."

As she spoke, everyone in the room sat riveted.

With an almost icy quality to her closely cropped blonde curls, there was an otherworldly quality to the young woman, an aura to her presence. Sylvia had readily seen from the moment she'd met her late husband's true love just why he'd been so captivated. And then she'd come to know her for herself, and realized how grand of a personality she was. In short, she was a figure to elicit interest and intrigue, where Sylvia had simply been . . . Sylvia.

"We had discussed deterring family members who might attempt to guide us toward that state, and instead, turn the tables so that the obligation and responsibility falls to the male members of the household. The Kearsleys, who explicitly stated they were indifferent either way as to whether their brother married as long as his attentions weren't on their unwedded states, were to employ some of the strategies we'd discussed as a group to put guardians and brothers and fathers or mothers off." Valerie concluded her reading.

Sylvia and the room on the whole looked to the trio of young ladies, aged seventeen to twenty-four, all crammed onto a settee really meant for two: the Kearsley sisters. The sisters of her late husband's best friend, the Viscount St. John, the young women had proven an unexpected but surprisingly welcome addition to the Mismatch Society.

Anwen, the eldest of the sisters, stood and smoothed her palms down the front of her skirts. "We began by summoning our brother for a family meeting."

As one, the other members leaned forward in their chairs, hanging on to the young lady's words. Just as she opened her mouth to continue, her younger sister Brenna Kearsley hopped up.

"And we each agreed to take on the sacrificial role," she finished, stealing her sister's thunder as all eyes swiveled to her.

Her elder sister glowered, but oblivious to anything other than the attention now trained on her, Brenna continued, sharing the clever, intricate way in which they had gone about bringing the viscount around to being the one to sacrifice his freedom, all the while preserving theirs. "We each of us took a turn, insisting that we would be the one to make the noble sacrifice."

"Everyone from Mother on down to my four-year-old sister," Anwen hurried to interject.

The pair went back and forth, each filling in the masterful details of a plot that had been hatched in this very room and orchestrated . . . to flawless perfection. When they'd concluded, both ladies curtsied and then sat beside Cora, who, as she so often did, had buried her head in a science periodical.

"Brilliant," Annalee whispered, lightly clapping four fingers against her open palm. She reached for another cheroot and lit the scrap with a burning candle. "Hear, hear," she said, banging the table.

All the women stomped the floor with their feet, sending up a rolling applause.

"You fended him off attempting to see any of you wed, while he took on the sacrificial role. *Well done!* I would classify this as a triumph." Valerie looked to Sylvia, who gave the nod for their secretary to make the statement official.

That triumph proved short-lived.

The doors flew open, and the rotund head housekeeper, Mrs. Flyaway, burst into the room. "There is a . . . man!" she announced, out of breath and her cheeks red.

Everyone flew to their feet.

What in blazes?

"My—" *Father-in-law.* Sylvia attempted to get the rest of that out. And failed.

"Not the duke"—Lila's husband—"and not your brother, my lady." Mrs. Flyaway pressed her hands to her cheeks. "And he is . . . *inside.*"

What?

An unheard-of silence descended upon the room . . . followed by a rapid flurry of staggered whispers.

Mrs. Flyaway hung her head. "I'm ever so sorry, my lady." Fire sparked in the old woman's eyes. "I'll be knocking Mr. Flyaway good upon the head for this."

Sylvia made a soothing sound, and crossing over to her head housekeeper, she gave her a gentle pat of assurance. "It is not your fault."

"It's that horrible man. A right brute, he is."

A brute?

That managed to stymie the chattering as each lady hung upon the words being spoken by the housekeeper, who in turn grew several inches over the attention now swung her way.

"All men are brutes," Valerie muttered, earning another concurring stomp from the group.

"But this one," Mrs. Flyaway went on. "He is the absolute worst. Big." She flung her arms wide on each side of her. "As tall as my Mr. Flyaway." She stretched her palms high above her head.

Shock brought Sylvia's eyebrows shooting up. "As . . . tall as Mr. Flyaway?" She couldn't stifle the unease that crept into her voice.

Her housekeeper nodded furiously. "Indeed he is, my lady."

Seven inches past six feet, the head butler was a veritable monster of a man. It had been why, when unwanted visitors, disappointed and angry papas, and husbands had come calling, it had been so very easy to turn them away. Until now. Until it appeared the old fighter had found his match in size. Panic gnawed inside her.

Lord Prendergast. There was no one else as manipulative or as dangerous as to fight his way inside. He had vowed he'd be unrelenting in seeing Sylvia's son, and that he'd ultimately have his way.

"And an angry beast he be." Mrs. Flyaway quickly lifted her hands into makeshift claws, wringing gasps from the group. "Has to be to have gained entry past my sweetie."

Several of the ladies clamored to hide behind one another.

"He is just a man," Sylvia said to the room at large in a bid to both assure and ease the over-the-top panic.

"And did this gentleman give a name?" she asked quietly, for the other woman's ears only.

"Not that I'm aware of, my lady," she returned in an equal quiet . . . that lasted only as long as her next words. "I overheard him talking to my dearie, and he informed Mr. Flyaway that he knew you were not receiving visitors at this time but said he'd not be deterred, and that he would *wait*"—every emphasized word earning a greater gasp amongst the ladies in the room—"as long as need be for an audience."

Determined to calm their members, Sylvia held up a hand. "He is not the first gentleman who has shown up these past weeks." Every last insolent one of them had been run off by their unconventional butler.

Mrs. Flyaway's eyes bulged, and her voice dipped when she spoke. "But this one, my lady . . . he . . . *sat.*"

Pandemonium ensued.

"Sat?" Annalee seethed.

Whispers born of horror and outrage all buzzed throughout the room.

While Valerie came to her feet and tried to bring the group together, Sylvia inhaled slowly. Perhaps it wasn't her father-in-law. Why . . . why . . . it could be *anyone.* Weren't unwanted visitors— fathers, guardians, and mothers of existing members showing up to collect their "wayward" child—becoming something of the norm?

The more prominent their group became, the more attention they earned from displeased members of the peerage who insisted on taking their daughters or wives with them. But those men had all been turned away, adhering to the strictures of Polite Society because they were operating under the norms of the life that Sylvia and her friends, and the women they called friends and compatriots, now lashed out at. Yes, it was surely that. It didn't have to be her late husband's father . . . this time.

And as the head of both the society and the household, she had a responsibility to assert herself . . . before whichever insolent guest had arrived. If she allowed whoever it was out there entry to this parlor, then this parlor would fall.

And she would be damned ten times to Sunday if she let this new society created by herself, Annalee, and Valerie crumble because some man disapproved of their purpose. Brutish monster be damned.

Setting her jaw, Sylvia lifted her hem slightly and marched for the door.

"Where is she going?" someone called.

Several girls cried out.

From behind her, the commanding voices of Annalee and Valerie rose above the racket as they called for order from the group.

Sylvia didn't slow her stride. In fact, with every step that brought her closer to the insolent nobleman who'd camped himself in her foyer, her ire grew. This was their world. One where, even after marriage and as a widow, she'd still be expected to answer to displeased gentlemen. Men who wanted her and the women who came here or resided here to be a certain way. To fit a certain bill.

Well, that stopped now.

Sylvia skidded to a stop at the entrance of the foyer.

Mr. Flyaway, her gruff, towering bear of a butler, who inspired fear in all guests . . . was shaking.

Nay, not shaking. He was laughing.

The tirade she'd mentally composed en route to the brutish beast Mrs. Flyaway had described left her. *What in the Devil?*

Whatever the horrifying *monster* said just then earned another round of laughter from Mr. Flyaway.

Humph. And here these past two months she'd believed her butler knew only two sentiments: stern-faced or stone-faced.

Sylvia folded her arms at her chest and waited for the pair to notice they were no longer alone.

"Nottingham reel . . . I would have thought it was the only way to go . . . ," Mr. Flyaway was saying.

"I wouldn't have disagreed with you, either. It has that wide drum—"

"Aye," her butler interjected, excitement bringing his tone up an octave from its usual deep baritone. "Spools out freely, it does."

Just a handful of the gentleman's response peppered the air and reached her. ". . . geared multiplying reels . . ."

Mr. Flyaway scratched at the small patch of coarse black hair he'd still retained at his advanced years. "You don't say?"

"Oh, I do say, though it is a secret I don't share with just anyone." The latest interloper said something that brought a loud guffaw.

Sylvia angled her head this way and that in a bid to glean the identity of the latest intruder, this one who'd managed to charm her butler, a butler who seemed to barely tolerate Sylvia, Valerie, and Annalee most days. She knew that voice. *How* did she know that voice?

Sylvia cleared her throat.

"Never would have thought of it . . ." Her butler laughed once more.

Ruthless visitor, indeed.

"Ahem."

Mr. Flyaway jumped an inch, turning quickly to face her, his tall frame blocking the gentleman behind him. "Forgive me, my lady. Didn't hear you coming. I was talking to the gentleman caller."

"I see that," she said dryly. She gave him a pointed look.

The butler hesitated a moment before ducking his head and stepping aside so she could, at last, face her nemesis head-on.

"I was informed that you were refusing to . . ." The diatribe she'd prepared on the way here and mentally shelved while her intruder spoke to Mr. Flyaway left her.

Sylvia cocked her head. At five inches past six feet, he was as tall as Mrs. Flyaway had braced her for. Only, she'd imagined the monster painted by the older woman as not broadly muscular.

With his cloak on and his hat perched atop a close crop of blond curls, the gentleman with a prominent square jaw and broad Roman nose, hooked slightly at the bridge, *was* familiar. Nay, *more* than familiar.

His arms were folded from the conversational exchange he'd been engaging in with Mr. Flyaway, and a copy of *The Times* hung from his fingers.

Surely there was a mistake? And the brute savage who'd invaded her household was not in fact this man . . . but another? Alas, just he and Mr. Flyaway remained.

His heavy features froze, giving way to a mask of disbelief and confusion.

The newspaper slipped from his fingers and fluttered to the marble floor.

Yes, well, that made two of them.

For the same man before her should be none other than the one who, on Sylvia's wedding day, had stood beside Norman in friendship and support. Unlike her husband, who'd been a charmer and had an ease with his words, Viscount St. John had been given to long pauses and stiff politeness. He'd been . . . different from her urbane late husband, the friendship having been an unlikely one.

Except he had certainly charmed her usually ice-cold butler.

His jaw went slack, and he did a search throughout the foyer before settling his gaze once more on Sylvia . . . this time, his expression perfectly pained. *"Youu?"* The elongated syllables squeezed into the one, indicating he was, in fact, the one who'd come demanding an audience.

From the hallway came the rapid pitter-patter of footfalls as the society gathered upon them, and she found herself jerked out of the haze of confusion, taking strength in the support of the small army of might, the women behind her.

"Were you looking for another, Lord St. John?"

Chapter 5

Had he been looking for another, she'd asked.

The answer was absolutely, unequivocally, and undoubtedly yes.

He was to have met with some cold, unfeeling stranger who'd unintentionally dismantled the norms of society and left his friend brokenhearted, and Clayton with the problem of trying to find a wife when no women wanted to be found as wives.

Nay, the last woman in the whole of the United Kingdom whom he'd set out to meet was . . . *her*. In fact, for the better part of three years, he'd made a concerted effort to avoid her.

Sylvia.

His gaze went to the small army of women glaring back at him with their fearless liege at the front and center of the group.

The audience he'd imagined had always been private.

All his muscles seized up, clenching painfully in a taunting reminder of just how damned foolish it had been, setting out as he'd done.

He who, as Landon and Scarsdale had pointed out, never did anything . . . irrational.

"He doesn't look like a monster," someone whispered from within that gaggle of ladies.

To give his hands something to do, he doffed his hat and fiddled with the article. "Uh . . ."

He'd known precisely what he was going to say.

That knowing, however, wasn't something innate that simply came to him. Rather, he'd planned and plotted each detail of the impending meeting because that was the way he had to move through life.

Where some men were glib with words and capable of disarming with a look and an effortless reply, Clayton had always been one who'd needed a whole menu of discourse prepared within his head.

All that suited him in parliamentary matters and business meetings and social affairs . . . as long as he'd an ability to prepare and everything went to script.

It was when it did not that he found himself slack-jawed and empty of a proper response . . . as he was in this very moment.

A member of their rather large audience groaned. "Whatever is *he* doing here?"

That voice, even more familiar, added to his absolute befuddlement. Furrowing his brow, he searched the group, his gaze landing on the flame-haired spitfire amongst them.

His eyebrows went shooting up. *"Cora?"*

What in hell?

A second figure amongst the masses slipped backward from the group, hiding behind the taller lady beside her, but not before Clayton made out the identity of another member of the party aggrieved by his presence.

He drew back. He might have expected Delia—with her of late very vocal disdain for men—would have found her way here. But . . . "Brenna?"

Both young women stepped forward . . .

Followed by . . . yet another.

He rubbed at his eyes.

The sight remained.

Well, this was really too much. *"Anwen?"*

"Whatever are you doing here?" Cora demanded, preparing to throw her periodical at him the way Cook had once taken down a mouse loose in the kitchens.

His sister would ask what *he* was doing here? *Him?* "It appears I am extricating you."

It was the wrong thing to say.

Bedlam ensued. The fifteen or so women marched forward, moving in tandem like a wave crashing toward him . . . and he backed up several steps away from the crowd out for his blood.

Salvation came from the unlikeliest one of the group.

Sylvia stepped between Clayton and the gathering of snapping and hissing ladies.

And without so much as a word or hand gesture, she commanded that loyal legion to silence. "If you'll excuse me? Lord St. John requested a word."

"But . . . but . . . he interrupted our session," Brenna said on an angry whisper to one of her compatriots. "How is she meeting him? How?"

She'd rather throw him to the lions, then.

Only Anwen cast a slightly sheepish glance his way. Tiptoeing over, she rescued his forgotten-until-now copy of *The Times* and held it out.

"Anwen!" Cora hissed.

Hurriedly releasing the newspaper into his hands, the eldest of his sisters rushed off to join the line of ladies now filing from the foyer until he was left alone with Sylvia . . . and Mr. Flyaway.

An awkward silence was all that was left of the departed group.

Returning his hat atop his head, Clayton beat the newspaper against the side of his leg, and that seemed to spring the butler into action.

He came limping over to collect his hat.

"No need," Clayton assured. "It was splendid chatting. Be sure and look for one of those triple-gear leads." He made the motion as if he were reeling something.

Sylvia creased her brow. What in blazes was a triple-gear lead?

"Not even sure where I might find such a thing," her butler was saying. "But if you return—"

"Ahem."

Mr. Flyaway glanced over at Sylvia and blushed.

"Anything else you require, my lady?" the butler asked gruffly, his gaze directed at the floor.

"No, Mr. Flyaway. You've been help enough already." There was a dry quality to her voice that earned a blush from the stalwart butler. "If you'll follow me, Lord St. John." Sylvia didn't wait to see if Clayton followed, just turned quickly on her heel in a whirl of silvery satin skirts and marched off.

Her steps were measured, with a military precision that matched the ramrod stiffness of her spine. And not for the first time since Clayton had discovered the identity of whom he'd sought out, he contemplated making his excuses and getting the holy hell out of there.

"She's not so scary," Mr. Flyaway said on a loud whisper that brought the lady to a stop.

She faced the pair of them and lifted an eyebrow. "Is there . . . a sudden lack of urgency to your meeting request?" she drawled. Her low contralto carried from the hall and rose through the soaring foyer.

"Er . . ."

"I suggest you go before she changes her mind," Mr. Flyaway said from the corner of his mouth. "The lady of the household doesn't grant visitors. Especially those of the male persuasion."

Heeding the older man's advice, Clayton hurried to join Sylvia.

Sylvia, who did not pause to wait but continued on ahead without him.

Which was fine.

This was hardly a social call.

In fact, it was anything but.

The motives for his visit hadn't changed because of her identity. In fact, her identity—the woman he knew her to be—gave him the first hint of confidence in the outcome of their meeting. Sylvia had always been reasonable and logical, and as such, he'd no doubt it wouldn't take altogether much for her to see the concerns he'd brought her way.

They reached the end of the hall, and she pressed a handle, wordlessly motioning for Clayton to enter.

He hesitated, gesturing. "After you, my lady."

"I think I'm quite capable of establishing the rules of my household, Lord St. John."

"And . . . your rules are that men enter rooms before women?" he asked, slightly confounded and trying to sort through this unexpected battle.

She narrowed her eyes. "Are you being sarcastic, Lord St. John?" She clipped out each syllable of each word.

"Not at all." Alas, he wasn't capable of sarcasm. Directness, straightforwardness, yes. But playing with words and tones was something he'd never mastered—nor, for that matter, had he attempted to. "I assure you, I'm not one who—"

She jabbed a finger toward the room.

"Uh, right. Of course."

Clayton entered the parlor. Or—he passed his gaze over the room. It had some of the trappings of a parlor, and yet, with a French Mazarin desk at the center of the room and a series of cabinets beside it, the space had been converted into more of an office.

The moment she'd closed the door, she spoke. "I don't run a household where women are beholden to strictures that say when they may or may not enter rooms, or who should have the right to determine such a thing. Am I clear?"

"Yes. Very much so."

Just as it was increasingly clear that he had a good deal less control of this exchange than he'd hoped to have.

Taking a moment to reassemble the thoughts that had scattered upon his arrival, he went through everything he'd prepared at White's and on the way here.

She folded her arms. "I trust you disapprove?"

And just like that, the unexpected question knocked his thoughts off kilter.

"Who are you to come here and demand an audience?"

Clayton tugged at the collar of his cloak. "I didn't really demand an audience."

"Didn't you?" she challenged, taking a bold step forward that sent him into a reflexive retreat. "You come here, charming my butler into allowing you to remain."

This was surely the first, last, and only time he'd ever be known for charming anyone. "I was merely speaking to him until—"

"Until I was forced to receive you."

He shifted his hat awkwardly between his hands. When she put it that way . . . "You are right. Forgive me. I didn't realize it was you."

She winged up a thin blonde eyebrow. "And would it have changed anything had you known it was me?"

Absolutely. He never, ever would have ventured down Waverton Street, let alone lifted the bronzed knocker over her door. Clayton looking in on, and after, Sylvia, had been the one request that had been put to him before Norman's untimely death . . . and it was the one guarantee he'd never given. Avoiding her eyes, he did another pass of his gaze over her room. "Perhaps we might . . . sit?"

She stiffened, and for a very long, endless, awkward moment, he thought she'd reject that request. Nor would it be the first time in the course of his thirtysomething years that he had been met with rejection from a woman. Awkward and rarely in possession of the right words, he'd never had the charm that had allowed Norman to woo her. Or countless other women.

Finally, she stretched a hand to the upholstered purple sofa, waiting until he was seated before taking one of her own.

"I don't remember you to be one to storm households."

Nay, he'd never done something so . . . forward or improper. Alas, desperate times and all that.

"And I don't recall you as one hosting incendiary meetings."

Outrage had a sound, and it was the swift exhalation of offended air that slipped from her lips.

Oh, bloody hell.

"Not that your meetings are necessarily incendiary," he said on a rush, attempting to put out the fire he'd lit with his loose tongue. "I'm sure they are not. That is why I'm here."

"You are here to make sure my meetings are not . . . incendiary?" By the slow, measured way she drew out each word of that sentence, he knew he'd bungled it all over again.

Clayton set his hat down at his feet. "No." Returning to the script he'd composed on his way to the lady's household, he picked through to those words first. "There has been talk about—"

"And you are one to listen to gossip?"

He bristled. "Of course not."

She lifted another perfectly formed thin blonde brow. "And yet, here you are . . . because of *talk*."

Touché. She had him there. Only . . . it wasn't necessarily gossip that had brought him here. Not completely. "I'm here to discuss your club, my lady."

"Society."

Was there a difference?

As if he'd asked the very question aloud, Sylvia elucidated. "Clubs are where gentlemen meet for brandies and cards. Societies are where actual change happens."

His stomach sank. It was, then, as his friends had feared.

"Furthermore, Lord St. John, what gives you leave to come here to discuss anything going on in my household?"

That grounded him, as the lady brought him back to the purpose of his being here: Lord Scarsdale. Though, if he were being even a little bit honest with himself, his pressing need for a bride and heir was not a very small part of today's boldness. "I am coming to you from a meeting I just left with a close friend . . . a gentleman who has suffered a broken heart because of you."

Her lips lifted at the corners in a smile that so perfectly melded sarcasm and sadness. "I'm not the one known for breaking hearts."

And yet . . . that wasn't altogether true. Not really.

She, of course, spoke of Norfolk.

The husband who'd been unfaithful to her . . . who'd planned to leave her. It was too much, the memory of that day.

He turned the newspaper around. "Given the details here pertaining to Lord Scarsdale and Miss Gately, and"—he spoke over her interruption—"my meeting with the gentleman a short while ago, it speaks of a different story."

Sylvia's perfectly too-full lips formed a firm line. She reluctantly reached for the copy he extended her way, wafting the sweetest, summery fragrance of lilac and rose water that put a man in mind of a field of flowers and—

Good God, focus, man.

The lady's eyes moved quickly over the page, skimming the details there. When she'd finished, she set it down on the table between them with a decisive *thwack. "Hmph."*

Hmph?

He waited for her to say something . . . anything other than that. She, the same woman who'd regaled him with story after story, chattering all night as card partners, should now find herself ever so inarticulate and silent? "That is all?" he pressed when it became abundantly clear she'd no intention of saying anything further.

"What else is there to say? If Lord Scarsdale has suffered a broken heart, then perhaps you should look elsewhere to discover the reason for the earl's suffering, say . . . the gentleman himself? He has no one but himself to blame for either his actions or current state of affairs"—her acerbic warning threw cold water upon the haze momentarily cast by her alluring fragrance—"and certainly blame doesn't belong here, in my household."

Sitting up straighter in a bid to put some space between them, he tried again. "Lord Scarsdale's betrothed has recently become a patron."

"I don't have patrons, Lord St. John."

"A member, then," he continued. "And at these meetings, she—"

The lady exploded to her feet. "She *what*? Had a sudden realization that mayhap the gentleman's feelings were not as deep as she'd hoped or wished, and she would vastly prefer a different life, even if it is one without him in it?" Sylvia's chest moved fast, rising and falling hard. Her cheeks washed red, a flush extending down over that creamy expanse, and all words failed him.

Well, words, they generally did fail him.

But not like this.

Not with him noticing the last woman he should be noticing. And with her standing as she was, and him seated as he was, his gaze was in direct line with the generous swells of her breasts.

Look away.

Look anywhere but where you are currently staring.

And now he knew the tribulations that had led Adam to commit the rest of mankind to eternal damnation. Forcibly, he lifted his gaze, and looked the second-worst place.

A question puckered the place between her eyebrows.

Mortified heat splotched his face, and he froze, certain she'd gleaned that he'd been ogling her like some manner of cad, which he'd prided himself on never being.

"Have you nothing to say?"

His mind went blank. "I . . ." No, he usually didn't. This time, his inability to recall had nothing to do with his usual tongue-twistedness, and everything to do with her nearness and the curve of her—

Think, man. Think.

About what had brought him here. Whatever that source of contention was between them. Or the last matter they'd been speaking on. *What was it . . . ? What was it . . . ?*

"Scarsdale!" he shouted, at last landing on it.

The confusion in her brow deepened. Sylvia did a search about the room as if he'd summoned the gentleman himself. He came to his feet so that his gaze needn't get him into any more trouble than it had . . . since he himself was already seeing to that task.

No . . . not Scarsdale. "That is, I'm here as it appears your meetings have led to not only a series of broken hearts amongst many but also a revolt against the state of marriage, and that simply cannot be."

Chapter 6

When she'd been married and her husband living, Sylvia had never been friends with the men of Norman's social circle. In fact, she'd rather detested them. Given to still carousing when most gentlemen had settled down, and indulging in more spirits than was prudent, they'd not been the manner of men she'd ever understood Norman wishing to keep company with.

With the exception of Clayton Kearsley, the Viscount St. John.

Not that she and Clayton had been *friends*, per se.

At least, they hadn't *called* one another that.

In large part because her mother, and society at large, didn't tolerate friendships between men and women.

As such, they'd called one another "ballroom companions" in jest, their secret language that made a mockery of the rules that prevented friendships.

By chance at one of Lady Waverly's affairs, Sylvia had happened to find herself beside Clayton. They'd exchanged teasing words and jests and then gone off to the card rooms. From that moment on, she'd found herself . . . friendly . . . with him. They had been equally poor at playing, and had laughed over the inanity of card games and dice. Just as they'd bonded over their equally poor footwork, which had them keeping one another company on the side of every ballroom dance floor—"wallflowers," the two of them, as she'd coined them.

And for a brief time, before Norman had entered her life, she'd believed that Clayton might offer for her. But he hadn't. And then her late husband had swept Sylvia off her feet . . . quite literally. Norman, who had waltzed flawlessly and insisted that he was capable of carrying her, should she so need it. And anyone present at the ball or who'd read of it in the papers, who'd not been given to sighing, had spoken longingly of the grand love between Sylvia and society's *reformed* rogue, Lord Norfolk.

From that moment on, her heart had been lost, and Clayton had . . . disappeared. She'd seen him but two times after that: at her wedding, when he'd stood beside Norman as his best man. And the day of Norman's funeral services, when Viscount St. John had come to pay his respects.

Until today.

Now he should arrive—he should come here to call her out and question her motives?

But then, wasn't that the way when it came to gentlemen? Nay, to *all* men?

Your meetings have led to not only a series of broken hearts amongst many but also a revolt against the state of marriage, and that simply cannot be . . .

Moving back several steps so she didn't have to look quite so high to meet his eyes, Sylvia fixed a cool stare on him. "And tell me why this . . . 'revolt against marriage,' as you call it, cannot be?"

He blinked—at her question? Or at being so called out? Either way, her days of meek servitude where men were concerned were at an end. "Well, *because*," he said, as if she were a child to whom he'd just doled out a commonsense lesson that she should have already gleaned.

That was it? That was all he'd say? A single elongated syllable tacked on to one word as his defense? "Because it is in your best interest?" she quipped.

"Yes," he said. She flared her eyes. "No," he hurried to amend. "Both yes and no. It isn't in my sole interest. You're twisting what I am saying."

"Oh, you are doing a fine enough job of that all by yourself, Lord St. John. Let us be clear." She shoved a finger in his chest, and repressed a wince at the solid wall of muscle that digit struck. "You are not to enter my home and instruct me or any of the young women in my household on what we should or should not be doing." She poked him again for good measure, and with every jab of her finger and word from her lips, he retreated . . . and outrage fueled her footsteps forward.

"I'm not attempting to instruct you but help you."

Sylvia gasped.

He tugged at those closely cropped golden curls. An angel's halo was how she'd thought of them when she'd first met the smiling lord at Lady Waverly's. More like a Devil come to visit.

He flinched. "That is to say—"

She'd had quite enough. "Are you in the habit of paying visits to people, demanding entrance to their homes?"

"No. Not normally. My unannounced visit, I acknowledge, is unconventional."

And it was even more so from the slightly socially awkward lord she recalled from the past. Now, he should simply show up to school her? Her fury mounted—with him. With Polite Society. With the world at large and how women's views and desires and interests were secondary to all men's. "You are not to come and volunteer help that I neither need nor want."

He backed into a small leather footstool, and came down backward over it. The pace of Sylvia's forward motion was too great, and she toppled over.

Clayton shot up his arms to catch her, settling around her hips and easing the brunt of her fall some.

Some.

She grunted as she landed on his barrel-size chest.

Her heart thudded. How had she failed to realize the sheer power and size of the viscount?

Because he's never been under you before. As he is now . . .

And she'd never been so very close to any man who'd not been her husband. A husband who'd made love to her only with the intent to get an heir, and not with great regularity. And from that moment on, he'd not come to her bed again.

She felt every contour of the muscles under her fingers.

He tensed, and those muscles rippled under her touch.

Remove your hand . . . Say something.

Except, she couldn't form words through a mouth that had gone suddenly too dry. Nor did he speak.

There was an inadvertent standoff in the matter of word production, triggered by the thrum of energy that came from the shock of their nearness. Sylvia's fingers reflexively smoothed the fabric of his sleeve. The carved planes of his triceps jumped. The burn of embarrassment at her own boldness brought her yanking her palm back, making words impossible for an altogether different reason—mortification.

In the end, she was saved from speaking.

The door exploded open.

Sylvia whipped her head so quickly toward that commotion her butterfly comb snagged the button of Lord St. John's jacket.

Bloody hell on Sunday.

And there was a new, and different, humiliation.

Pushing against Lord St. John's chest, she struggled to extricate herself from the viscount's arms, but her hair comb, still tangled on his button, thwarted her attempts.

Sylvia gasped.

As did all the ladies from their morning meeting. The group struggled in an impossible feat to squeeze as one into the doorway.

"Oh, dear, he is hurting Lady Norfolk."

Lord St. John's sputtering drowned out her response. "I am not hurting her," he said, indignantly. "Not . . . intentionally, that is."

More exhalations of outrage filled the parlor. "He said he is intentionally hurting her," one of the girls cried out.

"Oh, for the love of all that is holy." The viscount let his head fall, knocking it with a loud enough *thwack* to make her wince.

"Who is hurting Sylvia?" a concerned Miss Gately cried from her position at the back of the group. "I cannot see."

"I believe they said he is killing her?" Miss Dobson whispered.

"No one is hurting me or killing me," Sylvia hurried to assure the room at large. Lord St. John had annoyed her. Insulted her. And challenged her. But he'd certainly not harmed her. In fact, he'd made all attempts to keep her from the fall she'd ended up taking anyway. "Lord St. John and I . . . simply became tangled," she finished lamely.

Annalee and Isla Gately spoke as one, though Annalee's snort reached Sylvia first. "I'd say."

"As in a fight?" the youngest Miss Gately asked, sounding thoroughly befuddled.

Sylvia turned quickly to level a silencing glare on her roommate, but winced as the snagged strands of her hair pulled sharply at her scalp and ruined her efforts.

"Here. Allow me," the viscount muttered, and then with surprisingly quick, effortless movements, he freed those captured strands.

Those were the long, capable fingers of a man who'd far too much experience with a lady's tangled tresses.

Hands and motions that belonged to men like her husband, who'd had so many lovers that he'd learned the ins and outs around things such as . . . a lady's hair. Or untangling themselves from compromising situations.

She set her teeth so hard her jaw slid sideways. Bracing her hands on that solid wall of muscle that was Lord St. John's chest, Sylvia scrambled to get herself off him and on her feet.

Nine young ladies had maneuvered their way into Sylvia's offices and formed a half crescent at the entrance of the room. And just like that, the impossible had been achieved—the complete and utter silence of the Mismatch Society.

"Er . . . I believe it was the other way around," came another whisper from the group. "If she was on top of him, wouldn't *she* be the one hurting *him*?"

Kissing him.

She'd nearly been kissing him.

"I don't know any murder that looks . . . like that," Annalee said, and the knowing sarcasm contained within her response sent another rush of heat to Sylvia's cheeks.

One of Lord St. John's sisters piped up eagerly, with apparently more concern for gathering up those details than for the brother who, for all intents and purposes, might or might not be suffering harm or death at Sylvia's hands. "Have you seen a murder?"

"This will be my first." Emma's sister, Isla, clapped her hands with a disturbing amount of zeal for the proposed state.

Sylvia briefly closed her eyes. "No one is killing anyone. Or harming them. Or . . . doing anything else nefarious," she rushed to assure the crowd of onlookers. "As I said, Lord St. John and I stumbled."

Which wasn't *untrue*. He had stumbled in every sense this day.

"You should really go, Lord St. John," she said quietly in a steadied voice that was belied by the shaking within.

His sisters hung outside the doorway in various states of glaring disapproval for their brother.

Escorting the quartet of Kearsleys from her offices, Sylvia headed for the foyer, eager to have him gone so she didn't have to think about the momentary lapse in her judgment. A moment of wantonness and wickedness.

Mr. Flyaway drew open the door, and a wild figure stumbled in. "Trouble!" she cried. "Fetch Her Ladyship immediately. My son"—Lady

St. John's gaze landed squarely upon the tall figure framed between her daughters—"is here," she blurted. "Oh, dear."

"Mother," he drawled.

Sylvia braced for his outrage.

Only, it wasn't there. Not any of the tangible hints of fury and annoyance at his mother's and sisters' roles in the Mismatch Society. Or at the scandal they were causing.

Which was preposterous. It went against everything she knew about men and their attempts at preserving and protecting their dignity and pride at all costs.

Lady St. John laughed nervously. "We were just going . . . for now. Business and all that." She clapped her hands once, and her daughters sprang into motion.

The moment the Kearsley women had taken their leave, Clayton tipped his hat. "Lady Sylvia."

She inclined her head. "Lord St. John."

The other ladies seemed to take that as their cue to leave, collecting their cloaks from the footmen and following after the viscount and his family.

When Mr. Flyaway shut the panel behind the last of the members, only Sylvia, Valerie, and Annalee remained.

"That was the most exciting meeting yet," Valerie remarked.

"That isn't saying much about our meetings, then," Sylvia mumbled, earning a laugh from Annalee, who removed a cheroot from the deep V between her breasts.

"Before you go, Mr. Flyaway?" she asked, holding the scrap out before the old servant took the leave he so desperately wished for.

The butler used one of the crystal candlesticks to light the tip of that scrap.

With a word of thanks, Annalee accepted the cheroot and took a deep draw. "They are an unconventional lot. I like them. Especially the mother and the sisters." She waved away the little plume of smoke that wafted in the air between them. "You knew him."

It wasn't a question.

"I know most members of Polite Society." With that, Sylvia headed back for her offices, both women trailing close.

"And I know most members of Impolite," Annalee pointed out with a robust laugh. "What of it?"

And Sylvia had been friends with Clayton Kearsley, Viscount St. John, before she'd gone and married his best friend. Though, in truth, their friendship had come to an end the moment she'd met and danced with Norman. She chose to pretend and misunderstand that question. "I wouldn't turn away young women interested in our messaging simply because they happen to be related to those whom my late husband called friends." Just as she wouldn't have rejected or blamed Valerie for Norman's actions.

"I didn't think you would," Annalee said.

"Nor I," Valerie added for measure.

"What I was asking about was the gentleman . . . the Saint." Laughter filled Annalee's voice.

The Saint. It had been a nickname her husband and most in society had reserved for the viscount; polite and kindly, he'd not fit in with the sinners he ran with.

"He disapproves of what we are doing here," Sylvia said. This was safer than talk of just how she had been found with the gentleman. "However, when he set out to speak to me, he didn't realize I was"— *Norman's widow*—"one of the women running the society."

There was a brief somber silence.

"Nor did he realize several of the ladies included amongst our members were in fact his sisters and mother," Annalee said with her usual levity, and the three women shared a smile.

That ability to lighten any exchange or topic was a singular gift the woman had, and just one of many reasons Annalee so fascinated the *ton*. That and her scandalous penchant for daring dresses, fine—and not-so-fine—spirits, and of course, her use of a cheroot.

"There also seemed to be . . . tension there," Annalee said, ever so conversational as she took another drag from her cheroot. "Between you and him . . . being together as you were."

And just like that, Annalee revealed her other skill—disarming a person in a bid to elicit the truth.

Sylvia prayed the cloud of smoke left by that noxious little scrap was enough to conceal the blush heating up her cheeks.

Valerie stepped into the role of peacekeeper, as she so often did when they were at odds over opinions. "Any woman would be uncomfortable at being discovered so."

Annalee shot up her spare hand. "I wouldn't. If it were the correct gentleman, I'd quite enjoy it . . ." She sharpened an already too-astute gaze upon Sylvia. "And you did seem to be enjoying it."

Valerie swatted the other woman on the arm. "That is *enough*."

"I fell down hard, and on top of that, I snagged my hair upon his buttons. I assure you, I could name all manner of pleasures I'd enjoy a good deal more than losing several strands to a gentleman who'd come to lecture me on our society."

Annalee eyed her for a long moment before nodding slowly. "All right. I'll allow it." Sylvia no more believed the tenacious woman would let it go than she believed the King of England would give up his throne. "But—"

KnockKnockKnock.

They looked over as Mrs. Flyaway let herself in. "A young lady has arrived. Asking questions about joining the club."

"Society," Sylvia, Annalee, and Valerie corrected as one.

"Aye. That." The housekeeper looked amongst the women. "I took the liberty of showing her to the parlor. Unless you'd rather I send her away?"

"We'll see to her," Valerie said quickly.

As the two women started for the door, Sylvia looked down at the newspaper Lord St. John had left behind, detailing Lord Scarsdale's broken heart.

Broken heart, indeed. According to the gentleman's former betrothed, theirs hadn't been a love match. Far from it. Betrothed as children, in an entirely medieval manner. As such, it had been altogether too easy to guide the young woman away from a future with Lord Scarsdale . . . and on to whatever future she wanted.

But what if he had, in fact, been in love? What if Lord St. John had been correct with the charges he'd alleged? That Sylvia and Valerie and Annalee were actually responsible for shattering unions that might have been born of more than the empty one Sylvia had found herself trapped within? One that she'd not realized had been unloving until after her husband's passing?

"Sylvia?"

She jerked her head up. *"Hmm?"* Guiltily, she jammed the copy of *The Times* behind her.

Valerie paused in the doorway and looked questioningly back. "Are you joining us for the interview?"

"Of course." Hurriedly dropping the rubbish column on the very stool that had taken her and Lord St. John down, she headed after Valerie and Annalee.

And as she went on to join her friends and Mrs. Flyaway, Sylvia could not help but feel that she'd protested entirely too much.

For she had been very aware of Lord St. John in ways she shouldn't.

Chapter 7

There was a traitor in his midst.

Four of them—not only three sisters but also a mother to boot.

If ever there was material for one of their sister Delia's Shakespearean plays, this was it.

That quartet of traitorous kin had managed to cram onto a single carriage bench with Eris on their mother's lap, impossibly squeezed in like sardines in a can, all so they didn't have to sit near him. Or mayhap to give themselves a sense of power by numbers.

And yet . . . looking back, there wasn't a hint of shame or regret from a single one of the four of them.

Landon's words from White's whispered forward . . .

They school their members on how to instead push that task off onto brothers, guardians, and fathers, who will then see to the responsibility of raising a family's wealth and status through marriage . . .

And his breath caught on a hiss. "My God, you plotted it all."

"What would you prefer?" Brenna asked. "That one of us marry instead?" She didn't even pretend to misunderstand.

Clayton found himself in the same ranks as the "tricked," the pathetic brother duped by conspiratorial sisters, and just as his friends had rightly predicted.

It was a rather swift descent into ignominy.

"But . . . how in hell is a man supposed to marry if your club's entire mission is to encourage other women to avoid the matrimonial state?"

All the women collectively rolled their eyes. "That isn't our *only* mission. We talk about our rights, or rather, our lack of them, and the ways in which we can extend our influence over not only our households but also society."

He shuddered. "Terrifying. Utterly—*oomph.*"

Cora kicked him in the shin, abruptly ending the rest of his sarcastic response. "*And* for that matter, not *all* potential marriages, either. Just the bad ones," she said in tired tones, as if she'd already covered this particular topic a dozen times with him, and not just this once. "Why, Perenelle Flamel and Nicolas Flamel were quite content."

His confusion deepening, Clayton shook his head slowly. "*Whooo?*"

Cora released an exasperated sigh. "Perenelle Flamel, the famed alchemist, and her scribe husband."

"That's just a legend." Brenna spoke in the bluestocking tones she used to elucidate the Kearsleys on obscure topics that only she knew about.

"How dare you!" Cora reached across, making a grab for Brenna, but Anwen angled herself between them.

"Ahem. If we might focus."

With a final glare for her younger sister, Cora sank back against the squabs.

"Now, as Cora was correctly pointing out, we're aware *some* women will prefer to marry, and as such, there are plenty for you to choose a bride from."

"How considerate," he drawled. "Thank you ever so much."

Anwen beamed. "You are most welcome."

"I think he's being sarcastic," Brenna said from behind her copy of *Treasons Master-peece, the Powder-plot Inuented by hellish malice . . .*

Leaning across the bench, he flicked a finger at the gilded letters upon the cover. "A rather apropos choice of book, I'd say, given the circumstances."

Her earlier sisterly grievance apparently forgotten, Cora leaned closer to Brenna. "He's calling you a traitor," she said in a loud whisper that sent Clayton's eyes rolling.

"Yes, I quite gathered that." And in a clear demonstration of just how bothered by that insult she in fact was, Brenna licked the tip of her finger and flipped her page with a flourish.

His mother turned a disapproving look Clayton's way. "You are being quite overdramatic, Clayton, and it does not become you."

"Really? I am overdramatic? This from a mother who stormed the countess's household like she'd unveiled a traitor at the Home Office?"

His mother gave him an arch look. "Now you're just being silly. A lady is not permitted a role in the Home Office. More's the pity. I do think I'd make an excellent spy, do you not?" she asked Cora.

"Oh, absolutely," the devoted daughter praised, earning a beaming smile from the viscountess.

Clayton folded his arms before him, watching on. If a single one of them expected the matter would be so easily put to rest . . . *"Ahem."*

The viscountess's focus flew back his way. "Where were we?" Her wrinkled brow conveyed her confusion.

"I believe Clayton charged us with being given to histrionics," Anwen volunteered. At a look from Clayton, she winced. "Sorry," she mouthed, having the good grace to at least sink lower in her seat.

"That's right." The viscountess relaunched her earlier defense. "Furthermore, if we are speaking on dramatics, then we find ourselves in like ranks?"

It took a moment to register that the pointed look . . . the four pointed looks—five, if one included Eris—were all reserved for Clayton.

And then it hit him.

A laugh exploded from Clayton's chest. "*I'm* the one given to histrionics. This from a family where one sister quotes Shakespeare, another is in a perpetual state of mourning, and the lot of you orchestrate an over-the-top meeting to trick me into marriage." He laughed all the harder, earning a deepening scowl from the usually smiling viscountess. "Or where a mother who joins an antimarriage league bursts into strange households in a panic."

"Firstly, it is not a strange household," his mother said, her voice ripe with indignation. "It is Lady Norfolk's. Secondly"—she puzzled her perfectly unwrinkled brow—"or is that thirdly?"

"Oh, no. I'm fairly certain that Lady Norfolk's identity fits with your first point pertaining to Clayton's statement of a strange household," Anwen helped clarify for their mother.

Eris jumped off her mother's lap and proceeded to stomp her feet on the carriage floor. "I want to go to strange households and join antimarriage leagues."

Their mother made a soothing sound and drew her youngest daughter back onto her lap for a comforting hug. "Someday, dearest," she cooed. "Someday."

Clayton scrubbed his hands over his face. And he had no doubt Eris would, and that she'd also ascend to the rank of leader. Given the familial curse and Clayton's short length of life, he'd either perish long before that or it would be what did him in. "And furthermore, why is Eris here?"

"There was trouble again with her governess . . . I had to let her go this morning, and—"

Yet again. Either way. "Forget Eris," Clayton said.

"Well, you brought her up," their mother pointed out.

"I know I did." He dug his fingers into his temples. "Can we please just focus?"

When the little girl had been properly pacified, their mother looked over the top of her head at Clayton. "Furthermore, fourthly—"

"Thirdly," Clayton and Anwen corrected in unison.

"I am not really a member of the society. I merely discovered the meetings and arranged for your sisters to attend."

Of course she had. She'd be the only mother in the whole of the realm to maneuver her daughters into a club of women disavowing marriage.

Cora smirked. "*Furthermore*, it should be pointed out, given the way you arrived at Lady Norfolk's unannounced with plans to shut down our society, that you must have acquired that trait for the outrageous from the Kearsley line."

Checkmate.

The carriage rocked to a jarring halt that sent them rolling back and forth.

His sisters all scrambled for the latch, with their mother finding it first and letting them out before the driver had even reached the side of the carriage. By the quick, steady pace they'd set for themselves, weaving and dodging around passersby, there could be no doubting what they intended: escape.

He narrowed his eyes. Like hell was this exchange at an end.

Jumping down, he followed swiftly on the heels of the rapidly retreating Kearsleys.

As he entered, he found the lot of them stacking their cloaks atop one another's in the arms of the family butler, Mr. Georges. The vibrant stack of fabric rose to the servant's eyes, blocking his vision.

"Halt!" Clayton called just as they reached the main corridor leading off to another wing of the household. "In my offices." From the corner of his eye, he caught a slight movement. Clayton sliced a glance upward. "All of you," he called, just as Delia and Daria, observing from the top of the stairway, would have rushed off. "Now."

Lifting their chins in unison, his sisters fell into line behind the viscountess; almost in perfect time, Daria and Delia descended to the bottom step and met up with the rest of the Kearsleys.

Clayton removed his hat and handed it off to one of the footmen rushing forward to rescue Georges from suffocation by ladies' garments. Shrugging out of his cloak, he handed it over and made for his offices.

All the while, indignation fueled his steps.

His kin had joined a subversive order.

His sisters and mother had all come together to try and dismantle Polite Society.

And they'd set out to deceive Clayton, using his own guilt as a tool to manipulate him into doing that which he didn't wish to do.

Clayton firmed his jaw. He could have forgiven their joining the ranks of a rebellious society such as the one they'd found themselves members of, had they not turned those lessons on him.

Entering his offices, he found them seated nearly identically to how they had been in the carriage. Only this time, with the addition of the absent-until-now rest of his sisters, each lady had squeezed herself upon a pair of curve-backed chaises. With the exception of their mother.

This time, his mother stood behind her daughters, with her hands on her hips and a rebellious glitter in her eyes, a mark of her defiance.

The moment he reached to close the door, the viscountess launched her attack. "I am very disappointed in you."

He pushed the panel shut. "*You're* disappointed in *me*?"

Such was the problem of being the lone male member of a family in a house of six women . . . they excelled at disarming a gent before he could find his feet for an argument.

"It was most impolite of you to go ordering your beloved mama and sisters about in front of servants as you've done, Clayton."

"Ordering us about in front of anyone." Anwen, the most loyal of his siblings, stared at him with a disappointment that was only emphasized by those enormous spectacles.

The viscountess gave a tight nod. "Indeed, your sister is correct. It was most impolite of you to go ordering us about in front of *anyone*. I've raised you to be far more—"

"Polite?" he furnished, lifting a brow.

She pointed a manicured finger his way. "*Precisely.* I've raised all my children to be polite and kind."

"It is also impolite for a beloved mother and sisters to go about betraying one's son and brother," he drawled, crossing over to the sisters who'd become members of this newest club. Clayton spread his arms before them. "And yet, here we are. Now, if you would, join me." He motioned for the Kearsley matriarch to take a seat. "Please."

Elevating her chin another notch, she swept around the chaise.

All the girls rushed to make room between them so that their mother had a place at the center of their group. She gave a toss of her slightly greying brown curls. "I'd begin by stating we've not betrayed you," she said once more when Clayton had settled into a French leather armchair.

His sisters nodded in concurrence.

He suppressed a snort. This he had to hear.

"We merely brought you 'round to realizing that there was no reason it shouldn't be you who weds," Cora said, lifting her shoulders in a matter-of-fact shrug.

"Your sister is correct, Clayton."

"*All* of you felt compelled to join an antimarriage society?" he asked the room at large.

Mother sighed. "That is how you men think of it." The Kearsley women shared a commiserative look as if Clayton were the only one incapable of seeing logic and reason, and mayhap they weren't off the mark.

"And that isn't what the Mismatch Club—"

"Society," his sisters and mother corrected.

"Is?" he finished.

"We've already told you," Cora said. "That isn't our sole purpose. That is what society thinks we do." Her shoulders drew back. "But we are about far more than that; we are dedicated to the overall enlightenment of the mind through discourse on controversial—"

"Yes. Yes," he said, cutting her off, saving himself yet another lecture on their lofty goals.

Clayton looked past his other sisters, focusing on just one, a lover of Jane Austen and gothic novels and romance tales. "*You* don't wish to marry, Anwen?" Anwen, who was on her fourth Season, who'd been preparing for her entrance into Polite Society and marriage and motherhood since she'd been in the nursery, forcing Clayton into the role of pretend groom when he'd been fourteen and she five.

Anwen's cheeks pinkened. "I don't know if I want to marry. I just know that I don't wish to marry *yet*," she murmured, her gaze on her lap.

That he didn't believe. But neither was it his place to challenge her on whether or not she wished to wed some gent.

"The girls just wish to be in control of their own fates and futures," his mother clarified.

"And that couldn't be assured without throwing me on the sacrificial wedding pyre?" he shot back.

"No." That negation came collectively from all the ladies present.

Their mother added an extra nod in confirmation.

"Either way," Cora put to him, "why should Anwen, and not you?" He looked toward the charge leveled by his latest opponent as she continued. "Hmm?"

Clayton bristled. "I never said she *had* to."

Mother clapped her hands once. "I'll not have this become adversarial."

"A bit late for that," Clayton muttered. "The timing for a friendly talk would have been better had it come before all the duplicity."

Cora stuck out her tongue.

"Do you not *want* to marry?" his mother asked.

All eyes went to Clayton.

Did he want to marry?

The answer was neither a simple yes nor no . . . but rather complicated in nature, with the truth all coming down to one simple fact: he was a Kearsley. Society referred to the Kearsleys as "unlucky," not attributing it to anything more than that, and he had never been able to correct even his friends on the matter because he knew how it seemed. Unbelievable. Overdramatic. Impossible.

But the truth remained: he was destined to die young, as had most every other male Kearsley ancestor. That knowledge—nay, that burden—had been with him early on . . . along with regret regarding his fate. That same knowledge had driven him to live as safe a life as possible, as risk-free . . . so that he would be here as long as he could for his sisters and mother.

The same sisters and mother who'd embraced their notorious line and lived with an almost careless abandon—those were luxuries not permitted him as head of the family. There was no escaping or getting around that connection and the fate that awaited him because of his bloodline.

"Why isn't Clayton saying anything?" Eris whispered loudly, bringing Clayton out of his silent musings.

"I know why he doesn't wish to marry."

All eyes swiveled Daria's way.

Daria peered at him and spoke, her voice unearthly and haunting. "It is the curse."

He sighed. "It is—"

"Of course it is." Murmurs of assent and understanding went around the room, interrupting his answer.

"We are all shaped by the curse, Clayton," Anwen said ever so gently.

"Yes, I know," he allowed. But where his sisters lived their lives fully, daring the curse to smite them, he chose a cautious path . . . and one filled only with worry. As close as they were as a family, this was something they'd never understood about him . . . and something he never felt comfortable speaking about. He adjusted a cravat that had gone rumpled under Sylvia's hands upon him. "Might we return to talk of the Mis—?"

"Well, I think it is silly to be so bound to the curse. 'The world's mine oyster, Which I with sword will open,' and you should let it be, too," Delia said to a round of stomping feet of consent from their sisters.

He waited until that rumble of noise quieted before shifting them away from the uncomfortable matter of the curse, over to a different and slightly safer topic. "I simply feel it might be best if you consider not attending—"

Brenna burst to her feet. "You think to tell us not to go to Lady Norfolk's?" she cried out, her voice sharp with shock and disbelief.

"Yes. No." He dragged his hand through his hair. "It is just . . ."

They stared back. "Yes?" they asked.

It was just that the last person he needed his family having dealings with was Norfolk's widow.

He'd spent the better part of three years avoiding the lady, and with his siblings forming a friendship of sorts, that distance he'd kept between them grew tenuous. Those were details he couldn't share with his family. Or anyone.

Cora gasped, stifling that sound behind her fingertips; all the while, from over them, she scowled at Clayton.

"What is it *now*, Cora?" he asked, drawing upon the patience that could come only from being the eldest sibling in a family of six others.

"Why . . . why . . ." His sister stretched out another several "whys" until she'd ensured all eyes were upon her. "You disapprove of Lady Norfolk."

He sputtered under that false and erroneous assumption. "That is prepos—"

"And I should expect better of you, given her connection to Lord Norfolk," Mother added, *tsk*ing her disapproval, to which all his kin present added until they had the sound of the chicks from Eris's collection of fowl at their Kent estate.

He set his teeth hard enough that his jaw ached. The illustrious Lord Norfolk, whose family, along with most of society, believed him to have been a paragon while he lived. Clayton himself had also believed that at one time.

"It has nothing to do with the lady and everything to do with . . . with . . ."

"Yes?" they prodded when he went silent.

And yet, what was there to say? Neither he nor his father, when he had been living, had been ones to stifle and silence the women of their large family. He wasn't one who'd dare prohibit them from forming friendships where they would . . . or dissuade them from speaking their minds. But this newfound relationship his sisters had with Sylvia . . . it went beyond that. It dragged forth the past and a connection with Sylvia that he was better off not thinking about.

His mother rested a hand on his sleeve. "What is it, Clayton?" she urged in the same gentle voice she reserved for any of the Kearsleys when they were sick, hurt, or sad.

He'd have been wise to summon them all later and give himself time to prepare just what to say to bring about a proper end to that connection. "I have no objections to your connection with Lady Norfolk and her society," he finally brought himself to say. "I would just ask that, going forward, you speak candidly with me and not set out to deceive me."

"You are a dear boy, Clayton," his mother said, beaming from ear to ear. "Now, if there is nothing else?" She clapped once, springing all her suddenly obedient daughters to their feet. His sisters dipped a curtsy on their way past, before taking their collective leave.

Obedient, his arse.

He eyed their swift retreat with a wry grin.

The only reason for that sudden docility had to do with an urgency to flee lest he reverse course and press them on their jiggery-pokery.

Finding himself at last alone, Clayton sat back in his seat and stared distantly at the doorway his sisters and mother had just passed through.

All his earlier memories of his time at Eton and Oxford with Norfolk contained distant echoes of laughter. A free spirit who'd pulled pranks and caused harmless mischief, Norfolk had been so very different from Clayton's dull self. Clayton had always been driven by the knowledge of the early end that awaited him. Mayhap that was why he'd appreciated the other man's friendship as he had. Because through Norfolk, Clayton had been permitted a way to live vicariously the life that would never and could never be his. He'd admired Norfolk for being able to live as fully as he had . . . which was why it had made so much sense in Clayton's mind that Sylvia make a match with Norfolk. There'd been no doubt that two people so passionate in life would be passionate . . . and happy . . . in marriage together.

Or that had been what Clayton naively thought. How mistaken he'd been.

All the admiration and respect he'd carried for the earl, however, had suffered a swift death, one that could be traced specifically back to the day the other man had met his end. From then on, Clayton had struggled to battle back that day Norfolk had died at Gentleman Jackson's. Not just because of the other man's tragic death but also because of the favor Norfolk had put to Clayton just before his fight.

Guilt.

There had been, and still was, and always would be, a searing sense of responsibility for so much where the lady and her late husband were concerned.

After all, Clayton had been the one to introduce them—a pair he'd believed had been so very much in love. A sentiment between the love-birds that had earned equal parts horror and envy from Clayton. And that sense of responsibility for being the one to coordinate a pairing, even if Clayton's role of matchmaker had proven accidental. Even if it had been the earl who'd all but begged for Clayton to coordinate a meeting between the lady and himself, Clayton had done so. And in the end, there'd been a lack of love and a plethora of faithlessness . . . on Norfolk's part.

For the man Clayton had called friend for the better part of his life—nay, his best friend—had intended to leave his wife. His pregnant wife, at that.

And now Clayton's sisters would kindle a relationship with that very woman, reminding Clayton of his mistakes and the inadvertent role he'd played in her misery.

He slumped in his chair.

Yes, his sisters' friendship with the lady spelled the makings of disaster.

There was only one course, however, for him: to stay far, far away from Sylvia.

Chapter 8

Since Clayton Kearsley, Viscount St. John, had stormed her household and demanded a visit, seeking to school her on the purpose of her meetings, she'd not been able to stop thinking about him.

His visit, that was. His *visit*.

After all, it took a staggering degree of insolence and arrogance and . . . and all manner of other nasty adjectives she'd crafted about the gentleman.

And this when she'd not even known St. John to be insolent or arrogant. Always polite and respectful, and endearingly awkward. He'd been that, too.

She wrinkled her nose.

To think she'd found him endearingly *anything* was a wonder.

In the two days since he'd taken his leave with his sisters in tow, she'd ruminated on that exchange over and over.

Which was likely why, lying flat upon her stomach at the crest of a hill, she was seeing him even now.

Because *no one* was here.

And yet . . . he was.

At this early-morn hour in Hyde Park at the edge of the Serpentine River, when the sun had only just begun its slow creep over the London sky.

Sylvia squinted.

In fairness, mayhap he didn't intend to be here?

Because he rather had the look of one who was . . . lost.

His hands on his narrow hips, the gentleman did a slow, deliberate circle.

"Are they *lost*?" Vallen's nursemaid whispered with the same abject confusion as Sylvia herself.

"Shh." Sylvia touched a silencing finger to her lips.

Not that she needed to have worried that the "they" in question would discover her and her son and nursemaid over the rise. Lord St. John and her late husband's other friend, the roguish Earl of Scarsdale, strolled the park. As they did, they held their hands over their eyes, looking about and talking to one another. Between Clayton and Lord Scarsdale was the earl's illegitimate son. While his father and Clayton scoured the grounds, the ten-year-old boy kept his head buried in a book before ultimately meandering away from the pair.

"I don't want to be taking part in this," the child said loudly enough for his annoyed tones to carry over to Sylvia and her maid.

"Seamus!" Lord Scarsdale called out. Trotting after the child, he left Clayton . . . alone in his search—Sylvia dropped back into hiding— whatever his search *was*.

It really wasn't her business. *He* wasn't her business. Something about Clayton, however, commanded her singular attention until the sheer curiosity of it proved too much.

Exactly what did the boy not wish to be taking part in?

She peeked her head out and did another search for just whatever it was he was looking for. *Mayhap his horse?*

"Haven't heard a horse, my lady," Marin whispered, confirming Sylvia had accidentally spoken aloud.

"Of course he has a horse. That was undoubtedly it."

"Are you playing, *too*?"

They emitted matching shrieks and looked sideways to the little girl who, unbeknownst to Sylvia and Marin, had found her way to their hiding spot.

"Eris?" Lord St. John called with an urgency in his tones. "Is that you?"

Reclined on her belly as Sylvia and Marin were, the little girl—Eris?—stole a glance out and then promptly ducked once more. She favored them with a glare. "With all that caterwauling, you're going to give us away," she scolded.

Confusion lit Marin's gaze as she looked hopelessly to Sylvia, who had even less clue as to the peculiar visitor they'd picked up. "Are you . . . hiding from Lord St. John?" she ventured, her protective maternal instincts kicking in.

"Oh, yes. I do it quite often." Then placing a finger against her lips, the small girl urged them both to silence and burrowed deeper in the grass. "He makes it so very easy to hide from him, too," the girl added for good measure in her barely audible tones.

Sylvia's mind was sent reeling. Why would Clayton be out with Lord Scarsdale and his son—Sylvia gasped as it hit her. Clayton, too, had an illegitimate child. One who sought to hide from him? And just like that, everything she'd believed about the gentleman being polite and respectable was flipped upon its head.

Disgusted both with herself for believing he was somehow different, and with him for being like all the others, she glared his way. At some point, he'd set off in the opposite direction, heading west back toward Hyde Park Corner.

Good. Let him go.

Given everything she'd discovered about her own faithless husband, was there still reason to be surprised when it came to men? Lords kept mistresses . . . whom they more often than not truly loved. Those sweethearts, in turn, gave them children. And the gentlemen couldn't be bothered with acknowledging the existence of those children.

The heel of the viscount's boots ground up gravel as he went, his footfalls moving farther away.

"Where in hell are you . . . ?" The gentleman's murmurings, however, reached them crystal clear.

Sylvia's brow climbed another fraction. Scaring children. Cursing. It so happened she'd known the gentleman even less than she'd thought she had. She assessed her unlikely visitor, the girl's brow furrowed deep with concentration, her gaze trained on the spot before her.

As if feeling Sylvia's stare, she glanced over.

"Why are you—?"

Little Eris slapped a palm over Sylvia's mouth, effectively cutting off the rest of the question she'd intended to put to the girl. "I said, you are going to give us . . ." Her whispered warning trailed off as she looked past Sylvia and Marin. "What is *this*?" The girl was already scrambling over them until she'd found a place beside Vallen. "It's a boy child!" Excitement made the girl forget her own rules and directives on hushed voices.

Sylvia's lips twitched with mirth.

"*Shh,*" Vallen ordered, slapping a tiny, dirt-stained palm over her lips and finishing the girl's previous worrying for her. "You're going to give us away."

"I didn't know you were here," Eris said, this time quiet enough not to earn Vallen's disapproval.

He preened; even stomach-down as he was, he managed to puff out his small chest. "I'm the best at hiding."

The little girl scowled. "*I* am the best. I can remain hidden for hours on end."

A wide smile split the boy's chubby cheeks. "You didn't see me."

"Blast and damn, Eris!"

Their unusual quartet looked out at the gentleman stomping around, and scanning the area as he went.

"Oh, dear," Eris whispered. "This is the point where he gets very, *very* angry."

Sylvia saw red. This was really quite enough. There were many things she could and did and would always tolerate. Bullying gentlemen was not, however, amongst those things . . . nor was scaring a small girl.

Scrambling out from behind the rise, Sylvia collected her skirts and stomped off toward that broad figure with his back to her. "Tell me, is it your habit to go about scaring children, Lord St. John?" she shouted into the morning quiet.

Releasing a blacker curse than she'd ever heard, the gentleman turned quickly enough on his heel to unsteady his balance. He effortlessly righted himself.

Of course he did.

Sylvia finished her march, taking care to leave a pace between them so it was easier to glower up at him.

The viscount eyed her with an appropriate guardedness. "More of an owl than a lark, are you?" he said, offsetting that sardonicism with a deeply executed, respectful bow.

Or rather, attempting to nullify that insolence. She narrowed her eyes. He'd jest . . . about *this*?

"And I'm not in the habit of scaring children?"

She arched a single brow. "Is that a question?"

"No!" he exclaimed, a blush that under other circumstances might have been adorable climbing the harshly set, angular planes of his cheeks. "It's a statement. I don't go about scaring children," he repeated.

"Don't you?" she shot back. "What of Eris?"

"What of her?" He scoffed. "I hardly think she's going to be frightened of me. Why, Eris could scare Satan if she so chose."

Sylvia gasped. "Lord St. John! You would speak so about your daughter."

His head tipped sideways. "My daughter?" he echoed back. "My daughter." He strangled on some manner of sound that might have been a cough or a laugh.

Fury iced her vision, briefly blinding her to his smug, smiling visage. "You should think she is somehow less because she's illegitimate."

Confusion cleared away all hint of Clayton's earlier mirth. "What in blazes are you speaking about? Of course I wouldn't. If she was. But Eris isn't my daughter."

The scathing castigation she'd prepared in her head died. "She . . . isn't?"

"No. Eris is my *sister*."

"Your . . . ?" She tried and failed with that revelation. Why, the girl couldn't be more than four or five.

"My sister," he repeated. When she was capable of offering nothing more than a blank, befuddled silence, he clarified further. "As in a female offspring having both parents in common with another offspring. A female sibling."

She lightly swatted his arm. "I know that." Except . . . "That is to say, not that I knew the young lady was your sister, but rather I'm familiar with the definition of a sister." And yet . . . her gaze whipped back toward the rise where the girl even now hid with Vallen. "She cannot be more than five."

"She is four, *nearly* five, as Eris would happily instruct you and anyone else who dare accuse her of something as shocking as being 'just four.'"

Oh, good God. Sylvia blanched. She'd stormed out here, calling him out, and all along the small person who'd been taking shelter over the rise was his sister? "But . . . but . . . that isn't possible," she blurted.

"Your reaction was much the same as mine when I learned the happy news from my then forty-eight-year-old mother and fifty-eight-year-old father, my lady." Using the wide brim of his top hat as a shield from the rising sun, Clayton continued his search for the very subject of their discussion. "Alas, I assure you, Eris is in fact a sister, born of my mother and late father."

And he was out here in Hyde Park at this early hour, not riding but escorting the girl about? Something shifted in her chest, something conjointly so warm, and yet at the same time so acute, it caused a tightening band about her that made it a struggle to breathe.

Envy. Regret. Those darker, deeper sentiments commanding control of the tingles of warmth that came in thinking of a man so devoted to a small child. It was a reminder she neither wanted nor had allowed herself to believe since her husband's death . . . that there was simple good in a man.

"Where is she?" Clayton murmured distractedly. His gaze shifted, colliding with hers.

And the tension eased from Sylvia's breast as altogether different sentiments sprang to life. More dangerous ones that she was hopeless to control.

For his eyes . . . they were an impossible shade of blue reserved for a painter's canvas: a blend of azure and turquoise that melded with periwinkle. The glitter within their depths sent a restless little quiver through her.

How had she failed to realize before this moment the striking beauty of those irises?

A light breeze danced around them, sending the leaves overhead into a soft, quiet dance. That air, drawing the bergamot scent of him closer, flooded her senses.

His lashes swept down an almost imperceptible fraction she'd never have noticed had she not been studying him so, and yet, she could not force her gaze from him.

He lowered his head a fraction, bringing them nearer. Bringing his mouth closer to hers . . . as if he intended to kiss her.

Her heart thumped a peculiar rhythm. Or was that she who leaned nearer to him? This moment was as jumbled as the one two days ago when she'd landed upon his frame.

Oh, goodness. It was the wrong thought. It conjured the same wicked memories that had robbed her of sleep since he'd taken his leave that day.

He cleared his throat. "Uh . . . yes. I don't suppose you might be so good as to point me to her, Sylvia?"

His mouth had moved . . . only it wasn't on hers, and words had come out of those thin, sensuous lips.

She froze, trying to make sense of what had happened. Or rather, what had not happened. A kiss that she'd been so very certain was coming. And hadn't. And . . .

His sister. He was asking if she'd reveal the little lady's location.

And he'd *not* been intending to kiss Sylvia.

Mortification scorched every last swath of skin upon her person. Her cheeks burnt up with heat at noticing this man . . . any man, in any way. Not when she'd resolved to never be so charmed or aware in a romantic way, or in any way that could only bring her more hurt. "Er . . . uh . . . right." That she could help with. Which, considering she'd accused him of siring an illegitimate child and also neglecting said issue, was the very least she could do. Gathering the hem of her skirts, she set off back toward the rise, which she very much regretted leaving moments before. As it was, the sooner she sent him off with his young sister, the sooner she could return to a clear head. "Let me lead you to her."

With Clayton's long, muscular legs, he kept an easy pace beside her. "I appreciate your help. I'm usually far better at this."

At . . . ? She stole a sideways look.

"At hide-and-seek, that is."

That slowed her stride. "Hide-and-seek?" Consternation brought that question out haltingly.

"Indeed." Clayton scanned the grounds, in search of his sister still. "I fear you've caught me at one of my least fine moments. I'm not usually one who'd enlist assistance," he said with a self-deprecating smile that managed to elicit the same havoc within her. "That is, when it comes to hide-and-seek."

And damn her heart for dancing once more.

It was a child's game he'd been playing, and one she had no recollection of her father joining her in. And certainly not her brother. Wholly disinterested in Sylvia when she was carrying his child, Norman would have followed a similar suit, she knew. And before this . . . she'd simply expected his detachedness was the way of all men born to Polite Society.

The late-spring breeze toyed with Clayton's neatly combed blond strands, and as he brushed that lone piece back behind his ear, she could not resist wondering as to whether it was as soft as it appeared, for surely nothing *could* be. And before she could recall the action, Sylvia stretched a hand up and tested the texture of that errant lock. Warmed velvet to the touch, it was.

Clayton froze.

Or perhaps that was her?

Mayhap it was the both of them?

Everything again was unclear.

A vague, powerful energy sizzled to life, sprung from her boldness and fed life by her wantonness.

"You had a strand loose," she finished lamely, jerking her arm down and swiftly tucking both limbs behind her back, lest she once more do something born of folly.

In the end, she was saved from embarrassment by the shout of her maid.

She and Clayton looked off to the rise where Marin stood, waving her arms frantically. "They're *gooooone*. The little ones have gone."

"Oh, bloody hell," she whispered as reality came crashing through that momentary madness. Gathering her skirts once more, Sylvia charged on.

"I'll look this way, my lady!" Marin shouted, pointing beyond her shoulder.

Panic threatening to swarm her, Sylvia raced off in the opposite direction.

Catching up to her, Clayton took her lightly by the arm and halted her flight.

She looked questioningly back and opened her mouth to speak, but just as his sister had done a short while ago, he touched a fingertip to his lips. "When she has the upper hand, she always laughs," he said from the corner of his mouth. "It gives her away every time."

As if on cue, from somewhere near came the paired giggling of two children even now delighting in the havoc they wrought upon the grown-ups attending them.

Together Sylvia and Clayton set off racing through the copse of narrow birch trees, onward to the laughter that grew in frequency and sound. He sprinted through the brush, and she trailed along at a slightly slower pace, panting hard as she ran after him.

She came crashing through the brush and found them at the lip of the shore with only water and a small gathering of pelicans floating upon the serene lake. Vallen and Eris had been effectively trapped.

Dropping her hands to her knees, Sylvia fought to get her breathing under control. All the while, she gave her son the look she'd inherited from her own mother. His lower lip quivering, Vallen dropped his tear-filled eyes to the ground.

Clayton folded his arms at his chest, and the little girl, Eris, studied the tips of her boots.

Sylvia frowned. "I am very disap—"

Jumping with his front foot forward in a fencing position, Clayton held one arm before him, and the other stretched toward the two children. "Caught!" he exclaimed, waggling a makeshift sword at that pair and startling Sylvia into complete silence.

Vallen and Eris immediately dissolved into laughter.

Clayton joined the pair of children and, falling to his haunches, said something that only caused a redoubling of their mirth.

And Sylvia stood there . . . wholly unfamiliar with all of this. Any of this.

Her family had always been a loving one, her siblings endlessly loyal. And yet, they'd not ever been so free with mirth. They'd been strictly instructed by the sternest governesses—and for Henry, tutors. Everything about how they'd conducted themselves had come down to being proper and following the rules laid forth by the *ton*. There'd certainly not been games and teasing the likes of which Clayton engaged his young sister with.

It was foreign, knowing that a gentleman could be this way, and that he could be this way with two small children.

From over the tops of their heads, he caught Sylvia's gaze and winked.

That little flutter of his lashes as devastating as that earlier glimmer in his eyes.

Smile. A breezy one. That is what is expected of you, here . . .

She needn't have worried, however, at feigning breeziness, as his attention was already back on Vallen and Eris.

"Can we play still, Clayton?" Eris pleaded, gripping the lapels of his cloak. "It is only fitting since I defeated you that I should claim a prize." The girl scowled up at her brother. "I'll be ever so upset if you say no."

Clayton jumped to his feet and sketched a low, gallant bow. "Far be it from me to be the brother responsible for your upset." The pair had started to race past him when Clayton spoke, staying them in their tracks. "Alas, I fear the decision as to whether you two scamps are free to continue playing after the tomfoolery you've been up to is not mine to make." Clayton gestured to Sylvia.

Both children looked hopefully at Sylvia.

Ambling over, Vallen yanked hard at her skirts. "Please, Mama. *Pleeeease?*"

Being free of Clayton—and his family—was the wisest, safest, and necessary course. And yet . . . the excuses she'd intended to make died upon the hopeful, eager glimmer in Vallen's eyes. Vallen, who had never had other children to play with. Who'd never had and never would know the affections of a father. And not even fear of herself around Clayton, the Viscount St. John, was powerful enough to be the one responsible for Vallen's dashed hope. "Oh, off with you now, but you are to stay with Marin." She called that last part more loudly after the two children, who'd already set off running toward the maid still calling for them in the distance.

Until Sylvia and Clayton were left . . . alone.

Another faint breeze sent the tree limbs gliding back and forth, their leaves swaying like an emerald canopy that let the occasional slash of sunlight through.

The earlier levity was gone with the children who'd left, so all that remained was a palpable tension that now sprang up between them.

Clayton returned his hat to his head. "I take it we've arrived at a truce from our last meeting?"

And it was the perfect thing for him to say, the ultimate reminder of the reason she'd been so put out with him that day . . . which was vastly safer than everything she'd witnessed from him and experienced with him. Only . . . he'd allowed his sisters to remain as members. "I . . . suppose a truce is called for," she said grudgingly, "given that you've acknowledged you were wrong about the Mismatch Society."

His high brow puckered. "I didn't admit I was wrong."

Sylvia narrowed her eyes. "What did you say?"

Chapter 9

What did you say? she'd asked him.

Apparently the wrong thing.

Again.

Nor were those verbal missteps an awkwardness he reserved for this woman. It had once been quite the opposite, in fact. He'd had a rather easy time speaking to her.

Alas, he'd returned to his same fumbling-about-for-the-correct-words state.

When he didn't immediately speak, her lashes came sweeping down in a dire warning.

"I . . ." To give his hands a task, he doffed his hat and knocked it against his leg, as he was wont to do.

"Yes," she pressed in a husky, smoky voice he'd no place noticing was husky or smoky. "You were saying?"

It would go better for him if he let Sylvia to her incorrectly drawn opinion, one where he'd come to see the error of his ways and she was left triumphant in their disagreement.

A lifetime living amongst a houseful of women of all ages had given him sense enough to know the never-failing way out of what promised to be a contentious matter.

And yet, his mind had gone to all mush where she was concerned.

"All men of the peerage require heirs."

That dangerous spark flashed bright in her eyes. *"Annnd?"*

There was a warning there. A grave, big, flashing warning that urged retreat.

He tried again. "And it's . . . certainly unfortunate for both men and women."

She stalked over, leaving a foot of distance between them so she could better hold his gaze. "Do you truly believe that requirement the *same* for men and women?"

"Well, in a way it is."

Once again, by the flash in her eyes, it was the wrong answer.

He edged away from her. "I'm not saying that it is fair. I am not saying that it is a system without flaws and that it shouldn't be changed. But rather that it is a necessity for both. There cannot be a legitimate issue without a legally recognized union. It is simply the way. It is what ensures property lines maintained and inheritances retained. As such, men and women both stand to benefit from the security provided by marriage."

She was motionless, and then a little bark of laughter burst from her. "You speak like one who'd committed to memory your every tutor's lesson on viscountly responsibilities."

That's because I have . . .

She cupped a hand. "What was that? I cannot make out what you are saying."

"I was simply remarking that it sounds like words uttered by my tutors because they *were* words uttered by them."

Her eyes lit, and then she dissolved into a bout of laughter. "Of course it is."

And her laughter transformed her from magnificent into otherworldly. It was a joyous expression, contagious, and he found himself laughing with her.

Sylvia abruptly stopped, and with it cut a knife right through that shared merriment.

"Security for whom, exactly, Lord St. John?" she shot back, all earlier levity gone. Sylvia didn't allow him a word in. "Men get their heirs, and women receive what, exactly? A broken heart. A life of tedium and solitude while their husbands go off and enjoy their freedom?"

His gut clenched into a thousand painful, twisted knots. She spoke of herself. She spoke from experience of the marriage she'd had with the man she'd loved and trusted. And he hated himself just then. Not for the first time. He hated himself for having been the one who'd introduced the pair.

"Hmm?" she pressed, sweeping back over so quickly her skirts whirled and slapped at the tan fabric of his trousers.

This new, mature Sylvia was also . . . a good deal more confrontational than he'd ever known her.

When Clayton again spoke, he did so in a way meant to calm and placate. "The truth of the matter is, the way of the world isn't fair. Not for men, and certainly not women. The requirement expected of both is that in order to ensure security and prosperity, one must marry. Do I think that is fair? No. Is that the way it is? Yes."

"You'll marry, then, all to do your duty by the line."

Bitterness iced the lady's question.

Once more, was it a product of her union with Norfolk?

"Will I protect my sisters by sacrificing myself in marriage?" He took a step toward her. "Yes. Yes, I will, because they need their futures secure, and I need to know that if"—*when*—"something happens to me, they will not fall at the mercies of a relative. And perhaps you'll judge me for that, but they come first, and I will happily make that sacrifice for them."

They stood there, chests heaving, volatile emotion thrumming in the very air they breathed.

And all at once, he became aware of other details: their nearness. Just how very close they stood to one another.

His throat worked . . . painfully, the reflexive motion of swallowing suddenly a struggle.

He lowered his head . . . and she raised hers, and almost as one, their mouths were on one another's.

Passion blazed to life in all its reckless, delicious glory.

He passed his mouth over hers again and again until a little moan escaped her, and he swept inside a cavern so moist and hot it threatened to consume.

Sylvia kissed him back. She dueled with him, tasting him. Possessing him as he possessed her. Setting him afire until his length throbbed, an acute sensation that brought pain and pleasure together in an unlikely harmony.

And it was the first time in his life that he'd ever known a passion so powerful as to cloud reason.

A desire that crushed good judgment.

A hungering that erased thoughts about what was proper and what he should or should not do.

Because making love to Sylvia's mouth certainly fell into the very firm category of forbidden.

He nipped at her, tasting and teasing her lush lower lip, and she bit him back with a feisty aggressiveness that nearly drove him to the brink of madness. They dueled with their mouths, each fierce joining of their lips, each glide of their tongue against the other's a battle for mastery and control in a skirmish he'd be content to see without a winner so that it could go on forever.

Clayton filled his hands with her ample hips, sinking into that flesh as he reversed their positions so she was anchored against the trunk of the birch tree.

Sylvia panted, her body sagging and her legs slipping apart, and he slid a knee between them to steady her. To keep her aloft.

Except . . . she only sank lower onto his thigh. She rubbed herself against him in frantic, jerky little movements.

Clayton groaned, sweeping his tongue against hers, lashing at that delicate flesh, and she returned every stroke. Tangling her fingers in the front of his cloak, she dragged him closer, all the while pressing herself against him.

And it was bliss the like of which he'd never known, and he fell, sinking deeper into the web of desire that had been spun over logic and reason and—

Wait, no. Clayton really was falling.

He wrenched his mouth away, but it was too late.

He tumbled back into the water, inadvertently taking Sylvia with him. They landed with a damning splash that sent the pelicans into noisy flight. The water closed over Clayton, flooding his nostrils, burning.

Gasping, he shoved himself up on his elbows and gave his head a hard shake, dispelling the water from his eyes.

Sylvia's hair was a tangle of wet curls plastered to her cheeks, several strands crisscrossing her face, forming a curtain across her eyes.

Bracing his weight with his left shoulder, he reached up and brushed those locks back, clearing the tangle so she might better see.

"It . . . seems we're developing something of a habit of this," he murmured.

The lady blinked several times, slowly, and then her eyes went wide.

With an impressive curse, she pressed her palms against Clayton's chest, levering herself upright . . . and consequently dunking him under the water once more. The moment he emerged from the freezing depths of the Serpentine, he wiped the water from his eyes once more and found her.

She'd gotten herself onto the shore, and was frantically wringing the hem of her skirts out.

He winced, not having the heart to tell her that her efforts were in vain. Her cloak and dress were plastered to her frame . . . a voluptuous figure that not even moments ago he'd had against him, and his hands on, and—

Sylvia glanced his way. "You are still in the water," she whispered furiously. "Why are you still in the water?"

Because apparently logic ceased to exist in her presence. He managed to bring his lips up in a half-hearted smile. "I was rather thinking it was a good time for a swim and all."

She paused midwring and looked at him like he were half-sprung. "Not a time for jest?"

"Noooooo," she said, her voice creeping up several octaves. "Certainly not the time."

Yes, he could rather see that.

Muttering to herself, Sylvia set to work once more in her futile attempts at wringing the remnants of the Serpentine from her garments.

Clayton got himself to his feet and trudged to the shore. Sitting down on a patch of grass, he proceeded to wrest free his boots. He'd managed to get the left one off when he felt eyes on him. He glanced over.

"What are you doing *now*?" she whispered, her voice pained.

"My boots are wet, and I am attempting to dry them, just as you are attempting with your skirts," he said, laying out that matter-of-fact breakdown.

"You aren't supposed to be *undressing*. You are supposed to be doing the opposite, Clayton."

"But my—"

"Mama!"

"Oh, bloody hell," she whispered.

The two laughing children crashed through the brush, and both staggered to a stop.

Eris and Vallen stared, goggle-eyed . . . with the seemingly impossible now proven true: Eris could be brought to silence. And shock had made her do it.

That silence proved short-lived. Planting her hands on her hips, she alternated a fiery glare between Clayton and Sylvia. "This is unforgivable. You should be 'shamed of yourselves."

"Ashamed," he and Sylvia automatically corrected.

"I expect you are," his military general of a sister said. Eris's expression darkened further with her displeasure. "Swimming without us?" she shouted, scaring the remaining pelicans into flight. "What manner of brother or mother *are* you?"

He stilled. *Oh, hell.* No . . . "Eris!" But it was too late.

The little girl had already taken Vallen by the hand and tugged her partner in crime along, out, and into the water. The duo giggled and squealed as they went swashing about.

Sylvia slapped her palms over her face.

"Eris!" he called.

To no avail. The girl had long been a fish—part mermaid, their eccentric father had proclaimed—and it had been a lore that remained that Eris had dangerously come to believe. Clayton waded back into the water after her and Sylvia's son.

Alas, the naughty duo slipped and slithered about like the damned silver eels at Loch Carron, all the while expertly evading Clayton.

"Vallen, come over here this instant," Sylvia demanded. Hiking her skirts to her knees, she waded out from the shore, but brought herself up short at where the drop rose to meet her.

Her commands were met with only more merry giggles.

The nursemaid burst into the clearing, short-winded, and she took in the exchange: Clayton in the water, racing after the naughty pair at play. Those ebullient children expertly evading his attempts. Her mistress.

"Oh, my lady. I am ever so sorry. I should have been the one chasing after them." And with that, the loyal nursemaid dashed in to retrieve Eris and Vallen, splashing water as she went. "Having to go into the waters yourself after them."

Clayton and Sylvia avoided one another's gazes. Saints be praised, however; salvation came in that incorrect conclusion the maid had arrived at. One that explained away any other potential reason for Clayton and Sylvia to be soaked from head to toe as they were.

"Got him!" the maid called triumphantly, scooping up the little boy.

Sylvia rushed to collect her son and carried him back to shore.

"I'm sorry," he whispered, his lower lip quivering.

"You do make it impossible to be upset," she murmured, touching her nose to Vallen's and rubbing the tip back and forth with hers until he was giggling once more.

Captivated, Clayton stared on at mother and child, that freedom of affection he'd experienced in his own family, but one that was otherwise so very rare amongst Polite Society.

"I am not sorry," Eris announced when the trio had left and only they two remained.

"Of course you aren't, scamp." He tousled the top of her damp brown curls.

Eris giggled and swatted at his hand. "What? I'm not. A person should not apologize for having fun, and I did have a good deal of it. More so than we usually have together."

"Thank you for that," he said dryly, and scooped up his boots. He sat down once more, and proceeded to wring them out again.

Skipping over to join him, Eris plopped herself down cross-legged. "I don't mean to attend you."

"Offend," he automatically corrected. "And none is taken."

His sister watched him as he made futile attempts to dry out his boots. "Yes, there was," she said, dropping her chin onto her hand. "I *do* appreciate that you play with me. Seamus *never* plays with me. He's ever so serious," she said of Scarsdale's illegitimate son. "He always wants to go off and read. And you're far better at it than Delia with her

Shakespeare and Cora with her insects and the rest with all their boring pastimes. And they do play with me, too, but it's not the same as . . ."

He paused in his efforts to look at his unusually somber little sister. "But it's not the same as playing with other children," he said gently.

Her face brightened. "Exactly. There are no children about, but now there is your friend with her son, and he can be another child for me to play with."

His friend and her son? Another child to play with?

And then what his sister was saying hit him.

"No. Absolutely not. Impossible." Impossible for so many reasons. She was Norfolk's widow, and being near her raised the risk of her again caring for him as a friend when he was destined to die.

Eris kicked a foot out, catching him in the shin.

He grunted and rubbed at the offended flesh. "What was that for?"

"I quite like her."

"She is quite likable," he agreed. Sylvia always had been affable and charismatic. In short, it was why she'd been a perfect match for one such as Norfolk.

Eris rolled her eyes. "Gentlemen are supposed to have better compliments and words for special ladies."

Yes, gentlemen were. And many of them did. Clayton, however, had never been amongst them. Oh, he'd kept company with rogues, those fellows with glib tongues. But he'd never been like them.

This meeting, however, had been problematic. Because she was so likable. Because he'd no place admiring or ogling her.

Or kissing her. You have even less place doing that.

And yet, that was what he'd done with risk of discovery from anyone . . . including his youngest sister.

He cringed.

Mayhap he was a rogue, after all.

"Furtherless—"

117

"Furthermore," he corrected. Reaching for her foot, he helped her free of first one soaking-wet boot and then the other.

"If you like her, then why wouldn't you want to be her friend?"

Clayton squeezed the excess water from her left boot. It was a good question. One he couldn't answer. Not without explaining all that complicated any relationship between him and Sylvia. "Because men and women aren't friends."

"That's silly. I shall be friendly with whomever I wish."

And Clayton was going to be miserable for it. For there was no doubting that Eris would find friendship if she so wished with men and women alike, and there'd be no stopping it. He shuddered, not wanting to look too far into the future and see the trouble that awaited him there.

"Anwen says the lady was friends with Norfolk."

He stiffened.

"Is that why?" his sister pressed, entirely too astute for her almost-five years. "Is it because you are sad because you think about the earl and how you miss him?"

"Something like that, poppet." It *was* because of Norfolk, just not for the reasons his sister imagined. And one that none of his family or friends could imagine. For unlike society, who still carried remembrances of the free-spirited, jocund earl, for Clayton all those illusions had been shattered . . . as had the high opinion and esteem he'd once held the other man in. No, it was entirely Clayton's guilt for having been the matchmaker between Sylvia and the late earl that served as the source of his distractedness.

"What is it?" Eris murmured, scooting closer.

"I'm just thinking of what Mother will say, finding you soaked as you are," he said, tweaking one of her damp curls and earning another giggle.

"She will not be surprised by me. You, however . . ." She waggled her dark brows.

He winced. "Perhaps we'll both sneak through the servants' quarters, escape notice, and then meet in the kitchens to steal pastries together."

"You're bribing me?"

"Is it working?"

Her smile deepened. "Of course it is."

Giving up on trying to dry out their wet footwear, he tucked the articles into the crook of his right arm and came to his feet. Clayton extended his left hand to help her up. "Let's be on, then."

He tugged her to a standing position, and as they headed through the thankfully still-empty grounds of Hyde Park, he resolved that this would be the last run-in he had with Sylvia.

She could carry on her friendship with his sisters, and Eris would be free to strike up one with Vallen, but anything between him and Sylvia was absolutely forbidden.

And the embrace they'd shared today was proof of it.

Chapter 10

Yesterday morn had been nothing short of a disaster.

Only fate or fortune or good luck, or whatever it was, accounted for Sylvia and Clayton escaping scandal.

Or . . . a misunderstanding on Vallen's nursemaid's part as to the reason Sylvia had been soaked from head to toe in Serpentine water.

Either way, Sylvia had been spared from questions as she'd returned home with an equally drenched son and nursemaid in tow, and neither Valerie nor Annalee had probed.

For the understanding had been clear: two troublesome children had led her and Marin into the waters.

Not a passionate embrace with the estimably proper Viscount St. John.

"Sylvia?"

That gentle prodding brought her back to the moment.

Valerie's eyes revealed her concern.

"She's not listening," one of the girls was saying. "I do not think she heard . . ."

Jerked back to the moment, Sylvia felt her cheeks warm as the eyes of all members of the Mismatch Society landed upon her.

"Oh, dear, did you catch chill yesterday?" Valerie came quickly to her feet, and crossing over, she pressed a hand to Sylvia's cheeks.

Her heated cheeks.

"You're warm," her friend murmured, glancing over at Annalee.

"I am fine," Sylvia hurried to assure her protective friend. Of course, she couldn't very well say that she'd been reminiscing about the embrace she'd shared in Hyde Park. She, who'd never felt passion with her husband and believed herself incapable of it, had behaved like a wanton, rubbing herself against Clayton like a cat in . . .

Sylvia fanned her cheeks as she caught herself. She forced her hands onto her lap. "I am fine," she repeated for good measure, attempting as much to convince herself as she did the young women who were all too concerned with her well-being.

"She is flushed," Miss Gately unhelpfully pointed out.

"Yesterday was warm. How might she have taken chill?" Miss Dobson put to the group at large.

Drinking deeply from a glass of whiskey, Annalee swiped at the corners of her lips. "She took a swim in the Serpentine."

Whispers went up around the room.

"I did not take a swim," Sylvia called loudly to no effect from the shocked group. She gave Annalee a look.

Her friend winked and lifted her glass in salute.

"That is so peculiar," Anwen Kearsley murmured. "Because my *brother* also went for a swim in the Serpentine yesterday." And just like that, Clayton's eldest sister brought the group to a collective quiet. "He *tried* to keep it a great secret, sneaking inside through the servants' entrance, but my youngest sister sang like a lark. It was all rather shocking, as Clayton does not tend to do anything scandalous like swim."

There were several beats of silence.

Please, have them speak of something else. If only they would let the matter rest.

Sylvia would not ever be so lucky.

"That is . . . rather interesting," someone murmured at the back of the parlor. "That they were *both* swimming at the same time."

"We were not swimming," Sylvia said, exasperated to the extreme. "And certainly not together."

"Vallen and Lord St. John's sister Eris did, however, go for a swim," Valerie explained to the room at large.

The collective heads tipped back in understanding. *"Ahhh."*

"But it was like you were swimming, wasn't it?" Miss Dobson ventured. And apparently she didn't require confirmation, for she went on, speaking in halting tones that grew increasingly quick, as if she were a detective who'd at last assembled the details to solve her case. "Because the two children were swimming, and you both saw the children swimming, and you decided to join in the fun."

"No," Sylvia said emphatically. "That is not what—"

"And I think it is admirable for Lady Norfolk to prove that a woman can be so free as to swim at Hyde Park, or at any lake if she so chooses." Miss Dobson clasped her joined hands to her chest. "How often were we told as children that it was forbidden of us to swim?"

Yes, because that was the way. How many times had Sylvia and her sister been forbidden from partaking in those pleasures when they'd gone off to their family's country seat? And she'd always complied.

"And now Lady Norfolk decided that she wished to swim with Lord St. John."

Bloody hell with this. "No. That is—"

"I swim at my family's property in Loch Carron in Scotland," Cora piped up, as all attention went swiveling to the pale-green parcel-gilt armchair and the lady who occupied that pretty seat.

By her wide, dimpled smile, Cora reveled in the collective admiration she'd gathered from the group. "For why shouldn't a woman swim?" she went on. "Isn't that right?"

All the girls nodded.

And Sylvia let some of the tension go from her shoulders as she and the subject of her ignominious swim in the Serpentine were forgotten as all focus shifted onto Clayton's sister.

The young woman looked Sylvia's way, and the two shared a smile . . . so that Sylvia almost believed the young lady had known precisely what she was doing in diverting the crowd's attention.

"And why shouldn't she swim with my brother or any other man if she so wishes?" Cora added, just like that, quashing the illusion of shared camaraderie and ending the all-too-brief reprieve. "Men and women should be able to be friends and do wild things without judgment from—"

Lila cleared her throat. "Perhaps we should return to the focus of today's agenda?" she ventured, and Sylvia would be forever grateful for having a loving, devoted sister.

"Agenda. Agenda," Valerie muttered to herself, skimming the back of her charcoal pencil along her notes. She glanced up. "Are all *wantons* ready to begin?" she said teasingly, earning laughter amongst the members.

All thoughts of Clayton and their embrace yesterday vanished as Sylvia's belly churned. For even as it might sound and actually be ridiculous that Polite Society had applied the title of "wanton" to them, it was still . . . damning.

"Or should I say . . ." With a flourish Annalee brandished in her hand the latest scandal sheet and held it out for the room at large. "Harlots?"

Valerie gave the other woman a look.

Sylvia's stomach sank even further. This was so much worse.

Society had already begun looking unfavorably upon them because of the perceived scandalous nature of their meetings. But this? Being referred to and thought of as a harlot? It only opened Sylvia to the very trouble her mother had predicted she would find.

"Mayhap it's not in all the papers?" Lila put in with her same hopeful optimism. Scoffing, she reached for the newspaper still held in Annalee's hand. "After all, being written poorly of by a reporter with the name"—Lila turned the paper around and skimmed the headline—"Busy Bottoms of *The Tattler*, it's hardly reason for worry."

Anwen timidly raised a copy of the morning's *Times*. "It is here, too."

"And here." Cora lifted up a different newspaper whose title Sylvia could not see. Nor, however, did it really matter. The fact remained the same: the Mismatch Society and, by default, she were at the center of Polite Society's gossip.

Silence descended upon their usually voluble group.

"Mother said as long as our group was not immoral, I was welcome to be part of it," Emma's sister, Isla, whispered to herself.

Emma gave her a firm look. "We are *not* immoral. It is simply what some small-minded, insecure men are writing about us. Men," she spat.

That was the rub, wasn't it? Ultimately, it all came down to perception. And if it were only Sylvia, she wouldn't care. She'd happily tell all the busybodies and bastards where they could go. But she didn't have that luxury. She *had* to care. For Vallen.

"It isn't hopeless; if we simply reveal that we are a gathering group of scholars, then surely we can cut off the gossip," Valerie volunteered.

Anwen perked up. "I agree. Why, we are no different from the French salons! They'd be inclined to let us be and go on to gossip about someone else."

"Ah, yes," Cora drawled. "Drawing a connection between those societies that led to the guillotine and the heads coming off the nobility should go over smashingly."

Anwen tossed a satin, circular pillow at the other woman, catching her square in the face.

Annalee banged the gavel several times and hard enough to penetrate the sisterly squabble. "Enough! There is no resolving the *ton*'s gossip. To waste our time speaking about them and what they are saying about us squanders any moments to create real change for us and all women. Is that clear?"

Except it wasn't quite so black and white for someone like Sylvia. For a young mother who had a child dependent upon her, and said child could be taken away if she were deemed unfit. And the missives her father-in-law had persisted in sending, demanding to see Vallen, had also begun to include scathing opinions on her character.

"With the misery they bring, is it really a wonder that women don't want to marry?" Cora muttered to herself. "When this is the manner of rubbish we have to deal with?"

One of their newer members, Miss Kate Milsom, coughed lightly into her gloved hand—a tightly clenched hand. She was all of ten inches past four feet, and slender enough to be knocked down by a London breeze. "Not all women are unamenable to the idea of marriage."

"All the women *here* are," Brenna said with a slight emphasis.

Sylvia looked to Brenna and spoke loudly enough so she could be heard over the quiet chattering. "Let Kate speak."

All eyes went to the young woman.

That, however, had been one of the rules that had guided their group, that each woman listened to her fellow sisters.

Miss Milsom's cheeks blossomed pink.

Those blushes and averted gazes and quietly uttered words were a mark of most of the women who'd arrived in the parlor. That obsequiousness was an indication of how women of Polite Society were expected to be. Along the way, just like Sylvia and every other lady of the *ton*, they'd become empty shadows, murky figures that people looked through but never at.

Invariably, after but a handful of meetings, each lady tended to grow more comfortable in having her voice heard.

"Uh . . . yes," Miss Milsom began in halting tones. "It is just . . ." She stared down briefly at her joined hands, and then back to Sylvia.

Sylvia smiled patiently, allowing the young woman the time she needed to form the thought that was so important to her.

"His Grace created a beautiful gavel." There were murmurings of assent that seemed to give the girl courage, for Miss Milsom's voice grew steady and clear. "That is . . . I thought of it a good deal the other day when it was first revealed. And he supports her business." A boxing club that trained men and women in self-defense that had both scandalized and intrigued the *ton*.

Valerie guided Miss Milsom back to her point. "And what is it you wish to say?" she urged.

Miss Milsom turned up her palms. "It's simply that, I'm not sure why, if Lila has shown that young women can have loving, devoted husbands, we should not wish for the same for ourselves?"

"This was already settled earlier in the week," Cora pointed out. "We discussed the possibility of considering marriage, and decided collectively against supporting that state."

"Men are the worst," Brenna muttered from where she sat with her knees drawn to her chest.

Yes, they absolutely were.

A memory flitted in. Not a glum one sprung from a bitter past, but a recent one, from just yesterday, when Sylvia had discovered Clayton playing a child's game with his young sister.

I fear you've caught me at one of my least fine moments. I'm not usually one who'd enlist assistance . . . That is, when it comes to hide-and-seek . . .

It had been easier to accept the idea that all men were, in fact, terrible when the only models for good had been her brother and her brother-in-law. But now there was also Clayton. Clayton, who was kind to children and playful, and who, regardless of whether she'd wished it or not, had forced Sylvia to look at him, and because of him, all men, in new ways. Clayton, who'd also stated his intentions . . . to marry.

"I don't find that to be the case," Lila was saying. That statement was met with another round of horrified gasps. "I don't . . . disagree with Miss Milsom. In fact, I very much agree with her." She paused to smile at the other woman. "Not all men are bad."

Miss Milsom grew several inches under that support and praise.

Chaos descended upon the room, with women shouting over one another, calling out Lila and Kate as traitors to the principles.

"If it weren't true, they wouldn't be destroying our names and reputations in their silly scandal sheets . . ."

"And voicing all their ill opinions of us . . . ill opinions when they do not even know us or what happens here . . ."

While the members shouted over one another, Sylvia sat there through the tumult, silent. She shared the same outrage as everyone present. If only—

She sat up straighter and turned to Brenna. "What was that you said?"

"Men are the worst!"

"No, the point after that," she urged. The girl puzzled her brow. "You said they have ill opinions of us . . . ill opinions when they do not even know us or what happens here . . ."

"Just like our brother," Cora muttered.

Excitement crested in Sylvia's breast as an idea came to her. "Precisely!" It was madness, and yet it was something she and the other ladies present absolutely had to consider. Not only for Sylvia and her son but also for the preservation of their group.

Not even a day earlier, battling wits and opinions with Clayton in Hyde Park, she'd been so very adamant that she would never allow him near her society. But that was before. Before the gossip. The bad gossip.

"What is happening?" Miss Dobson whispered. "Why is Lady Norfolk looking like that?"

Because she was equal parts horrified and hopeful at the very ideas now rolling through her head.

And yet . . . before she thought better of it, before she could talk herself out of the idea that had come, she said, "I propose we reconsider the policy of our membership." When the room looked back at her, she realized she had to say it. She just had to be completely specific in what she was calling for. "I am making a motion that we admit a male member into our society." There—she'd said it. She looked around the room at the stone-silent ladies before her. That wasn't so very—

The quill slipped from Valerie's fingers and clattered to the floor. *"Whaaat?"* she squawked.

Several girls rushed over at once to retrieve the other woman's pen, with Cora rescuing it first.

"Don't like that . . ."

"Not at all . . ."

"Terrible . . ."

All the responses rolled together, but their meanings remained clear.

Valerie ignored her feathered quill, all her focus on Sylvia. "Surely you aren't suggesting we admit men into our society?"

"Rather defeats the purpose of an all-female society," Annalee drawled. "Doesn't it?"

"I don't understand how speaking ill of us and our society should merit membership within our group," Cora said.

The ladies around them murmured their agreement.

It was a fair point, and yet . . . "If we allow them to continue and the *gossip* continues"—Sylvia picked up a newspaper in each hand and held them both aloft—"then what happens to Miss Dobson's presence here?" The bespectacled lady dropped her eyes to her lap. "Or what, then, happens to Emma and Isla? Or Miss Langston?" Sylvia dropped those gossip sheets onto the mahogany center table alongside a tray of untouched refreshments. *Thwack.* "And those of us here who are young mothers: Lady Caroline. Myself. We run the risk of having our children taken away." Sylvia drew in a slow breath through the fury, refusing to give in to the uncontrollable rage she felt at her and so many other women's circumstances.

"How does having a gentleman amongst us make any of this"—Annalee waved at those newspapers that had derailed the day's agenda on the topic of marriage—"go away?"

"I'm not speaking about just *any* man," Sylvia clarified. "A specific man. One who is beyond reproach and admired and liked by all, a gentleman who is respected but also respectful." Clayton had proven himself all that over the years. And also, a gentleman who had shown respect for the decisions, strengths, and capability of women within his own household. Granted, he'd shown a great lapse when he'd come to her and questioned her about the Mismatch Society. But he had not been stubborn in his opinion. She'd been able to reason with him, and he'd respected her enough to speak with her. And, of course, there was still the matter of him not interfering with the wishes of his sisters, as most any other man in Polite Society would have.

The women collectively eyed her like she'd sprouted a second head.

"Oh, and where do we go about finding such a paragon of a man?" Annalee asked around a robust laugh. "After all, if such the gentleman did, in fact, exist, then there'd be a good deal fewer of us advocating against that miserable state of marriage."

Sylvia smiled. "The Viscount St. John."

There were several lengthy beats of silence.

"As in . . . my *brother*?" Anwen blurted, adjusting her spectacles as if that might somehow help her properly hear what Sylvia was saying.

Sylvia nodded. "The very same. He was so very determined to ask us to cease our meetings, while having no idea of what truly happens here. We can understand why these gentlemen feel so threatened, and can bring him around to our progressive thinking."

The Kearsley sisters collectively recoiled.

She'd get no help there. "This would be an honorary membership. A temporary one . . . where we"—Sylvia searched her mind—"peer within the minds of the male species."

"Go on," Annalee said suddenly, looking far more interested in Sylvia's shocking proposal.

"The benefits could be twofold."

"Finding even a single benefit to having a man around, let alone two good reasons? Now, *this* I have to hear," Valerie said under her breath.

Sylvia neither blamed nor faulted her friend for that opinion. After all, they'd both been betrayed by the same man. They'd both learned a cold, hard lesson at his hands. This, however, was different. In the sense of who Clayton was, in the past she'd had with him, and the purpose he would serve for all of them. Ignoring the other woman's sarcasm, Sylvia warmed to her idea. "I recently had"—*a discussion with Clayton*—"thoughts," she substituted, sidestepping any further talk about her exchange with the viscount, "that mayhap we might learn why men make the decisions that they do where ladies are concerned."

"So . . . use a man to study them," Annalee murmured, her brow creasing contemplatively.

Sylvia expanded further. "How they think and why they think as they do . . . And we, in turn, might educate our honorary member . . . this *temporary* member," she hurried to elucidate, "which might bring him and other men around to our progressive thinking."

That pronouncement was met with a long silence.

Lady Olivia was the first to speak. "And why, exactly, do we care what the gentleman thinks of us and our society?" she asked without inflection.

Indeed. Why should they? And yet . . .

Sylvia sat forward in her seat. "Men are of the opinion that we don't have real thoughts or real dreams. They go to their clubs and sip their whiskeys"—Annalee toasted with her glass of that very spirit—"but we are foreign to them. The idea that we might exact change that is necessary is something they cannot fathom. And mayhap if he sees it and shares those realizations with the men he calls friends, and that spreads, perhaps we can influence even greater change than we'd believed. Perhaps the lords who previously looked at ladies as solely the means to continue their line will see real people, and in so doing, mayhap we might alter the marriages that women who must marry make."

There came another roll of murmurs throughout the parlor as the membership collectively considered that proposal, and Sylvia braced for an inevitable rejection.

"I, for one, do not disapprove of Clayton being here," Anwen announced.

"You wouldn't," Cora muttered, turning a page in her book.

The eldest Kearsley sister pinched the other girl in response.

"Ouch," Cora exclaimed.

Anwen scowled. "I'm merely saying Clayton will *eventually* want us to marry. Having him here, viewing us in a new light, can only benefit us."

"I . . . hadn't considered that." Cora wrinkled her nose as if it were painful to admit her eldest sister might be correct in any regard.

"And I, for one, rather like the idea of having a society that is open to both men and women," Miss Dobson chimed in.

"Well, I, for one, despise it," Emma Gately shot back. "I have no interest in hearing what they think or feel about anything."

"Hear, hear, to that," Annalee said, exhaling another cloud of smoke from the corner of her mouth.

"A vote. We put it to a vote." Valerie accepted her pen from the lady still holding it, and turned to a new page in her notebook. "Those of us opposed to naming the honorary member Lord St. John, who is also temporary to our ranks, raise your hand and acknowledge your vote with a 'nay.'" Six hands shot up. "And those in favor of naming and adding the temporary member Lord St. John, raise your hand and acknowledge your vote with an 'aye.'"

Along with Sylvia, Lady Olivia, Miss Langston, Miss Dobson, and Anwen and Cora Kearsley added their votes as one.

The last voter, Brenna, undecided, shifted in her seat, and then ever so slowly lifted her hand.

Silence fell.

"It is decided, then," Valerie announced. "Lord St. John is our newest member."

She banged the gavel, making the decision official.

"Now there just remains the part of convincing him," Anwen said. "Which one of us will be tasked with that impossible job?"

Slowly, each member slid her gaze over to Sylvia.

"Me?"

"You were the one who suggested it," Annalee pointed out, her words beginning to slur as they invariably did when she reached her fourth glass of whiskey.

Yes, that much was true. And yet, having presented the idea and had it be a realized, actual thing that was happening now forced her to consider that which she'd not allowed herself to: facing him again after their embrace in Hyde Park.

"Unless you're having second thoughts and wish to change your vote?" Valerie volunteered, her tone filled with hope.

"No." Sylvia shook her head. "This is best for the society. We cannot properly dismantle society and change it without knowing the subject of our discontent. I shall speak to him."

It was decided.

Chapter 11

The following afternoon, Clayton found himself nearly escaping his sisters and mother.

Nearly.

"Your sister has requested your presence in the parlor," Georges murmured as Clayton reached for the worsted wool overcoat from a nearby footman, who helped him into the article before immediately scurrying off. But not before Clayton caught the sympathetic glance he shot in the old butler's direction.

This boded ill. "Which sister, Georges?" he asked, hastily buttoning the hard tartan garment.

"Misses Anwen, Cora, and Brenna." Georges dropped his gaze to the floor. "And . . . your mother."

His three eldest sisters *and* mother? Well, that decided it. "If you can let them know I have business to attend and I will speak to them upon my return?" He reached for his hat.

Georges tucked the article behind his back. "They suggested you might have said as much, in which case I should tell you that it is solely Miss Anwen," he said, his expression pained.

Clayton could commiserate. He knew what it was to accidentally thwart whatever games his sisters were up to.

For a moment, he considered taking the meeting. For a moment.

Alas, he was more a coward, and a selfish one at that. "Just tell them I'd already gone off for a meeting before you were able to locate me and deliver their instructions," he suggested.

"You have turned to lying now, have you?" a voice cried from overhead.

They looked up to where Eris sat perched on the upper hall railing, as if she were on a swing a foot off the ground and not a precarious, makeshift seat fifty feet high.

His stomach flipped over. "Eris," he said in slow tones meant not to agitate his sister into doing anything that might see her plunge accidentally to her death. Clayton started for the stairway. "I want you to please come down and meet me." White hair. Forget grey. He was going to go straight to white before the girl even reached her fifth birthday.

"You're worried I shall fall, Clayton." Her voice echoed around the foyer, highlighting even further the enormity of the space between her and the marble floor. "But you needn't. I intend to be a funbottomist."

A—? He looked desperately over to his butler, who shook his head.

Eris pumped her legs and, somehow even fifty feet above him, managed to roll her eyes. "A funbottomist," she repeated for them. "You know, like when you took me to the Royal Circus."

Understanding dawned. "A *funambulist*."

"Yes. And it is going to be such fun."

He stopped at the middle of the stairs. "How about we strike an agreement. You come down, and I'll go see what the sisters want?"

The proposed agreement hadn't even left his mouth before she was hopping safely back to the pine floor. "Splendid. They are in the Brodie Parlor." With a cheeky smile and even cheekier wave, Eris skipped off in the opposite direction.

Clayton glanced back to Georges. "Have I just been . . . ?"

"It appears you have, my lord."

Again.

Bloody hell. Annoyance filled him as he took the stairs quickly and headed for the Brodie Parlor, so named for the poor sod of an ancestor whose appellation not only translated into mud but who also had fallen face-forward from his horse, perishing, not unironically, in a puddle of mud. Drowning in mud was an apt way to describe all his meetings of late with his sisters.

"Shall I take your jacket, my lord?" Georges called after him.

"That won't be necessary. This shan't be a long meeting." He'd go, hear what it was they intended to put to him now, and then he'd get the holy hell out of here.

The moment he reached the Brodie Parlor, he let himself inside. "You have three min—"

Sylvia sailed to her feet, and he was left with his warning hanging unfinished in the air.

Of any of the people he'd expected to find standing before him, Sylvia had not been one of them. Sylvia, whom, after their . . . exchange . . . in Hyde Park, he hadn't anticipated he'd again see. Ever. Which would have been expected, given his forwardness. What he'd not thought about, however, was that, given her relationship with his sisters, he would have to one day face her. He glanced about for his family. Trying to make sense of their absence, and more, the presence of the lady before him. "Sylvia. Forgive me. I trust you are here to meet with my sisters. They should—"

"With you."

He tried to make sense of any of that . . . of any of this . . . and failed. "I beg your pardon?"

"I said, I am here to meet with *you.*" She placed a delicate emphasis on that last word. A little smile teased at those bow-kissed lips. "With you, Clayton," she repeated, the husky quality of her voice enveloping the two abrupt, coarse syllables, transforming them into something melodic and enthralling.

"I don't understand." Which was an increasingly familiar state he found himself in where the lady was concerned. "There isn't a meeting between me and my sisters, then?" He did another glance about, more than half expecting his brood of unruly siblings to jump out and yell "Trapped!" as they caught him in whatever scheme they'd concocted this time.

"There isn't. As propriety doesn't permit ladies and gentlemen to meet privately, they were helpful, however, in coordinating an exchange between you and I." Her lips slipped into a wry half grin. "Propriety hardly permits a lady the right to visit a gentleman, and as such, we ladies are required to use creativity to conduct private meetings."

At her pointed look, he followed her stare, searching for the sisters at his back.

"The door," Sylvia gently urged. "I was suggesting that you close the door so we might steal a private moment."

Steal a private moment.

Four words that conjured all manner of improper thoughts. Heat flared to life, just as it had yesterday in Hyde Park, when in a moment of madness he'd taken her in his arms and—

She lifted an eyebrow, startling him into action.

You are a Devil. A caddish, wicked Devil. Clayton pushed the panel shut a tad too hard, shaking it in its frame. "Is there something you require assistance with?"

Just see that they are well. Occasionally check in on them . . .

And yet, as that perfectly formed mouth moved, that last meeting with Norfolk was there. Haunting him. Taunting him. How much did she even really know of that treachery? The depth of it?

"Are you . . . all right, Clayton?" she asked hesitantly.

"Forgive me," he said, clearing his throat. "I'm fine." Except he wasn't. He was the exact opposite of anything even remotely all right.

Shoving thoughts of that day and the guilt to go with them into the place in his mind where he wrestled it shut and forgot it, Clayton joined her. "Please?" He motioned to the seat she'd quit upon his entrance.

After she sat, Clayton claimed the more functional George II Chippendale armchair. "You were saying?"

"Following our last meeting"—the one where he'd pinned her to a tree and had his leg between hers . . . He found himself staring at a point just beyond the top of her head—"I had much time to think about what you said. That is, regarding the weekly meetings which occur at my household."

His gaze flew back to hers. "You are closing your club." Well, this was even better than he'd anticipated. He'd be able to go about his business of finding a—

"Society." She frowned. "We are a society. And no, I'm not shutting down the Mismatch Society. Just the opposite. We intend to grow our membership."

Splendid.

"However, we have adjusted some of our policies, which had previously been resolute."

Hope stirred. This was interesting . . . and faintly promising. "Indeed?"

"Following your visit and, more specifically, our meeting in Hyde Park . . ." He did not imagine the faint pink blush that delicately splotched her cheeks, indicating that even for her assuredness around him this day, she, too, recalled their embrace. "It is not your fault that you wished for our group to be shuttered. You couldn't have any idea of the important exchanges that take place amongst our members. It also occurred to me that we might just as much learn from you as you could stand to learn from us."

What, exactly, was she saying? "I'm afraid I don't understand, Sylvia."

"We've decided to allow the very brief, and very temporary, membership of a male member." Sylvia smiled. "And I'd like to congratulate you on being our first and only honorary male member."

And just like that all his hopes of an uncomplicated closure of that society were lost.

Bloody hell.

⚜

Sylvia had spent the night working herself up for this very visit . . . and not because she believed she'd fail in securing Clayton's cooperation.

But because of their kiss.

Nay, what they'd shared in that copse in Hyde Park hadn't been a kiss.

Kisses were chaste.

Kisses were curt and usually wet and entirely unmoving.

Or that was what they'd been with Norman, anyway.

Not a single embrace she'd shared with her husband had managed to curl her toes and burn her up with heat. Nor had his touch or caress caused that throbbing wetness that had settled between her legs yesterday.

She'd thought there would be awkwardness.

Fortunately, however, there'd been no awkwardness. In fact, there'd been no indication that they had in any way shared that embrace that had seen them doused in the mercilessly frigid Serpentine.

But then there'd always been an ease between them. A comfortableness that went back to her first Season—those days when they'd so often found themselves seated across from one another at a whist table.

That reminder erased all the nervousness she'd felt at having to face Clayton again after she'd behaved like a wanton with him, and brought her back to the reason for her being here.

"You are speechless," she supplied when he still didn't say anything.

"I . . . uh . . ." That thought from Clayton went unfinished.

She would take that as a yes, then. "You're flattered?" she predicted, favoring him with a smile.

"Given our last discussion about my opinion of your society, I confess I am rather at a loss," he replied.

"You were determined to shut us down, Clayton." At the time, she'd been so overcome by indignation to not consider there might have been value to his presence there. For her. For Vallen. For all the other ladies who were at risk of being barred from attending.

Clayton rubbed the back of his neck. "And . . . that is somehow grounds for admission?"

From his wrinkled brow on down to the hesitancy of his speech, he was flummoxed. She couldn't help it. Sylvia laughed, that free, robust sound that had made her mother wince and that she, as a result, had fought to stifle over the years. And that after her husband's death she'd thought to never again know. And yet now, numerous times with Clayton, she had.

Clayton looked at her a moment, and then he joined in.

His whole frame shook, sending his knee jolting against hers.

"You're teasing me. I forgot your tendency to do that," he said after his amusement had abated.

Her smile faded. "I'm not teasing you. Not about this. I'm serious." Sylvia looked him square in the eye. "Deadly so."

"That sounds ominous."

"It is just the opposite. We've decided there are benefits to allowing you entry to our society, and I'm here to extend that invitation."

"What *possible* benefits could there be in having *me* there, Sylvia?" He was humble.

And also straightforward in ways that her late husband and most men were not. Gentlemen tended to prevaricate, offering pretty words and ways around what should just be up-front and direct speech. Sylvia appreciated that forthrightness. Her days of attempting to sort out what a person truly meant or did not mean had come and gone.

With that in mind, she launched into the argument that she'd gone over in her mind both last evening when sleep had eluded her and this afternoon on her carriage ride over. "As you're aware, gentlemen are going about trying to shutter our society."

"And?"

He really didn't see. "And," she said, as patient as she would be when explaining something complicated to Vallen, "your attendance can only help the Mismatch Society."

"I . . . see."

And yet, oddly, by the befuddled little glint in his deep-blue eyes, she somehow doubted that. She sighed. He really needed her to spell it out. And here men were allowed to rule the world, when all the while the ladies had to handle the strings, helping them along. "You really aren't aware of your influence, are you, Clayton? You are very well respected and honorable; you are friends with rogues and gentlemen alike. You don't have an enemy amongst the bunch. As such, when you join our ranks, it shows your peers that there is nothing to be threatened by. The Mismatch Society can only benefit from your being there."

He scrubbed a hand down the side of his face.

And she narrowed her eyes . . . as it hit her. "Why, you still believe the society should be shut down."

A blush turned his cheeks a ruddy shade of red. "I didn't say that."

"You didn't have to. You did that thing with your hand and your face."

"What thing with—?"

Sylvia gave him a look, halting him midmovement of that very action. "It's the same one you give when you don't approve or seek to hide something. Like that time I suggested we sneak off and sample Lady Clermont's French brandy."

"It was the middle of the ball."

"Or when I challenged Lord and Lady Castlerock to their entire pot and ours at the game of hazard?"

"It was a terrible wager," he muttered.

"That we won," she felt inclined to point out.

"That is neither here nor there."

"Yes, you are right," she agreed. They had gone into the weeds here. And she'd inadvertently moved them away from the sole purpose of this exchange. "You *do* disapprove." Sylvia couldn't keep the hurt from creeping in. She'd simply—and erroneously—believed he'd come to trust the purpose of the society when he found her and his sisters at the center of it.

His features were pained. "Does it matter whether or not I approve or disapprove, Sylvia?"

It didn't. And yet somehow . . . it still did. Because when she'd set out to request his help, there hadn't been a thought in her mind that he would reject her plea. The friend of long ago would have automatically lent his support. Instead, she made herself say, "I suppose not."

Because, ultimately, he was correct. It didn't matter what he thought of her or her society. What did matter, however, was the perception of his approval. The rest would come later, when he joined their ranks and saw the good that did, in fact, exist.

"Our membership, as you know, has disavowed the state of marriage, and yet, we've not heard the other perspective. Your perspective."

"Mine?" he echoed, his expression blank.

She nodded. "Yours. Of course, we can invite any number of gentlemen—"

"Thank you," he said with a droll twist to those two words.

"But as someone I know and trust, you also happen to be related to almost a quarter of my membership, and as such, you are the safest."

Clayton snorted. "I don't know whether I'm insulted or honored."

"Oh, honored." Sylvia smiled up at him. "You are most definitely honored," she said, resting a hand upon his knee to deliver him a reassuring pat.

That movement so reflexive. So very natural. As automatic as drawing in breath and exhaling it out the next. And yet, at the same time . . . it was scandalous, too.

Her touching him.

Her being alone with him here.

Remove your fingers from his person this instant. It helped that those directives pealed around her mind in the tones of her prim and proper mother.

But it didn't help enough to make her draw back her palm and cease touching him.

Just the opposite.

In another reflexive movement, Sylvia curled her fingers into that hard flesh, those small digits barely budging the solid brick of muscle.

Her husband had been wiry. Lean to the point of gaunt. And not at all powerful as this man whom she now touched was.

Just then, the smooth wool fabric jumped under her palm, and, blushing, she managed to guide her hand back to her lap. For good measure, to keep herself from any further boldness, she clasped her palms.

Mayhap he'd not even noticed that forwardness.

She stole a sideways peek up at Clayton.

His heavy features were pained; had it been her brazen touch? Or the question that still hung in the air between them?

Reaching for the reticule at her feet, Sylvia fished out the folded sheet written in Valerie's hand. She held it over.

Clayton eyed it a moment. His gaze went to Sylvia's before moving guardedly back to the note she still held.

She shook the sheet, and he jumped. "It's words on paper. It's not going to bite you."

"Many men would say words on paper have proven at various points in history more dangerous than any physical threat."

That wasn't incorrect. "Take it, Clayton," she said impatiently.

Mumbling to himself, he unfolded the sheet and proceeded to scan his gaze along the words she and the other members of the society had crafted.

Several moments later . . . he was still reading.

Sylvia peered down at the handful of sentences there, hardly enough to merit this lengthy break in dialogue.

Invitation and Requirements for Honorary Membership.

1. Clayton Kearsley, Viscount St. John, has been approved as an honorary and temporary member.

2. Membership is to commence immediately, and your presence is requested each Tuesday and Thursday of every week for a period of one month.

3. The Viscount St. John is expected to share with his peers the goings-on of the Mismatch Society, as specifically allowed him and agreed upon by the membership.

4. Any information that is not approved but revealed to society at large will result in immediate expulsion.

"Ahem."

At last, he looked up. And by the endearing little pucker between his brows, he was as befuddled as he'd been before.

Sylvia leaned in and whispered, "This is generally where you explain how honored you are and say you're looking forward to your first meeting."

Clayton neatly folded the official document along its crease. When he spoke, he did so with measured words, as if he had carefully picked out and delicately handed over each one. "Please, let me begin by saying I am both grateful and deeply honored by your invitation."

She frowned. "This has the sounds of a declination."

"But I must decline." He confirmed that supposition. Clayton held over the note.

That was it? A handful of pretty words was all he thought to turn over for his rejection?

Sylvia refused to take the paper. Just as she refused to accept his eminently polite but wholly unacceptable no. "Why?"

"I can't attend your meetings."

He'd said no. It should not surprise her, given the fact that he already had such a low opinion of her society that he'd come around to shut it down. And yet, this was Clayton. Clayton wasn't the manner of man to treat a person differently because of their gender. It was why he'd kept company with Sylvia's wallflower self when she made her Come Out years earlier. Sylvia made no move to take the page. She was not letting him off that easy. "And whyever not?"

This time, there was a pained look to his features. "Because I have responsibilities." There was the matter of him finally getting to the business of finding a wife and securing his family's future. "Because it isn't proper. Because—"

Storming to her feet, Sylvia snatched the page from his fingers. "Because we are female," she finished, glaring down at him. Angry with him for being like the others. And even angrier for allowing herself to be disappointed by and in a man, yet again. "I expected different from you."

Clayton stood. A frown settled on his heavy features. "It isn't that, Sylvia."

For survival's sake, Sylvia opted to believe it was what she said, and that also helped refocus her on the sole reason for her presence this day. "I wanted to again speak on how . . . your sisters and I will expressly benefit from your presence at our meetings."

Clayton folded his arms at that barrel-wide chest. "Go on," he said warily.

Encouraged by that first real sign of engagement, she went on. "We've earned increasingly unfavorable attention from members of Polite Society." Specifically, gentlemen. Small-minded, arrogant gentlemen. Although with his arrival earlier in the week he'd demonstrated a similar thinking to those gentlemen, he was not like them. Their shared past together, along with the support he showed by allowing his sisters to attend the Mismatch meetings, was proof enough of that.

"And you are *concerned* with the unfavorable opinions you're receiving?" He sounded genuinely confused, only highlighting the fact of their past friendship. Because he knew she was not one who cared much about gossip.

And that there was a luxury Clayton, along with every man of every station, was afforded. A luxury no woman had: the ability to care or not care about opinions. Sylvia threaded her needle carefully. "Women are expected to be above reproach in every way. Ladies are expected to conduct themselves in a way that is seen as flawless. Having one's own opinions about life and institutions and politics and . . . and simply *living* are luxuries we are not permitted."

His gaze held hers. And within those deep, endless blue depths, she felt the connection. She felt him hearing her when not even her own mother did. As unfair as it was. As wrong as it was.

Resentment brought her mouth firming into a hard line. "I don't want to care, Clayton." She really didn't give a jot what opinions the world carried about her. "But at the same time, I have to." Yes, she was in the unfortunate position of having to care. Because of her son. Because of Vallen. However, she held herself back from mentioning him. Because she'd not secure Clayton's cooperation by invoking her son's name. No, even as she'd explain why she and the others had issued the invitation, she would not have Clayton come out of pity. She'd have him there because he wanted to be there.

Sylvia felt Clayton move his stare over her face. That smart, gentle gaze that looked at her. Truly looked at her. And that allowed her to ground herself and share with this man all the resentment that she had long carried, a resentment that had been exacerbated after she'd become a mother.

The tension left her jaw, and she angled herself so she might better face him. "When"—*I*—"women flout the rules of convention and society, their suitability as mothers and caregivers are called into question." As her mother had warned when Sylvia had moved out of her townhouse and in with Annalee and Valerie.

His gaze sharpened, and he drew up straighter. "Has someone threatened your claims to Vallen?" he asked, his tone sharper than she'd ever heard it. Because of her.

"No. Not . . ." Directly. But implicitly. If she said as much, if she indicated it was a possibility, she'd no doubt he would intervene and involve himself. She, however, didn't want him . . . that way. "Women have to be above reproach on everything. Even when they are doing something as simple as meeting with other people and sharing their views on society and existing institutions within that society, they run the risk of being deemed unfit. A wanton. A blight on society. All the while, men are permitted all those freedoms, whereas women have to acquiesce by establishing the veneer of respectability that society deems appropriate by having a man." She gestured to him.

"Me."

"You," she confirmed. "Provide validation. And if that means extending my membership to you, Clayton, so that the male members of society can have their fragile confidence and even more fragile egos massaged, then I'll do it. Because unfortunately my reputation, and the other ladies' reputations, do matter. And as such, if we have to entertain doing things repulsive to us, like asking you to report back out to the world at large about who we are and what we are doing, then I'll do it."

"Thank you for that," he said dryly.

"Even there." She pounced. "What I'm speaking to you about shouldn't offend, and that certainly shouldn't be the focus of what you heard from what I shared. Do I like you? Of course I do, Clayton. But I would be lying if I didn't express my frustration at having to care whether or not Polite Society approves of the Mismatch Society."

"Sylvia . . ."

"You cannot do it," she finished bluntly. "That is your decision. I'll not ask you again, and neither would I allow someone to join our membership who doesn't wish to be there."

He winced.

"I thank you for your time, Clayton. I shan't bother you again." Grabbing her reticule, she headed for the door.

Chapter 12

When Sylvia shut that door behind her, it didn't come with a slam, as he was certainly deserving of. But rather, it came with a faint and somehow more damning soft click.

More than half fearing he'd change his mind and charge after her, Clayton kept himself absolutely motionless.

Because he had no place attending her meetings. Or joining her society. Or having any intimate dealings with her. That was something he'd known as far back as her first London Season, when they'd kept one another company through the monotony of tedious affairs.

Knowing all that, however, didn't change anything.

For it had been one thing to turn his back on the request Norfolk had put to him all those years ago, to look after her. It was an altogether different matter when she had come to him, asking for help.

Clayton scrubbed a hand over his face.

It was the wrong thing to do.

You did that thing with your hand and your face . . .

For it forced him to recall Sylvia's visit, and remember her words. Ones that suggested she knew him too well. Those little details she was in possession of needlessly reminding him how, at one time, they'd been so very close. As such, she deserved far better from him.

He stared at the doorway, braced for an explosion from an army of Kearsley sisters storming in and blasting him as he deserved.

And yet oddly . . . that invasion did not come.

They did not come.

And proving to be a coward for a second time that afternoon, he headed quickly for the door, determined to get himself out of this and the overwhelming guilt threatening to drown him, and from the inevitable *visit* from his siblings.

Georges stood outside, his hand holding out Clayton's hat. "Thought you might be needing this, my lord."

"Thank you, Georges."

"I took the liberty of having your horse kept out front, waiting for you."

"I don't pay you nearly enough." In no small part because there were hardly the rich amounts they were all deserving of.

Guilt; it was the flavor of the day.

Georges bowed his head. "You are as generous as you are able, and gracious enough, for me to put that first."

It was another reminder of the precariousness that awaited not only his family but also the loyal men, women, and children who served this household.

Just like that, Sylvia and her favor and the quick leave she'd taken took root once more. Nay, his sisters were never going to be forgiving of this. Nor should they.

He made his way, with Georges following close behind, through his household, eyeing older crevices and nooks his sisters had a habit of popping out from behind. Only, the places were . . . empty. Eerily so. It only increased the greater sense of urgency of getting the hell out of here.

He reached the entrance to the foyer and skidded to a stop. Ah, so that was why they'd not invaded his offices or scared him at various turns.

All six of the Kearsley ladies—seven, when one included their mother—stood in wait in the foyer. That line extended out through the front door that sat open. Not a single one of them said anything. They just looked at Clayton with cynical stares better suited to an old lord with forty years of age on the oldest one of them.

"Forgive me, my lord," Georges said sheepishly. "Did I not mention the ladies had assembled?"

"No, Georges," he replied out the corner of his mouth. "You may have left out that detail."

"My apologies, my lord."

Though in truth his loyal butler, who even now rushed off, waving to each young lady as he went, didn't have the look or the sound of one who was apologetic. Of course, Clayton could well commiserate with being cornered by the Kearsley sisters.

"Hullo, Mother. Anwen, Cora." He greeted them one at a time as he went, forced to make the ignoble march of shame past each of his kin, and all for daring to reject Sylvia. "Delia . . ."

At last, he reached the outside steps.

Clayton's sisters' disappointed stares followed him all the way out of the townhouse.

"Shame!" Eris said from behind him. "For shame, Clayton."

"Cowards die many times before their deaths," Delia shouted.

He winced, that particularly accurate quote from Shakespeare finding its mark.

The moment he accepted the reins from a waiting servant and swung himself onto his mount, his sisters were forgotten and only one person remained the source of his focus.

Sylvia.

She'd assumed the reason for his rejection had been because she was a woman.

And in a way, she was not wrong. But it was not for the reasons that she'd believe. That low opinion that he'd let her to.

It was because of who she was, specifically as a woman. She was a lady he had spent the better part of three years avoiding. The woman whom he'd wanted, and if there hadn't been a curse, the one he would have pursued a future with. Instead, he'd put his yearnings aside, as the desire to see her happy above all else had driven him. It had driven him right into playing matchmaker between her and the ideal chap: Norfolk. Clayton's best friend in the whole world. In the end, she had known only hurt. And he was too much a coward to be around her, drowning in the guilt and regret at all the ways in which he'd failed her. Sentiments that would always be there.

And the situation surely wasn't as dire as she'd feared. Society gossiped about everything and everyone. *Or are you just saying that to alleviate the guilt of not being there for her? Of not doing what Norfolk asked and making sure she is well?*

Clayton fought off those uneasy musings.

Either way, there could be only one certainty: between her palpable disappointment and the manner in which she'd stormed out, this would mark the last time Sylvia voluntarily sought him out. And he should be only glad for it. At last, he'd created the separation between them that he'd desperately been trying to resurrect since her reemergence in his life. Albeit he'd done so unwittingly.

That satisfactory outcome should be all he focused on and, more, what he should be grateful for.

So why wasn't he? Why, as he rode through the crowded streets of North London, could he see still that glimmer of disappointment in her expressive blue eyes?

He arrived at his club, grateful to escape the company of females determined to be disappointed by and in him.

Landon lifted his hand in greeting. "I think the end is nigh," the other man said as Clayton pulled out a chair and seated himself. "First Scarsdale, suffering a broken heart. And now St. John, showing up late to a meeting."

"It's not a meeting. Not a formal one anyway," he muttered. A glass had already been set out in anticipation for him, while the two before his friends sat nearly bone dry at the bottom.

"He's hiding something."

"I'm not hiding anything," he said with a frown sent to Scarsdale that went unseen as both men were, at present, sharing a look. "It's not a secret. Not really."

This time, his friends fixed annoyingly amused stares on him. They'd try to upend him? "And really, a little notice would have been appreciated before you sent me flying off to Lady Norfolk's."

Landon broke into a laugh. "I tried to tell you."

"Yes, next time, when in possession of those details, try harder," Clayton said under his breath. "My sisters have formed an alliance with Lady Norfolk and . . ." He silenced himself. He'd already said too much. The "and" was definitely too much.

"And?" Landon leaned over with the bottle and poured some into Clayton's glass, fully attending him.

Alas, Landon wouldn't ever be one to let it go.

Scarsdale, less dejected but also with a heavy beard on his cheeks, stared on with more interest than he'd shown anything since his betrothal had fallen apart.

Clayton resisted the urge to squirm. "Following my visit, the members of the society—"

"Club," both men corrected.

"Actually, they prefer to be considered a society." He scoffed. "Something about clubs being for men who only do things like drink and . . ." His gaze landed squarely on the snifter of brandy and the glasses held by his friends and—he looked out—all the gentlemen at the club. Clayton set his drink down and pushed it aside. "Anyway, as I was saying, following my visit, the members spoke, and they believe it would be a good idea if I becameanhonorarymember."

Landon leaned forward. "What was that?"

"An honorary member. A temporary one, was how it was explained."

Landon laughed. "Surely you aren't considering th—"

Scarsdale shot up an arm. "I'll do it!" he croaked, scrambling forward so quickly he sent his glass tumbling. The remnants of the nearly empty snifter splattered amber drops upon the smooth mahogany. Unconcerned for that mess, Scarsdale rested an elbow in the tiny puddle of spilled brandy. "I should do it. Be the one to go there. And . . . see . . ."

"And see your former betrothed, the lovely Miss Gately," Landon drawled.

A flush splotched the swath of his face not covered by that hideous beard. "And see how she is doing," he said gruffly. "To make sure she is well and happy. Yes. That would be the purpose of my being there. Because then I would know . . ."

Clayton went absolutely still.

See how she is doing . . .

Make sure she is well and happy . . .

That would be the purpose of my being there . . . Because then I would know . . .

He closed his eyes. He'd spent all these years hating Norfolk so much that he'd failed to see that, in this, his former friend had been . . . correct. Clayton had let his hatred and guilt cloud his sense of right. He *should* have visited Sylvia. Not even out of an obligation to Norfolk but because she'd once been Clayton's friend.

And now, you choose this time, the moment when she probably won't want to see you . . .

Bloody, bloody hell.

"What is it, Saint?" Landon pressed Clayton.

"Someone should go there, and . . . verify that she is, in fact, well," he finally admitted. To himself as much as his friends.

The marquess's brow dipped. "We should verify that Scarsdale's Gately is well?"

The other man bristled. "I beg pardon. If anyone is going there to see if my Miss Gately—"

"Not Miss Gately," Clayton said, exasperated. *"Lady Norfolk."* Silence met that pronouncement. He cleared his throat. "She is . . . Norfolk's widow, and as such, one of us should be certain the lady is well. The lady's brother has been occupied with his new family. We should be certain she's . . . well."

Clayton's gut clenched. He had known that and still chosen to look the other way.

He braced for the onslaught of amusement, the deep chuckles. The robust laughter from Landon, who was given to fits of hilarity. There was an aberrant sobriety to the always lighthearted lord.

"Hmm," the marquess said, rubbing his chin in a study of contemplation. "You aren't wrong. I've heard Lord Prendergast has been troubled, thinking of his grandson living in such a household."

Clayton tensed as Sylvia's words from earlier came back to haunt him. He'd specifically asked if her role as mother had been called into question. She'd insisted that hadn't been the case. But . . . there had also been a hesitation there. And bastard that he was, he'd allowed himself to believe that which had been easier to see.

"Between the three of us," Landon was saying, "we should have invested at least some time into making sure the lady is doing fine. Widows are prey and all that."

Those muscles in his belly balled up all the more.

Yes, widows, in fact, were marks for bounders and scoundrels.

Just see that they are well. Occasionally check in on them. I know you have your own obligations and responsibilities . . .

Me. It was supposed to have been me. And in the face of Landon's virtue, he was struck with the depth of his own cowardice and absolute lack of honor. He'd owed it not to Norfolk. For what the late earl had intended, he could rot. But to Sylvia. Clayton's sense of obligation and responsibility belonged firmly with the young woman whom he'd paired with a faithless, feckless husband.

"Yes, as always," Landon murmured, "St. John isn't wrong." He nodded. "It shall be Scarsdale, then."

Clayton looked back at Landon in confusion. "*What* shall be Scarsdale?"

"The one responsible for visiting with the Mismatch Club," the gentleman in question clarified.

Landon pointed a finger in the other man's direction. "Precisely. That. The responsibility should fall to Scarsdale."

Clayton dragged his chair forward, the mahogany legs creaking along the floor noisily enough to attract the attention of nearby patrons. *"Whaaat?"*

Scarsdale bristled. "And just what is so shocking about the idea that I should be the one to go there?"

"I . . . You . . ." The other man hadn't seen much beyond the bottom of the bottle since the end of his betrothal. Not that Clayton would ever say as much. He wasn't the manner of man to go about kicking a fellow when he was down.

"Yes?" Scarsdale prodded.

Clayton looked to Landon for help.

Alas, there'd be none forthcoming there. The marquess turned up his palms, his meaning clear: Clayton was on his own with this one.

"It just makes sense that it should be me." He should have done this long ago. How was it that only today, after Sylvia had left, he should realize as much?

Frowning, it was Scarsdale's turn to make a silent appeal to Landon.

Landon tapped the table twice. "It actually makes sense that it's Scarsdale. He'll have the opportunity to check on his Miss Gately and also ensure that Lady Norfolk is well, and steer them from any potential scandals or precarious situations. Birds and stones and all," Landon explained, taking a sip from his brandy.

Killing two birds with one stone was really what he'd say?

"It's decided, then," Scarsdale said, wearing the first real smile Clayton had seen on him since he'd gone and made a muck of his betrothal.

"No."

Both men looked to Clayton. "No?"

He tried a different angle. "The lady asked for my help." *As had Norfolk* . . . That voice taunted and tormented. It was something he should've done long ago.

"And did you consent to do so?" Landon put to him.

Clayton squirmed. "I'm doing so now."

Scarsdale slapped a palm on the table, attracting more looks. "But you don't have a betrothed in there, St. John," he said tersely in a rare lack of affability.

Clayton spoke before he thought better of it. "Neither do you." As soon as the words left him, he flinched.

The brokenhearted lord's eyes bulged, and he scrambled forward, and Clayton hastily backed his chair away. "That came out entirely wrong." Words invariably did with him.

"Enough," Landon ordered, and Scarsdale sat back in his chair, glaring blackly at Clayton. "I don't see why this is a fight. It seems fairly straightforward. We were all friends with Norfolk; as such, any one of us attending Lady Norfolk should suffice."

"I agree," Scarsdale chimed in quickly.

With that both men proceeded to talk as though the matter had been settled. And mayhap for them, it had.

And Clayton should allow them to it. He should relent. He should happily let the other man to the task, and in that, he would be assured Sylvia was looked after by one of them, and he'd be spared from involving himself in her life.

Except she was his friend. And that had to matter more than his own selfish need for self-preservation. "He asked me." He spoke in tones so quiet that it failed to penetrate whatever discourse Scarsdale and Landon had moved on to. Clayton made himself say it again, this time more distinctly and loudly enough to be picked up on. "I said, he asked me to do it."

All focus shifted his way. And he wanted to leave. He wanted to flee. Anything other than admitting to this.

Landon shook his head. "I don't understand. What are you saying?"

Clayton's palms grew moist and his stomach revolted. How was it possible that even as he'd had years to wrap his brain around those final moments with Norfolk, he still didn't know *what* to say to the two men who had also called the earl "best friend." Forgetting his earlier resolve to leave the spirits untouched, Clayton, in search of liquid fortitude, grabbed his glass and drank deeply from it. He drained the contents, and wiped a hand across his mouth. "I was the last person he spoke to before that fight at Gentleman Jackson's."

Then he told them, taking care to leave out the most damning details, ones he would never breathe aloud for the pain they would surely bring Sylvia. Sylvia, who'd already been hurt far more than she ever should have been. He told them of Norfolk's request that day.

When he finished, he stared intently at the lone amber droplet clinging to the edge of his glass, unable to meet either man's gaze. Alas, the time for hiding had come to an end. Clayton looked up but could make nothing out of Scarsdale's or Landon's expressions.

"Why did you keep this to yourself all these years?"

With that, they proved better friends than Clayton, for they didn't bury his face in the shame, as he was deserving. Emotion formed thick and unforgiving in his throat, and he reached for his glass to drink it down before remembering the snifter was empty. But how to give voice to the truth—that he'd been unable to bring himself to face Sylvia in all her misery and know that he was the one responsible for it. He'd been the one to encourage a match that had proven disastrous and painful to her.

Wordlessly, Scarsdale refilled his glass.

"I didn't know what to say," he finally said, and there was no absolution, even in this. Because ultimately, the person whom he'd wronged most hadn't been Scarsdale. It hadn't been Landon. It hadn't even been Norfolk.

It had been Sylvia.

But to have mentioned her in any way would have invited questions that he himself wasn't even comfortable thinking in his own mind.

"I told myself the lady was well cared for and hardly needed further assistance from . . . us. Everyone knows Waterson to be a respectable, honorable chap." *Just like Norfolk,* a voice inside his head taunted. *You freed yourself of responsibility with the same assurances Norfolk did.* Guilt sent his stomach muscles spasming. "And then when Waterson found himself beaten up on the streets, we should have been there. One of us should have stepped up to at least inquire as to whether she was well."

He stopped, realizing he was rambling.

They didn't press him for the reason he'd been so defiant of Norfolk's wishes, and whether that lack of questioning was intentional or not, he was grateful for it.

"The fault is not yours alone," Scarsdale murmured, more magnanimous than moments earlier, when he'd been close to leaping across the table for Clayton's daring to snatch the role of honorary Mismatch Society member out from under him. "We all had an obligation to see that the lady was well . . . and we all collectively failed Norfolk."

Clayton clenched his hands so tight he left marks upon his palms. Norfolk could rot for his treachery. Would the other men feel the same were they to learn of those crimes? He couldn't say either way, and neither could he say it mattered. Spilling Norfolk's ugliest sins and crimes solved nothing.

"Well, there is a change to our original consensus." There'd been no consensus; Clayton bit the inside of his cheek to keep from pointing out as much to Landon. "It is decided. St. John will accept the invitation to join the lady's society, and confirm that all is well with Norfolk's widow . . . help keep her out of scandal. And then, perhaps, even Lord Prendergast might worry less, knowing we are involved?"

Yes, there were many benefits to Clayton joining Sylvia's group.

It was decided.

Neither would I allow someone to join our membership who doesn't wish to be there . . .

Now came the matter of finagling a second invitation to the society.

Chapter 13

"He *rejected* you." Emma Gately's whisper filled the meeting room.

"Did we truly expect anything else?" Brenna asked the group at large. "My brother is quite proper and would never do something as shocking as join a room full of revolutionary ladies."

"We are no revolutionaries," Miss Dobson whispered, stealing a frantic glance about, as if discovery were imminent. "Tell them, Annalee."

"Oh, I can say it aloud, but it doesn't mean it's not true." That other member of their leadership slurred the last word, then promptly dissolved into a great big snorting laugh.

She'd already begun drinking for the day. Not for the first time since Sylvia had issued Annalee an invitation and the other woman had moved in, Sylvia worried after her. Emotionally scarred by the memories she carried from whatever it was she'd witnessed at the Peterloo Massacre, the young woman's dependency on spirits and free living was well known amongst all. The other young ladies, the majority unjaded by life, however, appeared oblivious to Annalee's need for drink. Sylvia caught her slightly bloodshot gaze.

"I'm *fiiine*." Her roommate's assurances, however, emerged sloppy.

"Who is fine?" Anwen elevated her head and scanned the room. "Who is fine?"

"It is fine," Sylvia hastily put in, sparing her friend from scrutiny.

"What is fine?" the youngest of Clayton's attending sisters asked quizzically. "I'm confused."

Oh, hell. Sylvia had always been rot at dissembling. Fortunately, Valerie stepped forward to the rescue. "It is just fine that Lord St. John rejected our offer of membership," she put in smoothly, effortlessly redirecting the group away from Annalee's current inebriated state and back to the focus of the day's agenda.

"Whoever should say no to Lady Norfolk?" Miss Gately cried.

There were murmurs of assent from a loyal group of women who'd been more devoted to her than the man she'd married. It was a loyalty she didn't understand, and yet one she was so very deeply appreciative of.

"It does not matter," she lied. For she didn't know that it didn't matter. She'd seen so many benefits to Clayton's being part of their group. "It is important that all our members want to be here. As such, he didn't prove a fit."

"Hear, hear," Annalee said from around the cheroot clamped between her lips. She hammered away with her gavel, and a rumbling clamor went up as each member stomped the heels of her boots upon the floor.

While each woman had that moment of shared solidarity, Sylvia allowed herself her disappointment with Clayton. Nor had it been the first time that day. She'd not ever thought he would reject her offer. Before he'd introduced her to her husband, she and Clayton had been friends. Nor did she resent him for arranging the meeting that had ultimately led to her disastrous marriage. After all, it was hardly his fault that she'd gone and made a mistake, falling for the idea of Norman. But Clayton's having disappeared from her life? That was proving hard to understand . . . or forgive. She'd expected that he'd be supportive of her *and* his sisters. And that she could be a friend to him again.

"But," Anwen ventured when the room had quieted once more, "if Lady Norfolk believes it vital to secure support for our continued prosperity, does Clayton's rejection not mean that we are still at risk?" A pall descended on the parlor. "Are we still not at risk of losing members because their families worry about perception and reputation?"

Miss Dobson twisted her fingers.

Yes, that much was true. And Sylvia had even more to lose if her name continued to have scandal tied to it. Resentment burnt strong inside her at the double standard that was a woman's life. And frustration with Clayton, who could have helped her, but who'd chosen not to.

"What of Lord Waterson?" Miss Gately ventured.

"Married to a former courtesan and current music hall owner?" Annalee drawled. "Stuffy Waterson's days of lending respectability with his name are at an end."

Yes, that much was also true.

Sylvia glanced around at the young women who made up her membership. There was a despondency and silence to them. A dejectedness, the likes of which Sylvia had never witnessed from the always hopeful, feisty lot. Women she felt not only protective toward but also responsible for. From the moment they'd arrived at her doorstep, looking for her to lead a wave of change amongst Polite Society, she'd committed herself to them and their futures. They wouldn't become this quiet gathering for her. She'd not allow it.

Sylvia came quickly to her feet, and began to pace. "Yes, Lord St. John rejected our offer, but that doesn't mean our society must or will close." With every word spoken, the spines of the girls within her audience grew stiffer and straighter. "We will continue to talk. We will continue to discuss the future as we want it to look. We will continue to fight against the injustices that exist, ones that relegate women to the role of ornamental figures, where our opinions aren't welcome." She stopped in the middle of the room. "No matter how hard they try, they will not take from us the dreams we have for change and our plans to exact them."

And that was where she lost them.

"They are trying to shut us down!" Lady Lisbette Davies cried. "We are not going to meet anymore?"

"No," Sylvia hurried to interject. "That isn't what I . . ."

Alas, it was too late.

"It was rather inspiring . . . before that last part," Valerie said over the din.

Sylvia winced. "I should have stopped before that very last part."

"Given the current fears, I think that might have been the wisest course," her friend confirmed.

Cora slammed her fist against her open palm. "My brother *would* be the one to destroy the Mismatch Society."

That was enough. She'd not hold Clayton to blame. She'd not wanted his assistance because he pitied her or because he felt a sense of obligation. She'd wanted him, yes, because it benefited her and the group, but she also wanted him to want to be there as much as their other members. Sylvia lifted her hands in the air in a bid to bring calm to the members. "He did not destroy—" Her efforts were for naught. Each lady was lost in her own outrage.

The door opened, and Mrs. Flyaway appeared, wringing her hands, her face a study of agitation.

"What now?" Annalee laughed uproariously, as though she'd told the funniest of jests.

"What is it?" Sylvia called loudly enough to be heard over the group.

"There be another visitor, my lady. A gentleman. Insists on seeing you."

Again with this? "I'm not accepting visitors. If you would . . ." She attempted to turn her attention to the other ladies, but Mrs. Flyaway would not be deterred.

"But he insists he speak with you, my lady. Said it's his right."

That proved the shot necessary to quiet the din in the room. Or, at least, divert it to a new source of outrage.

"His right?" Valerie spat.

Miss Gately gasped. "How *dare* he?"

Annalee tapped the remnants of her cheroot next to the chocolate biscuit on her small porcelain dish. "Which angry papa is it this time?" she drawled.

Yes, such was how members were plucked from their midst. Previously *tolerant* fathers reached their limits and showed up, demanding their daughters accompany them home. Only for those ladies to never again be seen at the Mismatch Society.

Lady Lisbette and Miss Dobson drew closer to one another, clasping hands.

"Not a father," the old housekeeper said, then rushed to clarify. "At least, not anyone here's father."

"Then there is even less reason to see him, isn't there?" Sylvia said calmly, in a bid to instill a sense of ease amongst the troubled members. She turned back to the group. "Now—"

"It be the Marquess of Prendergast, my lady."

Sylvia's entire body jolted, her knee crashing against the side of the center table. Pain radiated up her leg. That discomfort was, however, forgotten. Her heart knocked a sickening thump against her rib cage.

She'd avoided him. She'd avoided all contact with her in-laws. From the moment she discovered her mother-in-law's involvement in a childhood fight ring and the role she'd played in coordinating her son's death, Sylvia had vowed such people would never be allowed near her or Vallen. Before this, her father-in-law had made a pest of himself, sending notes requesting and then demanding to see his grandson. Never, however, had he shown up at her doorstep.

And neither was it so uncomplicated as just sending him away. Because whether she liked it or not, his connection to her late husband and the child she'd given birth to had created a link that made the complete dissolution of a relationship between them impossible.

Out of the corner of her eye, she caught the looks the other women were casting one another.

"Do you want me to handle it?" Valerie's invitation came in hushed tones, a loyal, loving offer from a woman who'd been egregiously wronged by that family.

It only cemented that Sylvia needed to take this meeting herself. "No. I'll see to it. Where is His Lordship?"

Mrs. Flyaway cleared her throat. "Showed him to the drawing room, my lady. Didn't want to risk a repeat of when the last lordship arrived."

The housekeeper spoke of Clayton.

Whereas Clayton had adeptly handled a gathering of boisterous females calling him out and challenging him, Sylvia's father-in-law wouldn't prove as tolerant or as understanding. Stuffy and proper, and yet complicit in that fighting ring his wife had been willing to kill her son over, given the lengths he'd gone to protect his wife from being prosecuted, he was a dangerous man in his own right.

As Sylvia made her way through the household to meet her father-in-law, a pit formed in her belly. She'd made every effort to avoid any dealings with these people. They were a family of monsters and couldn't be trusted in any way. No good could come from his being here.

She reached the drawing room. The door stood open, with Mr. Flyaway waiting outside. After a quiet word of thanks, she dismissed the old fighter. He lingered a moment, his gaze straying over to the visitor and then back to Sylvia, then gave a reluctant nod and shuffled off. Sylvia drew a deep breath, eager to have this meeting over and done with, and entered.

Her father-in-law remained stationed at the front windows with his back to her, examining something he held in his fingers.

"Lord Prendergast," she greeted coolly, not wasting her time with false pleasantries.

The marquess tensed but didn't immediately face her. Rather it was a pointed pause, one where he was determined to deny her complete control over their meeting.

At last, he turned, and she struggled to mask her surprise.

It had been a year since she'd last seen him. That night, she'd been in disguise, a guest at his masquerade, secretly there with her sister to search for evidence of the marquess and marchioness's nefariousness.

Since then, his black hair had gone streaked with strips of white at his temples and wrapping about his head, like a crown that marked his advancing age. His eyes appeared sunken and his cheeks gone, and for a moment, she found pity for the haggard figure before her.

That weakening sentiment proved short-lived.

"You've ignored my letters," he said bluntly.

He'd always been direct, but before, when his son was alive, he'd possessed a charm that had dulled what had now become sharp edges. Edges that had grown increasingly more jagged with his wife's mental state having unraveled as it had. And as much as Sylvia wanted to hate him, she felt more pity for him . . . and his wife, whose unstableness marked her ill. Ill in ways that society went out of their way to avoid discussing, like a dirty secret people were more concerned with sweeping away than providing help that others—in this case, the marchioness—so desperately needed.

Sylvia pushed the door shut behind them. "There didn't seem a reason to respond, beyond the first one you sent." One where he'd put demands to her that involved Vallen's life. And where she promptly severed all ties in a bid to keep her son from the vicious family she'd married into.

The marquess compressed his thin lips into a harsh, cold line. "It is unnatural for a boy to be cut off from his grandfather."

There'd been a time when he would have never abandoned the veneer of civility. They'd all changed, though. "Why don't we sit, Lord Prendergast," she urged as she swept over and indicated the painted fauteuil near her. This discussion with her father-in-law had been inevitable. That he was a man of such power and influence that he'd even managed to sway the courts and spare his wife's life and imprisonment at Newgate, which she was deserving of, was proof enough of that. It was even more reason for Sylvia to be wary in her dealings with him.

His mouth hardened before he joined her. He waited until she was seated before doing so himself, revealing a hint of the polite gentleman he'd once been.

"I understand you have a desire to see Vallen," Sylvia began, proceeding with the utmost caution, drawing from years of practiced pleasantries and a perfect ladylike demeanor. "However, given the circumstances, I trust you understand my reservations."

"I understand nothing of the sort," he blustered. "The boy was born of my son and you'd deny me a relationship with him."

My God, the arrogance that was the man. He'd really make her spell it out, would he? Did he truly want her to breathe aloud the treachery and evil tied to the marquess and his wife? Sylvia had agreed to be silent, not only for her son's future but also out of consideration for Lady Prendergast's mental state. And still, that would not be enough for them? Sylvia resisted the powerful emotions boiling inside. He'd expect that of her. "You speak of natural versus unnatural, and yet, I believe we can both agree, after everything that has happened these past years, with your wife . . . it defies naturalness," she said as gently as she could. Filicide was a manner of heinous evil reserved for sick Greek tragedy.

A florid color splotched his crypt-like cheeks. "There is nothing wrong with my wife, Sylvia," he snapped. He immediately glanced about, his eyes filled with fear. At the prospect of discovery, of course.

She tightened her jaw.

Perhaps if he'd been less concerned with protecting his wife's reputation these years, and more focused on helping her when he knew just how very sick she was, then Norman wouldn't now be dead and their families in turmoil. Then it would have been a different turmoil Sylvia would have been dealing with: an empty, loveless marriage.

"You and I know that isn't true, Lord Prendergast," she said, letting go of some of the patience she'd shown him. "And you should have a care, as that is one of the reasons I have offered my silence."

"I am not speaking of my wife. Not with you and not with anyone. And it is in your best interest to not mention her."

His meaning was clear: Sylvia's reputation, as well as that of her son, were inextricably intertwined with the marquess and marchioness. It was yet again a great travesty and an unfairness that a person could be so judged just by their connection to such a vile group. It was why she allowed he was right in this, and that for the sake of her son, she had to be conscious of just how much she said. Sylvia tried a different appeal. "You loved your son very much, Lord Prendergast."

The way his haggard features twisted served as more confirmation of her statement than any words would.

"You hate that you were unable to protect him," she said softly. "You no doubt regret that he found himself hurt." The marquess sat stock still, his throat jumping as she spoke. "That is what I seek to do with my son." Sylvia willed him to see. "I want to keep him safe."

That was the moment she lost him. His eyes formed thin, merciless pricks. "From me?"

To hell with all men and their fragile egos. They were too self-centered to see that it wasn't really about them. But somehow, those were the only parts they ever heard. "Yes." And to hell with him if he couldn't understand that.

"I . . . see."

Sylvia tensed, hearing more within those two words, deciphering a deeper meaning. The woman who'd fallen in love with and married Lord Norfolk had been too naive and innocent to detect subtleties in speech. Not anymore. Still, she didn't give in to the overwhelming urge to demand an answer as to exactly what he was saying.

With a deliberate slowness to his movements, he stretched forward a hand and collected the child's soldier he had been holding upon her arrival.

Do not let him see how he's affecting you. Do not let him see you care in any way.

Lord Prendergast studied his palm, that crimson figurine a splash of garish red upon the sickly white pallor of his hand. "It hasn't been easy, finding a time to see you, Sylvia. Between all the letters that went without a reply from you, one can only gather that you've been inordinately busy. Of course"—as if distracted, he turned the soldier upside down, and she could connect with how the inanimate figure felt—"reading the papers, I'm learning the news. I've seen that with your little club"—*little club*—"you don't have the time for things ladies generally have time for."

Her son.

No, he would expect her to be above reproach, when all the while, his wife had been responsible for the greatest of atrocities. Sylvia slanted a look his way. "If you have something to say to me, I suggest you say it. Let's dispense with games."

Using the gilded arms of the rococo piece, the marquess levered himself to standing, his efforts more lazy than struggling. "Oh, I'm not playing games. I find the matter of being kept from my grandson deadly serious business."

Sylvia resisted the urge to shiver. She refused to give in and allow him the satisfaction of seeing that he'd caused her either unease or fear.

"I want to see my grandson. And I intend to. I've come today, respectable and nice, and that will not always be the case, Sylvia." He set Vallen's toy back on the table. "I'll give you some time to come 'round to the idea of me being in his life."

Or else.

Lord Prendergast took his leave, the unspoken words of warning hanging there in his parting. Real. A palpable threat that sent another frisson of fear through her. Because she knew this family, had learned the depth of their ruthlessness. Considering the marchioness had given the command for her son to be killed, and her husband had been willing to turn his cheek and forgive that evil, Sylvia did not doubt they'd think nothing of destroying her and those she loved.

There came a tentative knock at the door.

Mrs. Flyaway entered. "Company, my lady," she announced, and there could be no doubting by her beleaguered tones that she or her husband had been listening at the doorway through the marquess's visit.

Prendergast had returned. "Send him away," she clipped out. "I don't want the door opened to my father-in-law again."

"But it's not the marquess, my lady," Mrs. Flyaway whispered to Sylvia.

She frowned. Not the marquess? Who . . . ?

Clayton stepped forward, a smile on his face. "Hullo again, Sylvia."

Chapter 14

He'd not really expected a cheerful welcome, given the ending of their last meeting.

But neither had he anticipated the absolute blank set to her features. In her eyes.

It was gone in a moment.

"Claytonnn?"

The slight emphasis there on his name, along with the extra syllable she'd managed to squeeze into it, indicated the lady's surprise.

But not displeasure.

He'd take it.

"What are you doing here?" she blurted.

It was a fair question. And also one he'd expected. He'd spent the whole journey from White's to Waverton Street trying to think how to play this very exchange. In the end, what he'd come up with were the next words he spoke. "Well, given your earlier invitation, I thought it should not be such a surprise, my being here."

That was what he'd decided on. Pretending the outcome of their earlier meeting had been altogether different. After all, she'd been clear that, with his having rejected that membership, he would not be afforded the gift of joining, and as such, the only way to make that go away was to act as if it had never happened.

Endearing little creases of confusion puckered the place between her eyebrows. "But . . . you declined my offer."

"*Ohhhh, did* I?"

"Yes," she said with a slow nod.

He tapped his hand against the side of his leg. "I'm sure you might have misinterpreted what I said." Sylvia's eyes formed dangerous little slits, and Clayton quickly coughed into his fist. "That is to say, I was likely unclear and no doubt the cause of any misinterpretation."

She smiled wryly. "'Please, let me begin by saying I am both grateful and deeply honored by your invitation . . . But I must decline.' I should say that seems fairly clear."

Mrs. Flyaway snorted back a laugh, and Clayton felt his face go warm.

Sylvia showed him more mercy than he deserved. "Mrs. Flyaway, would you see a tray of refreshments readied?"

The housekeeper started to go.

"Refreshments really aren't necessary."

The old woman stopped in her tracks.

"Refreshments, please," Sylvia repeated.

"Yes, my lady." The housekeeper dropped a curtsy and bustled off.

"Do you know how long it takes to prepare tea and a tray of biscuits, Clayton?" Sylvia asked the moment they had the room to themselves.

"Uh . . ."

"Between the time it takes to make a walk to the kitchens and provide the instructions, it's no less than twenty-two minutes in this household. Do you know what that allows? Hmm?" She pushed the panel shut and leaned a shoulder against the lacquered door.

Clayton scratched at his hair. "I . . . do not." He wasn't really sure about much anymore.

"Twenty-two minutes where we might speak alone."

"Ah, of course. I did not think . . ." A rogue would've known. A gentleman adept at seduction and clandestine meetings would know how to steal those private interludes. All his friends would've known as much.

Pushing away from the door, Sylvia drifted closer, stopping before him. Her fingers found purchase along the sleeve of his forearm, and he couldn't breathe. He couldn't move. Or think. He very well may have ceased to exist, beyond the tunneling of sensation where she touched him. "What is this really about, Clayton?" she murmured.

He tried to open his mouth and tell her but found himself frozen. Not, this time, because words eluded him, but because her touch bewitched him. His muscles clenched and unclenched under her innocent caress. His body, however, cared not for the casualness of it. He was incapable of feeling and knowing anything other than the slight sensation, the magic, that came with her delicate touch.

He glanced down at the top of her bent head. Her loose curls, a hundred different shades of browns and blonde, glistened in the sun's rays. And the way she remained speechless with her stare fixed on his jacket sleeve, the both of them silent, he might almost believe she was as captivated by him. Which was preposterous.

She'd never been aware of him. Certainly not the way . . . a way he had no place noticing her.

That sobered him and gave him back his voice. "I'm accepting your offer of membership to the Mismatch Society." He paused. "That is, if it still stands?"

Sylvia slid her palm along his sleeve, and he swallowed rhythmically, that butterfly caress muted only by the light fabric of his wool coat. She twined her fingers with his. "That's not what I'm asking, Clayton," she said gently. "I'm asking *why*." Sylvia lightly squeezed his hands, and he glanced down, once again briefly distracted by the feel of their palms kissing.

"Because I want to." His baritone was grave and low to his own ears. A hoarse intonation he didn't recognize as his own. But his words were true. He did want to be here. "I want to be here," he repeated.

After all, he'd fought his friends for the right to that responsibility. But being here with her, in this moment, didn't feel so very much like obligation. And his mind backed off and shied away, terrified.

She drew back her hands, and he curled his fingers to keep from reaching for her. "What changed between your rejection and your leaving?"

What, indeed.

Clayton clasped his hands behind him and wandered several steps away from her.

Their friendship, if that was what one might've called those earlier days they'd shared, had taught him Sylvia was a proud woman. As such, she would never accept his being here if she believed he was motivated by pity. At last, he let himself face her. "I thought I had no place being here." And as he spoke, he uttered only truths—just ones, however, that were borrowed from the demons that had gripped him these past years. "I didn't see how I could help or contribute, Sylvia. Or think that you could truly want me here. What could I offer, really?"

The delicate planes of her heart-shaped face softened. "You always underestimated yourself, Clayton," she said softly, drifting over, floating, her step so graceful her skirts were silent as she moved. "You didn't realize you were better and more honorable than any man I've ever known."

I am undeserving of this, of her praise. I've failed her, and in so many ways.

"Yes," she murmured, "you are." Her fingers came up to stroke his cheek, staying his head, and he hadn't realized he'd been shaking it. In denial. And in rejection of the praise she offered.

"Does that mean you've reinstated my membership?" he asked hoarsely.

A smile danced at the edges of her full mouth.

She wore so many smiles. He'd never known there could be so many, and he wanted to find out just how many more there were.

It was a dangerous thought that should've sent him running fast. And one he'd allow himself the proper fear of later.

Because in this moment, as her smile dipped, some emotion flickered to life in Sylvia's eyes, darkening their already fathomless depths. Those eyes that moved as if in tandem with his own, searching his face as he searched hers.

He couldn't say in the moment who moved first. He didn't think he'd ever be able to say. Whose lips found the other's. Whose hands roved the first path.

Or perhaps it was just that they moved as one in perfect tandem.

Sylvia slipped her fingers inside his jacket and curled them in his long shirt, her nails pressing little crescents upon his chest. Marks he wished would remain forever imprinted upon him so he could commit the memory of her, and this embrace, for all time.

Moaning and panting as his mouth took hers in a primitive rawness he'd never believed himself capable of, she backed him up, and his knees collided with the edge of the sofa. He let himself collapse into it.

Sylvia went with him. Climbing atop him, she straddled him so that her skirts lay in a decadent tangle about them. He worked those silk garments up higher, and groaned at the feel of her. She was temptation incarnate, the real-life Eve of flesh and blood and fire and passion. And he Adam, hopeless to resist her. Clayton stroked his hands over the smooth, satiny expanse of her thighs, kneading the flesh, massaging it until keening little moans spilled from Sylvia's mouth and into his.

And he devoured that sound, the thrum of vibration caused by it an aphrodisiac. At the edges of his brain, reason attempted to chip away the hedonistic joy of just feeling.

I should stop. We should stop.

"*Nooo,*" she moaned pleadingly, confirming he'd spoken aloud.

And he was lost all the more.

Upon her marriage, Sylvia had come to believe there was something wrong with her.

Before her wedding night, there'd been an eager anticipation about all that was to come, lying in the arms of the man she'd believed she loved. That excitement had proven short-lived, to be replaced with a keen disappointment. For the moment she'd built in her mind to be something magical had instead proven awkward and uncomfortable and, upon her husband's hasty departure, lonely.

The sense of her inadequacy as a woman had been only strengthened with each hasty encounter that had felt—and she later realized had, in fact, been—obligatory.

It had been her fault. She was incapable of grand passion. Of the manner of butterflies and delirious sentiments she'd read about in the romance novels she'd sneaked and read without her mother's notice when she was a girl. That was why her husband hadn't sought out her bed. Or kissed her mouth. It was why he couldn't be bothered to remove her nightshift when he'd been trying to get his requisite heir.

Only to learn, after Hyde Park, and again, in this same man's arms, in Clayton's arms, that there was nothing at all wrong with her. That she was capable of passion. And now that she'd tasted it twice, she wanted to feast on it forever.

Curling her fingers against his nape, she angled his head so that she might better taste of him. Sliding her tongue against his, tasting that sleek flesh, tasting him.

There was a hint of figs, and it was no wonder that savory fruit was the nectar of the ancient gods and goddesses. And she wanted to eat more of it.

Sylvia suckled on the tip, and he returned the favor.

An ache, so sharp, so powerful, throbbed between her legs, a hunger that didn't know whether it wished to be pleasure or pain and had therefore spawned its own, more acute sensation. Sylvia pressed herself against Clayton and rubbed in the desperate desire to fill that empty void. It only deepened that yearning within.

And then he reached between them, finding that delicious pleasure pain, pressing a palm against her moist curls.

A hiss exploded from her, a surprised exhalation that emerged in the form of his name and was swallowed within the heat of his mouth.

Sylvia rubbed herself against him. Searching for more from that hand pleasuring her. Demanding more.

Needing it.

He slid a finger deep within her channel and stroked her. Teasing that nub.

The rise and fall of her hips grew more frantic, and overwhelmed, she drew back from Clayton's kiss. Burying her head in his neck, she ground herself harder against him and that relief he dangled before her.

He sank his spare palm into her buttocks, bringing their bodies even closer and deepening the glide of those long digits stroking her.

She moaned, and arching, she tossed her head back. She clenched her eyes tight, the brightness of the sun's rays too acute with the pleasure coursing through her.

"Sylvia." He panted her name. Again and again. Over and over. And the sound of it, hoarse and graveled, his melodious baritone unrecognizable for the shades of darkness and deepness to it. Because of her.

That threw her over, to a magical place she'd never thought to know, and she gave herself freely to it, exploding in a blinding flash of white. She screamed, and his mouth was immediately on hers, a beautiful absorption of the sound of her release that only drew the moment on. And she wanted it to. She wanted this bliss to go on forever. Desperate to prolong it, this, her first climax, she ground herself against the hand so expertly working her. Clenching her thighs about him.

Until she was replete.

Her entire body went weak.

She sagged against Clayton. Their chests heaved in a like, frantic rhythm, their breaths a tangle of ragged rasps. Closing her eyes, she turned her cheek against his chest, the soft wall of his jacket tickling a smile from her lips.

He pressed a trembling hand upon her back, and smoothed it over her. That tender touch soothing her, continuing to offer her body that which it needed in this new moment.

She'd never felt anything like this. She'd never imagined it could be this way.

She'd wanted it to. But she'd never believed this manner of dream would ever belong to her. And it had been . . . Clayton, her fellow wallflower, as she'd named them.

And her mind was too muddled from the pleasureful aftereffects of his touch to make sense of this. If any sense ever could be made of it. For now, all she knew was that—

Footfalls sounded in the hall.

She and Clayton stiffened.

Oh, hell.

As reality reared its unpleasant head.

"Was that twenty-two minutes?" he whispered, frantically tucking the damp curls that hung loose about her face back behind her ears.

She scrambled off Clayton's lap, hitting the floor hard and landing on her knees . . . just as Clayton came down on the opposite end of the rose-inlaid table.

The door opened, and this time, Lydia and Ava, two young servants Mrs. Flyaway had brought with her from the Rookeries, returned.

"Where is it?" Sylvia muttered to herself, scouring the floor for some imagined—

"I've found it!" Clayton cried, holding the crimson soldier aloft.

And she closed her eyes as he found that cover.

"You found it!" she cried, rushing to her feet. "How can I ever thank you?" Sylvia raced over to him, as if she hadn't just moments ago been coming undone in his arms and grinding herself against—

"Too much," he said, his lips barely moving as he issued that hushed warning.

They both went silent as Lydia and Ava deposited their respective trays upon the table, carefully arranging plates.

That mundane act brought Sylvia crashing back to the reality of social propriety. And what they'd done. She'd been shameful. A wanton in his arms. The wanton, in fact, that all society had recently taken to calling her.

Perhaps she was. Because she couldn't bring herself to care. Men took their pleasures and reveled in their passions, every day. Why should she allow herself to feel guilt for having shared what she had with Clayton?

"Anything else you need, my lady?" Ava asked.

"No. That will be all. Thank you."

"I have to leave," he said the moment the pair had gone.

He wouldn't meet her eyes. And she hated that. Because it suggested there was something wrong with what they'd shared.

"I recall business I have to see to." He was already rushing for the door.

That sprang Sylvia into movement, and she hastened after him. "Do you still intend to join our next meeting?"

"Of course." Clayton directed that answer to his timepiece.

With his return into her life, she only just recalled how much joy had come from being with him. Her marriage had been so miserable and, until Vallen's birth, her days so empty that she'd forgotten the happier times. And she would hate it forever, how that magical moment she'd longed for the whole of her adult life had become a divide between them . . .

"Clayton . . ." She laid a hand on his sleeve, and the muscles bunched under her fingers. "Nothing has changed between us. I don't want anything to change between us." *Please.*

He briefly closed his eyes. "Of course not, Sylvia."

And with that, he left.

Chapter 15

Upon his abrupt departure two days earlier from Sylvia's, she'd been adamant that nothing would change between them. And that nothing need be different because of their embrace.

She'd insisted there was no room and no place for awkwardness between them. She'd sworn none of what had transpired should result in any change in their relationship.

Nothing has changed between us. I don't want anything to change between us . . .

Nay, that hadn't been an embrace. That had been passion come alive.

She'd been in his arms, hot and hungry, and had keened and cried his name.

On the way out the door, he'd breathed the requisite sigh of relief that had come with her pronouncement.

Because that had been the fear. That he, in a moment of passion fueled by lust and insanity, had altered the once comfortable ease between them. And if he were being honest with himself now, he could acknowledge that fear had likely factored in his decision to not court her—the desire to not ruin what they'd had. Yet after he'd fled, there'd been fear, too. Her assurances had been made in the immediacy of the moment. Now, braced to join her and the members of her society, he didn't know whether those sentiments had held.

What if he had altered the special camaraderie they'd always shared?

For how could anything ever be the same between them?

Climbing the steps of her household on Waverton Street, he feared he was about to have confirmation of those very worries.

Clayton knocked and was greeted almost immediately.

Mr. Flyaway's expression lit when he saw him.

"Snagged yourself an invitation, did you?" He hurriedly stepped aside to allow Clayton entry.

"It appears that way. Unless the lady has changed her mind," he said as the unconventional butler used the heel of his boot to push the door shut.

Mr. Flyaway laughed.

Alas, Clayton held off on confirming that he hadn't in fact been kidding.

The servant nodded to the pole in Clayton's hand. "What have you there?" It was yet another boldness that would not be permitted in almost any other lord or lady's household. Not Clayton's, however. With their closeness to the lady and lack of formality, Sylvia's staff was very much like Clayton's household, and he was made all the more comfortable for it.

"Ah, following our last meeting, it occurred to me it would be far easier to get you one of the geared multiplying reels. Didn't want to send you on an almost impossible hunt for an American reel in our too-proud country," he said, handing over the gift.

Mr. Flyaway's mouth moved for several moments before he at last found his voice. "For me, is it?" He accepted the fishing pole with reverent hands. "Never had a gift, I did." While he tested the serpentine crank, the old servant angled his shoulder in a bid to conceal the tears in his eyes.

One of the many things his parents had passed down was the understanding that life was to be lived, shared, and enjoyed. And though Clayton vehemently disagreed with his father's and his grandfather's and his great-grandfather's willingness to marry for love, when they'd ultimately known the only end result was a shattered heart, he had come to appreciate sharing those items that might bring other people joy.

"I think you'll find this a superior reel to the Nottingham. Although"—Clayton dropped his voice—"it's unlikely you'll find another Englishman who'll agree about an American fishing reel."

Mr. Flyaway guffawed loudly. "You forget you're an Englishman, too, did you, my lord?"

"Only half. Other half Scottish." The cursed side that would smite him down in his youth. It was a sobering realization that was always with him.

With a degree of interest to rival his fascination with the rod, the butler looked up. "Scottish, are you?"

"Indeed. And quite proud of those roots."

Where most of their English family shunned those connections, the Kearsleys had been taught early on to celebrate that rebellious, strong, unconventional side.

"Well, now it explains me liking you and all." The butler flashed a largely toothless smile. "That and your taste in fishing. No doubt that's why Her Ladyship likes you!" Mr. Flyaway's eyes widened and he lowered the rod. "Her Ladyship! Distracted, I was; I forgot to tell her you'd arrived."

Clayton handed his cloak and hat off to a young footman who came to relieve him of those things.

"Early you be. Her Ladyship is going to like that," the old man said approvingly.

"Will she?" It was a detail, likely one of many, that Clayton didn't know about Sylvia, and it served as a reminder that with every moment spent with her, he acquired a deeper and deeper understanding of the lady and who she was. It also represented vulnerability for Clayton . . . this dangerous wanting to know even those little pieces, such as what Mr. Flyaway had revealed.

"Oh, yes. Doesn't much like people who can't be bothered with respecting her time. Not that I can blame the miss."

No, neither could Clayton.

A memory intruded.

Of a different sunny spring day.

"You're going to be late to your own damned wedding, Norfolk. Get on with it, would you?" Clayton demanded, checking his timepiece for the fifth time that morning.

Adjusting the diamond stickpin in his cravat, Norfolk belly-laughed and slapped Clayton on the back. "A better friend might be helping me plan my escape. And here's you trying to get me there on time."

"Clayton!"

He spun toward the voice, and any of the worries and reservations he'd had about seeing one another this day were put to rest. A wide smile wreathing her cheeks, Sylvia swept forward. "You're early!" She glanced about.

"I had business to attend this morning, and came from there." It was brotherly devotion that kept him from mentioning two of the society's four Kearsley members had still been sleeping.

Her gaze went to the fishing rod Mr. Flyaway had returned to caressing. Her brow creased. "What is—?"

The butler looked up. "This fine gent brought me a fishing rod, he did. An American one," he said on a loud whisper.

Sylvia's gaze whipped to Clayton. "That is . . . most generous," she said softly, and the tender glimmer in her eyes sent heat climbing up his neck.

"Aye, not a finer fellow there is," Mr. Flyaway declared.

Clayton coughed into his hand. "It was nothing, really."

"Of course it was," the old servant insisted. "Quite a fellow you are." And with that, Mr. Flyaway proceeded to launch into a lengthy soliloquy praising Clayton and his generosity. Through it, Clayton felt Sylvia's gaze upon him, and he resisted the urge to shift with the discomfort of her watching him. Because there was a warmth as she did. A claim of admiration and respect and something more . . . none of which he was deserving of.

Not from her.

Not when he'd turned his back on her for all these years, when he'd been responsible for introducing her to the last man who'd ever been deserving or worthy of her. Not that there had ever been one who was worthy of her. He'd known that the moment she'd made her Come Out, back when they'd first met.

"Most lords can't be bothered with a servant," the old butler was saying. "Not this one . . ."

While he continued on, lavishing praise on Clayton still, Clayton clasped his hands at his back and smiled sheepishly at Sylvia, who shared his smile.

"Some might find it peculiar," the old butler was saying. "A gent would join a ladies' club."

"Society," Clayton and Sylvia corrected as one.

"Aye, that. All the other gentlemen who've come around or written think they are better than what the misses are doing here. Not you. You are here."

"He is, isn't he?" Sylvia murmured, as if more to herself, her blonde lashes slanting down as she assessed him anew.

And for an endless moment sprung from the seeds of his own guilt, he expected she could see all the way through him to the secrets he carried, the real reason he stood before her now—atonement. It was there, and would be there, until he met whatever end awaited him.

Clayton cleared his throat, eager to cut off that exploratory search the other man had inadvertently brought to his being here. "Forgive me for arriving early," he said, fumbling for his late father's timepiece and directing his focus on the numbers there.

But he needn't have worried . . . for rescue came from the unlikeliest source.

A wild hammering that he knew all too well fell on the front door. Mr. Flyaway was already rushing over to let the guests in.

"Surprised?" Cora asked, sticking her tongue out. "Thought we'd still be sleeping, did you?" she asked as several unfamiliar ladies streamed through the entryway.

"Actually, I did," he drawled. The majority of the Kearsleys were notoriously heavy sleepers. And late wakers. He'd always been of the frame of mind that if he was to be cut down too soon, he'd not have wasted his time sleeping.

Cora's gasp of unwarranted indignation and outrage was drowned out by the growing assembly in the foyer.

"Oh, yes?" Brenna countered with a little smirk. "Is it that? Or were you just looking to spend a little time alone with Lady Norfolk?"

It took a moment to process that question over the cacophony, and when he did, Clayton's eyebrows shot up. "What?" he croaked.

His sister gave him a peculiar look. "That's it, isn't it? You were looking to speak with her about today's agenda before the rest of us. *Tsk-tsk.* That's presumptuous of you to join late and expect you should be privy to that information first."

Clayton didn't blink for a moment. And then a wave of relief swept over him. "Yes," he said quickly. Too quickly, by the suspicious narrowing of Brenna's catlike eyes. When he again spoke, Clayton made himself modulate his tone. "That is . . . you are correct. I hadn't thought of it in that light. I wouldn't presume to do so, again."

His sister continued to regard him distrustfully, and then she nodded. "See that you don't."

And when she hurried off to join the ladies now headed to the parlor, Clayton fell back and waited until he was the last in line before carrying on to join his first Mismatch Society meeting.

At the end of each meeting, the Mismatch Society drafted an agenda for the next gathering.

The agenda was an important one. All of them were. It was at each meeting, where the women present discussed and broke down existing ideas forced upon ladies since birth, and thought about them in a new way.

Some might argue the present discussion already taking place also represented the most important of any other to precede it. For it was at this one where they entertained the possibility each woman had been adamantly opposed to before—the prospect of marriage.

As such, Sylvia should be attending the ladies in the midst of that most important of conversations. After all, she was only one of three existing members to have entered into that expected-of-women state.

And yet, she wasn't at all able to focus . . . on the meeting. On the day's topic. Or any of the speakers.

Instead, her gaze continued to stray away from the other ladies present, and over to the newest addition to the Mismatch Society.

The most attentive of the group, Clayton leaned slightly forward, his brow furrowed with a deep intensity as he attended Miss Gately while she spoke about what she had previously desired in a marriage, and why she had no interest in reconsidering that uncertain state. Had she ever known a man to attend a woman so? Her own brother was usually so distracted—as if he were constantly sorting through parliamentary papers in his mind—that Sylvia was often an afterthought. After her quick courtship and then marriage, her husband had ceased to see her. It was as though she'd no longer existed as a person. He looked through her but never at her.

Clayton listened. He attended both his sisters and the women who had been, until this moment, strangers to him, with a like intensity.

And she didn't know what to make of it. Just as she didn't know what to make of his unconventional relationship with her butler, Mr. Flyaway. Earlier in the week—had it really only been a week?—when she'd come upon Clayton and the old fighter, she'd believed Clayton's kindness and friendliness toward the servant were orchestrated by nothing more than a desire to force his way into her household. Yes, her family had been friendly with the staff, but neither had they formed intimate connections with them.

Then he had come with a gift for Mr. Flyaway. Gruff-until-now Mr. Flyaway had all but melted under Clayton's unexpected kindness.

But was it really unexpected? Was it, when she'd known Clayton years ago and he'd kept company with her, treating her as though she were an equal, her gender not mattering as they'd conversed on the side of ballroom floors and formal card parties. He—

". . . what say you, Sylvia?"

Oh, hell.

All gazes swiveled her way, including that of the gentleman who'd been occupying all the corners of her brain and hadn't allowed space for . . . whatever it was the other members now looked to Sylvia about.

At her side, Lila's knee discreetly nudged Sylvia's own, and she peeked down at the notebook open on her sister's lap.

Lila circled a bubble around the words written there, and ever so faintly tapped her pencil against it.

What qualities would make a woman consider or reconsider marriage?

"My God, none!" she exclaimed.

Miss Gately gave a pleased nod as a series of protesting murmurs came from a larger number of the ladies present.

Sylvia had apparently delivered the response Miss Gately had sought, but also one that had been largely unpopular amongst the other members. She felt that disappointment as a livable force from the sister who sat beside her.

"It was merely a hypothetical," Anwen Kearsley said, pushing her loose spectacles back into place.

"We don't do marriage here, ladies," Annalee drawled. "That is why we are the Mismatch Society. Not the *Match* Society."

Sylvia froze . . . her heart thumping a little harder as it came to her in absolute, stunning clarity. "What if we've been wrong?"

"About marriage?" someone asked in a confusion-laden voice.

"No!" Sylvia was quick to explain. "About our restrictive policies that exclude women who might want to marry."

"We don't exclude all," Valerie pointed out, gesturing to Clara and Lila.

"But that is Lady Norfolk's family," Anwen pointed out, glaring when her sister threw her an elbow. "What? They are," she protested on a loud whisper.

And the other woman was not wrong. "We shouldn't be in the habit of dissuading conversation about marriage, either."

The young bespectacled woman grew several inches under Sylvia's support.

Sylvia felt Clayton's stare most keenly. Unlike the chattering group, he sat silent, his eyes probing.

It had never been easy for Sylvia to bare herself before anyone, particularly as it pertained to her marriage. Her failed marriage. No, Polite Society didn't know the ugliest details, ones that involved Valerie Bragger. But it had been no secret that Norman, just like nearly every other married lord in England, had a lover.

To consider and speak aloud an answer to the question the group now put to her, required her to share that which would exist only as dreams she'd once carried for herself and the marriage she had hoped to have.

Sylvia folded her hands, locking them at the fingers, in the dowager Countess of Waterson's manner, instilled in Sylvia since she'd been a little girl as a way to mask emotion. "Very well . . . If I were ever to con-template marriage"—which she wouldn't—"the gentleman would need to be as loyal as he was loving . . ." Her gaze inadvertently drifted over to Clayton. Clayton, who sat as still as a stone. His features as conceal-ing as the mask she'd worn to her in-laws' masquerade the night she'd hunted down the details around her husband's death. And she faltered. How much did Clayton know about what her marriage had been? She preferred the answer to be . . . next to nothing. For she didn't want Norman and his treachery to be something Clayton knew about and pitied her for. "He would be a friend," she murmured, making herself continue. "That love and loyalty and friendship would extend to my son and any children we had together."

"Such a father doesn't exist," Miss Gately muttered.

"I must disagree." Anwen spoke insistently. "My father was such a man."

In one of the first shows of agreement they'd come to in all their weeks at the Mismatch Society, the other Kearsley sisters nodded their concurrence.

Then their family had been blessed . . . And it also explained how Clayton had come to be tolerant of his sisters' visions and interests and accounted for the closeness that she'd come to see him share toward the ladies present, along with the littlest of his sisters.

Warming to her talk, Sylvia continued. "To even begin to think about marrying, the gentleman would need to value both me and my opinion. I would be permitted equal say over all decision-making as it pertained to estate business and not just"—wryness brought her lips twisting—"household affairs." Leaving that dullest task for her responsibility, which her husband had refused to take a role in. All the while never discussing any other business matters with her. "In short, I'd be a partner and not a prisoner in that institution." She turned up her palms on the now silent room. "As such, it is something that cannot be. For men are simply incapable of it."

Lila protested.

"That is, with the exception of a handful of men." Sylvia, however, wasn't inclined to find herself digging through that haystack in search of a lone needle.

Her cynical but matter-of-fact, accurate speech brought the group to a collective quiet.

"*Ohhhh . . .* is that *really* true?"

All gazes—Sylvia's, too—swiveled over to Clayton, the lone male member, who'd chosen this moment to speak his first public words at the Mismatch Society.

An adorable blush filled his cheeks, and he squirmed uncomfortably in his chair. "That is, not what Sylvia . . . Lady Norfolk"—he amended when eyebrows went up—"said about her wishes."

"Requirements," Cora corrected.

He shook his head slowly. "I don't . . ."

"See the difference?" his sister drawled. Leaning across Cora, Brenna patted him on the knee. "*Of course* you don't."

The sisters, delighted in their efforts to educate their brother, weren't wrong. But neither were they being entirely fair with Clayton, either. In his being here and his willingness to listen and discuss, he'd already proven himself the exception to most men.

Anwen took mercy on a floundering Clayton. "Wishes imply Lady Norfolk would hope for but might settle for something different," she said in a gentle way that indicated a deeper closeness to this particular pair of siblings. "A *requirement* means she wouldn't even entertain the possibility unless a gentleman was in possession of all the attributes and qualities she so listed."

"Men, by virtue of being men," Sylvia explained, bringing Clayton's focus back to her, "are incapable of offering all that. Those, however, are my requirements." She turned back to the group, looking for the next woman to share an opinion of what would allow her to contemplate that prison sentence of an institution.

Alas, Clayton was apparently not content to let the discussion take that next turn. "But . . ."

"We've moved on, Clayton," Cora chided.

"No." Sylvia raised a palm. "We should hear him as we would any other member." She returned her attention to Clayton, as did all the other ladies present.

There was still a tautness to his frame; however, he appeared more at ease than when he'd first begun speaking. "It would be unfair to cast all men as the same."

"Yes, it would be." Pouring her first whiskey of the morn, Annalee snorted a laugh. "If they *weren't* all the same, that was." She toasted Clayton, her movements slightly jerky, and she sloshed tiny droplets of the blond brew onto her fingers, indicating it was likely only the first drink the society had seen her take that day.

To Clayton's credit, he didn't so much as blink at the sight of a lady indulging in spirits, and at this early hour, no less. Nor did he visibly chafe at being laughed at, either, as all other too-proud men would. "Some men are both capable of that love and devotion and would allow their wives to be actual partners." His gaze slid from Annalee and leveled on Sylvia, his words, along with his stare, penetrating her. Slicing into her with all the wishes and hopes she'd carried and leaving her exposed once more to the regrets for what had been, and what she'd wanted her life to be.

All things that could never be. "You and I both speak of an ideal. But it's nothing more than that," she said, both regretting and resenting her inability to stymie the bitterness that coated her response. "Men want to protect and defend. They want to coddle and keep safe. And even more, they want their power: Over politics." Parliament, where women couldn't even attend to observe the laws in discussion. "Over their families. In short, they do not want a partner. Not truly."

And all those painfully learned truths were the collective reasons Sylvia would never marry again. Ever.

Clayton looked stricken. As no doubt any man would be upon listening to Sylvia's opinion . . . And yet there was something more there.

Some emotion, some thought . . . just something she couldn't identify or name. And it sent unease traipsing along the small of her back.

"I don't see it that way," he said, his baritone a shade deeper and darker, his gaze and attention entirely hers, as hers belonged to him. At some point, the rest of the room and members had melted away. "Just as I don't see the desire to care for and worry after and look after someone a selfish one."

She came forward in her seat, the painted-blue French tea table all that was between them. "A woman doesn't require someone to care after her. She isn't a child. She isn't a babe in need of protecting from herself. Women, like men, are born with free will. And with that comes the right to make decisions and mistakes, even if that means she is hurt for them. They are still her own. Or they should be . . ."

As it required clarifying, several members chimed in, "Men . . ."

"I would argue the desire to see a person cared for and loved isn't reserved for men alone," Clayton said quietly. "I should hope women would seek to offer the same to their husbands."

And just like that, he knocked her back in her seat, and the argument from her lips. For he hadn't been speaking of an arrangement that elevated a husband into the role of provider and protector, but rather one that saw women as equally capable. And God help Sylvia . . . Her heart unfurled from the black cocoon of cynicism it had been wrapped within as a giddy lightness she'd never thought to again know burst back to life in her breast.

"Lord St. John isn't at all wrong in believing that such marriages exist," her sister-in-law, Clara, put forward, and Sylvia was ever so grateful for the interruption that broke the enigmatic pull between her and Clayton. "I should know . . ." The former courtesan smiled. "I have one. However"—she raised her voice a slight decibel when a chatter rolled around the room—"I should also remark that Sylvia is also correct. Men have this sense of needing to look after a woman. It is ingrained into society. All men. They can come to believe, as Lord St. John does, that women are equal partners, as entitled as any man to their business and lives and dreams; however, it also often requires a woman to train them in as much . . ." Clara shrugged. "And then, of course, only if a woman decides it is something she *wants* to invest her heart and energy in."

Valerie held up her pencil. "Should our next new order of business include the ways in which to train men for those women who decide they might or wish to enter into the married state?"

"I would vastly prefer we stick to the important task of advising women how and why to avoid that miserable state," Miss Gately volunteered.

Annalee hiccuped. "Agreed."

And Sylvia should, as well. And yet . . .

Valerie stared intently at Sylvia. "What say you, Madam Leader?"

Madam Leader.

It was a term that had been affectionately and teasingly coined by her living companions after a trio of ladies had arrived on their doorstep and asked to join the society Sylvia hadn't known they'd formed.

"I . . ." Once more, she felt Clayton's gaze like a physical touch. Had even her brother, father, or husband given her such undivided attention? She'd always been an afterthought in the lives of the men who were supposed to love her. And there was something empowering in commanding that attention.

She drew in a breath and, before her own past resentments and bitterness could overwhelm her once more, spoke. "I believe that it would be wrong"—and had been wrong—"for us to be closed-minded of members who are interested in entering into that state . . . Affection and love should guide marriages." Sylvia, however, needn't have bothered with that latter statement, as chaos had already overwhelmed the room and drowned her out.

Her pronouncement was met with a series of gasps and shouts. "But . . . but . . ."

"Doesn't that go against shattering the institution of marriage?" Miss Dobson asked in a scandalized voice.

Unable to look at Valerie and Annalee, lest she see the disappointment there, she found Lila with her gaze.

"She is disbanding us, isn't she?" The fear-laden whisper sounded from somewhere in the room.

Cora glared at her brother. "This is all your fault."

Clayton lifted up his hands as if in surrender.

Annalee gave the gavel an emphatic *thump*. "We are not disbanding."

Valerie slid onto the love seat beside Sylvia. "What is it?"

What could she say to a gathering of women who'd coalesced under a vision of something different, a society without strictures placed upon them?

Her younger sister caught her eye, and with a smile, she nodded slowly.

That support gave her the strength to continue. Sylvia glided to her feet. "We came together with the purpose of helping women avoid marriages to unworthy men. Our mission grew to where we came to challenge the position we find ourselves in, as objects. Property. Maneuvered by our family and the world's expectations into the matrimonial state." As she spoke, she moved throughout the room, speaking directly to each lady, and to the room as a whole. "And yet"—she paused in the middle of the parlor—"we aren't a society that disavows the marriage state altogether." She just decried it for herself.

"Aren't we?" Lady Annalee asked on an exaggerated drawl.

Sylvia gave her friend a long look.

The other woman winked in return.

"I am confused," Lady Florence whispered loudly. "I thought that was the whole purpose of the society?"

Yes, and by the writings in the societal pages, that was what the world had come to see them as. And that was what they'd allowed themselves to be.

"Precisely." Valerie pointed a finger in agreement at the young lady's musings. "First admitting male members, and now contemplating marriage." She grimaced. "Not I."

Sylvia pounced. "And not I, either, but . . ." She turned her attention to the group. "Who are *we* to dictate whether a woman should or should not wish to marry? To do so makes us no different from everyone else who is dictating that a woman feel or think or do a certain thing. We can encourage others to imagine a world of freedom from marriage, should they so wish it, but to tell them not to marry? Is that truly our place?" Sylvia didn't allow them a chance to answer that rhetorically posed question. "We want a woman to have the right to choose what she wishes. Every woman must decide for herself whether or not to trust her heart to a man who is worthy."

It was a risk she, however, would never again take for herself.

When Sylvia concluded, she could have heard a pin dropping, that silence broken by the rustle of the rapid turning of Valerie's notebook pages. "So . . . you are proposing that we encourage freedom, liberty, and equality for women outside the bounds of marriage, but not dissuade members who find themselves . . . who . . ." The other woman's large lips curved in a grimace.

"Who fall in love," Lila helpfully supplied.

Valerie jabbed a finger in Lila's direction. "That." She glanced back at Sylvia. "Do I . . . understand the motion correctly?"

Sylvia nodded. "I believe you've summed it up sufficiently."

A hand went up.

"Yes, Brenna?"

"We don't have to marry, though, do we?" the young lady asked, even as she troubled her lower lip with her teeth. "You aren't advocating we be open or amenable to that state."

"Of course not. In fact, I would personally urge you to steer clear, but neither do I believe we should turn away young women who would like to marry."

Sylvia paused.

Will I protect my sisters by sacrificing myself in marriage? . . . Yes. Yes, I will, because they need their futures secure, and I need to know that if something happens to me, they will not fall at the mercies of a relative. And perhaps you'll judge me for that, but they come first, and I will happily make that sacrifice for them . . .

Her gaze slipped over to Clayton. An idea rooted around Sylvia's brain. "Or men," she murmured to herself.

Cora nodded. "We shall stay, then."

"Oh, hush," Anwen muttered. "Neither of you were going anywhere."

"Are there any objections to the proposed amendment of not completely shunning those amenable to the institution of marriage?"

All the women looked at one another and shook their heads.

"Those in favor of avoiding any possible redeeming discussions on the institution of marriage, indicate so with a show of hands." Miss Gately was the first to let her hand fly, along with three of the other women present. "And those in favor of helping women train their spouses or prospective spouses, indicate with a hand and an 'aye.'"

There had been a time, not so very long ago, when even a positive discussion on marriage would have been anathema to her. Since Clayton had reentered her life, Sylvia had reconsidered the absolute way in which she looked at women entering into marriage.

While Clayton sat there, the lone abstention, Sylvia couldn't quell the fear at all the other ways she found herself weakening toward this man.

And she realized there was just one thing to do . . .

Chapter 16

There were one thousand and one things Clayton should be doing and business he should be attending to. Such was the reality of the cursed Kearsley family. There were estates to get in order. There were sisters to look after. A mother. And with his recent decision, the need to find a wife. One whom he got along with, but also one who wouldn't be heartbroken when he died like his father before him. And an heir. He needed to see to that, too.

And yet, seated in his offices as he had been for the past two hours, since the conclusion of dinner, the page of his journal, but for one sentence, an assignment, remained blank.

Good God, he was going to be party to young women *training* men.

Or, he was . . . if he put words to paper.

As it was, he could think only of her.

Sylvia had this effortless ability to make other people look to her. Whereas some of the ladies present that morning had been adamant, refusing to consider Anwen's question about marriage, Sylvia had been tolerant. She'd been patient when most women in Polite Society had been only cruel toward her. She'd been open-minded, not shutting down those who were in possession of a different opinion than her own.

And he was reminded all over again of all the many reasons he'd liked her and respected her and enjoyed being with her. And he hated that he'd allowed himself to remember *all* that. Because it had been easier to forget just how very much he wanted her for his own. How he'd not even allowed himself the dream of a future with a woman such as her, because he'd known what his future was.

Of course, there'd been an arrogance even to that very thought, an improbable possibility that she could have loved him. And even as unlikely as it had been that Sylvia could have loved him, he loved her too much to risk the idea of hurting her. And so he'd let go of his dreams, sacrificing them so that she could have the real love she deserved.

Norfolk.

Resentment and rage brought his hands curling into fists.

What had it all been for? The life she'd thought she'd have, and the one Clayton now desperately wanted for her, had never been. Her cynicism toward marriage and love was a testament to that. But then it hadn't been a secret to the world that Norfolk had a lover. Such was the way of the peerage. They married and gave their name, but not their devotion. Those faithless unions so very different from that of Clayton's parents, who had entered into a love match. As such, Clayton had been so naive as to believe that because Sylvia and Norfolk had loved one another, their marriage would be a happy one.

Because he could've never known, he could have never imagined, that Norfolk wouldn't have fallen completely head over heels for Sylvia, forgetting and forsaking all other women. Just as it had been even more inconceivable that the affable man Clayton had called his best friend would have turned his marriage into any other cold, empty societal one.

Not for the first time since he'd departed Sylvia's household and that meeting, her words haunted him.

You and I both speak of an ideal. But it's nothing more than that . . . Men want to protect and defend. They want to coddle and keep safe. And even more, they want their power: Over politics. . . . Over their families. In short, they do not want a partner. Not truly . . .

And with that handful of sentences, she'd revealed so very much about her marriage to Norfolk . . . and what she had originally dreamed of.

She'd believed herself an obligation of Norfolk, the responsibility he was seeing to as the future marquess. Nor had she been wrong.

And in a way, wasn't that precisely what had brought Clayton back into her life? A sense of duty to see that she was happy and safe? His gut turned. It was entirely different. For so many reasons. The ultimate being he cared about her. And that surely superseded the original and main motive.

One that she would despise were she to discover the truth.

He steeled his jaw. *She won't.*

She couldn't. There was no way.

A figure slid into position at the front of his desk. "What are you doing?"

With a shout, Clayton exploded to his feet, his heart hammering wildly.

"Darling," he greeted the pale twin with the moniker he'd used since she was a babe, the only of his sisters to crawl over to him to be picked up. There'd always been a shared bond between them. "I didn't hear you."

"Yes, that much was clear," Daria said in her usual monotone voice. Leaning forward, she peered at the sheet that was upside down before her. "I *seeeee*." This time, it was the slightest uptick in the delivery of that elongated word, the tiniest bit of inflection to convey her disapproval.

Resplendent in the customary voluminous bombazine, black skirts she'd begun wearing before their father's death, since the age of five, a combination of sick morbidity and her own conviction that she, too, would die young, she plopped herself onto the arm of the leather armchair across from him. The wide hoop under the dress flipped up, exposing equally ample layers of midnight crinoline underneath. "You're working on the same assignment, too." There was an accusation there. No one else would've gathered it by the absolute lack of variation in her tonality. He, however, knew her too well for her disappointment to be a mystery.

He eyed her with a new wariness. "You know about the assignment?" Lord help him . . . Sylvia was going to admit all his sisters from four on to twenty-four.

"Of course I know about it," she said in that still deadened voice. When she'd first begun speaking in that peculiar cadence, it had been horrifying. Now, it was just part of who Daria was.

Clayton reclaimed his seat. "And you disapprove."

"Immensely so. I should miss everything. I shouldn't take part in any of the pleasures and experiences of my sisters that even *you* get to take part in." Her brow dipped ever so faintly in the lightest wrinkle. "Why, even *Eris* has been to the society."

"Not really. She never made it through the front door." He winked.

Daria remained singularly unimpressed. "You think to make light?"

Oh, hell. It was to be one of these somber sets with her, then. She alternated between carefree and fully consumed with the prospect of her own demise. "I would never presume to do so," he said, altering his original course, and meeting her solemnity.

"I shall never live life. I am destined to die experienceless."

From another girl, the words may have been melodramatic. But Clayton understood those fears. And the Kearsley experience was not the same as almost any other family's. Giving up his seat once more, he came around the desk and knelt on his haunches beside her. "The days you live are only unfulfilled if you let them remain unfulfilled. All you can do is live."

"*Pfft.*" Her little features tightened. "That isn't true, and you know it. Otherwise, you would have been married long ago. You always liked children. You would have had a babe by now. But you're afraid about time running out, too."

It was a chillingly accurate reading that delved entirely too deep. "No," he allowed. "You . . . are correct in some of that." All of it. She'd been right about all of it. And yet, he still couldn't bring himself to admit as much to his sister . . . or anyone.

"What is she like? Lady Norfolk, that is."

It took a moment to realize the conversation had taken another turn. And ironically, it was more dangerous and more uncomfortable than all the talk of dying young and unfulfilled dreams.

"She is . . . clever. And tolerant. And patient and kind. Willing to consider other opinions."

"If you're going to marry, I vote you marry her."

He swallowed wrong, saliva going down the incorrect tube and promptly choking him on his own spit.

Daria patted him quite sturdily and methodically between the shoulder blades. "Worry not," she said in those haunting tones. "You shan't die like this. I've already told you. It happens in a bedroom on a red blanket."

Yes, he was well aware of her prediction for how he'd meet his death. She was happy to inform each of her siblings as to how they would one day die.

"Furthermore, after Father, I've done research on preventing a person from choking to death."

"Splendid," he managed to get out, the word garbled.

"Are you quite done?" she asked without inflection when he was again properly breathing.

"If I say no, does that mean we don't have to continue this discussion?" he asked teasingly.

"Oh, this isn't a discussion, Clayton."

"Isn't it?"

Daria shook her head. "This is a lecture."

Yes, well, he wouldn't disagree with her there.

"It isn't enough that I've agreed to marry? Now I have you ladies hand-selecting my bride for me?"

His sister's gaze remained the barely blinking, always wide one that it was. "I have decided that you should put a good deal more effort into the woman you take for your bride. Otherwise, you run the risk of saddling us, and yourself, with someone who will only bring further heartbreak . . . and the last thing a cursed family needs is more reasons to be sad."

That was certainly one way of looking at it. Someday, when Daria was older, perhaps when he was gone, she, with her knowledge of the Kearsley curse, would understand, in terms of matters of the heart, how and why Clayton had come to live his life the way he had. But he knew for her to have sought him out that this was a matter that troubled her. As such, he buried his smile behind proper somberness. "I promise to think on what you've said, darling."

"Very good. See that you do. Carry on." With an almost ghostlike quality, she drifted to her feet and let herself out.

The moment the door closed with the faintest click behind her, he shook his head.

They wouldn't be content until he was married. Of course, they weren't wrong in the reasons they wished him to wed. Daria, however, had been the first to raise the very intimate and difficult-to-think-about question of who that woman would be. Because he'd always known who he wanted it to be. Just as he'd known all the reasons it couldn't be.

Sylvia.

He buried his head in his hands and shook it back and forth. Mayhap he was already dead. He was dead, and this was his hell. A world where he was thrust back into close and daily dealings with Sylvia, wanting her so desperately, and knowing all the reasons she couldn't be his.

Taptaptaptaptap—taptap.

That light, almost musical, rhythmic knock belonging to Cora served as all the announcement he needed for that particular sister. So Daria had sent reinforcements. "Enter. But be warned," he said even

203

as she opened the door. "Neither of you are discreet in your intentions for— Sylvia!" He remained kneeling on the ground, his head still cradled in his hands as he stared sideways at the visage of Cora and the woman beside her.

"What are you even saying?" Cora exclaimed, her tones entirely put out. "What intentions can I possibly have for Sylvia? She just arrived, asking to see you, and I only offered to show her."

"No! That isn't . . . I thought you were . . ." Yes, well, he couldn't very well say something about the fact that Daria had just left, after she'd sprung the idea of marriage between Clayton and Sylvia. "Cora." He cleared his throat before realizing he still knelt on the ground.

Sylvia stood over him, one of her very many smiles on her lips. "Lord Clayton," she greeted, extending a hand toward him, and he stared at those long fingers encased in a silvery satin that shimmered. And all he could think . . . All he could see was that hand pressed against his chest, curled in the fabric of his jacket as she keened his name.

His sister snorted, yanking him out of that desirous reverie. "My brother is entirely too male to do anything as commonsensical as accepting a lady's hand in help."

His whole face went hot, having been caught lusting after Sylvia as he had been. He gave thanks for his sister's incorrect assumption. "Hardly," he said, taking Sylvia's still extended palm. That attempt to show Cora and Sylvia that he wasn't such a pompous bastard proved the wrong decision.

Heat. It fired up his arm. A lightning strike of tingles that radiated from where he and Sylvia touched.

The moment he found his feet, Clayton swiftly drew back his palm and flexed his fingers, the feel of her too much. Every tendon and every muscle in his palm tensed with the need to again hold her.

"Do you require anything?" Cora asked, so casual and innocent and oblivious to the undercurrents of tension thrumming in the air.

"Refreshments," he blurted. "Can you see that Cook prepares a special tray?"

"Of course!" Cora's face lit as she gathered Sylvia's hands in her own. "You are going to absolutely adore her chocolate biscuits. You shall never want to leave!"

Sylvia slid her gaze briefly over to Clayton. "Between the chocolate biscuits and the company, I fear you might be right."

Clayton's heart jumped a beat.

Only to resume its very normal, very safe cadence at his younger sister's next words. "We ladies do have the most wonderful time together, don't we?"

"*Always,*" Sylvia said, squeezing Cora's hands in her own.

He should feel only contentment that his sisters had so connected with Sylvia and the Mismatch Society. And yet, with the envy he felt for his sister, in that moment, Clayton, who had thought himself to be a rather good brother, realized just how much of a selfish bastard he in fact was. For a moment sprung of irrationality, he'd thought Sylvia had spoken about desiring to be with him.

Clasping his hands behind him, he watched as his sister hurried off to see to the refreshments.

The moment the door had closed, Sylvia smiled. "We've secured twenty-two minutes."

"No. Given Cora's habit of sitting down in the kitchen to personally taste-test each of the dessert options, we have at least thirty-eight."

They shared a smile.

"Please," he offered, motioning to the leather seat previously occupied by Daria.

Sylvia did so, removing her gloves and resting them on the arms of the chair. Instead of taking a seat at the head of his desk, Clayton claimed the one nearest to Sylvia. "I wanted to begin by thanking you for being open-minded enough to attend our meetings." She reached for her gloves, toying with that fabric, revealing an unfamiliar uncertainty.

"Since we've begun spending time with one another, I've had time to consider what you said back in Hyde Park." Back when he'd made love to her mouth. "And you weren't wrong. In fact, you were correct about much where marriage is concerned."

"I was?" He sat up a little straighter. "That is . . . I *was*," he amended, altering that question into a statement.

Another smile, this the ghost of one. "Marriage is a requirement for most . . . women, and as you pointed out, men, alike. But being an obligation does not mean that there couldn't—that there *shouldn't*—be more." Her gaze grew distant, passing through him, so that he knew she wasn't seeing him. Rather seeing another. The ghost of the man who'd betrayed her in every way a man could betray a woman.

He went completely still on his seat, afraid that if he so much as moved she'd glance over and see the dreams he carried but had never allowed himself because of a damned curse. A curse he sometimes selfishly wished he could convince himself was silly to believe in so that he could pursue what he'd always hungered for—a future with her.

Sylvia glanced briefly down at her lap, and beat her gloves together in a distracted little rhythm. Except, when she lifted her eyes to his a moment later, he may as well have crafted the imagining of her earlier melancholy. "It doesn't mean that those who have to or choose to marry should not find a person who is perfectly suited for them." He nodded as she spoke. "It does not mean they aren't capable of forming a match with a person who brings them happiness, and who they might love and be affectionate with." She inhaled quietly. "I confess, your thoughts on marriage have had me reconsider that state."

He was still nodding before that last statement registered. Clayton stopped midshake of his head. He froze. His heart did that funny little jump again. At what she said. At the *implications*. Only because she'd allowed herself to consider the possibility of the future that she'd wanted and dreamed of and deserved. Not because of the possibility that she spoke of him. *Liar.* "That is good, Sylvia," he said quietly. "I would hate for you to not think of a different future for yourself."

Her bow-shaped lips moved, but no words were forthcoming. She recoiled and then found her voice. "My God. I'm not speaking about marriage for myself."

"You aren't?" Then what . . . ?

"No." She laughed. "I'm speaking about you, Clayton."

All words but for one failed him. *"Me?"*

Looking entirely too pleased with herself, Sylvia nodded.

Yes, he'd already resolved that he would marry. But it was not a conversation he intended to have with this woman. He shook his head. Praying that negative gesture would be enough to end any further talk on this topic with Sylvia.

Alas . . .

She nodded once more.

He sharpened his gaze on her. "Did you speak to my sister?"

"Which one?" She did a search, and then when her eyes landed back on him, they brightened. "Has one of them had a similar thought?"

"Never . . . mind. Just . . . no." And that was the truth. Everything she spoke of and suggested and raised here was "just no."

Clayton should have known Sylvia would never be so deterred. Catching the underside of the chair, she dragged her seat nearer his, so close their knees briefly touched, and he was grateful when she edged away, as that physical contact proved a distraction he didn't need through whatever *this* discussion was.

This time when she spoke, there was an excitedness that lent a rapidity to her words, perfectly paired with the animated glimmer in her eyes.

"After seeing you with Eris and observing the manner of brother you are to Cora, Anwen, and Brenna . . . that you aren't one to force them to make matches, but rather to do so yourself so they might be spared that decision, it occurred to me that you shouldn't have to settle into a cold union. That you should, in fact, be paired with someone who will be supportive of your sisters and the lifestyles you encourage them to live." Her eyes grew solemn. "And then I heard you speak at the Mismatch Society. And I listened to what you were saying. And I really heard you. Your words resonated, here." Sylvia touched a fist to her breast.

Whatever she'd heard hadn't been what he'd intended for her to hear.

The George I striking musical bracket clock marked each prolonged passing beat of silence following Sylvia's pronouncement.

Tick.

Tock.

Tick.

Tock.

Tick.

The clock proceeded to play a crisp, clear tune marking the start of a new hour.

And yet, somehow, when two minutes later the song had ceased and silence remained, Clayton was as dumbfounded as he'd been since the lady had finished speaking. Sylvia didn't press him through that protracted silence. Instead, she sat there, ever so patient and smiling, as if she'd just herself come up with the solution to achieving the world's peace. "You are offering to play . . . matchmaker for me?"

Sylvia beamed. "Yes!"

"No." Good God, no. A million times no.

Her expression dimmed, stealing the light from the room. "No?"

"No." As in, absolutely not. Any closeness with her was too much. Allowing this woman to be part of his life in such an intimate way? In *this* way? Never.

Ever.

And damned by the lady's hangdog expression if he didn't feel like the very worst of bullies. Clayton tried again, softening his rejection this time. After all, this was Sylvia. "Let me begin by saying I am grateful for your offer to help." He couched his reply in all the polite respect she was deserving of. "However, at this time, I am graciously declining."

"Why?"

She'd ask . . . why? But . . . he'd been polite and gracious and very decisive. That had merited a surefire end to this discussion that was absolutely not a discussion. And yet, he'd long known Sylvia was unlike anyone and everyone. As such, her defiance in accepting "no" should have come as no surprise.

He tried again, this time opting for bluntness. "I don't wish for your help . . . in this, Sylvia." He'd find a wife. But not like this.

Her smile found its way firmly back in place, dimpling both of her gently rounded cheeks. "Ah, but not wanting my help, and perhaps benefiting from it, are altogether different matters, aren't they, Clayton?"

Yes, she was correct on that score.

Once again, she tugged her chair closer to his, repositioning it so they faced one another, her pale-pink skirts against his sapphire-blue wool trousers, those colors clashing . . . not unlike they two as man and woman in this exchange, and so many times before. "What are you searching for in a wife, Clayton?" she murmured.

He tried to attend to her, and yet, near as they were, the rosewater scent she dabbed upon her skin proved a dizzying distraction.

"I don't . . ." His voice emerged gruff and garbled.

"A potential bride," she clarified, as if his distractedness were a product of that particular word, and not because of the effect she had upon his usually well-ordered senses.

It was a question that brought him up short.

What was he searching for in a bride? He'd not given specific thought to that question, having just arrived at the conclusion that he'd dragged his heels enough. That he needed to at last do this. He'd known he would one day have to do his responsibility by the St. John line. He'd known it would be to a woman who valued his sisters, but a match built on convenience and mutual respect . . . and certainly not love. Not when he knew he'd die young and leave a family behind.

It was what he'd known back when he'd first met this woman now before him.

He knew it because it was the very reason that, wanting her as he had, Clayton had stepped aside so that another man could have her.

When she'd always been all he'd wanted.

His pulse hammered away in his ears, nearly deafening and dulling all sounds and senses. The longer he spent with her, the more dangerous it was. The more he recalled just how badly he wanted her. He didn't doubt that he would spend his days making her as happy as he was able. But it was the uncertainty of their number that had always made her forbidden to him.

"Clayton?"

"You think to find me a bride." One who would be good for his family, and one who would keep him from Sylvia.

And he also wanted and needed to be sure that Sylvia was well. Allowing her, someone who cared as much as she did for his sisters, and who knew his sisters, made some weird kind of sense. "Fine," he gritted.

Her mouth formed a circle with her surprise. "You won't regret it."

And yet, as she rested a hand on his knee, he already did.

The muscles bunched up under her touch, and his eyes slid closed, and it was sheer lunacy to think about talking of marriage to another woman when this woman was touching him as she did. It was an innocent touch. And yet, her fingers began to move. She unfurled them, and let them glide up and down. Higher. And then back and forth. A siren's touch. And his breath grew haggard to his own ears.

Sylvia continued to stroke him, and he fell back in the leather folds of his seat, refusing to be the dastard who turned an innocent exchange into something she didn't intend.

Except . . . she followed him, climbing astride him so that her skirts fanned out about them.

He gulped, his throat struggling through a simple swallow.

"I'm wanton, aren't I?" she whispered, her question laden with both desire and guilt, and only one of those sentiments he wanted between them in this moment.

"You are perfect," he groaned, arching up as she leaned down, and their mouths met.

Chapter 17

You are perfect.

There had never been headier words spoken to Sylvia in a moment of passion than those three spoken by Clayton now.

Though there'd never really been *any* moment of passion. Not before Clayton.

And not after him.

Mayhap that was why she so desperately wanted to steal these moments in his arms. Because there couldn't be a forever with Clayton. Not for her. And he'd one day belong to another, but in this moment, like her, he, too, was free, and so they might make this magic where they could. There was no theft in this.

His mouth consumed hers. And she devoured his in return. Biting and licking and tasting of one another. She curled her fingers hard against his nape, anchoring him so that she could explore all of his mouth.

And while she did, his large palms moved over her thighs. And unlike the earlier gentleness to their previous embraces, this caress, this touch, was infused with a primal roughness, and she reveled in it. Moaning his name through their kiss, she thrust her hips, grinding herself against the flat wall of his muscled belly.

Then he filled his large, powerful hands with her buttocks. Squeezing her. Kneading her flesh until that place between her legs throbbed to an unbearable point that straddled the line of pleasure and pain, and moisture collected.

Overcome, she broke their kiss and buried her face in his neck. Sylvia inhaled deeply of him. The scent of bergamot that clung to his skin flooded her senses, and she'd never again taste of an orange without thinking of this man and the citrusy hue. Sylvia, however, wanted to know all of him. Even as her late husband had shamed her whenever she'd attempted such boldness. She didn't care. With those three words, "You are perfect," Clayton had freed her. And she wanted only him in this moment, and as such, she buried away old thoughts of the past, unpleasant encounters. Shimmying back on his lap, she reached between them and wrestled with the front flap of his trousers. And ultimately, she freed him. Her chest rose and fell, quickly and painfully, as she sat back to admire his length. Thick. Long. The enormous flesh had a perfect plum-tipped crown. Sylvia wrapped a fist about him.

He hissed through his teeth. "Sylvia." Just that, her name.

Desire clogged her senses and her veins as she began to stroke him. She, who'd previously been shamed whenever she expressed curiosity over lovemaking. She, who'd married a man who would make love to her only with the candles out and the blankets up. But at last she knew passion, and now having had a taste, how would she ever be sated?

Emboldened, she lightly squeezed Clayton's shaft, silken steel under her fingers. She pumped him. Working him in slow and steady up-and-down, rhythmic strokes.

Clayton's breath came in harsh, ragged respirations. She lifted her gaze; the harsh planes of his face were screwed up tight, his expression a study of concentration, as if he were tunneled on the feel of his pleasure and didn't want to let go. And the sight of him, the evidence of the effect of her touch, sent a sharper ache between her legs. Unwittingly, as she pleasured him, her hips moved in time to each glide of her fist.

Clayton's head fell back, and an endless groan spilled from his lips. Because of her. For the first time in her almost thirty years, she knew a woman's sense of triumph. She thrilled in his desire. A bead pearled on the tip of him, and she stroked the pad of her thumb over it, smearing the whole head in that soft crystal glaze.

Clayton's hips shot up, and she took that as an invitation for her curiosity. Bending her head, she flicked her tongue over him, indulging in her curiosity of that taste. Salty and purely masculine, and unlike anything she'd ever consumed.

"Sylvia," he groaned, dragging her up and into his arms.

Coming to his feet, Clayton lifted her from his lap, and she whimpered her protest. But he was only laying her down on the cool, smooth surface of his desk, an unlikely makeshift bedding under her as he came down over her. When all she'd ever known of lovemaking was a mattress and discomfort and awkwardness. Never had there been this beauty and splendor. Sylvia panted, fighting to get air into her lungs, and she pushed herself up onto her elbows as he shoved her skirts up and stepped between her legs.

He reached between them, untying the flimsy laces that shielded her mons, and then he was cupping her. Sliding a finger within her sodden channel. And then another . . . with such an infinite, agonizing slowness. Sylvia bit her lip, and moved against his hand. Sweat beaded her brow as she lifted into his forbidden caress.

"Do you like that?" he rasped, his voice harsher than she'd ever heard. This question, spoken in those ragged, gravelly tones, demanding in a way she'd never before heard him speak. And it raised her passion to an intensity that threatened to burn.

"*Yessss,*" she moaned, arching in time to the glide of his fingers.

He found the particular spot, one so heightened she cried out, and he buried that sound with his kiss, but not before it pealed around the room and lifted to the rafters, echoing there, lingering like an erotic symphony created by her and Clayton's passion for one another.

Nudging her legs apart with his knees, he spread her wider, and positioned himself against her damp curls. "Yes," she panted. "Yes." She needed this. She needed him. She needed all this. Just once. Once would be enough.

Clayton gripped her by the hips, sinking his fingers into that flesh, and then with one flex of his hips, he thrust deep. She screamed into his mouth, the feel of his length within her wet channel a bliss unlike anything she'd ever known.

Clayton grunted, those guttural sounds so raw and primal she moaned in time to them. Stroking her fingers down his back, hating the fabric that was a barrier between them, she held on tight to him as he moved. Rocking himself inside her. Withdrawing slowly and then filling her. All the while, his features were tight, as if every stroke was that blend of special torture that it was for her. Clayton pressed his damp brow against hers. "You are so beautiful."

She wasn't. Oh, she'd long known she wasn't ugly. But neither was she a manner of beauty who inspired sonnets or could make men fall in love at a glance. With this man, in his arms, she believed it. For the first time she felt beautiful, and she thrilled in it.

Clayton guided the bodice of her gown down, bearing her breasts to his gaze and attention. Lowering his hands, he palmed them, and Sylvia's eyes slid shut as she luxuriated in the feel of his touch. Then he buried his head within that flesh, and he worshipped the tip of the right mound. "Clayton," she pleaded, wrapping her legs about his waist and lifting into his thrusts. He suckled and teased. Flicking his tongue across that agonizingly sensitive crest.

She wanted this moment to go on forever. But also knew they danced with danger, discovery, and scandal. God help her again for the wanton she'd become, because she couldn't bring herself to care about anything beyond assuaging the incessant ache between her legs.

He withdrew from her and stilled; the head of him throbbed against her.

Agony. It was sharp and acute, and she whimpered.

"Do you want this?" he breathed against her ear.

And she knew that question moved beyond a need to confirm that this was, in fact, what she wanted. He wanted to hear the words. He wanted them from her lips. "I want this," she panted. Forcing her heavy lashes up, she lifted her eyes to his. "I want you."

His eyes darkened, passion turning them nearly black. And covering her lips with his once more, Clayton buried himself deep inside her.

There grew an increasing frenzy to his movements. Nay, to theirs. For in this moment, it was confusing who each of them were, as they'd merged as one. They moved together in passion's dance. Neither capable of words. Each of them reduced to animalistic grunts and moans. Ones that should have shocked and induced shame in her. But perhaps it was because this was Clayton, and she'd always been so very comfortable with him. It was only natural that they should be free in this, as well.

That pressure built, increasing. Steady. At each glide of his hips, at each stroke, he pulled her higher and higher to that magnificent precipice he'd brought her over several days ago. And she wanted that. She wanted to tumble from that magnificent cliff, so all she was, all she became, was that blinding flash of light and color.

He pumped himself deep inside her. And she lifted her hips to meet each downward thrust.

"Come for me," he ordered, his command a harsh rasp against her temple.

And that was all it took. Sylvia exploded, her body reaching that peak, and she surrendered to it on a cry she pressed against his mouth. She shuddered and shook, weeping from the force of her release.

Clayton's entire body stiffened, and then he withdrew, coming in shimmery arcs upon the surface of his desk. His hips still pumping all the while.

And then he collapsed atop her; catching his weight with his elbows, and framing her within the shield of his arms, Clayton held her.

Closing her eyes, Sylvia struggled to control her breathing.

"That probably shouldn't have happened," he whispered, his chest still rising and falling quickly. "But I am glad it did."

Her lips curved in a smile. "And I am, too." Her back throbbed. Her legs ached. And she'd change nothing. Not a single part of this moment. She wanted it to last . . . forever.

Even as it couldn't.

As if Clayton's unspoken thoughts followed her own, he straightened, and she bit the inside of her cheek, silently crying out at the loss.

And yet, inevitably reality needed to rear its head. Refreshments would be coming. Which meant so would people. Either his sister or a maid, and as such, they had to make the return to the present. There should be a greater sense of urgency and panic at the possibility of impending discovery. All there was, however, was regret at what was coming to an end.

Clayton used his kerchief to ever so gently clean Sylvia, before then seeing to himself. After he'd wiped the remnants of his seed from the desk, he saw to his garments, and Sylvia straightened her own. All the while, there was a silence between them. One that she was grateful for, as it allowed her some time to sort through and attempt to steady her tumultuous thoughts and everything she was feeling.

This moment with Clayton had been unlike anything she'd ever known. Nay, so many moments she'd shared with him these past days. From their explosive embrace in Hyde Park to their exchange in Sylvia's townhouse when she'd first tasted the most complete form of passion. Now . . . *this* mind-numbingly overwhelming passion.

When she had gone into his arms today, she'd done so with the understanding and expectation that this would be the last intimate encounter between them, given the terms of what she'd gotten him to agree to—helping him find a wife. It had made so much sense. It had also been how she'd rationalized making love to him here and now.

Only, when the door opened shortly and his sisters streamed in to see Sylvia, and Clayton ceded his offices to the women, one question whispered around inside her head: How could this one time with him ever be enough?

Chapter 18

Later that evening, determined to quash whatever madness this was with Clayton, Sylvia set herself up in her offices and devoted the night to the task of finding a perfect bride for him.

It was the only logical course to take. For every encounter with him proved dangerous in weakening her toward things she'd vowed to never again want—being so completely and thoroughly head over heels in love with a man. When love had already destroyed her.

It was why she was determined to do this thing now. She *should* be able to complete the list.

Given the members who were part of the Mismatch Society, there should be any number who would be a matrimonial fit for Clayton. And as his friend, it was a task she'd signed on to help him with.

Except she hadn't been able to bring herself to compose that list. The one with eligible ladies he might marry.

Drawing her knees up to her chest, Sylvia wrapped her arms around them and rested her chin there.

Why was it so difficult to put names upon that paper? After all, it had been her idea. And as a friend, it should be a relatively easy task to help him with.

What it shouldn't be was impossible.

But maybe that was because she cared so very much about him. Because their friendship went back years.

When Sylvia had made her London debut, she'd not been the diamond of the first waters. There'd been no rush of suitors or a bevy of admirers. Or even one.

Nor had she found herself the object of society's meanness.

Rather, she'd been largely invisible to them, standing on the side of ballroom dance floors. Partnered during sets with men whom her brother worked on parliamentary matters with. Or Henry's friends.

And then along had come Clayton. Entirely by chance. They'd found themselves standing beside one another at Lady Waverly's . . . and from that moment on, they had become friends. When until that time, until Clayton, she'd not known men and women could be friends.

In the earlier days of their friendship, however, Sylvia had thought there might have been more between them. And through their discussions and the stolen, laugh-filled moments they'd shared in alcoves, escaping the crush of crowds, it had seemed like an absolute certainty.

But there hadn't. Their friendship hadn't moved beyond that. There'd been no exchange where they pushed or challenged the boundary of that to see whether there was or could be something more.

Now, she wondered.

If the passion they'd now shared had come then, would their relationship have metamorphized into a romantic one?

There came a light knock, and she glanced up, grateful for the interruption.

Valerie hovered in the doorway. "You look busy. I can come back."

"Not at all," Sylvia said. She set aside her notes and stood to meet the woman who'd become her closest of friends.

Valerie joined her on the sofa and looked Sylvia's abandoned notepad over. "You're matchmaking."

Yes, because that's what she should be doing. "I was . . . composing a list of potential matches for Lord St. John." Or trying to. Trying and failing.

"I . . . see."

Sylvia didn't know what to make of that slight pause. Feeling the need to explain, she said, "I promised I'd help Lord St. John."

Nay . . . she'd offered to help. That was entirely different. She'd all but pleaded with Clayton for the pleasure of this very task.

"And . . . is this something you want to do?"

Was it something she wanted to do? It should be. "It's something I've agreed to take on." Feeling her friend's eyes on her, Sylvia made a clearing sound with her throat. "I know you're likely thinking, with my responsibilities to the society, that it's not a proper use of my efforts."

"No. That isn't what I'm thinking *or* saying." Valerie angled herself so she better faced Sylvia. "Is this something you *want* to do?" her friend repeated, with a slight emphasis added to her inflection this time.

Avoiding her eyes, Sylvia stared at the still empty page. "He's a friend."

"You are deliberately not answering," Valerie said gently.

Her friend wasn't wrong. And where these past months Annalee very much lived a separate life in the evenings, spending nights out at various balls and affairs, Sylvia and Valerie had come to spend most of their time together. Perhaps that was why the other woman saw things that Sylvia desperately didn't want her to.

"You like him," Valerie murmured.

"I do." She always had. "We've been friends," she hurried to explain. "We knew one another before Norman. It isn't more than that."

"But do you want there to be?"

"No!" That denial burst from her. Because she didn't. "Perhaps, if life had been different, and less complicated and . . ." Less everything.

She would have allowed herself to consider marriage. But she couldn't. Not again. Her husband's betrayal had nearly destroyed her. She wasn't strong enough to risk her heart again.

"Mayhap you can have more with him?"

"Would you give your heart to another?" she asked without intent to wound, wanting only to cement that connection they shared.

"Never," Valerie responded almost instantly. "But not for the reasons you believe." Pain twisted the young woman's features. "I haven't been entirely truthful with you or the society."

Sylvia tensed. "I don't . . . ?"

"I've said what I have about marriage and men, and yet . . ." Valerie's voice broke. "I don't feel all those things I've said I do. Even though he hurt me, and even though he betrayed me and lied to me, I still can't hate him as I should."

As Sylvia hated him. Her feelings for her husband had hardened long ago. And that was something she, no matter how close she became to Valerie, could never understand.

A little sob escaped the other woman, and Valerie tried to catch it in her fist. "And . . ." She briefly closed her eyes. "This surely makes me the worst friend in the world to admit this aloud, and to you of all people . . . but I love him still. And if he was still here, I don't know that I wouldn't want a future with him"—those words came as a nearly indistinct whisper—"not that I would have allowed myself to that future, had I known about you."

Sylvia's heart pulled. What must the other woman's heartbreak have been? Her relationship with Norman had predated Sylvia's courtship and marriage by years. And had there not been the obligations and responsibilities thrust upon the nobility, then Norman would have pursued the future he'd wanted with this woman before her.

"You hate me for saying that."

"God, no. *Never!*" Sylvia exclaimed. "I . . . can't myself understand how you're able to feel what you feel." Except . . . She paused. Perhaps because she'd never really loved Norman. She'd been entranced by him. Charmed. But there'd not been a deep, abiding love. She knew that now. And yet, their situations, hers and Valerie's, were not entirely the same. At all. Because Norman had loved Valerie. "But I would never pass judgment on you for feeling what you feel."

Valerie's eyes gleamed with tears, and she folded her arms around Sylvia. Sylvia hugged her in return. When they parted, Valerie scrubbed the backs of her hands over her cheeks. "And . . . the only reason I'm telling you this, when I'd rather let the guilt of it devour me, is because if there is even some small, remote chance that you do in fact love this man, then do not set him free."

"Oh, no. Clayton and I are just . . . just . . ." Sylvia floundered. What were they exactly? *Friends* was the immediate answer. Friends, however, did not make love. They didn't embrace as Sylvia and Clayton had, numerous times now. Fear sat low in her belly, and her mind continued to balk at that question she'd been forced to ponder as she played matchmaker that night for Clayton.

Her friend lifted an eyebrow.

"I don't know what we are," Sylvia brought herself to whisper.

"Dearest *friennnds*!"

They both looked up at that interruption. Her coronet of blonde curls slightly disheveled, her hem ripped and dragging behind her, Annalee staggered into the parlor.

The inebriated young woman giggled, that little laugh giving way to a watery hiccup as she collapsed onto the opposite edge of the upholstered settee and missed the seat, landing on the floor. "What are *weee* talking about?"

Her own concerns forgotten, Sylvia rushed to help Annalee up. Valerie was immediately at the other woman's side, and together they got her onto her feet and into the chair.

"It's our latest member, isn't it?" Annalee said in an outrageously loud, exaggerated whisper. She shook her finger under Valerie's nose, and then squinted. "Oops. Wrong one." She giggled, and this time proceeded to wag that digit in front of Sylvia's face. "I've told you before. Men, bad. Husbands, worse." Her eyes went to round circles. "Never tell me you're going to marry him."

"I'm not marrying anyone," Sylvia said in the soothing tones she always adopted when Annalee found herself in her current state. And even though the young socialite rarely found herself quite as blisteringly drunk as she was, the moments came often enough to indicate a real problem. "Annalee—"

The other woman cut her off with a groan. "No lecture now. Promise."

Valerie and Sylvia exchanged a look.

The talks she'd had with her sister's best friend were often met with resistance, an insistence that Annalee, in fact, didn't have the problem that she very clearly did. And because no good could come, and never had or would, in trying to reason with an intoxicated Annalee, Sylvia wouldn't. But it was still a matter that needed to be addressed, not just out of concern for Annalee, which Sylvia did feel plenty of . . . but because Sylvia had a son who resided here. Not only for his well-being but also for the image which Sylvia had to be cautious of.

"*Thasss* good . . . Do not like lectures. He tried to do it once," Annalee rambled. "And I told him precisely what I think. No one likes a lecture."

"He?" Valerie asked.

"Doesn't matter. *He* doesn't matter. Something does matter." Annalee tapped an index finger against the center of her forehead in a repeated motion. "What is it? What. Is it." Then she stopped. "There is one small problem," she slurred, reaching for the little flask she kept in a pocket sewn along the front of her skirts.

Sylvia hurried to relieve the other woman of her drink. "What?" With Annalee, when she was in her cups, it could be anything from the torn hem of her dress to the volatile relationship the young lady had with her family.

Annalee eyed her silver flask, which Sylvia handed over quickly to Valerie, who rushed across the room, depositing it on a table far away from the other woman. "It *miiiight* have to do with your father."

"My . . . ?" Sylvia glanced once more to Valerie; however, the other, equally confused woman lifted her shoulders in a shrug. Sylvia's father had been dead for several years now. Both friends were well aware of that.

Annalee shot an arm out, so quick that she nearly unseated herself once more. "Father-in-law. *Thassss* it."

Sylvia's heart dropped. "What is it?" she asked with an ever-growing dread.

"Came up to me, he did. Forlorn old man. Asking questions about you and Vallen."

Oh, God. Norman's father was tenacious. Unrelenting in his efforts to see her and have a relationship with his grandson. But blood did not family make. The marquess had done everything in his power to silence the scandal and the sins his wife was guilty of. Terrible ones that he had been well aware of over the years. And he'd been so eager to protect his image and his murderer wife, even at the expense of proper justice for his son. He'd sent notes to Sylvia. And most recently had paid a visit. But this? Seeking out one of the women with whom she lived? This was a new level that spoke to his desperation. "Why . . . how . . ." Sylvia made herself take a steadying breath and tried again. "What exactly did he say?"

"Cornered me when I was in the corridor, doing . . ." Annalee flashed a sheepish smile. "Well, that is neither here nor there." It was . . . but that again would have to wait until tomorrow. Until she was sober enough to have the talk and hear Sylvia's and Valerie's concerns.

"What did he say, Annalee?" Sylvia prodded, striving for patience even as panic was knocking around her breast. Her in-laws were ruthless.

"And then he said something about it being a scandal that I live with you. Because I'm a scandalous woman. And that no grandson of his should live in a house with a woman like me."

Storming to her feet, Sylvia began to pace. "That bastard," she seethed.

"He was also verrra curious about Lord St. John . . . said it was quite unconventional annnd interesting that a gentleman as respected as he would ever join us . . . He was pressing me for information about the viscount, but I refused to sayyy anything other than how honorable and good he was to join his sisters and us and have an open mind about the work we were doing."

Adrenaline added a quickness to Sylvia's strides as she walked the same path back and forth over the Aubusson carpet. She gave a pleased nod. "Good. That was perfect." Mayhap this wasn't so very terrible, after all.

Annalee ducked her chin against her chest and slumped in her seat like a child prepared for a good scolding. "And I might have said some other thiiings . . . ," she mumbled.

Annalee's words brought Sylvia to an abrupt stop.

Concern flashed in Valerie's eyes. "What did you say?" Her friend asked the exact question Sylvia had wanted to but was too afraid to formulate.

"I told him he had no power over us. I told him to leave Sylvia alone. I told him we didn't answer to anyone." Sylvia's eyes slid closed at Annalee's recitation. For she knew, with a knowing of who the marquess and marchioness were, how he would respond to that. And worse, the implications for Sylvia and her son.

When no one was quick to respond, Annalee dropped the back of her hand over her eyes. "I *wasss* trying to prove we did not fear him."

"Instead, you baited him," Valerie whispered, with horror blanching her skin of color.

Sylvia made herself take a small, quiet breath. For all the fear that came about her and Vallen, she was not so selfish as to be unaware of the terror that her friend likely felt. Valerie had been made to fight as a child at the pleasure of the marchioness. Those were the only details she'd revealed about her dealings with Norman's family. But it had been enough for Sylvia to know Valerie had endured an everlasting hell. None of them were safe if he decided to come after them. And if Sylvia had only had herself to worry about, she'd tell the bastard to come and get her. She'd dare him to do his worst.

But there wasn't just herself to think about.

There was her son.

The need for respectability wasn't something she had the luxury of *not* caring about. That had been the entire reason she'd made the effort to include Clayton in the Mismatch Society—he, a pillar of society and a friend but still a man, when their group had agreed to not allow membership. And now, the threat posed by her father-in-law had only been exacerbated.

The life went out of her legs, and Sylvia collapsed onto the edge of the nearest seat.

"I'm so sorry," Annalee whispered as she entered what Sylvia had come to find was the melancholy that inevitably followed her euphoria from drink.

"It is fine." Except . . . it very likely wasn't.

Damn it all to hell. She hadn't doubted, when the marquess had visited and then left, that he would have simply accepted her rejection for what it was. But all this time she had spent with Clayton, Sylvia hadn't let herself worry. Because she'd been so very busy laughing and smiling and just generally being lighthearted again.

Another person might have judged her on that admission.

And how her life would have been so different had she married such a man.

But there was little point in thinking of it. They had not been romantic . . . and Clayton had ultimately introduced her to his best friend, and the rest of Sylvia's relationship with Norman and her friendship with Clayton had become history.

Putting on a brave face, Sylvia stood. "There is no point worrying about anything this evening. Why don't you find your rooms?" Together, she and Valerie helped their inebriated friend stand.

Annalee let her head roll against Sylvia's shoulder. "You are so very good to me. Better than I deserve." She let her head fall the other way, against Valerie. "You're both so very good."

"We are going to talk again when you're more yourself tomorrow," Sylvia promised when they reached the door.

Annalee released a sigh that ended on a watery little hiccup. "*Stoooop.* I am perfectly well. Very very very well," she slurred as they headed from the room. Annalee stopped in her tracks, forcing both young women to stop with her. "Did I already say 'very well'?"

"You did," Valerie murmured, her arm around the other woman's narrow waist. They reached the hall and nearly collided with Lydia, one of the maids. It was either a sign of the young woman's professionalism that she didn't so much as blink at the sight of one of her mistresses three sheets to the wind or, the more likely, that she'd become accustomed to such a sight.

"Sorry, my ladies. Miss," she added for Valerie. Lydia dropped a curtsy. "The little master is awake. He had a nightmare and is asking for his mum."

"I have her," Valerie said in hushed tones. "Go see to him."

"I can help, my lady." Lydia was already moving to Annalee's other side and stepping in for Sylvia.

Sylvia rushed onward for the nurseries . . . the threat posed by her in-laws lingering still.

Chapter 19

The next day, Clayton received the most unlikely summons: one that requested his company and presence at Hyde Park . . . along with the company of his youngest sister, Eris.

"Daria was quite upset, she was," Eris prattled happily as she skipped at his side down the graveled walking path. "She wanted to come. All of our sisters wanted to." The little girl puffed her chest out with pride. "But I get to."

"Quite the lucky one you are," he said, ruffling the top of her already tangled brown curls.

Eris continued to chatter on.

No, this was certainly not the next meeting he had anticipated between him and Sylvia.

What did you expect? That when she sent around a note, it would be exclusively for you? That after their passionate encounter, she should wish for more continued time alone? "You're a damned fool," he muttered.

"What was that?" Eris asked.

"Nothing. Nothing at all."

And yet . . . he had hope that she might have just wished for his company. Not for the purpose of matchmaking him. Not because of a child's wish to play with another child. Just because she wanted to be with him. Even as he knew there couldn't and shouldn't be more between them, that hadn't been able to stop him from wanting more.

This should be enough. And it would be enough. Because it had to be. For then his not taking a chance with the future on her years and years earlier would have been in vain. Otherwise, what had it all been for? Clayton not pursuing so much as the possibility of a future with Sylvia, out of a fear for a lack of his own future. Instead, he'd ceded her to Norfolk, because Norfolk would have been better for her anyway: Charming. Witty. Smooth with his words. The lady's life would have been a happy one. That was, anyway, what he'd told himself.

Norfolk's passing changed nothing. In fact, it only made whatever had grown between them even more complicated.

For either way, past, present, or future, she still couldn't be his.

Not that, given her intention to help marry him off to another, she appeared interested in that impossible future between them anyway.

Eris slipped her hand into his as she skipped along, pumping her little arm back and forth as if she used his hand as a half swing. "It isn't that I don't like you or playing with you," his sister was saying. "You're good . . . *enough*," Eris said matter-of-factly.

He chuckled. "Thank you for that."

"You're welcome," she said, wholly oblivious to sarcasm as only a child could be. Her eyes lit. "He's here!"

Clayton followed her chocolate-stained fingertips to the "he" in question.

His gaze landed on the little boy furiously waving his arms back and forth, before Clayton moved his focus over to Sylvia.

The early sun's rays played with the many shades of browns and golds that made up those luxurious strands he'd had between his fingers when they'd made love.

With a squeal, Eris went charging after Vallen, and the boy had already taken off in their game of chase. The young nursemaid hurried after the pair, close at their heels. Lengthening his stride, Clayton went on to meet Sylvia.

Once again, even with the intimacy of all they had shared, there was no awkwardness or discomfort. They had always been easy around one another. The moment he reached her, he removed his hat and bowed.

She smiled in greeting. "Thank you for bringing Eris to play."

"Thank you for thinking of it. She has been without other children for too long." Forever. Really, it had been as long as she'd been born. Clayton glanced about, noting other details.

Along with ten or so crimson-clad metal soldiers, a little makeshift desk had been set out.

"I thought we could begin," she said, urging him over to the blanket.

He took in that space with a new and wary interest. "Begin?"

Sylvia collected a leather notebook . . . the same one he'd observed her using during the Mismatch meeting. "To speak about your bride."

So it was to be a matchmaking date. Splendid. "I don't have a bride," he said dryly, desperately wishing to change the subject.

Her eyes twinkled. "No. That is rather the point."

It was likely wounded male pride that accounted for the flash of hurt at how quickly she'd moved on to partnering him off with someone else. Which was unfair on his part. After all, he was the one who'd stated his intentions to marry.

Humming to herself, Sylvia fished about the inside of her mahogany writing slope, and he was grateful that her attention was elsewhere, lest she see just how very miserable he was about the prospect of having this discussion. Nor was it just her. The idea of courting a woman, one whom he'd inevitably marry and leave a young widow, was generally not his favorite thing to consider. "Aha! Here it is." She held a larger, sharpened pencil aloft. Her triumphant expression gave way to confusion as her gaze landed on him still standing there.

Swallowing a sigh, Clayton made himself sit . . . as far as he possibly could from her, directly opposite, but with enough space between them so he didn't have to recollect all the ways in which they'd touched one another. And all the ways in which he wanted to do so again, here and now.

"An ignoble start to a marriage," he mumbled under his breath.

"What was that, Clayton?"

His mind raced. "A *noble* start to our . . ." Oh, hell . . . He was bad with words. He was rubbish with rhymes. And he was even worse at trying to feign an alternate response. "Let us begin." Because the sooner they started, the sooner they could stop.

"What do you wish for in a wife, Clayton?" she murmured, scooting closer to him so they sat side by side, hip to hip. Shoulder to shoulder.

This was to be his punishment, then. For having failed her, he would be forced to endure this close contact with her. Wanting what could never be. Wanting what he could never have.

He glanced down at the top of her brownish-blonde curls; the early-morn glow of the sun again played with her tresses, highlighting traces he'd never before noticed there. How could he be guilty of such an oversight? Clayton made himself focus on her question. What did he wish for in a wife? "She'll be kind to my family." Which wasn't and hadn't always been the case where his mother and sisters were concerned. "And we'll be faithful to one another."

"And love, of course."

It wasn't so much a question, but more of a statement from Sylvia. "Absolutely not." That was the last thing he would allow himself or the woman he eventually married.

Sylvia's head came flying up from that page, and he squirmed under the intensity of her frown. "You're jesting."

"I'm deadly serious." It was his pathetic attempt at humor, one she would not gather unless she knew all the details about the curse that followed his family. Which she didn't . . . And now, because of the agreement they'd struck, he had to share all. Less than eager to have that conversation, he shifted the course of their discussion. "And . . . this is something you want for yourself? Love." Because she deserved that. Because he'd always desperately wanted that for her. With her.

"I did," she said softly, her gaze falling briefly to the notes she'd made. "I don't . . . not anymore."

Clayton waited for her to say something else. To confide in him about her marriage.

"We're talking about you."

"Yes, but I'd rather talk about you."

A sharp little bark of laughter escaped her lips, and she nudged her shoulder against his in the same way she had when they'd stood keeping one another company on the side of ballroom floors. And he let her to the belief that he'd been speaking to her in jest. Her levity faded. "Of course you want a loving marriage."

Yes, it was what he wanted. But not what he could have. "No. I"—*need*—"want a partnership with a woman whom I respect and who respects me in turn."

Eris's laughter trilled in the distance, and he searched and found her racing over a slight rise with Vallen following suit. The boy paused and did a sweep of his surroundings; he stopped, his gaze landing on Sylvia.

Her son waved his fingers frantically, and Sylvia returned that acknowledgment, shaking both her palms in an overeager hello before blowing him a kiss.

Vallen shot a hand up, and closed his fist. Then he pressed his hand against his cheek as if he were planting the kiss there. The little boy raced off once more.

A wave of melancholy swept over Clayton. He was blessed to have the moments he did with his youngest sister. But he wanted to know children of his own. He wanted to know the close bond he saw play out daily between his mother and siblings. And the one Sylvia shared with her son. And he didn't want his time with that child cut short.

"You don't really mean you don't want love . . . Clayton," she said when she returned her focus to him, as though they hadn't even missed a beat.

"I am serious."

"But . . . but . . . you speak about having a real relationship with whomever you marry. You talk about a partnership, one that is not built on anything more." Sylvia tossed her book aside, forgotten. And it was then he knew her questioning had ceased to be about her role as matchmaker and came instead from a friend. "Is it that you don't believe in love?"

Clayton scooped up a handful of gravel and rock at the edge of the blanket, and sifted through the remnants. "Oh, no. Quite the opposite, really." He settled on a particularly flat stone, and from where he sat, he skipped it upon the otherwise serene Serpentine. The little missile skipped four times upon the surface, rippling the river. "I very much believe in it. I come from a long line of ancestors, my parents included, who either married for love or came to find it in their matches." Clayton skipped another stone, this one making five jumps before sinking under the water. He selected another, and held it out for Sylvia.

She ignored the offering. "But . . . it doesn't make any sense, then. If you believe in love, then why would you not want it for yourself?"

"Oh, I would want it very much," he said, and skipped the stone she'd passed over.

Sylvia tossed up her hands. "Then why wouldn't you seek it for yourself?"

"I'm going to die." Clayton let another stone fly, and this one sank with a dreary little *plunk*.

Her knee jolted against his as if her entire body had been dealt a shock to the system. "What?" she whispered. There was such horror and terror in that query, he looked over . . . and found the sentiments reflected back in her eyes. "You're sick."

And the sight of that, her palpable concern for him, caused something to shift in his chest.

"No." He grimaced. "Or at least I don't think I am. Not yet anyway." His late aunt Barbara had perished of a wasting illness . . . at twenty-eight years old. And as a small boy, paying his respects to his father's beloved sister, Clayton had tucked his hands behind his back, crossed his fingers, and said a prayer that his fate wasn't hers. He sighed. "I'm cursed."

Society often spoke of the Kearsleys' "rotted luck." And given that Sylvia had never been one to gossip, it came as no surprise that she didn't know that detail about his family.

Sylvia's features remained a study of confusion. "I don't . . . understand. Are you making a jest?" she ventured hesitantly.

"Oh, no. Rather wish I was." What would his future and hers have been then? Could he have wooed her and won her as Norfolk had? Or had she always been an illusion just beyond his grasp? "I'm going to die young." And probably a miserable death, at that. He kept himself from adding that particular detail. "Or, if not very young, live a shortened life . . . Yes. I do believe it.

"The Kearsleys, my father's family, are notoriously cursed. From my understanding, it goes back nearly two centuries. One of the earlier St. John viscounts, John Kearsley, was visiting his Scottish properties on the Isle of Arran. He had a fascination with archaeology, and went digging in a field of stones. That field of stones also happened to be ancient burial chambers. From that moment on, the Kearsleys were cursed."

"Surely . . . not all of them," she asked skeptically.

"John Kearsley was journeying back to England when he was set upon by bandits and killed with the very point of the stones he'd stolen, and all his loot went with those bandits, too. His son went back to fetch him, and when he was sailing over, his ship went down. He was never found."

Sylvia's eyes rounded. "I'll allow you, that *is* bad luck."

"His grandson reached the age of twenty-one. Possessed of the same fascination with fossils, he launched a search for those pieces his father had taken . . . and snuck inside the household rumored to have them. And he was shot for his efforts."

She gasped. "There . . . is more."

"Oh, there is more. There was a great-great-nephew whose household caught fire while he slept. A beam fell across the doorway, barring any servants from helping to free him." Clayton continued with his telling, and with every tragic ancestor revealed, Sylvia's expression grew more and more bereft. "And then there was my father . . . who choked on a plum pit not even three years ago." Old enough to know six of his children, but denied the gift of knowing Eris beyond just eighteen months of her life.

"I didn't know," she whispered. "I . . . had been so very preoccupied with . . ." He waited for her to say more. To cast further light upon what those years with her husband had been like. But she didn't. Instead, sadness wreathed her features.

"It's fine." Now. At the time, there'd been only devastation over the loss of the father he had so loved. The pain had dulled with time.

"I should have known. You were my friend." Her hand slid over his, covering his knuckles with her palm. "You *are* my friend."

And how much he'd always wanted for there to be more.

"But, Clayton," she said softly, "all people inevitably die. Surely you believe we make our own fate?"

"I do . . . until we don't." His gaze moved out once again to the children happily at play.

"Well, I think it is cowardly," Sylvia blurted.

He stiffened.

She spoke on a rush. "No offense intended."

"None taken," he said dryly, tossing the remaining stones in his hand at the Serpentine. They rained down in offbeat plunks as they hit the surface. Of anything he'd thought she'd say or expected her to say, that certainly hadn't been it.

"It is just . . . by your own admission, you are going through life *wanting* love but denying yourself the possibility of it out of fear that it won't be long enough?"

"This from a woman who doesn't even believe in love." As soon as the words left him, he wanted to call them back. He didn't want to hurt her. He shook his head. "Sylvia," he said, regret hoarsening his voice. "I am sor—"

"Don't." Sylvia touched a finger to his lips, ending the remainder of his apology. "That is fair," she allowed when she let her hand fall back to her lap. "Do you know what I was to my husband?"

He knew what she hadn't been—loved as she deserved—and Clayton hated it. And even more, he hated that she knew it.

"I was a responsibility, Clayton."

And it wrenched even more inside.

"I was a responsibility. An obligation." Each of those words ripped from her with an intensity that may as well have come from deep within her soul. Sylvia's eyes held his, and they were ravaged. "I was nothing more than that to my husband. I don't ever want to be that again." She shook her head. "Not to anyone." Sylvia glanced away, out at the Serpentine, and when she again spoke, she did so with a renewed calm. "I might not have the grand love that everyone dreams of and deserves, but at least I can say I tried my hand at it, Clayton. I gave myself completely to it." Tears glazed her eyes, making a lie of her attempt at matter-of-factness, and the sight of those drops hit him square in the chest. "And I lost." With jerky, almost angry movements, she brushed the backs of her hands over her eyes, and it was too much. He'd never be able to just sit silent and inactive as she faced her grief.

"Here," he murmured, and snapping his handkerchief, he wound the corner of it around his thumb and brushed a drop free.

Sylvia brought her hand up and cupped it around Clayton's, freezing his efforts and commanding his full attention. "You cannot say the same, though, Clayton. You can only say that you've shut yourself away in the fear of what might happen."

"Will." He implored her to understand. He wasn't speaking about possibilities and hypotheticals. "What *will* happen."

"Perhaps," she said, tenacious in her denial, "but perhaps not, Clayton." A light breeze toyed with a loose curl that hung artfully at her shoulder. Sylvia brushed it back distractedly. "You deserve love, Clayton." She went up on her knees beside him so their eyes were level. "You find a woman who is good. And you steal whatever moments you can together. No one is promised another day."

"Mama!"

They both looked over, the moment between them ended as Vallen came hurtling forward. Gathering her skirts, Sylvia jumped up and went rushing off to meet the boy.

Clayton came more slowly to his feet. As he did, he stared on at the tableau of mother and child together, Sylvia scooping him up and holding him close as she did, spinning in a dizzying circle. All the while, her words lingered, remaining there with him.

And he couldn't let himself think that perhaps she had been correct. Because that would mean the sacrifice he'd made, the decision to not pursue anything more, had been for naught. And that all these years he'd spent pining for her, in actuality, they could have been together.

No, it was best not to think of any of that.

Rather, he intended to enjoy being in the only place he wanted to be . . . here with her.

Alas, the moment appeared to be short-lived.

Over the rise, Anwen came hurtling, waving her arms as she went, brandishing a little scrap of paper.

What in hell?

Clayton started for the eldest of his sisters.

The moment they met, Anwen sagged, dropping her hands upon her knees and gasping for breath.

"What—?"

"A letter arrived." She spoke in little spurts. "From Lord Landon. His servant indicated it was a matter of some urgency." Anwen pressed the letter into Clayton's palm. "Mother sent me to watch after Eris so that you might go."

Clayton unfolded the note.

St.

Meet me at GJ. Urgent business.

L

That was it.

He stole one last glance over to where Sylvia was now playing with her son and Clayton's sister.

"Go," Anwen ordered, her tone strident. "I shall tell Sylvia a matter of importance came up that you had to see to."

"It might not be," he said in an attempt to alleviate some of her worry. "With Landon, more often than not, it's hardly a matter of seriousness." She had been the one who had brought him a note about

Norfolk's death that day. From that moment on, whenever a missive came, she responded with the level of urgency that she did now.

Anwen gave him an impressively sturdy shove between the shoulder blades.

And he proved to be a bastard because, as he took his leave, the only place he wanted to be was here with Sylvia.

Chapter 20

13 Old Bond Street

God, how he despised this place.

There was no place he hated more. For the memories here. For the guilt. The resentment. And for the reminder of that one fateful day when life had been irrevocably changed.

"Shocking to see you here," Lord Landon called from where he stood alongside Scarsdale at the back of Gentleman Jackson's.

Yes, Clayton went out of his way to avoid this place whenever he could. The only exceptions he made were when Landon sent 'round some vague, cryptic note requesting Clayton's company. Experience had come to show that invariably there was nothing of any real urgency behind those notes. But the friend and person within him waiting for the next worst thing to happen never ignored those summons for fear that the one day he did would be the one day he was really needed.

Clayton stopped before the pair, presently checking their hand fastenings. "Is it really something of a shock, when you called for me?"

Landon's eyebrows both went flying up. "What's this now? Sarcasm, I do detect? From the affable, always agreeable Saint St. John?" His childhood friend staggered back with his hands to his chest in exaggerated shock. *"Impossible."*

"Go to hell," Clayton muttered.

"And cursing?" Scarsdale nudged the marquess with his elbow. "The *scandal.*"

"And you can go to hell, too, Scarsdale," Clayton added for good measure. Though he was happy to see the other man in his usual spirits, Clayton rather wished it weren't at his own expense.

"So *this* is what they are teaching at the Mismatch Club."

"I've told you," he said with a concerted effort that had come only from being a brother to six unruly sisters. "It is a society . . ."

Both men erupted into an uncontrollable fit of laughter.

He consulted his timepiece. "And I have another meeting coming up shortly."

His friends only laughed all the harder.

Clayton started to go, and Landon sobered up immediately and called out after him. "Come back. We do need to talk."

This time, there was an unexpected seriousness to Landon's words that stayed Clayton and brought him back to the pair.

"Tell him," the marquess said to Scarsdale when he reached their side.

"What?" Clayton asked, unease tripping along his spine as he looked back and forth between his friends. "Tell me what?" he prodded when neither man was quick enough to respond.

Scarsdale was the one to answer. "Gentlemen have begun remarking upon your joining the Mismatch Society. And . . ."

"And?" Clayton snapped when no further information was forthcoming.

"And people have noted that you've been attending the Mismatch meetings," Landon said.

"Yes, Scarsdale just said as much." Some of the tension went out of his shoulders. Talk of his attending them had been inevitable. That had also been Sylvia's reason for issuing the invitation in the first place. He caught the look both men exchanged. "What now?"

"Well," Scarsdale went on, "it is, of course, that people are naturally curious and wondering as to why you were attending them."

"There have been wagers placed at White's," Landon clarified. "Some believe it is motivated by your desire to keep a careful eye on your sisters." The marquess brightened. "Which is entirely noble and fits with your character."

"Spying on my sisters?" Clayton asked dryly.

"Ohhhh, it's all semantics, really. You call it 'spying,' while every other man would call it 'looking after.'"

Indeed.

"And in a way, it kind of is spying, though. They just have it wrong as to which woman it is," Scarsdale pointed out as he fiddled with his hand wrappings once more.

"*Shh,*" Clayton demanded, frantically looking about him. Fortunately, at the early hour, there was just one other pair of boxers, and they were in the midst of a lesson with Gentleman Jackson. "And I'm not . . . spying on the lady. I'm . . . I'm . . ."

"Looking after her?" Landon supplied with a smirk. "Which was precisely my point, thank you for making it, old chum."

Clayton opened his mouth to counter the point, and yet . . .

Was Landon really wrong? Hadn't the whole reason Clayton had accepted Sylvia's invitation and begun attending the meetings been so that he might look after her?

Landon tossed an arm around his shoulders. "Come now, St. John," he said. "We know your motives and actions are honorable. We were just making light."

But were they honorable, though? That question persisted.

Clayton dragged a hand down the side of his face. What the hell was it with the friends he had who seemed to think the best place to conduct private business was in a crowded private club or a boxing studio?

"If it makes you feel any better," Scarsdale put in, "others are saying if you, Saint St. John, have given your approval, then the society cannot be all that bad. Gentlemen have been less fearful about the motives of that organization since you've come along."

Clayton perked up. Well, that was certainly good news. After all, the entire reason Sylvia had invited him about was to achieve the very ends Scarsdale now spoke of. So in that, some good had come of his efforts for Sylvia.

"And then others think . . ."

Clayton snapped back to attention, and in a bid to make sense of Landon's muffled words, he cupped a hand around his ear. "What was that?"

"Others are of the opinion that you have your eye on one of the ladies in the bunch. Not in the fraternal kind of way."

He sputtered. His neck went hot.

"That's what my reaction was as well," Scarsdale said. "Now, if it had been Landon, I'd probably wager the same as those gentlemen."

The two gentlemen began to play at sparring over the pretend insult.

While they boxed like little boys, Clayton shook his head.

Wagers. This was certainly a first . . . for him. Never before had he done something to land himself in the betting book of White's.

"What the hell is he doing here?" Scarsdale asked as he abruptly let his arms fall to his sides.

All three of the trio looked to the front of the studio, and Clayton went stock still.

Whereas he had forcibly made himself stop thinking about Sylvia, he'd not had to do so with the older gentleman now making his way through Gentleman Jackson's. But he should have. If for no other reason than the closeness Clayton had once had to the gentleman's family.

"Prendergast," Landon whispered.

"Yes, I see that," Clayton replied out of the corner of his mouth.

"What is he doing here?" Scarsdale again asked the question they all had.

By the purposeful stride and the focus of his gaze, there could be no doubting they were, in fact, who the marquess sought out. Of all the places for this man to be, he should choose this one? This place where his son had died?

The marquess reached them. "Boys," he greeted them, the same way he had when they'd returned from Eton with his son.

Each of them hurried to sketch a deep bow.

"Landon and Scarsdale." Gentleman Jackson summoned the pair.

As they rushed on for their session, both men looked tangibly relieved at that reprieve. And as Clayton was left alone with the marquess, never more had he wished he'd been a fan of the sport, and in the middle of the ring where Scarsdale and Landon now found themselves preparing to spar.

To be left here with Norfolk's father in the very place where his friend had died was a level of discomfort Clayton had never known in his thirty years. To the marquess's credit, he gave no outward action to the agony this place surely caused him. Clayton had been gutted by the death of his father. To this date, he couldn't enter the breakfast room at his family's country estate without reliving the agony of that loss. As such, he studiously avoided it, taking his meals either in the kitchen amongst the servants, or in his offices. Or even on occasion in the formal dining room. Never, however, that room. And yet, Prendergast should be here. In this place.

His hands clasped behind him, Clayton watched on as the two men settled into their fight. The silence between him and the marquess was magnified by the shuffle of Scarsdale's and Landon's feet as they moved about the ring, and the increased respiration that their efforts brought.

"I sometimes come here to feel closer to my son. I trust that sounds peculiar," Lord Prendergast murmured.

"Nothing sounds peculiar where lost loved ones are concerned." But then there was no explaining how each person navigated their own grief. Hadn't Clayton and his sisters all responded in different ways following their father's death?

"I have kept in touch with Landon and Scarsdale over the years." Clayton masked his surprise at that revelation.

"They've been good enough to indulge an old, lonely man," Norfolk's father said as his gaze followed the dancing fighters around the ring.

They'd been good enough to indulge an old, lonely man . . . where Clayton had not. The meaning, whether intentional or not, Clayton did not know. Once again, his own guilt could be the entire reason for internalizing what the older man was saying. "Forgive me for—"

Norfolk's father waved him off. "None of that. You are here now, and it is so very good to see you again."

They fell into another silence, this one more comfortable than the one before. "I have read about my daughter-in-law in the papers."

That change of topic came so quick, Clayton blinked.

Lord Prendergast sighed. "That is the only way I can find out anything about her . . . or my grandson." Pain twisted the old man's features into a mask of grief. "Though there isn't much one can glean about a three-year-old boy in the gossip columns."

This felt very different. And he may be the optimist his friends insisted upon calling him, but something in that statement stirred his unease. "No. I expect that is true," Clayton said carefully.

"I don't think there's anything untoward about your being at whatever club she has."

"Society," Clayton automatically corrected, as he found himself having to so often do. People couldn't even respect what Sylvia and the members chose to call themselves.

"I think it is admirable," Norfolk's father said. "Your going there."

Clayton, however, wasn't looking for the older gentleman's praise or compliments. The last thing he wanted or intended to do was share anything about his private dealings with Sylvia. With him, or with anyone. Still, something in the steel of the marquess's ice-blue eyes and the hard lines at the corners of them served as a contradiction to the smile on his mouth and the words on his lips. As such, Clayton proceeded with caution, directing Norfolk's father away from talk about his daughter-in-law. "I trust that you and Lady Prendergast are well?" From what his mother had shared, the marchioness had retreated to the country and hidden herself away . . . with none invited to visit, and her visiting no one.

"You've not come by. Not like Landon and Scarsdale." There was an oddly detached, emotionless quality to that statement, which shifted them back to the older gentleman's original words for Clayton. "That took me by surprise. You were closer with my son than any of the others." The marquess spoke as if he were dropping casual comments about the fine London weather they'd been enjoying and not as though he were casting the aspersion upon Clayton's character that he now did.

Nor did it escape his notice that Norfolk's father had failed to answer his question. And yet, the older gentleman was entirely right to that disappointment. "Forgive me, my lord. You are, indeed, correct." There'd been an obligation to many whom he had failed. Not just Sylvia. Clayton, after all, had spent many of his childhood days visiting the household of the man who now stood before him.

Clayton had never minced words. He'd only ever been direct and forthcoming. That did not mean, however, he was incapable of picking up on the subtleties of when someone was saying more than he was.

"As close as you are with your own family, you see how wrong it is that she keeps me from my grandson."

"I was unaware that you have not been seeing your grandson." Clayton pulled his focus away from the pair in the ring. But then he'd studiously avoided Sylvia, along with Norfolk's father.

The marquess dabbed at the corners of his eyes, in the first real show of emotion Clayton had ever recalled the other man sharing. "Oh, yes."

This was who Sylvia had believed was visiting her the day Clayton had first shown up, the person who'd been determined to see her. And yet, why would she turn the older man away?

She wouldn't have made the decision she had to cut out her in-laws if there hadn't been some reason. That, Clayton would stake his very life on. Whether it pained her to do so . . . or for other reasons, he didn't know. But there had to be *something*.

"She is seeking to punish me," the marquess whispered, his voice breaking. "It is her revenge against Norman for . . ." Having had a lover. Nay, not just a lover, but a woman whom he'd loved when he'd not Sylvia.

And yet . . . "Lady Norfolk is not capable of unkindness." That did not fit with everything Clayton knew about Sylvia or the woman she was.

"Do you know how many letters I have written her? Daily," he said, not giving Clayton a chance to answer, nor himself concurring with Clayton's assessment of Sylvia's character. "I am not guilty of sins that should keep me away from my grandson."

God, how he despised all the torment and unrest Norfolk had left behind. Now he felt compelled to help this aged man before him.

Norfolk's father rested a hand on Clayton's sleeve. "You will speak to her." There was an entreaty there.

"Of course," he promised. Although he could not promise to secure Sylvia's permission, he could at least offer to try to help. And in that, in doing this, he could secure peace for the marquess and relieve himself of any obligation to the man who had been so kind when he was younger.

In this, and by helping Sylvia, Clayton would be free of these two responsibilities.

Clayton had left early, without time for even a goodbye, and since his sister had announced his departure from Hyde Park, Sylvia had spent the whole day thinking of him . . . and their exchange. Specifically, their discussion about marriage. Never had she believed a man could speak, would speak, as he had.

Even when her late husband had been courting her, she'd once overheard him jesting to Lord Landon about the struggles of rogues giving up their bachelor ways. Sadly, she'd come to realize only after they'd married that'd been no jest on his part.

Then, there'd been her brother, who—until he'd fallen in love—had thought of matrimony as a business arrangement.

And then there was . . . Clayton.

Clayton, who saw the woman he'd one day wed as a partner.

We'll be faithful to one another.

Her heart spasmed and squeezed all over again at just how effortlessly those words had flowed from his lips.

Of course, he'd said. As if he was absolutely certain he wouldn't relent on the terms of his eventual marriage. He spoke of honoring his vows and being faithful, and she found herself jealous of whichever lady he ultimately made his bride.

Devotion. Fidelity. Honor. They were all gifts that his eventual wife would be the recipient of.

Her heart hammered hard in her breast, knocking there painfully.

Not envy of the woman . . . but rather, of the marriage the couple would have. One that, following the forbidden embraces she'd shared with Clayton, would include passion, and not the cold, awkward exchanges Sylvia had known with her own husband. Yes, it wasn't that she was jealous of the idea of Clayton with someone . . . rather, she was jealous of what that couple would share. That was all there was to it.

Finding some solace in those silent reassurances she gave herself, she let her legs fall to the floor, grabbed her notebook, and snapped it open.

Brides.

Potential matches.

Sylvia tapped the tip of her pencil against that heading, drumming it on the page. "Potential matches. Potential matches."

To give her fingers a purpose while her mind searched for names, she underlined the title. And then underlined it a second time for good measure. She needed to provide more than one for Clayton's consideration. One would never do. He required choices.

There was . . .

Or mayhap . . .

Why do you have to add others?

Because the moment you present Clayton with one name is the moment this becomes more real, a voice taunted. When she suggested this lady, then everything would continue in a forward motion, and then her friendship with Clayton would be no more. Not given all the intimate moments they'd shared together. For even though she would never act on her passions with a married man, the undercurrents of it would always be there . . . a sexual tension that, when combined with the ease of their friendship, would never be fair to whomever he married.

And the more time Sylvia spent with him, the more she found herself longing for the last thing she should be. Her mind shied away from putting labels to all those things. Institutions she'd shunned. Sentiments she'd sworn never to let herself be weak to, again.

It was why she needed to be done with this.

She underlined that name on the page.

Miss Milsom.

Miss Milsom, who'd only really just begun to find her voice in the Mismatch Society. A woman who, unlike many other members of the group, had expressed interest in the possibility of marriage. Yes, and the lady required a husband who would be supportive of her challenging propriety and societal norms. Furthermore, Miss Milsom was friendly with Clayton's sisters.

In short, Sylvia couldn't think of a reason the match would be a bad one.

There, she'd come up with one.

And for some unexplainable reason, she felt an overwhelming urge to cry.

Chapter 21

Clayton had completed his first two weeks as a member of the Mismatch Society.

When he'd initially signed on, the sole motivating factor had been checking in on Sylvia. Without her awareness, of course. In fact, there had been a mutually beneficial part to his being here. First, there was the opportunity to just freely visit with her. And she would receive that which she had hoped to attain—an easing of the fears amongst gentlemen of the *ton*. In providing Sylvia with that, he could relinquish some of the guilt he'd felt at his real motives for being here. Because there seemed something almost underhanded to it. If, however, he served some benefit for her, then he hadn't really done anything wrong. That was what he told himself to alleviate the guilt. And it helped . . . some.

But seated directly across the room from the leader of this eclectic group of ladies, he could acknowledge that he'd come to enjoy his time here.

Listening in on what Sylvia, his sisters, on one occasion his mother, and the other women present were saying had been nothing short of enlightening.

After all, men and women were treated as if they were entirely different species with nothing in common. Men oversaw parliamentary matters. Women were excluded from Parliament. Gentlemen attended their clubs, and ladies were barred entry.

After formal dinners, men retired for their brandy and billiards, while the women went to some other parlor . . . and did Clayton still knew not what.

Even when married, they kept separate chambers. Or . . . most did. Such a detail had been pointed out to the roomful of ladies, much to his horror, by his mother. And yet, regardless of how little he cared to think about his mother and late father being intimate in any way, there was no disputing the important point she had made about spouses living their separate lives . . . and the wrongness of it.

The list went on and on.

Always apart, never together. And therefore, by the very way in which society had been structured, completely unable to truly understand one another or live shared experiences.

Nay, what had begun as a responsibility had transformed into something more.

And as he was being honest with himself, Clayton could freely admit that much of his found joy in the Mismatch Society came from simply being with Sylvia. Near her. And listening to her.

Just then, it was his sister Cora who commanded the floor.

"Rousseau and Aristotle and vast numbers of the other Enlightenment thinkers didn't believe women were deserving of an equal place amongst society and in their own household, and I find it highly doubtful to expect a single one of us can locate one, let alone *multiple*"—Clayton's sister jabbed her finger at the air, punctuating that word—"English gentlemen who are elevated in thoughts above and beyond the great philosophers."

He was equal parts appreciative of his sister's articulate positioning and regretful at such a level of cynicism from a girl of just eighteen.

"A female wit is a scourge to her husband, her children, her friends, her servants," one of the ladies—Scarsdale's almost sister-in-law, Isla Gately—called out to the hisses and boos of every woman present.

The woman sitting next to him, a birdlike, petite young lady near in age to Cora, took mercy and explained, "Miss Gately wasn't speaking ill of women, she was quoting Rousseau's *Emile*. It was one of our first readings that we discussed."

"Ah." He needn't have bothered with a reply, however, as his seating partner had already returned her full focus to the lively debate unfolding around the room.

"I assure you, my role is that of equal in my household," Lila said.

"But we've already ascertained that your husband is the exception."

Wordlessly, Clayton leaned over to Miss Dobson in hopes for some insight here.

"Because he was raised outside the peerage," she whispered in return.

Yes, everyone knew the story of the Lost Heir who had been restored to his rightful rank of duke.

"What of Wollstonecraft?" Sylvia spoke loudly enough to be heard over the ever-growing volume. "One of the greatest Enlightenment thinkers, did she not call for women's rights in both public and private spheres?"

"She was a woman," Anwen pointed out.

"Precisely," Lady Annalee drawled, kicking up her bare feet on a nearby side table so that her skirts rucked up about her legs. "Now, if Sylvia was suggesting it would be wiser for women to marry their fellow women, to avoid all the headache that comes with having to fight men for freedom and equality within one's household? I agree with the point."

Laughter rolled around the room.

Sylvia, however, remained steady in her seriousness. "Very well, then, what of Montesquieu?" There came the stirrings of disagreement. "Just a moment; hear me out." And just like that, they did, giving her the space she'd requested to make her point. "Montesquieu was of the opinion women were weaker than men and expected them to obey the commands of their husband . . . *but* he also believed women had the ability to govern." And Clayton hung on to every word Sylvia uttered. Before this, he'd been captivated by her humor. Bewitched by her touch. And enthralled by her intelligence and wit. But this? Witnessing her complete and magnificent mastery of this discourse would be one thing he remembered for the remainder of his days. "Or what of Voltaire? He deliberately wrote women to be like men and, in so doing, highlighted the idea that women and men are interchangeable and that we all possess the same potential."

How effortlessly she guided the meetings. She'd defused the volatile exchange, bringing them away from a place driven solely by emotion and to one where the members were using reason and intellect to defend any divergent opinions they possessed in a way he'd never witnessed any member of Parliament capable of doing.

She was nothing short of awe-inspiring.

"Are you then defending marriage?" Miss Bragger asked Sylvia.

And Clayton didn't realize he held his breath until she slid her gaze his way. Only because her answer mattered in the sense of knowing Norfolk hadn't ruined her for love. Not because it meant there might be a chance for a union between them. No, not when he'd already turned his back on that possibility. That couldn't be the reason he hung in a suspended state, waiting for her answer.

"I am pointing out that if we generalize old men as being one way, then we are no different from those closed-minded thinkers," Sylvia explained.

"She is quite amazing, is she not?"

It took a moment for Clayton to register that faintest of whispers . . . now coming from his seatmate.

For one horrifying heartbeat, he believed he had been so transparent in his admiration for Sylvia that this stranger, Miss Dobson, whom he really knew not at all, had detected it.

Except as he glanced at Miss Dobson, Clayton observed the frank appreciation she had trained on Sylvia.

"We are not inferior . . . We should never settle for anything less than a relationship where we are treated as the equals that we are," Sylvia was saying. "Do I believe it is likely to find such a husband and such a marriage? No. I do not. Did I have that when I was married? No, I did not. But neither should we believe and speak in absolutes."

⬦

The day's Mismatch Society meeting was proving to be one of the most lively and thought-provoking ones since their inception.

Sylvia herself had been completely and entirely engaged.

That was, however, until she had happened to glance across the room, in the midst of the point she'd been making, and seen Clayton leaning close to Miss Dobson. Just as he had been since the members had broken up into pairings, as they did at the end of each group discussion.

Miss Dobson . . . was perfect. Why had Sylvia not thought of it before now? In her mind, she kept a mental inventory of the potential bride for Clayton. Fact: the young lady was clever and possessed of a genuine sense of humor. Fact: they were comfortable with and around one another . . . as had been evidenced by the stolen exchanges they'd shared during the meeting. In short, Miss Dobson was perfect for Clayton.

Fact: for some reason, instead of triumph, Sylvia was overwhelmed by the need to have herself a good cry.

Then she made the mistake of looking across the room to where Clayton sat . . . on the same bench as Miss Dobson. Their heads bent close, they were completely engrossed in whatever topic they now spoke on.

"And it is quite shocking, but I rather approve," Clara, her partner in discussion for the day, was saying.

"I agree," Sylvia said for the sake of saying something.

What were Miss Dobson and Clayton *talking* about?

And was it really so funny, whatever it was they were talking about? Because it shouldn't be. The manner of the day's business was serious stuff. Was there really all that room for hilarity?

Just then, Miss Dobson laughed. Louder and longer than she'd ever heard. In fact, Sylvia couldn't think of a time when the generally quiet young lady had ever been so exuberant.

"Though I'm sure many will disagree with me," Clara continued to carry on with what had become an entirely one-sided discussion.

Miss Dobson giggled. *Giggled.* The sound of innocence and everything Sylvia was not.

"Do you not think so?" Clara asked.

Sylvia gritted her teeth. She thought they should get on with more serious talk. "I do." She absolutely thought that.

"Then I shall make it official . . . I shall order my club shuttered . . ."

Sylvia blinked slowly. What in . . . ? She whipped her attention away from Clayton and his future bride over to her sister-in-law . . . and found the beautiful woman smiling back.

"Of course I've no intention of closing up my music hall." Clara winked. "I do, however, have your attention."

Heat slapped Sylvia's cheeks. "Forgive me." Since she had happened to glance over earlier at Clayton and found him charming his seating partner, Sylvia hadn't been able to properly focus on anything. In fact, since then, she had been useless. "I was . . . distracted."

Another of Miss Dobson's laughs filled the room. This time, that innocent, bell-like sound that Sylvia had once been in possession of, too, was followed by Clayton's deeper and more rumbling one. *Do not look. Do not look.*

"I see that." Her sister-in-law lifted a perfectly golden brow and arched her head ever so slightly in the direction of his partner for the day. "You care about the gentleman," Clara said softly, her tones so hushed they were reserved for Sylvia.

"Of course I do," she said automatically. "He is a friend."

"A friend," Clara repeated.

Sylvia's back went up defensively. "Yes, friend. We have known one another for many years." Even if there had been a few in between where she had not seen him. They had resumed all this time later, picking up as easily as if there had never been a parting.

"I know friends. They do not glare at poor Miss Dobson, the way you are, for her speaking to the gentleman."

Sylvia blanched. Good God, had she been so very obvious?

Her sister-in-law covered her fingers and squeezed them lightly. "Everyone is thoroughly engaged in today's discussion. I likely wouldn't have noticed . . . what I did, had I not been partnered with you today."

Sylvia sank in her chair from the relief of that. "Truly?"

"Well, not me. I notice everything, and as such, I have also paid attention to the looks you and the viscount steal of one another during the meetings."

They didn't *steal* looks. They happened to look at one another at various points. It was all by coincidence and chance. Why, it was no different from when each of them happened to glance at other members in the room. Why . . . why . . .

She was lying to herself. And if she was, what exactly did it mean?

"You yourself have pointed out numerous times, Sylvia," her sister-in-law whispered, "that you have seen marriages that are actual partnerships. You have seen there can be love. And you know there are some good men. Not a lot," Clara allowed, "but some. And as you have had a long friendship with the gentleman, then you *know* that he is one of the good ones. Which might be why you were struggling so much, setting him free for someone else?"

Clara's words sent terror clamoring inside her. What her sister-in-law said . . . it all made sense. "It is more complicated than that," she said, glancing down at her tightly clasped hands.

"How so?" Clara gently pressed her.

"Because I swore never to . . . to . . . lose myself so completely to a man." And this? What her sister-in-law was proposing? It challenged everything Sylvia had sworn to never again do. "It broke me when Norman rebuffed my love," she said on a ragged whisper. "And he rejected me. He rejected me in every way. I lived in a constant state of feeling terrible about myself. Why can I not be enough?" But he had been an ideal. The unattainable rogue who could never be interested in someone as ordinary as herself . . . and it had been so thrilling when he was. Like pretend. A fairy tale. Clayton, however, was a man whom she'd admired and respected and cared about and trusted . . . And if he were to break her heart, she would be destroyed. That would shatter her beyond the place that she could ever recover from. "I cannot lose like that again."

"Sylvia," Clara said, shifting even closer to her on the sofa. "I was not hurt in the same exact way you were. But I was one who thought just like you . . . that it was too dangerous to trust a man. All they ever wanted to do was control me and make me their plaything. They didn't respect me. They treated me as an object for their pleasures. And I hated them for it. I hated them all." There was a surprising lack of sting to those vitriolic words she now spoke. "I even hated your brother when I first met him," she continued in that matter-of-fact way. "I believed he was just like all the others. And do you know, Sylvia?" Clara held her eyes with her own. "If I had not taken a chance that was different and better, think of all I would have lost. What if you do not think of it so much as losing yourself in a man, but finding yourself in new ways?"

Clara spoke of loss. And yet Sylvia had lost so much from her marriage to Norman. And even as her sister-in-law was making the most sense, Sylvia didn't know if she was brave enough to do it all again.

Annalee banged the gavel, marking an end to Clara's questioning and the latest meeting. Sylvia came to her feet, and caught Clayton's gaze. She discreetly motioned to the floor, silently asking for him to stay.

While he spoke to his sisters, Sylvia made a show of tidying her notes. She waited until all the young women and members had filed from the parlor, until it was just Sylvia and Clayton.

They stood across from one another, and spoke at the same time.

"I very much enjoyed—"

"You probably already know—"

They both stopped at the same time. Sylvia gestured to Clayton. "Please, you first."

"I was going to say how very much I enjoyed today's discussion. The points you made were ones I hadn't considered; I wanted to thank you for including me in the society."

Sylvia bit the inside of her lower lip. Why must he be so wonderful? It only made it all the more difficult, relinquishing him to another. "Thank you for that." She swept her hand toward the upholstered sofa nearest them. "If you would?" After he sat, Sylvia joined him. "As I was saying, you probably know why I asked to speak with you." Good, she had managed unaffected breeziness.

He nodded.

"Miss Dobson."

Clayton glanced around, and puzzled his brow. "I am afraid I do not—"

"She is your bride," Sylvia clarified.

"My . . . ?"

"Bride," she supplied once more, and then Sylvia sat there, her body reflexively tensed. Clayton didn't recoil or immediately reject, and that which should have marked her decision and this exchange a success ushered in another wave of tears that she wanted to cry. "I see how well you suited one another. She is lovely. She's quite clever and kind and perfect with your sisters." And she was an innocent. Miss Dobson still wore the glow of that innocence in ways Sylvia never would again. That was what Clayton deserved.

"I have no interest," he began slowly, "in marriage to Miss Dobson."

Her heart jumped a beat. "You do not?"

"I'm sure she is quite lovely. And she is all those things that you say. However, she is young, and she is lacking in the maturity and life experience that I would hope to have in the woman I one day marry."

In short, he would not rule out a woman of more advanced years and experience . . .

A woman like yourself.

Unnerved, Sylvia jumped up. "This is helpful. Very helpful. Thank you so much. For clarifying, that is."

After Clayton took his leave, Sylvia thought about what he'd said he wished for in his future wife, and smiled.

Chapter 22

That evening, following her discussion with Clayton, Sylvia found her night like so many others before it . . . in attendance at a ball.

Lingering on the sidelines of Lord and Lady Waverly's ball, Sylvia found herself thinking back to a time when she'd enjoyed these affairs—back when she'd made her Come Out and she'd had Clayton's company to make the night joyous. The memories proved even stronger this night, given this was the place they had first met. When she had been so innocent, and capable of freely smiling and laughing. Things she'd never thought to be able to do again, but that had proven so easy since he'd reappeared in her life.

"You should drink champagne," Annalee shouted over the swell of the orchestra. With two glasses in hand, she offered one to Sylvia. "Wine makes them all the more enjoyable."

She waved off that offering, to which Annalee shrugged. "The more for me," she said, and alternated a sip from each glass.

"I thought you said you loved attending balls," Sylvia said, making the decision to accept that drink after all to hopefully slow Annalee's consumption of alcohol.

"I do." Her friend tapped Sylvia with the edge of the painted fan dangling from her wrist. "I said they make them *more* enjoyable." Annalee followed that with a wink and a laugh.

Smiling, Sylvia relieved the woman of her other refreshment.

"But . . ."

"You promised." Several times about the same topic, that of Annalee's concerning level of drink.

Annalee pouted. "You are terribly stuffy sometimes." She softened that by placing a kiss upon each of Sylvia's cheeks. "But I do love you so." The young woman's still lucid gaze caught on someone in the crowd, and she waved exuberantly at whomever she had spotted. "Would you be so very offended if I abandon you for a bit? I know you do not like these affairs."

Sylvia cut her off with a laugh. "Go. I am perfectly content. And I told you, I—"

"Or you can join me? We would so love to—"

"Go," Sylvia repeated.

She watched on, bemused, as Annalee cut a path directly through the crowded dance floor, the partners presently in the midst of a waltz, and all the while Annalee walked, she gestured with her arms as if she were conducting the orchestra, dancing gingerly between partners . . . until her form was lost to that crowd.

Giving her head a shake, Sylvia turned her focus to the two glasses she'd been left holding. An attentive footman immediately appeared. With a murmur of thanks, Sylvia deposited one flute. She made to set down the other before thinking better of it and holding on to the drink.

When the servant rushed off, she turned her gaze on the crowd once more.

Despite her friend's assumption, Sylvia did not dislike attending balls. In fact, she rather enjoyed them. She wasn't much of a dancer. But she enjoyed the music. She despised gossip. But she appreciated the swell of laughter and the din of people conversing. When she'd been married, it had been those affairs that had kept her from drowning in sorrow at loving a man who'd spent most of his nights away from her. Surrounding herself with crowds had allowed her to forget for a short while just how alone she was. And how lonely.

Upon her husband's death she, an expectant mother, had gone into mourning. Then as a new mother, she had been overwhelmed by a state of depression. Most of her days she'd spent crying. And when she hadn't been crying, she'd been fighting tears.

She had never imagined she would ever attend another ball. She'd never expected that she would want to.

Then she found her way back to the living, and had recently begun to attend these affairs.

And yet, since Clayton had reemerged, she found herself discovering . . . the artificial sense of fulfillment that was to be found here. Now she found herself thinking what it would have been like to spend her days and nights with—

"What is the wager on how many times Lady Waverly's brow turns up in disapproval?"

Sylvia gasped and looked up.

Clayton!

At some point, he had slid into the spot beside her. Arms folded across his massive chest, his focus turned out, there would have been the question as to whether he was, in fact, speaking to another. If another had been around. If it hadn't been just they two together in company.

Just as he'd been that night they'd first met.

Her heart doubled its rhythm. In a way it had not during their first exchange. How had it not? And how had this awareness of him changed so much all these years later?

Mimicking his body's positioning and his focus on the waltzing dancers, Sylvia spoke out of the corner of her mouth, delivering her exact same response from that night, too. "I believe the estimate was one hundred. Alas, she went through that number at the receiving line alone."

"Perhaps, then, we can try our hands at another wager in the card room?" And also just like that long-ago night, he offered his elbow to her.

At last, they looked at one another and smiled. Sylvia placed her fingertips upon his sleeve and allowed him to lead her on to those rooms. "You're here." Happiness drew that exclamation from her.

"My brotherly responsibility." As they walked, Clayton angled his head in a nearly imperceptible tilt, directing Sylvia's focus to the young bespectacled lady. Surrounded by the company of her mother and the viscountess's equally eccentric friends, Anwen was nearly three decades younger than all her companions. Just then, Clayton's sister laughed at something one of the matrons said.

"I worry about her," he said quietly as they proceeded along the perimeter of the room.

Sylvia stole another look, and puzzled her brow in confusion. "She appears happy. Is she not?"

"She should be with other young ladies her age. And this, since she joined the Mismatch Society, has really been the first time that she's interacted with women of similar years. Those who aren't her sisters, that is. Friends," he clarified. "And for that, I thank you. Prior to you, I have been at a loss as to how to help her."

Clayton's level of devotion was uncommon amongst the peerage. It wasn't driven by power or prestige, but a genuine caring. Whereas every other gentleman of the *ton* worried only about who and when one's sister would marry. But their friendships and happiness didn't generally fit into an equation with any real concern. "You needn't thank me, Clayton," she said gently. Sylvia continued to study the sister Clayton was so worried about. "And why must you help her? Why can she not simply find her own way without your guidance?"

His brow furrowed. "She can. She has. I just . . ." He paused, and it was as though he searched for the words to explain himself. And then he found them. "If I can help her or my sisters in any way, I will. I would not see them suffer in any way if I were capable of helping them." At Sylvia's silence, he glanced over. "You disagree." It wasn't a question.

They reached the card room, and he gestured for her to proceed.

"I didn't say that, Clayton."

"You didn't need to."

Because he knew her. That revelation, and understanding, stirred a little panic. Because no man had. Not even the one she'd given her heart, body, and soul to. And yet this man did. It was a level of intimacy that was still foreign and uncomfortable to her. For what did it mean to share such a bond with a man . . . when she'd vowed to herself to never want anything more from one? And as they took their seats at one of the spare tables, she was grateful for the brief reprieve over her jumbled thoughts. When they sat, Sylvia reached for the cards and proceeded to shuffle them. "I believe it is admirable you love your sisters so," she finally said.

"But?" he pressed, as she dealt him his first card for their game of vingt-et-un.

"*And*," she enunciated slightly, giving herself a card. They each made their bets. "I also believe your sisters are entirely capable of finding their own way. It doesn't mean you don't have to worry about them as you do," she was quick to say when he opened his mouth to interrupt. "But also, it is important for you to trust them completely and fully. To trust that they will be more than all right, and then at some point, you, as their big brother, can set them free and set yourself free of responsibility you feel for their happiness." Sylvia dealt their next cards.

He made no attempt to pick his up. "You think it is wrong to worry about the state of other people's happiness?"

Sylvia studied her hand. Sixteen. She raised her wager.

She waited to speak until he made his next move.

This time, he scrutinized his cards for a long while before adding his ante.

She dealt again. "I think it is wrong to let that worry supersede any person's right to make their own decisions." Not picking up that third and final card, she turned her hand around for his inspection.

Clayton winced. "That is not a wager I would have made." He turned over his cards, revealing his high hand of twenty.

Sylvia turned over her third.

The five of hearts.

He started.

"Twenty-one," she said with a smile. "Sometimes, the risks one takes in life pay off." Sylvia held his gaze. "Sometimes people lose. But ultimately, I believe what is most important is the power one has over one's decisions." Collecting the small pot of her earnings, she allowed him the next deal.

Clayton dealt their first cards. "That is where I disagree with you."

Throughout her marriage to Norman, she'd been so very worried about pleasing him. Because she'd loved him and believed if her opinion had aligned with his, he'd see her as his perfect match. With Clayton, however, she didn't worry about sharing or having an opinion of her own. Whenever they conversed, it was as equals, and it was so very refreshing and freeing from the constraints she had placed upon herself during her marriage.

"Life is entirely too short to not do everything one can to work toward bringing happiness where one can," he said.

Only, it wasn't *about* happiness. It was about the freedom to make one's own decisions. Just a handful of days ago, she would have said as much to him because she wouldn't have read the deeper meaning behind the worries he had—the fear he possessed of his impending early demise . . . and one she could not let herself the thought of. Because she couldn't and wouldn't allow herself to think of a world in which Clayton Kearsley, Viscount St. John, died young. More to give herself something to do than considering her wager, she pushed several coins into the middle of the table.

He made his wager and dealt their next cards. "I ran into the Marquess of Prendergast."

It took a moment to register what he'd said. That what had come between her and the miserable thought of Clayton perishing was that miserable marquess. Sylvia's . . . *father-in-law*? And in the end, she could manage just one word. "What?"

"He mentioned that he misses his grandson."

"Good," she gritted out before she could hold back the petty reply. She pushed a coin into the middle of the table, and gestured for him to continue.

"Sylvia," he said chidingly.

Chiding? He'd chide her. She made herself take a deep breath. Reminding herself that Clayton did not know. That few did. All those who knew the sordid, evil details had been compelled by reasons of their own to silence about the crimes that family was truly guilty of. The majority remained silent because of a deference for rank. Sylvia, however, and her family, had only done so, perpetuating that secret, for the sake of Vallen and his future and for the marchioness's delicate state. She looked across the table at Clayton, and hooded her gaze. Mindful of the nearby players, she spoke in hushed tones. "Let it go, Clayton. You know nothing of it." She tapped the table, indicating the need for her next card and the desire for him to cease this topic immediately.

"But I would like to," he said, proving tenacious.

He would. It fit with who he was as the son and brother and person who hated for there to be any unrest. And perhaps under most any other circumstance, she could understand and maybe even admire the intent behind it.

"I thought there could be an element of peace."

So this was why he'd been so intent to bring into their discussion the idea of another person's happiness.

He presumed much. "There can't be," she said tightly, with a finality; she intended to end any further discussion on that hated family.

It proved futile.

"But every aspect of life, for every person, is better when there is peace."

He was wrong on that score. The world was better when there was justice. Sylvia bit her tongue hard to keep from uttering a rebuttal that would only usher in more questions. Justice, which hadn't been served to Norman's family. *And I am complicit in that.* And she hated that reality . . . because it marked her a hypocrite. And yet she'd wear that badge, and proudly, if it meant she could protect her son from hurt. "You are an eternal optimist, Clayton," she said softly, directing her attention to the cards in her hands.

"You aren't the first to say as much." Clayton edged his seat closer to the table, and leaned across the velvet surface smattered with their cards and coins. "And perhaps I am. But it is just that they are old, and—"

Sylvia pushed back her chair quickly; the chatter in the card room and the noisy revelry from guests outside drowned out the scrape of those legs along the hardwood floor. She set her teeth hard enough to grate them. Of anything she wished to speak with Clayton about, this was decidedly not it. Ignoring the curious glances cast her way, she made a beeline for the doorway and continued back out into the main ballroom. Sylvia didn't stop. Outrage and annoyance and hurt fueled her movements, past the guests and onward. It was, of course, wrong to be hurt. Clayton didn't know anything about the secrets she carried. Nor should she have to share them for him to trust her judgment.

And yet he was a friend, too. And something told her that if she were to reveal all, they would be confidences that he kept. Because of the man of honor he was. That, however, didn't lessen the hurt, for the whole reason he'd sought her out this evening had been to speak on behalf of the people she hated most.

She reached an empty corridor; fast-approaching footfalls echoed behind her. Sylvia whipped around and faced Clayton. "This is why you came to find me tonight?" she cried. "So that you can play peacemaker between me and my in-laws?"

He shook his head. "No. Yes." Clayton dragged a hand through his loose gold curls. "Of course that wasn't the only reason. I told you already, I came to be with my sister. I always intended to speak to you about"—he looked around—"the situation."

Sylvia narrowed her eyes. "Always?"

"Not always. That isn't why I came to see you that . . ." He faltered, and the lit sconce revealed the flicker in his eyes. "This evening," he said. However, it felt as though it were a correction. One she didn't understand. "As you are aware, Anwen arrived with a summons at Hyde Park, cutting our meeting short that day."

Of their own volition, Sylvia's eyebrows went flying up. "He summoned you."

"No! It was Landon. You know Landon." She did. All too well. The most roguish and most reckless of the gentlemen her late husband had kept company with. "With him anything might be either tragedy or nothing at all. I went . . . While we were meeting, Lord Prendergast happened to arrive."

She stiffened. He just happened to arrive? "Nothing that family does is by chance."

"I am bungling this. Might we please speak alone?" he implored, gesturing to the doorway beside them. "Away, in the event someone comes by?"

Tense, she studied Clayton for a long moment before collecting her hem and letting herself into the nearest room. Not because she wished to continue this conversation, but rather, for the simple fact that at some point, she would need to. Sylvia would rather have it done now, as he pointed out, away from prying eyes.

The moment he entered the darkened parlor, joining her, he pushed the door shut behind them.

Sylvia folded her arms at her chest, and waited.

"I know you have your reasons for not wishing to see Norfolk's father. I am trying to understand."

"Does it matter?" she asked curiously. "Why do you need to?"

"Because I am your friend." She refused to let herself feel remorse at his wounded expression. Or she tried to. Tried . . . and failed.

Yes, he was her friend. Or that's what they had been briefly, what they'd only recently renewed. Still, she had resolved to share nothing of the details surrounding her husband's death. Yes, it had been in some small part to protect the dowager marchioness's struggles. Ultimately, however, what it had come down to was protection. Protecting her son from the vicious fallout and the scandal that would follow him if the world learned all those sordid details. "Is that all it is?" she asked softly, moving toward him. Sylvia kept coming, not stopping until the tips of their shoes brushed.

"I don't understand." An uncharacteristic frown formed on his lips, those hard, perfectly formed lips that she hated herself for noticing amidst this tense debate. "You are suggesting my reasons are somehow nefarious?"

Nefarious. And she fought to suppress her first real smile since he'd resurrected mention of her in-laws. "I'm not saying that at all, Clayton." He wasn't capable of underhandedness. "I know you are a good man." That was just one of the reasons she had always loved him. Every muscle in her face and body froze, and a pressure formed in her chest, a tightness, as if her heart were attacking her. Love him? Not like that. As a friend, yes. But it couldn't be more. And yet, what did it say about the passion that flared whenever they were near? Was this hunger she felt for his friendship? Or more . . .

Sweat beaded at her brow and moisture dampened her palms.

"Sylvia?" he asked, concern wreathing his deep baritone.

Sylvia took a deep breath. And in a bid to gain some control, she took a step away, turning, giving him her back. Nor did he press her, beyond just that, her name. Clayton had always been possessed of a patience and calm that had made it so very easy for her to speak to him. Even through the tumult of her confused thoughts, it proved steadying now. When she collected herself enough to just focus on their debate, she faced him again. "You are so very worried about other people's happiness. You're so concerned about the decisions they make. You hate conflict and would intervene in any way, just for the chance of erasing it."

"I don't . . ." He shook his head slowly. "Is that a bad thing?"

Sylvia smiled and took his hands in hers, briefly squeezing and then releasing them. "Your intentions are not bad, but neither is that decision always the right one."

"Would you be very offended if"—he wrestled with his immaculate-until-now cravat—"I asked for an example?"

A soft laugh shook her frame, and she covered her face with her hands. As endearingly unjaded as he was, he made it impossible not to love him. "Why did you reappear in my life all these years later?"

Clayton blanched as all the color drained quickly from his cheeks.

"It wasn't a condemnation," she was quick to reassure. "I know you have a life and a family of your own to care for. I would have never had you see me as an obligation." Did she imagine that his cheeks grew more pale? "I was referring specifically to the reason you arrived at my townhouse." Naturally charming Mr. Flyaway, whom she'd never believed *could* be charmed. But then that was Clayton's magic. "The sole reason you came, demanding an audience? It was because society had been speaking about Waverton Street, and even though you didn't know anything about us or our society, your ultimate concern was restoring peace.

"You are so concerned with tying up loose ends in life."

He frowned. "Anything I do is because I care."

"And I don't doubt that," she said, finding her earlier calm. "Or at least, I don't doubt you believe that. You have this sense of bringing closure to things . . . and I understand, from what you shared, why. And yet, those loose ends you feel the need to be tied are for *you*," she said, willing him to understand. "A sense that you are seeing to something that you feel should be seen to. The marquess. Your sisters. Your marriage.

"But if maintaining peace is your ultimate concern, you risk shuttering good ventures, like the Mismatch Society, where women are free to discuss the institutions that bind us. Just as you risk throwing your support behind a man who is entirely undeserving of it . . . all so that conflict can be avoided."

He stilled. "You are right," he whispered.

Sylvia blinked. "I . . . am?" She was, of course. It was not that she doubted it. Rather, she hadn't expected that he'd come 'round to see her point of view so easily.

"I . . . never thought about it in that way. My thought is only ever to see that there is peace, and I am sorry for twice now interfering without simply trusting that you know what is—"

Sylvia leaned up and kissed him. And when she drew back, his eyes were clouded with desire and confusion.

"Thank you," she said softly. "For trusting in me and my judgment. For not asking me to explain myself . . ."

"More than I already did?"

"You didn't ask. You asked me to speak with him, and I said no. And you listened but didn't press me for more, and for that, I am grateful."

The air crackled like the earth before a lightning strike.

Their gazes locked . . . and then she was lost. Or perhaps this was what Clara had meant when she had said to look at it as being found.

Sylvia grabbed him by the lapels of his jacket and dragged him down to meet her. And then she kissed him, thrusting her tongue and forcing her way inside his mouth.

Clayton's body tensed, and then his hands were on her. All over. As she wanted them. As she wanted him. Desperately and without apology, in this moment, raw and fast, and as wonderful as it always was in his arms.

With a groan, he filled his hands with her buttocks, cupping and kneading that voluptuous flesh, drawing her up and closer, so that he could press the hard ridge of his shaft against her belly.

They moved as one, with him backing her up and her retreating along with him, until she collided with the wall. He slid his mouth over hers. Again and again. Plunging his tongue inside to spar with hers.

Desire seared her veins and robbed her of restraint. She didn't care about the risk of discovery. She couldn't. She'd been reduced to nothing beyond her awareness of his like need for her. Shoving up her skirts, he stepped between her legs. With an answering moan, she let them fall wider, accommodating, but more importantly encouraging, him.

Clayton ran a path of kisses down the curve of her cheek to her neck. And in that place where her pulse beat hard, he sucked and nipped and tasted.

"Mmm," she keened, nudging him with her hips, and that movement appeared to enflame him, pulling an animalistic groan from deep within his chest.

She undulated and arched wildly against him. "Please," she begged.

Clayton rubbed himself against her, teasing her with that which she wanted. "Is this what you want?"

She moaned. "Yes. Desperately so." She craved it.

Reaching down between them, he freed himself from his trousers, and she whimpered, thrusting her hips toward it. Toward him.

"Now," she demanded, digging her hands into his neck so hard she left marks with her nails upon his skin.

He thrust home, and she cried out as he filled her. So very deep and throbbing inside her sodden channel. And as he pumped her over and over again, so hard the sconces and frames alongside them rattled, she wept. Begging and moaning, incoherent, as her body climbed toward that heavenly peak she wanted to jump and fly from again.

"Come for me," he demanded against her temple.

Except, even as she wanted it, she wanted to prolong this moment, to stretch it out until she was consumed and swallowed whole by desire. Clayton hefted her up, and she wrapped her legs around his waist, deepening that penetration.

The walls shook. She shook.

And then, she could take no more. She let herself hurtle freely into her climax, and she screamed his name, his mouth and his kiss swallowing the last syllable. The moment her body sagged, drained of all her pleasure, he pulled out, and spent along the side of her. His surrender coming in creamy rivulets as he groaned, low and deep.

They remained there, braced against the wall, breathing hard and heavy.

Clayton pressed a kiss against her temple in a caress that was so tender and somehow more intimate than when he'd been moving inside her. That intimacy continued a moment later as Clayton gently cleaned her, and then after he tended to himself and disposed of the dirty kerchief, he proceeded to tuck the curls that had escaped her hair arrangement back into the pearl-encrusted combs she wore.

He did so silently, and all the while she watched on, moving her gaze over his face, a study of concentration as he worked.

She trusted him.

She'd trusted him as a friend. As a lover. And she knew he would never betray her. And she wanted to share all with him.

As if he felt her eyes on his, he paused with a ringlet caught between his thumb and forefinger. "What is it?"

"What I am going to tell you, I've told no one." The truth would eventually come out. She knew that. She'd just been—and still was—stealing time for her son, whatever chance at freedom from the scandal she could. "Norman's death was not an accident."

"It was. Landon and Scarsdale were there. The club had brought in a famous fighter for them to test their techniques against. He—"

"He was sent there by Norman's mother," she quietly interrupted.

The curl slipped from his fingers. "What?" he whispered.

"The marchioness was involved in an underground operation. It was a fight society comprised of young children. Children from the streets, who were made to fight. One of those children grew up to be a woman my husband was in love with." She took a breath. "Valerie."

Any other person under the sun would have reacted with shock or horror to learn a woman Sylvia was housemates with had also been her late husband's lover. Clayton, when he spoke, didn't dwell on that sordid detail.

"How . . . ?"

"How do I know?" Sylvia hugged herself around the middle. "The day of his funeral services, I came upon Lord Prendergast going through Norman's desk. Afterward, when he'd gone, I went on to search for whatever he'd been attempting to find. I discovered the information there." Her words rolled together as she spoke, the freedom in finally uttering them making them come quickly. "I just assumed, incorrectly, that it was the marquess who was to blame. My sister and I launched an effort to uncover the truth, and from that we learned of Lady Prendergast's role over all of it."

She grabbed Clayton's hands. "He is not a good man. And she is even more evil than he. That is why I want my son nowhere near that family."

Clayton's cheeks were ashen. "Jesus." His whisper emerged as a prayer.

He didn't challenge her. He didn't question her. He trusted her. And in that confirmed what she had suspected when she'd decided to tell him. He was a man deserving of her confidence.

"She needs to be brought to justice. They both do. Everyone who had been involved in Norfolk's death and the cover-up."

Sylvia drew in a shaky breath. "My son—"

Clayton gripped her lightly by the shoulders. "Vallen is no more responsible for the crimes of his grandparents than you are, Sylvia."

A sound of impatience escaped her. "It isn't that simple. Vallen's life, his whole future, would forever be linked to that dark scandal, one that has been wholly beyond his control and had come before he'd even taken his first breath."

"But what a lesson would he have learned from his mother's demands for justice . . ."

How dare he? He knew nothing of it. He didn't know what it was to want to protect one's child at any cost. To keep that babe from all pain and suffering. "You are speaking of ideals and not real life. He'll be known as the grandson of a murderer."

"And the mother who saw them brought to justice when people of power would have rather made a crime go away."

"This from a man who'd protect his sisters at every cost?" she shot back. "You, who are so concerned for their happiness? Don't tell me you wouldn't have pushed your sisters into marriage if you thought it would have seen them secured."

He bowed his head. "That is . . . fair. Perhaps it is easier for me to say as I don't explicitly know what it is to be a father, or to navigate what you have been navigating these past years." Clayton stepped toward her. "But I do know that you, who speak to women of how society should be, are not one who'd tolerate the evil Norfolk's parents perpetuated."

She inhaled sharply through her teeth, wanting to send him onward to the Devil with his optimistic view of her and that which was right and wrong. And yet . . . she could not.

Sylvia's mouth moved. She'd initially sought justice against her in-laws. But then when Lord Prendergast had used his influence to hush the charges and see his wife settled somewhere in the country, Sylvia had also had the opportunity to consider the ramifications the scandal would have upon her son.

It had taken until this moment, until Clayton had pointed it out, for her to realize that no matter how well intentioned her efforts, they'd still been wrong. Wrong for so many . . . not the least being her brother-in-law, who as a child had been a victim of Lady Prendergast's. Still, Hugh had turned the other cheek for Sylvia's son . . . but he shouldn't have had to. She shouldn't have asked him to.

"I should go," she said softly . . . because she was still bound by respectability. Yes, she was a widow. But all society cared about, first and foremost, was that she was a mother.

"Forgive me if I—"

"You misunderstand." Sylvia touched her fingers to his lips. "Do not apologize. Not when you are correct. I see that now." And yet as she took her leave, knowing what, ultimately, she would have to do, she hated that Lord and Lady Prendergast had interrupted this time she'd shared with Clayton.

Chapter 23

Clayton stood there after Sylvia had gone, his heart pounding, his thoughts all twisted with confusion and shock at everything she had revealed.

And here, since Norfolk's death, Clayton had stayed away from Sylvia. When all along she'd been in possession of some of the darkest, ugliest secrets. And she'd been living alone with them, she, a woman of honor, battling between what she wished to do and what she felt she had to do for her son.

And Clayton couldn't love her any more. He always had. Back when she'd been an innocent young lady who joined him for a game of cards. And even more now, when he learned how much she'd suffered and endured and . . . triumphed.

God, how he wanted her.

Only it wasn't just her body in the splendor they knew making love. He wanted all of her. In every way.

All along he had convinced himself that he couldn't have a future with her. That protecting her from the possibility of his dying young mattered most.

But what could they be together? What if his sister, and Sylvia, had been correct in their charges against him? What if he let himself live as he'd been afraid to fully do? Yes, it would be acknowledging that in his failure to pursue a future with her all those years ago, there had been lost time.

There would be even more lost moments if he didn't pursue the possibility of them together.

Yes, she had indicated she didn't want to love or marry again. She, however, had opened his eyes to the possibility of living. Perhaps he could do the same in terms of her and her thoughts on love.

The door handle clicked, and he whipped his focus to the front of the room. She'd returned. "S—" *Oh, hell. "Siiir."* In a bid to mask the name he'd been about to call out, he settled for that weak substitute. "That is . . . my lord." His muscles tensed as he faced the same man whom only earlier this evening he'd attempted to help. Only to discover a monster now stood before him.

Lord Prendergast took the liberty of shutting the door and entering deeper into the room. The moment he stopped before Clayton, he gave him a brief up-and-down look. "I . . . saw you speaking with Lady Norfolk."

Perhaps before he'd discovered Norfolk's father hadn't thought anything of covering up his son's death, he might have missed that detail. Or at the very least attributed it to nothing but the old man's desperation to see his grandson. Now, knowing what he and his family were capable of, there was something very sinister in having been watched by him. "Indeed." Clayton made himself smile in an attempt to cover up his loathing. "If you would excuse me, my sister—"

Lord Prendergast slid into Clayton's path. "Is undoubtedly safe with your mother."

And he was aware of Anwen. Clayton struggled to battle back the panic that came in knowing those he loved—Sylvia, his mother, his sisters—had all become a subject of interest to this man before him.

"I take it by the lady's abrupt departure in the midst of your game that she was less than agreeable to what you proposed."

What he'd proposed.

"I did not say that," he hedged. He'd thought it, of course.

The older man narrowed his gaze on him.

Clayton forced a calm that he didn't feel into his features. How had he failed to see how Norfolk's father had been manipulating him? And the marquess had done so, all in a bid to see his grandson. Ruthless enough to present himself as the wounded party and enlist Clayton to work on his behalf.

Perhaps if he could put the other gentleman off for even just a bit, he could ensure that Sylvia had some distance, for some time, from Lord Prendergast. Clayton switched to a different tactic. "Lady Sylvia is a woman with a deep heart and intellect, and I believe in time, if she is not pressed, she will think about it." And ultimately decide to have nothing to do with the man before him.

The marquess removed his gloves, and dusted them together in a movement that felt like orchestrated distractedness. But then, considering everything Sylvia had revealed, Lord Prendergast was as much an actor as his wife.

"That is . . . disappointing. I had thought you might be able to reason with her. You were close . . ." Lord Prendergast elevated a greying eyebrow. "Were you not?"

Clayton froze. He'd never shared with a single soul, not even the friends he trusted, his feelings for Sylvia.

The marquess gave him an odd look. "You and my son."

He spoke of Norfolk. *Not* Sylvia. Clayton made himself take a normal breath. Of course that was what Norfolk's father had meant. "We were." Until that last day of Norfolk's life, when Clayton had learned of the betrayal his friend had intended to carry out against Sylvia. That treacherous decision had erased a lifetime of friendship, and it had also allowed him to feel as though there'd been no obligation to the other man . . . not even in death.

"Then I would expect you should see this is something my son would want."

Given the other man's late son had intended to abandon his child, Clayton didn't think Norfolk would have cared one way or the other what Sylvia allowed or disallowed in terms of Vallen's visitors. And Clayton's chest tightened sharply, not just for Sylvia, but for the boy who deserved a loving father. And who'd found himself a pawn in some sick, twisted game of chess Lord and Lady Prendergast now played. "I know it isn't my place to interfere," he murmured, trying once more to take his leave. "My lord."

"How interesting," the marquess called after him, so that if Clayton continued on, he risked presenting himself as adversarial when he knew this man before him had to be handled cautiously.

Clayton turned back. "What is that?"

Lord Prendergast continued to beat those gloves together in a grating fashion. "It is simply that today, just hours ago, you were sympathetic. You agreed to help me secure a visit with my grandson. And now here we are." He spread his arms wide. "And you are of an altogether different opinion . . . What accounts for that, St. John?"

Oh, hell. God, how Clayton hated this waltz. But for Sylvia and her son, he'd gladly dance it. "I am not unsympathetic to either of you," he lied. Clayton felt no sympathy for the conniving man before him. "Both of you have suffered, and suffered greatly. And as someone who has suffered loss as well, I understand that it shapes us. We all have to come to terms, in our own time, and in our own way." That part came easier for Clayton as he now spoke in truths.

The marquess appeared wholly unmoved by Clayton's attempts at forging a connection through their grief. "She is spiteful," he spat. "That is all this comes down to. You know my son was unfaithful to her, as did she, and that resentment is what drives her to hurt me as she is. Vallen is my last link to my son, and his widow would deny me."

Clayton fought to mask his rage. He'd never been a man moved to violence, except for that one day when he'd struck Norfolk outside

Gentleman Jackson's. That same sentiment burnt strong inside, now . . . for that other man's father.

Logic said it was more dangerous to debate the unhinged man. Loving Sylvia as Clayton did, however, he refused to simply take those smears against her in silence. "I would not say that," he said in frosty tones. "Lady Norfolk is a woman with an enormous heart, a champion of others, and has shown only kindness for my sisters and those who truly know her."

Lord Prendergast sharpened his gaze on Clayton. "Hmm."

There was a cryptic quality to that vague rebuttal that sent disquiet through him once more. "I trust nothing about this has been easy for Lady Norfolk," Clayton said in an attempt to defuse whatever tension his response had elicited.

"A woman who smiles so freely and hosts scandalous company hardly strikes me as one who is grieving." The marquess looked squarely at Clayton. "In fact, one might even begin to suspect that she doesn't grieve because she has replaced Norman . . . that she is having her bed warmed by some man, as all wanton widows do." He left that dangling there, his meaning clear.

Clayton balled his fists tightly to keep from letting them fly into the other man's face. "You dishonor the memory of your son when you speak so ill of his wife."

"Tell me, St. John . . . with your and Lady Norfolk's relationship, have you been honoring my son's memory?"

Heat climbed Clayton's neck. "I don't know what you mean."

The marquess smiled, but it was one that never reached his eyes. "*Ohh*, I think you do."

Desperate men were dangerous ones. And Clayton had never been more eager to end a meeting. He glanced at his timepiece. "Forgive me, I must leave."

"Of course," Lord Prendergast said with a slight inclination of his head. "If you *see* Lady Norfolk again soon, please send her my regards."

That slight emphasis did not escape Clayton's notice. "I confess . . . I am disappointed that you wouldn't help an old man meet his grandson again."

There was a level of coldness in the marquess's eyes that chilled him, and Clayton was hurrying to take his leave when the older gentleman called out, stopping him once more. "Oh, and St. John? Your cravat is askew, boy."

This time when Clayton made to go, Lord Prendergast let him to his departure. All the while, however, Clayton felt that hated stare boring into his back, and the promise of a threat following after him.

Chapter 24

It was not the first time an emergency meeting had been called. In the past when ladies were facing demands from their parents to withdraw their membership, the group had convened to discuss ways in which they might manage to keep those ladies with them.

This was, however, the first time that *Sylvia* had found herself the source of the emergency.

Numb, her stomach churning and threatening to revolt, she made herself read the words written in the newspaper. Even though she had already read them. Numerous times.

Over and over. They were unchanging.

A wicked . . .

A wanton widow . . . caught leaving the company of a gentleman whose identity is believed to be that of Lord S. John . . . though most have contested the gentleman's identity. It is highly unlikely, given the gentleman's reputation . . . Now, that of the mother? There is no doubting the manner of woman she is . . . A shameful mother . . .

A shameful mother . . . A shameful mother . . . A shameful mother.

It was that last one. That last one struck the blow that threatened all she held dear. And she read it, over and over, to torture and punish herself. It was one thing to be a wanton widow. But being a mother as well? In a world where women were expected to be godly, that was not allowed by society. And her in-laws had known as much. They had rightly timed the situation so that Sylvia's reputation and good name were called into question, and because of that, they could have Vallen's court-appointed guardian challenge her.

I am going to be ill . . .

The article went on and on, likening Sylvia to a cancerous poison amongst respectable ladies, pervading the norms of propriety and respectability. Perverting them. Nor could there be any doubt as to who the one behind this public shaming in fact was. Norman's father and mother had acted first. There was an overall simplicity to the plan that Sylvia had failed to see . . . until it was too late. Destroy Sylvia's reputation so thoroughly. Why hadn't she done that which was honorable before? Why had she agreed to the silence? Why? Why? *Why?* There were so many regrets. Too many of them.

"*A gentleman whose identity is believed to be that of Lord S. John . . . though most have contested the gentleman's identity.*" Anwen pushed up her spectacles and continued to read that piece aloud. "*It is highly unlikely, given the gentleman's reputation . . . Now, that of the mother? There is no doubting the manner of woman she is . . . A shameful mother . . .*"

She lowered the page. "That is really . . . something, is it not? The woman is a harlot, while the gentleman should be an afterthought. Not that I agree with their opinion on Clayton. That is neither here nor there."

"Enough," Cora whispered loudly, nudging her sister in the knee into silence, then casting a less-than-discreet nod in Sylvia's direction.

Oh, God, it was too much.

Sylvia looked away from the pitying stare over to where her mother sat between Clara and Lila. And Sylvia would hand it to her mother. Give credit where credit was due. She would have expected the dowager countess to be reduced to a blubbering mess of rage and tears, as she'd been when Sylvia stated her intentions to not move back in with her family, as they had both wished and expected.

What Sylvia had *not* expected, however, was for the dowager countess to join the Mismatch Society . . . and remain so very composed through Sylvia's scandal.

No, in the greatest of role reversals, Sylvia sat there, fighting to not give in to histrionics, while her mother was the composed one.

Nay, not composed—her mother was enraged . . . on her behalf. And that show of support proved somewhat steadying.

"A lover," her mother spat. "As if you would ever."

The other ladies present all added their support of the dowager countess. Sylvia briefly directed her gaze up to the ceiling out of fear that someone present might see an imprint of that wickedness she'd shared with Clayton. Only, it hadn't felt wicked. It had been wonderful and freeing, and there'd been no shame in it. And now to have their relationship called into question before all of Polite Society? In a scandal sheet?

Sylvia returned her gaze to the table before her, covered with various newspapers.

In many scandal sheets, she silently amended.

"It is . . . preposterous. You are *none* of these things," Anwen said in Sylvia's defense.

"Of course she's not," Cora said.

But it didn't matter what she was. Just society's belief and perception were the reality. And the reality was, a mother of ill repute could and likely would have her authority over her child questioned.

Oh, God.

KnockKnockKnock.

Sylvia looked over to the one wielding the gavel, the unlikeliest one. Her mother, having commanded the attention of the room, stood at the center. "Now, lamenting what has been said is a waste of our energies and efforts. What we must concentrate our attentions on is correcting the situation."

Correcting the situation. As if they were speaking about repairing a torn hem or retuning an old pianoforte, and not Sylvia's thoroughly shredded reputation.

"She is correct," Clayton's mother called out, her support earning a pleased little nod from the dowager countess. "We simply need to . . . fix it. Make it go away." Her eyes narrowed. "Find those responsible and see that we make their existence very, very uncomfortab—"

Approving cheers went up around the membership.

"That isn't . . . ," her mother tried again, struggling to make herself heard over the rambunctious group. "That isn't what I was saying," she said, and raised her voice—in vain—to be heard. "I said, that isn't what I was saying."

Clara stood and held her arms wide, silencing the group once more. "Our individual rage does nothing. Collectively, a show of support, however, is what Sylvia needs. Along with possible solutions."

The ladies all looked around at one another helplessly. As helpless as Sylvia herself felt.

"Society knows better," Brenna murmured. "Clayton would never go about . . . doing . . . doing . . . what it says he's done."

Actually, he had done that . . . and more. Such were truths, however, that Sylvia would never share with anyone, let alone his *sisters.*

"Perhaps if he and the proper gentlemen he is friendly with vouch for him?" Anwen volunteered with the same level of optimism as her brother.

"Yes, let's begin with Landon and Scarsdale. The two worst rogues should do much toward helping the situation," Cora muttered, earning a sharp kick from her eldest sister. "Ouch." Cora rushed to grab for the bespectacled girl when the Viscountess St. John placed two fingers to her lips and whistled sharply.

Both women instantly stopped their fighting.

Sylvia's mother winced and gave her head a faint, horrified shake.

"We might launch a campaign ourselves," Miss Dobson suggested. "Between the lot of us and our familial connections, surely we might quash the gossip?"

This wasn't going to go away. Because it wasn't supposed to. Lord and Lady Prendergast intended to bury Sylvia with her sins and scandals. *Think. Think.* Sylvia pressed her fingertips against her temples in a bid to drill a solution into her head and rid herself of the growing megrim.

"It is more likely it will lead to the quashing of the Mismatch Society," Emma Gately said on a pain-filled whisper.

Yes, there was that reality, too.

"Does anyone have any other solutions?"

"Have we even heard one?" Annalee asked with her usual dryness.

Valerie scanned her notes. "We have the idea of Lord St. John's influence, and the influence of the Mismatch Society, and . . ." She lifted her forlorn gaze. "That is all."

That was all, indeed.

"There is always marriage," Sylvia's mother put forward, her half-hearted suggestion drowned out once more.

This was going nowhere. Sylvia climbed to her feet. "I thank each of you for your support and unswerving loyalty. I am grateful. I also need to think."

Clara claimed the gavel, and banged it once. "I think that is wise for all of us. We need to reconvene. We need to come together when we're in a clear frame of mind and we've each had time to think individually on a way out of this."

Sylvia forced her features into a serene mask, one that belied the panic knocking around at her insides, as she said her goodbyes to each member of the society, until only her family and Annalee and Valerie remained.

"Do you want company?" Valerie offered tentatively.

No. There was no one she wished to see just then.

She was proven wrong a moment later.

Her son came hurtling into the room, laughing as he raced ahead of his nursemaid. Vallen tossed himself at Sylvia, and she caught him up in her arms, swinging him about. "I needed that," she said in all sincerity as he wrapped his chubby little arms around her neck and squeezed so tight she couldn't breathe for a moment. He planted a wet kiss on her cheek. "Go," she said to the group still gathered. "I am fine." Nothing would be . . . but in this moment, it was.

"Bye-bye, Grammy," Vallen said, waving a hand wildly at the reserved matriarch of their group.

And though she prided herself on her strict reserve, the dowager countess went all soft in the eyes, waving both her hands in a greeting and a goodbye.

Valerie was the last to leave, closing the door behind her.

And then Sylvia and Vallen . . . were alone.

"You're sad."

"I'm not," she said as she set him down on his feet.

He sucked on his thumb. "Scared?"

"Does Mama get scared?"

"You said everyone gets scared and—" He giggled wildly as she tickled him in the sensitive spots under both of his arms until she drove away his worry.

"Will we see Eris and Clay?"

Eris and Clayton.

How could they go out now without attracting more gossip and scandal? Sylvia felt tears sting her eyes, and she furiously blinked them back to keep her son from seeing them. "Not this morn, love."

"This afternoon?"

"No, I'm afraid Mama has things to see to." The important one of holding on to her son at all costs. Sylvia fought the rising panic. Damn her in-laws. Damn—

"What 'bout tomorrow?"

"I said I don't know when we can see them again," she cried, and then immediately hated herself. Vallen's lower lip trembled, and big tears filled his eyes, and she hated herself all the more. "I'm sorry," she said, gathering him into her arms once more, and just holding him for all she was worth. "I didn't mean to snap."

"I like them."

"I do, too, love," she soothed as he wept.

"I want him to be my da."

Oh, God. Her heart couldn't take this. For Clayton was the manner of father her son had deserved, and he was the manner of man she had always dreamed of and wanted and—

There is always marriage . . .

Her mother's suggestion danced in the air.

And yet the idea of it, her consideration, didn't come from a solution to her crisis, though it would certainly be one. It came from a place of finally being able to acknowledge to herself that she loved him. She always had. And when she imagined a future between him and another, it ravaged her. Because she wanted him in her life. Not as some secret. Not as a friend she had to surreptitiously steal time with.

She . . . wanted to marry him. She wanted to wake up in the same bed as him. She wanted to travel with him. She wanted to spend every moment of every waking day they had together. Sylvia waited for the rush of horror and the panic to come. After years of living in a loveless marriage and then learning of her husband's betrayal, she was now considering entering into that state . . . again.

Only, this time, it would be . . . with Clayton. Her friend. Her lover. Her partner.

It was Clayton. It had always been him. Then, she'd been a girl, waiting for him to move from friend to suitor before coming to accept there were no romantic feelings on his part. Now, she was a woman. A woman determined to take her future—their future—into her own hands.

And for the first time since her world had fallen apart that morning, Sylvia smiled.

Chapter 25

Clayton found himself with an unlikely quiet at the breakfast table. A rarity in a household full of women.

That silence proved short-lived.

"They've left me." Eris sighed, dropping her chin forlornly atop the table.

Clayton accepted a cup of coffee from a footman, and waved off the copy of *The Times* the young man offered. "Who?"

"*All* of them," she groused. "Mama, Cora, Anwen, Brenna. Even Daria and Delia went this time. I want to be old. Like you."

"Thank you," he said dryly, taking a sip of his coffee.

"You're welcome." Eris let out another aggrieved, exaggerated exhale.

He would miss these days when her innocent ability to let sarcasm go undetected was at an end. Clayton set down his glass and leaned over to whisper near her ear. "Trust me, you don't want to wish it all away, poppet." He rustled her curls. "The older you are, the more difficult and complicated everything else is."

She swatted his hand. "Don't patron me."

Patron . . . ? "Patronize?"

"That's what I said, Clayton. You go to bed when you want. You eat all the sweets you want. You stay out late. You see your friends whenever you want."

It was an impressively sturdy argument from his youngest sister, indicating that mayhap she wasn't so very far away from losing that pure child's innocence. It was a sad and sobering realization. "Point . . . taken. There are some benefits to being an adult. But there'll be time enough for all that. For now, enjoy being a child."

She glared at him.

And to soften that display of her disapproval, he offered her one of his two chocolate biscuits.

Eris gave him a look.

Clayton hesitated, eyeing the tray where the remainder of the chocolate biscuits had been, before they'd likely been devoured by his uncharacteristically earlier-rising sisters. With a sigh, he handed over the last one on his plate.

His youngest sister smiled around the mouthful of biscuit she'd already started devouring. "Thatsbevver," she said, dusting the back of her hand over her mouth. She swallowed a big bite, and then took another.

Footsteps sounded in the hall.

Alas, it appeared his sisters had returned.

Landon appeared in the doorway with Scarsdale at his side.

"There's a scandal, a—" He stopped midsentence and dropped a deep bow. "Lady Eris."

"I'm a miss." Eris rolled her eyes. "You should know that. I keep telling you."

"Alas, I'm still learning."

Eris promptly ignored him and turned her attention on Scarsdale. "Wherefsyourbow?" she demanded around another big bite of her morning treat. With a chocolate-stained finger, she wagged it in the gentleman's direction.

Properly scolded, Scarsdale bent low at the waist. "Miss Eris."

Clayton's sister nodded slowly. She took a long and audible swallow. "Better."

"Why don't you run along, poppet, so I can discuss whatever business has brought these scoundrels here to visit so early."

It was the wrong thing for Clayton to say. His sister set her jaw at a defiant angle. "I want to stay."

Of course she did. From over the top of her head, he caught the amused look exchanged between Landon and Scarsdale.

With a wide smile, Landon brandished a small leather sack from inside his jacket front; he dangled it by the two black strings.

Hopping up, Eris held out a palm and wiggled her fingers.

Taking that as an invitation to join her, Landon placed the item in her hand.

Her head bent, Eris opened it and peered around the inside, sifting through whatever those contents were. She nodded once. "Peppermints will do," she said, and with a jaunty little wave, she skipped off for the doorway before stopping midstride. Doubling back, she stuck the strings for the little velvet sack between her teeth and filled her hands with the remnants of her biscuits. Not bothering to turn back, she lifted them both, waved, and then was gone.

Scarsdale gave his head a rueful shake. "Remind me never to complain about my four brothers. Your sister is positively ruthless."

"Speaking of ruthless." Landon snapped his fingers, and Scarsdale waved a copy of *The Times*, which had until now been tucked under his arm. The marquess looked to the servants. "If you would?"

"Dismissing my servants, are you?" Clayton drawled when the young men had all filed neatly from the room. He picked up his coffee. "What crisis is it now?" he asked as Scarsdale took the liberty of shutting the door behind them. "A problem with the mistress? Another bad hand at cards?"

Landon laughed good-naturedly. "Alas, this time, there's a different naughty scoundrel amongst us. Scandal is a-brewing." Landon tossed a paper at Clayton's chest, knocking the grip Clayton had on his cup, spilling droplets of the black brew into what was left of his morning meal. "And it appears for once you are at the heart of it."

"What in hell is *this*?" he muttered as he scanned the front pages of the favored society paper.

"And cursing now, too," Landon remarked with a sharp bark of laughter. "It appears you have been corrupted, after all."

Corrupted.

And yet . . .

That was precisely what the newspaper was reporting.

Scandal!

What in hell was this? With every word read, he sat farther and farther upright in his seat.

A wanton widow . . . caught leaving the company of a gentleman whose identity is believed to be that of Lord S. John . . . though most have contested the gentleman's identity. It is highly unlikely, given the gentleman's reputation . . . Now, that of the mother? There is no doubting the manner of woman she is . . . A shameful mother . . .

"You're only just telling me of this?" he cried.

Landon bristled. "I had business at my clubs, and . . ." He angled his head in Scarsdale's direction. "Who the hell knows what he was doing. Disappearing with one of his mistresses or another, which you really shouldn't make him feel badly for, as he's been heartbrok—"

"All right. All right!" Clayton interrupted that seemingly never-ending defense. Not that any defense was needed. It was hardly Landon and Scarsdale's fault.

Flummoxed, he collapsed against the red velvet upholstery of his breakfast chair. Horror. Fury. Worry. So many emotions that he couldn't settle on just one and was left with a tumult inside. He didn't give a jot what the papers printed about him, but what they said about Sylvia? Nor did he have a doubt as to who was responsible for spreading the poison here.

Rage darkened his vision.

When he could properly see again, Clayton read and reread the words written there. And then he read them once more for good measure. Wanting them to change. Needing them to change. And yet, they did not. The vile, ink-black marks remained the same. About her. Shameful, unfair, and hateful ones she was undeserving of.

Hurling the paper across the room, Clayton let fly a string of curses.

With a contrasting calm, both men settled into chairs, each on the opposite side of Clayton. And what was worse . . . In place of their usual banter, there was only a damning, accusatory silence.

Clayton sat, staring at the wall ahead of him, avoiding looking at either man. For a moment, he thought the other men knew. That they suspected all the wicked and wonderful things he'd done to and with Sylvia.

"We know it's not true," Scarsdale said quietly. "You'd never do something in bad form . . . and certainly nothing so outrageous as pursuing the lady."

Their late best friend's widow. Why didn't they just say it? They were both thinking it.

"Of course he wouldn't . . . ," Landon scoffed, and then there was a noticeable hesitation. "Right?"

Clayton closed his eyes on his friend's question. This was certainly not a discussion he wanted to have now or ever. Particularly even less at this moment, when all he wanted to do was go to Sylvia. For years, he'd said nothing. For years, he'd concealed from his friends all he felt for Norfolk's wife.

"I cannot say that," Clayton said hoarsely. "I love her. I have loved her since I met her. And I would do anything to see her spared from pain." And yet, doing just that all those years ago, he'd inadvertently sentenced her to an unhappy marriage with Norfolk. He made himself open his eyes and look at the silent pair of gentlemen next to him. Braced for their condemnation. Waiting for them to call him out as a dishonorable friend.

Scarsdale slammed his fist on the table, rattling Eris's leftover porcelain plate. "I knew it!" he exclaimed triumphantly.

Landon cursed. Fishing a small purse from inside his jacket, he tossed it past Clayton, the sack landing with a noisy jingle near Scarsdale's fingertips.

"You . . . ?" Perplexed, Clayton couldn't get out the rest of that thought. He couldn't make anything of the bizarre exchange unfolding before him now.

"I knew it!" Scarsdale exclaimed again. Kicking his legs up, he rested his boots on the edge of the breakfast table.

"You knew?"

The other man shrugged. "It wasn't difficult to see."

"Except, apparently, for me," Landon mumbled under his breath. "How long?"

Clayton drew a breath. *Forever.* It was as though his and Sylvia's souls had been connected before they even met, and that relationship cemented upon their first meeting on the side of Lady Waverly's ballroom floor. "From the moment she made her Come Out."

"God dammit." Landon took out another small bag of coins and hurled those earnings over at a laughing Scarsdale.

The moment the other man's laughter died down, Clayton collected the newspaper and returned to his seat. He read through the front page before handing it back over for Landon's perusal.

"Why would anyone do this to you and Lady Norfolk?" Landon asked, scanning the words on that vile sheet. "You are probably two of the nicest people. Present self excluded, of course."

"Of course," Scarsdale said sarcastically.

"Norfolk's father," he clipped out.

That managed to again silence both men for a moment.

Taking care to leave out any and all details of what Sylvia had revealed about Norfolk's death, Clayton shared everything else about his dealings with Lord Prendergast . . . and the man's ruthless determination to see his grandson.

When he finished, they remained quiet.

Landon's cheeks were a sickly shade of grey.

Clayton straightened in his chair. "What is it?"

"I'm so sorry," Landon said, his voice weak. "He came to me, asking if I could help arrange a meeting between you and he." Gentleman Jackson's. "It was his idea . . . to meet at that place. Said he wanted to watch Scarsdale and me because of how Norfolk used to love boxing. Claimed he felt closer to his son." Which was not unlike some of the subtly coercive words he'd used to bring Clayton around to doing his bidding. "I didn't know," the other man said on a rush, misinterpreting the reason for Clayton's silence. "I thought I was helping. I thought—"

Clayton squeezed his arm. "It is not your fault. The man is a master manipulator, and he has been attempting to exploit us all." And now the marquess was playing a different game. One that threatened Sylvia's right to her own child.

"Why are you still here, St. John?" Scarsdale asked.

"Where should I be?"

His friend eyed him like he had two heads. "Wait, after sharing everything you've shared about Lady Norfolk, you really still believe you should be here?" Scarsdale leaned forward. "If you love her, why are you here even now with us miserable buggers?"

Why . . . indeed?

A hand touched his shoulder, and Clayton looked over at an uncharacteristically solemn Scarsdale. "For too long, you've worried about too much. Don't let fear of what others might think, or what might happen to you, keep you from your happiness . . . again."

Landon nodded, adding his support.

Clayton needed to go to her. He needed to see her now. Even as it was likely the worst thing to do for the increased scrutiny they would receive, he had to see her. With their names twisted and twined with scandal and gossip. Because everything between him and Sylvia was good and pure. Oh, society would never see it that way. Because society cared about an image of propriety. They, with their false outrage and sense of offended morals. And yet . . . it was not as uncomplicated as his friends believed it was.

"Go to her," Scarsdale urged. "Don't be a damned fool like I was, man."

He is right . . .

And it was as though Clayton were suddenly free. As if the chains he'd placed upon himself, restraints that had kept him from surrendering completely to Sylvia and a future with her, were broken.

He took off flying from the breakfast room . . . and collided squarely with a servant who had the inopportune timing of being in the entryway at that particular moment.

The small young man, Jones, went sprawling square on his arse, while a slightly unsteady Clayton managed to maintain his feet.

"I hope that's not a sign," Landon whispered loud enough for Clayton to hear.

Yes, he hoped the same thing.

"He didn't fall," Scarsdale pointed out, shielding his mouth as he spoke.

"Forgive me, my lord," Jones stammered from where he still lay on the floor. "Company arrived for your sisters, and when I informed her that they weren't here, she insisted that she would wait. And—"

Stretching out a hand, Clayton helped the servant to his feet. He really didn't have time for this. There was the matter of trying to convince Sylvia he was worth marrying.

"I have important affairs to see to; handle it as you would." With that, Clayton took off running once more down the hall, calling for his horse as he went.

"I did. But, my lord, your sisters aren't here—"

Whatever else Jones intended to say was lost as Clayton reached the next corridor and nearly ran headfirst into a maid.

The young woman gasped but managed to stay on her feet. "Forgive me, my lord." It was official: overeager servants were determined to get in his way, and delay a proposal that was years overdue. "I was advised to find you and—"

Clayton continued on and reached the foyer to find his butler in wait with the door partially open. At least someone in his household staff was not determined to thwart him.

"Thank you," Clayton called, not breaking stride as he stepped out the open door and into the street and— "Sylvia!" She had been the one waiting for his sisters. Of course.

Halfway inside the carriage, she froze. "Clay . . . Lord St. John!" Ignoring the offer of help from the servant, Sylvia scrambled down and, lifting her skirts as she went, glided toward him as if they'd met in a parlor.

And he hated that she had corrected herself in using his Christian name. He hated that formality because he wanted only the intimacy that had begun as a secret years ago, and had grown between them.

They met at the bottom of the steps of his townhouse. Just as much as he wanted to hear his name fall freely from her lips, he wanted to invite her in . . . and he hated that his sisters had not yet returned, and the perception that would come from her joining him inside. Instead, they'd be forced to steal several moments as if they were passersby compelled to exchange pleasantries.

He lowered his voice. "I heard . . . read . . . the gossip, and I am sorry. So sorry."

She waved off that apology. "Do not be, Clayton." The breeze toyed with those artful curls she always left to dangle at her shoulder, and he ached to gather them in his fingers as he'd done when they were alone. When they made love. And yet for the intimacy of this exchange, he was suddenly aware of the interested glances cast their way from residents in their windows. Sylvia brushed the strands back, and he envied her that touch and freedom. "You were correct," she said softly. "That was one of the reasons I wished to see you. To tell you that. Rather, to thank you. I should have had the courage to follow through with the demand for justice. I didn't. Instead, I made a deal with the Devil, and because of that . . . here we are." Her voice trailed off.

A pair of elderly matrons, holding the leads of two noisy pugs, came marching down the pavement. Neither woman made any effort to conceal her bald curiosity. And as Clayton and Sylvia stepped apart, allowing them to pass, it served as a reminder that their every move was being scrutinized. Making a show of holding out his elbow, he offered her an escort back to her carriage. They made a very slow stroll.

"How can I help you?" he whispered as they walked. Anything. Whatever she asked. Clayton would marry her to save her reputation, and make sure her son remained in her care. But now, he also realized, he would marry her even if there was no reason at all. That was, beyond the love he felt for her.

"An emergency meeting of the Mismatch Society was called today."

And he had not been invited. Of course, it made sense. They couldn't very well have the fellow whose name had been linked present. But still, he wanted to have been included. Because he loved her. Because she was his friend.

"The general consensus is that the situation is very dire. The options to restore my reputation are few. My mother suggested marriage."

Clayton's heart skipped a beat, and then fell with her next words. "I thought on it a good deal . . . I don't want a marriage because of necessity. One of convenience. I already had that. One where I was a responsibility."

It wouldn't be that with her. Yes, he'd reentered her life for the very reasons she hated and spoke against now. But deep down, it had been about something more. He knew that now. He couldn't say as much. "Of course," he said, his voice wooden to his own ears.

They reached the carriage, and he made to hand her up, but Sylvia ignored that offer of help. "And then I realized something . . ."

"What was that?"

She craned her neck back to meet his gaze. "It wouldn't be any of that. Not with you. Yes, of course it would be convenient, given the circumstances. But that isn't why I would marry you . . . why I want to marry you. I would do so because I love you." Her eyes softened. "I love you," she repeated.

Clayton's ears . . . They could not make sense of it. Of what she'd now said twice. What was she saying?

"I have loved you forever," Sylvia said softly. "I am asking you to marry me, not because you feel you have to. But because you want to. Want to, as I want to marry you. And I know what you are thinking."

He was glad one of the two of them did.

For he could make less sense of the latter part than the former. Sylvia . . . not only loved him . . . she was also asking him to marry her?

"You think this is about respectability and . . . the gossip sheets. And Vallen."

Nay, he couldn't put together one thought, let alone all those she'd strung together.

"And yes, given the circumstances, it would certainly be convenient. But that isn't the reason I'm asking you to marry me. You are the reason. When I am with you, I am happy." And in the greatest contradiction, a glassy sheen filled her eyes. He caught one of those tears as it rolled down her cheek. A watery laugh bubbled past her lips. "I always was, with you. And then I forgot to smile and laugh, and you reminded me how to do all those things again."

And you came to her on a lie. You came to her in what began as her being one more responsibility . . . and she will hate you if she knows that. She will question whether your motives were driven by a sense of obligation instead of friendship.

Sylvia's full lips quivered, and her smile faltered. "You don't want to." "No."

Her hands released his, leaving his palms cold and empty. "I see."

My God, no. "Not no. Yes. I mean, yes. Yes, I love you." Clayton's voice shook—his entire body shook from the force of his emotion. "I have loved you from the moment I met you, Sylvia."

"I don't . . . under . . ." Sylvia stopped, and then tried again. "You . . . do?"

"I was a damned fool." About so much, and for so long. Clayton moved his gaze over the cherished planes of her face. "I was scared. Scared of what my fate held and what that would mean to any woman I left behind. Scared I was undeserving of you, because I wasn't good enough for you."

"Why? *Why?*" she whispered. "Why would you ever think that? I thought you only saw me as a friend. Just a friend."

"I was so determined to see you happy, not even allowing myself to imagine a future with you as my wife, if it meant that you could have the grand love you were deserving of." Which he had thought Norfolk could provide her. God, he had been wrong about so much. He glanced over the top of her head to the steady stream of carriages passing by. "I thought I would be just fine with that sacrifice, but only destroyed myself and broke my heart when I saw you marry him." He briefly closed his eyes and relived the hell of watching her walk down the aisle to meet another man, lifting his glass in many marriage toasts to Sylvia's future with another. Even to this day, he struggled to breathe from the pain of that.

When he opened his eyes again, he found Sylvia's tears falling freely. "You foolish, foolish man," she said, lightly pounding her fists against his chest.

"Yes, I have been. But I'm determined to never be so again where you are concerned. I will marry you as long as you promise to be my partner in every aspect of life . . ."

"Clayton, Clayton, we will always be best friends."

Sylvia flung herself into his arms, and Clayton caught her to him. Laughing, she touched her mouth to his. And this, her in his arms and the promise of a future together laid out before him as a reality, was only all he'd ever wanted.

Reality, however, had a way of rearing its ugly head. He wanted all the things he'd just said, but he also wanted the absolute truth between them. He'd not have a lie clouding over that happiness, for then it could never be a true happiness. And it was that which chased away what should have been unadulterated joy, replacing it with a dread that tightened all the muscles of his belly. Reluctantly, he broke that kiss. "I need to—"

"Clayton is kissing Sylvia!" Eris cried. "Ew. Ew. Ew. Yuck."

Not that. He certainly did not need that.

All seven of them, to be exact. Clayton looked off toward the owner of that very public pronouncement. And cursed his and their timing. Like a small army on the march, the Kearsley sisters streamed down the pavement toward him and Sylvia.

"Kissing a lady in the street is sure to garner attention, and more attention is not something either of you are in need of," his mother said, loud enough to be heard by all, and Clayton flinched. She and her contingent of daughters reached them. "Granted, I mind it less if there is marriage and love involved," the viscountess prattled. "Not that marriage need be involved. As long as love is." Clayton's mother looked back and forth between Clayton and Sylvia.

"There is . . . both," Sylvia supplied. She nudged him in the side.

"Yes, both."

Clayton's mother clapped her hands. "Splendid! Not that I am one to require marriage for something as innocuous as kissing to occur, but other mothers?" She cleared her throat in an exaggerated manner. "Such as your mother, dear," she said on an equally obscenely loud whisper that sent Clayton's hand up to reflexively cover his eyes. "She would, I suspect, worry." Looping her arm through Sylvia's, the viscountess led Sylvia off. "Now, come. We shall celebrate first with our families before the public announcement."

And as the Kearsley women swarmed Sylvia, she stole a bemused glance over her shoulder back to where Clayton stood, left behind . . . trying to figure out how in hell to tell her now.

Chapter 26

All the *ton* was talking about Sylvia and Clayton still. But the gossip had shifted, and what once had been viewed as sordid was now a great romance. And the only thing Polite Society devoured more than someone's downfall was an unexpected and unlikely love story.

As such, there had definitely been more sighs at this latest Mismatch Society meeting than at all the other meetings to come before it. A surprising amount, given that what had brought most of them together was their disdain for anything romantic.

At that particular moment, the latest of the sighers was the eldest of Clayton's sisters. "How very—"

"Progressive."

Anwen favored Cora with a frown. "I was going to say 'romantic.'"

"Yes, I agree it is both," her younger sister said. "However, I prefer we lead with progressive. Lord knows a society of independent ladies has already gotten far enough away from our original intent."

Annalee held her silver flask aloft. "I'll drink to that." As the young lady lifted it to her mouth, Valerie leaned over and neatly slipped it from the other woman's hand. She set it down at her feet, away from Annalee.

"Spoiler of good times," Annalee groused. "We should acknowledge in some way that we've moved dangerously far away from what we'd set out to do."

"What did you set out to do?" Sylvia's mother, who'd shockingly decided to remain on as a member, looked around the room. "What was . . . the original intent?" she asked when no one made any effort to elaborate.

Leave it to Clayton's perfectly wonderful and eccentric mother to expound on that question. "To break down marriage."

The dowager countess fluttered a hand about her breast, fishing for the chain that dangled at her throat. "That . . . was real?"

"Very much so," Miss Dobson confirmed.

Wilting in her seat, Sylvia's mother grabbed her smelling salts and sniffed.

"Worry not, Hettie . . . Some of the girls have not entirely disavowed the state. Why, your daughter is marrying . . . that is . . . if she doesn't change her mind and wish to retain her inde—"

"Oh, *goooooood.*" Sylvia's mother collapsed against the back of her seat, and with a wry grin, Clara fanned the older woman.

Seated next to one another on the painted canapé sofa, Sylvia and Clayton shared a smile.

Yes, the dowager countess may be close to fainting, but she'd unconditionally and staunchly stood beside Sylvia through the whirlwind of a scandal . . . and she was here now, attempting to be part of the Mismatch Society. And it was also the closest Sylvia had ever felt to her mother in the whole of her twenty-seven years.

"Perhaps, as we are speaking about progressive marriages as being the only marriages we should consider, we might hear from Sylvia on her expectations after she weds?"

All eyes went to Sylvia. What did she want . . . ?

"I expect to have a partnership." Which they would. Because it's what they'd always had in terms of their relationship. "And I expect my husband—"

"Clayton," Anwen substituted.

Christi Caldwell

"Clayton will be supportive of me and my decisions. And there will be love," she said softly. "And honesty. Of what one another is thinking or feeling and wanting of life." None of which she'd had with Norman, and had despaired of ever knowing.

"I wish Sylvia much happiness," Miss Gately said. "However, I still fail to believe such a marriage exists."

When the group's attention shifted over to the young lady and the latest debate on marriage, Sylvia felt Clayton's eyes on her, and looked up.

"I do need to talk to you," he said quietly. "When the meeting is adjourned?"

"You've changed your mind."

"No," he said with a solemnity that made her smile.

God, how she loved him. Why had she, for so long, resisted the idea of a future with him? Leaning in, Sylvia touched her nose to his and whispered, "I was teasing." How very endearing he was . . . How had she for so long fought the possibility of a future as his wife?

"Oh, yes. Right. Uh . . . of course. But there is something we need to discuss."

Despite her attempt at teasing him, there was a . . . seriousness not only to those words . . . but also to the tone of his voice, an added layer of deepness that sent the first stirrings of unease through her since she'd had the idea to offer for him.

Stop it. You are imagining trouble where there isn't any . . .

She'd become so accustomed to all the worst happening that she was allowing that worry to creep into this unabashed joy.

And yet, no matter how many times she told herself as much throughout the remainder of the meeting, she continued to steal glances at Clayton . . . and found him . . . distracted. Serious. And unsmiling.

In short, no way that she'd ever remembered him being. And he should be this now, after accepting her offer.

And then there was the threat posed by her father-in-law. For she didn't believe for an instant that he'd simply concede the right to see his grandson. Just as much as she knew that if he saw Vallen once, it would never be enough. Unless . . . that was the reason for this change over Clayton?

All those panicky thoughts robbed Sylvia of the ability to concentrate on the remainder of the meeting, and when it was at an end and the ladies were filing from the room, she'd never been more grateful. She stared on as Clayton's sisters circled him, all taking turns teasing and ribbing. Periodically, he'd playfully tug a curl or ruffle the top of one of his sisters' heads, the way he might a small girl, in such a tender display of brotherly affection and warmth that it was impossible, from the sight of that closeness, to feel the same crippling fear she had during the meeting.

The tension eased as Sylvia watched on, a silent observer. "I believe he will make you a good husband," her mother murmured at her side, and Sylvia startled, having failed to hear her approach.

"I believe he will, as well." A man who loved so absolutely and cared so deeply and gave his affection so freely would be a good husband.

"I know it is ill to speak unfavorably of the deceased and in bad form to say, but I never much liked your husband, even before you were married."

No, her mother hadn't. When the *ton* had been entranced by Sylvia's whirlwind romance with society's most notorious rogue, her mother had alternated between sniffing her smelling salts and lecturing Sylvia on his unsuitability.

Her mother leaned in and spoke close to her ear. "Before him, though, I had thought for a bit that you and Lord St. John would be a match, and I am so very happy that you did not let the husband who stole so much from you also steal your ability to trust another." She paused. "But if he violates that trust, and he hurts you, I'll hurt him more."

Sylvia turned and placed a kiss on her mother's cheek. "Thank you, Mother."

Color splashed cheeks that were just showing signs of wrinkles. Waving a hand, uncomfortable with that display of affection, as she'd always been by any show of emotion, the dowager countess tossed her head. "None of that now. I'm still not like that woman."

"That woman" being Clayton's mother, who at that moment was in the midst of pinching Cora's cheeks and touching her nose to the girl's.

"I like her very much," Sylvia said. She loved all Clayton's family.

"I do, too," her mother confessed, and then elevating her chin, she swept out of the parlor and past the noisy collection of Kearsleys. "Good day, Julia."

"Hettie," the viscountess said as she passed.

Seeming to take that as a cue, Clayton's mother broke up the assembling of her children and paused to make her goodbyes to Sylvia. "We shall leave one by one for the carriage." A twinkle lit the older woman's eyes. "That way there is confusion as to who is outdoors and who is indoors." With a wink, she took herself off.

"I adore them," Sylvia said when she and Clayton were alone.

"I adore you. I love you," he said quietly.

And yet . . . "You are troubled." It wasn't a question. Rather, it was a statement of fact that came from knowing this man as she did.

Presenting Sylvia with his back, Clayton scraped a hand through his hair.

<hr />

You are troubled . . .

Troubled was the least of what Clayton was.

Terrified. Tormented. Tortured.

And ashamed. Ashamed of himself. One, for the initial reasons he had avoided her. Because that decision had been born of an act of cowardice. She spoke often of their friendship. And yet he had not been the friend she had deserved. Through so much. Friends were there for everything. The bad. The awful. And the really, really awful. Not just the easy times enjoyed beside a crowded ballroom floor.

And what was worse, he'd allowed his love for her to be the reason he'd stayed away from her. What did that say about the manner of man he was?

"Won't you say something?" she asked, her voice pleading.

Years. Clayton had been in possession of years with which to prepare a response about this. Only to find himself guilty of yet another failing. Because he had no good words, or even so much as a place to start.

Nay, that wasn't true. There was one place that made sense.

Clayton made himself face Sylvia. "We need to speak about the day Norfolk died," he said, cutting to the heart of it. "Perhaps you might want to sit?"

Sylvia dampened her mouth. "I don't . . . ?"

That was a restlessness he well understood. Clayton needed to be done with this telling. And the only way to end it was to begin. "Norfolk asked me to join him at Gentleman Jackson's. I hated fighting. I hated boxing. I hated that place long before . . . that day. I never understood, and still don't, the enjoyment in something so barbaric. Battering and bloodying another man?" *I'm rambling. Stop. Just get to it.* He took a slow and steadying breath. And then several more, until he found his way back toward words that mattered. "Norfolk knew it; I didn't understand why he should ask me to go that day." There was so much about that day, and that man he once called his best friend that he didn't, and wouldn't, and could never understand. Most of which stemmed from Norfolk's inability to love Sylvia. "He . . . informed me that he intended to leave you."

"What?"

There was no inflection in her tone to make sense of what she was thinking, and it was the first time in all the years he'd known her that he failed to gather what she was feeling. "He indicated that he was in love and wanted a future with her. He was going to leave you and Vallen, Sylvia."

Neither of them said anything for a long while. Or perhaps time ticked along quickly. Clayton wasn't altogether certain of anything . . . other than his love for her. That was the constant.

Sylvia rubbed at her arms. "I expect I should feel . . . something? Resentment. Hurt? But I don't feel anything for him. I don't feel anything where he's concerned anymore."

How was she this strong? God, how he loved her. And yet, the story couldn't end there, no matter how much he wanted it to. This . . . this proved the even more impossible part to get out. "There is still something more . . ."

"More than that?"

A commotion sounded outside the parlor, streaming in from the hallway, proving the salvation it wasn't.

"Can't go in there, I said." Mr. Flyaway's voice rose up, along with the distinct sound of numerous footfalls.

When the door opened, it wasn't with an explosion but with a measured calm.

Lord Prendergast entered, and Sylvia went motionless. "What are you doing here?" she seethed.

Just then, a parade of servants piled in behind Sylvia's father-in-law, each member of the staff colliding into the back of another. Everyone from the butler, to the housekeeper, to the footmen, and by the heavy pan wielded by one, the cook. It was both a remarkable display on the part of the loyal servants and on that of the man near his sixtieth year, who had outdistanced all of them.

"Company has arrived, my lady," the butler said quickly. "Refuses to leave. Demanding to be seen. I'll throw him out, I will. Or call the constable. Or—?"

Sylvia lifted a hand. "That won't be necessary." She spoke with an impressive level of coolness. And Clayton found he loved her all the more for her strength. "If you could just wait outside, so that you can then show Lord Prendergast out. This won't take more than a moment."

Mr. Flyaway hesitated, and then with a threatening glare leveled upon the older gentleman, he backed out of the room, pulling the door shut behind them. The absolute absence of retreating footsteps indicated there was a veritable household army waiting to storm the room, if Sylvia so needed it.

Clayton didn't doubt Sylvia's ability to handle herself, but even so, he moved closer to her. Because the level of ruthlessness this family had demonstrated had it so that Clayton would never trust they weren't capable of other ugly deeds.

Lord Prendergast took in Clayton's movement with a small icy smile before returning his attention to Sylvia. "How bold you are all of a sudden."

"I am bold? This from a man who invaded my household?" Sylvia shot back. She took a sweeping step toward Norfolk's father. "And let us be clear, the only reason you are here even now is because I want to say my piece and be done with you."

Instead of displaying a hint of having been insulted, the marquess chuckled, a laugh as cold and empty as Lord Prendergast himself. "If you had that spirit when you were married to my son, mayhap you could have kept him interested."

Rage pumped through Clayton's veins. "By God, I restrained myself out of respect for your age, but I will be damned if I tolerate this." He lunged, but Sylvia touched a hand lightly to his right arm. And that touch had an immediate calming effect. Not enough to quell his hatred, but enough to keep him from tearing Lord Prendergast apart with his bare hands.

"Unfortunately, it wasn't until I made the mistake of marrying your son that I realized I had no interest in keeping *his* interest."

She was magnificent. A fearless warrior.

"It did not play as you wished, did it?" she asked coolly. "Destroying my reputation, so that you could have a guardian call into question my fitness as a mother and thereby have the access you wish to my son?" She angled her chin up. "Well, let us be clear. You will never see Vallen. Neither you nor your wife. And I intend to see that which you managed to silence is silent no longer. The world will know about what your family did, and what you were involved in."

And yet, the marquess didn't so much as flinch at that promise of what she intended to do. And it was then warning bells went off.

Lord Prendergast dusted some imagined fleck of dust from his lightly puffed sapphire wool sleeve. "Given that insolence, I have more than half a mind to let you to your mistakes," he said to Sylvia. And those bells rang all the louder. He lifted a monocle and looked her over, before shifting that same focus to Clayton. "You have St. John here unnecessarily trying to play the role of a hero, when you clearly don't need his help. Alas, he doesn't seem to be able to help himself, does he?"

Oh, God.

Sylvia stiffened.

He looked down his hawklike nose at her. "How smug you must feel. How arrogant . . . believing you've secured your respectability and gained complete control of your child . . . But tell me, how will it feel knowing you are once again nothing more than a responsibility to a gentleman driven by a sense of duty?"

Sylvia faltered, her gaze sliding over to Clayton before returning once more to the marquess. "What are you saying?"

"I'm saying that the sole reason he ever came back to you was because my son asked it of him. The day he died, he insisted that Clayton watch after you, and that is what he was doing and that is what he's agreed to do forever."

She stared at him with a pained expression. "Is . . . this true?"

Clayton squeezed his eyes shut. "Not . . . yes . . . no."

And yet, his answer made even less sense.

"No yes no? Which is it, boy?"

Sylvia glared the marquess into silence.

Clayton lifted a hand that trembled. "I came because I cared about you. And I wanted to know that you were well." How empty, and how insignificant, that all sounded.

Sylvia's legs sagged, and she caught herself from crumpling by grabbing for the back of the sofa.

Lord Prendergast wasn't done with him. "You have always wanted what my son had. And you saw your opportunity."

"Yes, I always loved her, but I didn't see it as an opportunity," he said hoarsely. The marquess would make what Clayton had felt for Sylvia all these years something dirty and wrong.

Norfolk's father scoffed. "My son even knew it. He pitied you. Lusting after his wife."

Sylvia stood there, pale and silent, unmoving through that attack being launched on Clayton. And what was worse? Norfolk had known how Clayton felt for Sylvia . . . That secret hadn't been so very secret after all, and now his twisted father would use and contort it, as he did everything else, to suit the narrative he'd spun.

"Get out."

Clayton managed a wooden nod. "Of course—"

"You."

An earsplitting scream that shook a person's very soul came distantly but distinctly from somewhere outside the parlor. "The boyyyyyyyy."

Sylvia froze, then whispered one word, a name: "Vallen."

Lord Prendergast paled. And it was the first indication that the older gentleman wasn't infallible, after all.

This time, the door did explode open. The little boy's nursemaid appeared, out of breath, her hair disheveled, and her eyes wild. "Some woman is with the little master. Has a pistol, she does."

Lord Prendergast's cheeks went all the whiter. "She . . . she . . . wouldn't harm him. She just wanted to see him," he stammered. "I was trying to allow her time to see him. Just a visit, was all she said."

"Oh, God." Sylvia pressed a fist hard against her mouth.

Ignoring the older man's ramblings, Clayton strode over to the maid, who had dissolved into a blubbering mass of tears. He took her lightly but firmly to steady her. "Where?" he urged in gentle tones.

Sobbing, the young girl raised a trembling arm over her head and pointed at the ceiling. "The . . . the n-nursery. Second floor, th-third door—"

Sylvia had already gathered up her skirts and taken off, and armed with directions, Clayton went flying past the servants, who all appeared to be immobilized by shock, and then past Sylvia. The young maid's instructions played like a litany in his head, coming in beat to Clayton's footfalls as he ran. "Call the constable," he shouted at one of the footmen.

The young man nodded and rushed off in the opposite direction. Skidding upon the marble floor of the foyer, Clayton caught himself at the bottom railing, and used it to leverage himself upright. He took the stairs three at a time, and didn't stop until he reached the third door on the left, which stood hanging open.

Out of breath from fear and his exertions, he entered cautiously . . . even as every muscle and nerve within him thrummed with a frenzied energy.

He immediately found her. Norfolk's mother. But Norfolk's mother as Clayton had never seen her or remembered her. Her lips, always composed in a perpetual line of her own pomp and self-importance, were now turned up in a wide smile that bordered on maniacal.

But then, this was the same woman who had ordered her son murdered. And she now held Sylvia's son on her lap, bouncing the boy up and down. All the while she alternately hummed and sang a lullaby.

Goosey, goosey, gander,
Whither dost thou wander?
Upstairs and downstairs
And in my lady's chamber.

There I met an old man
Who wouldn't say his prayers,
I took him by the left leg,
And threw him down the stairs

Sweat slicked Clayton's hands—hands that shook.

Vallen looked over Clayton's way, and the boy's eyes brightened.

Clayton frantically shook his head and pressed a fingertip to his lips, but it was too late.

"Clayyyy!"

Lady Prendergast abruptly ceased singing midverse.

Clayton forced himself to stop three paces away. So close and yet impossibly far.

The older lady's smile widened all the more. "Clayton!" she called out happily. She pointed her gun at his chest, that deadly weapon a contradiction to the maternal look she wore and the cheerful greeting on her lips. "You have come to play with Norman. Isn't that wonderful, Norman?" she cooed against Vallen's ear. "Every little boy needs a friend. You always were such a dear boy," she said to Clayton.

Dear boy. He used that affection as his opportunity to continue forward once more. "I would very much like to play with him."

Vallen clapped, and bounced up and down on Lady Prendergast's knee. "We play!"

The old woman made to set the little boy on his feet, when her gaze landed on a place past Clayton's shoulder. Her smile immediately withered into a harsh, hard, and—worse—threatening line.

Even without looking back, he registered the small crowd of people behind him, hovering at the entrance.

"Stop," she cried, pointing her pistol at Clayton's chest, freezing him in his tracks. "I am angry at you. Very, very disappointed." As she spoke, she shook that weapon at him. "You are being very naughty." She wrapped her other arm tightly around Sylvia's son, dragging him close to her chest. The boy immediately began to cry.

Clayton detected an audible intake of breath, and knew it as Sylvia's. And even as that telltale mark ravaged him, he made himself concentrate all his attention on the threat before them.

Lord Prendergast stepped forward. "Libby, what are you doing?" he said plaintively. "You said you just wanted to see him. That was all you wanted."

"I am trying to play with my son. And all these people are interrupting me. And I don't like it. I don't like it at all." There was a strident quality that lent an added layer of danger to the volatile situation.

Clayton needed to get Vallen away from her. She was going to snap. It was a certainty.

"Libby, that isn't your son. Norman is dead," her husband implored.

Clayton did not know what the right words were to defuse the unfolding crisis, but he knew reminding Libby Prendergast that her son was dead was not the wisest of courses.

Her eyes flashed with unhinged rage. "You stupid, stupid man. I am holding him right now. Don't you see?" She jerked the sobbing boy so her husband could see him. Vallen cried all the harder. "Look what you made him do. You're making him cry."

Sylvia and Lady Prendergast spoke at the exact same time.

"Mama is here."

"Mother is here."

"Libby," her husband tried again. "Our son is dead."

"Stop!" she cried. "You will not take him."

Terror beat like a drum in Clayton's chest. At his back, he registered the cries that went up.

And then Vallen began to cry anew, and the marchioness's lip quavered. "Hush, dear boy. Mama is here."

"Libby, it is your grandson," the marquess tried once more.

"Don't you dare try to take him from me," she cried to her husband, now waving the pistol in the direction of the collective group behind Clayton, to that place where Sylvia stood at the center.

Vallen squirmed and cried all the harder.

"Shut up!" she screamed. Madness blazed from the depths of the older woman's eyes, and she blinked. "Oh, come, dear. Mama is sorry. So very sorry."

Her grip on Vallen slackened, and the little boy scurried from her lap and raced past Clayton toward Sylvia.

"Noooo!" Lady Prendergast wailed as she raised her pistol and pointed it once more at Sylvia.

Clayton moved quickly, charging the marchioness. Time unfolded in an unnatural way, a dizzying mix of rapidity and slowness that lent a cacophony to his mind and the moment.

The loud report filled the room, followed by the echo of the shot, mingled with Sylvia's scream and the dull thudding of Clayton's own pulse. Everything came distant, as if down a long tunnel, and then he pitched forward, collapsing onto the stark-white coverlet.

A spot of red appeared, staining the fabric, spreading out slowly, in a widening swath, of crimson . . . blood. It was his blood.

"I've already told you. It happens in a bedroom, on a red blanket . . ."

A red blanket. "By damn," he whispered weakly. "She was right, after . . ."

Clayton closed his eyes, and remembered no more.

❧

Heaven was noisy.

Or mayhap that meant Clayton had landed himself in hell. Now, that would make far more sense. Which would also mean hell included his sisters' chatter.

"I told you it would be a red blanket . . ."

"Oh, hush. Your brother is there, dead, and you're more focused on triumphantly predicting how he is going to die."

"He isn't going to die."

And from that, a fight ensued, with all the voices of his sisters rolling together as they fought about whether or not he would die. A sharp whistle cut across the noise, bringing them to silence.

Yes, this was very likely hell.

He forced an eye open . . . and then another.

Hell looked a lot like his bedchambers.

A pair of enormous brown eyes collided with his. Eris blinked slowly. "You aren't dead!" she said happily. And then, hopping up onto her feet on his mattress, she proceeded to jump up and down. "He's not dead! He's not dead! Huzzah!" Her jumping jostled the mattress . . . and his side that was on fire before she leapt off and onto the floor.

He groaned. Yes, no "very likely" about it. This was absolutely hell.

Another face appeared before his.

His mother's beaming, smiling one. "I told you my boy would break the curse upon him. Probably confused it, you did."

"Tricked it," Anwen reminded. "That is how we each have to cheat death, and you did it, dear brother."

"Who would have imagined that it would be Clayton to do so?" Cora marveled aloud.

"Not I," Daria said in her haunting voice.

Clayton attempted to push himself up onto his elbows, and a hiss of pain exploded past his lips. He collapsed back.

"Rest easy now." His mother kissed the top of his forehead the way she had when he was a small boy who'd suffered a bad dream.

"Yes, it isn't every day a man cheats death," Anwen said, sitting gingerly upon the mattress, at his feet, with an awareness that after Eris's bouncing he was appreciative of.

"What . . . happened?" he whispered, his voice weak as he tried to make sense of why his entire side ached with a dull, throbbing pain. Or why he was surrounded by his family, celebrating his triumph over the curse.

"Thou know'st 'tis common, all that lives must die, passing through nature to eternity . . ." Delia smiled. "But this is not that day, dear brother. You broke your curse."

He'd . . .

And then he remembered . . .

Lord Prendergast's visit.

The shock and horror as the marquess had revealed all to Sylvia. And hurt. There'd been that, too. Oh, God . . . the agony of that remembrance, her face etched in shock and confusion greater than the pain cleaving at his side. He'd never been capable of getting anything right with her.

Except . . . that hadn't been the sole source of his misery this day.

There had been the marchioness, gone mad, with . . . Vallen.

"Vallen," he rasped, surging upright so quick his ears buzzed and his vision went briefly black.

"He is fine. You are the one who is not. However, the doctor said you will live if you have a care," his mother said, firmer than he'd ever heard her.

And when he managed to open his eyes and look once more, it was Sylvia who stood there before him.

Why was she here? She surely hated him after what Prendergast had revealed. She'd ordered Clayton gone. "Sylvia," he whispered.

His mother and sisters shared a look, and then for the first time ever, they all fell silent at the exact same moment and filed in an orderly line past Sylvia.

The door closed with a click.

Perhaps he was dead, then, after all. Only this? This would be heaven . . . he and the woman he loved deeper than he'd ever loved a soul, together.

She was there. Her hands twined together before her, stiff, silent. Her features . . . ravaged. "Clayton," she said, her voice breaking . . . and then tears flooded her eyes.

He groaned. Nay, back to the original assessment. Indeed, hell. For the sight of her suffering, he owned as his. "Vallen is—?"

"He is fine," she said quickly. "Happy and entertained by my mother and Clara and Lila. Thank you. You saved me and my son, and I . . . I have no words to express my appreciation." She cleared her throat. "This time, they brought the marchioness to Newgate and all are aware of her sins."

That was why she was here, then. To express her gratitude . . . and to explain what had become of Norfolk's evil parents? He should just be grateful that she was here, and speaking to him. But he was selfish, because he wanted her and them the way they'd been . . . before Prendergast had outed Clayton for his lie to Sylvia.

"It was nothing," he said woodenly. "I would happily and gladly give my life for you or Vallen."

She swept over. "It was . . . *nothing*?" she cried. "My God, you could have died. You almost did," she corrected. "You lost so much blood, and we worried you would never wake." Sylvia hugged her arms around her middle while she continued to silently weep, that noiseless expression of her grief somehow all the more devastating.

"I am fine," he insisted, willing a greater strength than he felt into his voice so as to alleviate her pain. "Why, I was just shot, and look how sturdy I am. Already awake."

Sylvia looked at him as if he had lost control of his faculties. "Eight days ago," she whispered, and then moved swiftly, joining him at the side of the bed.

His eyebrows flew up. "Eight days." That much time had passed? "Yes."

"And . . . you are here, now?" Eight days later? Surely that meant . . .

Sylvia caught a sob with her palm. "Of course I am, you silly man. I've remained here, waiting for you to awaken. I love you, Clayton. That has not and will not ever change."

She'd stayed beside him. She loved him? He closed his eyes once more. "I am dead, aren't I?" There was no other accounting for the ease with which she stated her love.

She laughed midsob, and stroked her fingers through his hair.

Clayton tried to pick through the cobwebs clouding his mind and his memory of that day with Sylvia and Prendergast that may as well have been moments ago, as he'd been in this suspended state of rest with time and life after it unmoving. "But . . . you ordered me to leave." He'd not imagined it.

"No. I didn't. Silly, silly, *silly* man. I ordered *him* gone. I didn't want to hear anything else of what he had to say." Ever so gently, Sylvia claimed the spot beside him. She rested her palm on his, her fingers soft and yet so strong as they stroked his. "I know your sense of responsibility. I don't hate you for coming to me for that reason." She wrinkled her nose. "Perhaps I was annoyed and stunned when I realized, but . . . I could not, would not, ever let that be what kept me from living a life with you." She stopped that butterfly-soft caressing but left her hand there, covering Clayton's. "Because I know that even if it began as one thing, that when you continued to come, it wasn't all it was."

"No. No. You are right," he said hoarsely, struggling onto his uninjured side.

She made a sound of protest. "Please, don't. You need to rest."

But Clayton managed to get himself upright anyway. "I will be fine . . . as you are here with me, Sylvia."

Sylvia lowered her mouth close to his. "I will be with you, now and forever. I love you, Clayton Kearsley. I always have and I *always* will."

It was all he'd ever wanted. Nay, she was. A future with the two of them, together.

"And I love you," he whispered. "From the moment I saw you in Lady Waverly's . . . and joined you in a meeting that wasn't accidental."

She gasped. "It wasn't?"

"No. I couldn't stop watching you all night. I needed to—"

She kissed him, gently and tenderly, and he lay back against the pillow, with Sylvia coming carefully over him. Clayton surrendered to the warmth of that joining.

When they parted, there came a whisper of sighs and giggles.

"Whoever loved, that loved not at first sight?" Delia's muffled voice carried through the wood panel, and he and Sylvia shook with silent amusement.

And folding an arm around her, he pulled Sylvia onto the mattress and against his uninjured side. "Who indeed?"

And this time, as she curled into him, they gave in to the laughter that now came so very easily. For at last, they would be together.

And this time . . . it would be forever.

Clayton smiled.

About the Author

Photo © 2016 Kimberly Rocha

Christi Caldwell is the *USA Today* bestselling author of numerous series, including Lost Lords of London, Sinful Brides, Wicked Wallflowers, and Heart of a Duke. She blames novelist Judith McNaught for luring her into the world of historical romance. When Christi was at the University of Connecticut, she began writing her own tales of love—ones where even the most perfect heroes and heroines had imperfections. She learned to enjoy torturing her couples before they earned their well-deserved happily ever after.

Christi lives in southern Connecticut, where she spends her time writing and looking after her twin girls and amazing son. Fans who want to keep up with the latest news and information can sign up for her newsletter at www.ChristiCaldwell.com.